**Zack was seated at his desk and swiveled to face her as she stepped in, his shock evident by the slack in his jaw.**

For a moment, no one said anything. Taylor's heart was back to performing sixteenth notes on a snare drum. She tried to slow her breathing.

Zack opened his mouth to say something, but she couldn't let him have the first word.

"Zack…" That was all that came out of her mouth. She wanted to tell him she was so terribly sorry. She wanted to tell him why he hadn't heard from her in so long. She wanted to tell him how much she had missed him. But she said none of those things. No words came out.

Zack leaned forward. "Yes? Something you wanted to say?"

"Are you going to have a problem working with me on this case?"

"Uh… Yeah. Absolutely."

Dear Reader,

Every day, there are advances in technology. While there are many wonderful innovations, insights and opportunities, there is also the dark side of the internet where unsavory characters prey on our children. I wrote this book for two reasons: to shine a light on the fact that we must be ever watchful of those who would take advantage of the young, and to encourage people to step away from their devices and get involved in the world and the communities around them.

This is also a second-chance love story between Zack and Taylor. Both struggle with their own inner demons, which keep them apart. Resolving their differences and bringing them together was a challenge—but that's what keeps writing interesting.

I hope you enjoy reading *The Vanishing Trail* as much as I had fun writing it.

Xxoo

*Maria*

# THE VANISHING TRAIL

**MARIA LOKKEN**

**ROMANTIC SUSPENSE**

If you purchased this book without a cover you should be aware that this book is stolen property. It was reported as "unsold and destroyed" to the publisher, and neither the author nor the publisher has received any payment for this "stripped book."

ISBN-13: 978-1-335-47185-7

The Vanishing Trail

Copyright © 2026 by Maria Lokken

All rights reserved. No part of this book may be used or reproduced in any manner whatsoever without written permission.

Without limiting the exclusive rights of any author, contributor or the publisher of this publication, any unauthorized use of this publication to train generative artificial intelligence (AI) technologies is expressly prohibited. Harlequin also exercises their rights under Article 4(3) of the Digital Single Market Directive 2019/790 and expressly reserves this publication from the text and data mining exception.

This is a work of fiction. Names, characters, places and incidents are either the product of the author's imagination or are used fictitiously. Any resemblance to actual persons, living or dead, businesses, companies, events or locales is entirely coincidental.

For questions and comments about the quality of this book, please contact us at CustomerService@Harlequin.com.

TM and ® are trademarks of Harlequin Enterprises ULC.

Harlequin Enterprises ULC
22 Adelaide St. West, 41st Floor
Toronto, Ontario M5H 4E3, Canada
www.Harlequin.com

HarperCollins Publishers
Macken House, 39/40 Mayor Street Upper,
Dublin 1, D01 C9W8, Ireland
www.HarperCollins.com

**Printed in Lithuania**

A cozy reading chair and a romance novel are all **Maria Lokken** needs to have the perfect afternoon. The perfect evenings are spent with her husband—her real-life romance hero. Both her husband and her large family are inspirations for many of her stories. Besides being an avid reader, she loves popcorn, movies and walking around museums. You can find her at marialokken.com or on Instagram, @maria_writer_lokken.

## Books by Maria Lokken

### Harlequin Romantic Suspense

*Breaking the Code*
*Operation Blackout*
*The Vanishing Trail*

Visit the Author Profile page at Harlequin.com.

To the two people who helped me get this book out.

My husband—who has read every word I have ever written and whose critiques are always invaluable. Thank you for over four decades of the most adventurous, exhilarating, crazy, unexpected and fun ride of a lifetime.

My twin—my forever best friend. We waltzed into this life together and have shared every moment since. You're the one who turned me into a romance novel fanatic, and...well, I wouldn't have written a word without you. You get me.

And to my big, boisterous, loving family— too many to mention—who make my life better every day in every way. I love you all, and this is for you.

# *Chapter 1*

"I've got you now." His steel-gray eyes focused on her as he charged forward. "You haven't got what it takes to beat me. You are way out of your league." His muscular, six-foot-two frame charged toward her.

Sweat poured down her back, but Agent Taylor Shore stood her ground. She widened her stance, fists up, and when he was a foot away, she made a one-hundred-eighty-degree turn and, with her torso perpendicular to the ground, thrust her leg out to the side, her foot making contact smack in the middle of his solar plexus.

"Ooph. Good shot," Gil said.

Taylor wiped the sweat from her forehead as she danced in place. A slight hop from one foot to the other, fists raised to her chest. Without warning, she threw a right uppercut, a left cross, and a high kick to the chest.

With his kick shields in place, her partner, Agent Gil Clancy, withstood the pounding. "Not bad...for a girl."

"That's not even funny." She put her gloved hands on her hips. "After all this time, I thought we were done with the sexist remarks." The smirk on his face gave her the impetus for her next move: a roundhouse kick so hard it threw him back a foot.

"Hey, you didn't even warn me."

Taylor kept coming—kick, punch, turn, sideswipe.

"Enough!" Gil laughed. "You've made your point."

All five feet four inches of her danced in place, ready to pounce.

"Seriously, I think we've done enough for today. Looks to me like you've gotten out a fair share of aggression."

Taylor stopped dancing, dropped her hands to her sides, and looked around the FBI's state-of-the-art gym.

"What's going on with you?" Gil stepped closer. "Listen, Shore, we've been off assignment for over a month now." He paused as a tall male agent walked by, on his way to the free-weights area. Gil lowered his voice. "The boss gave us this time to decompress and get our lives back in order."

Her gaze focused on him, and she narrowed her eyes. She wanted to ask how he'd been able to put their last assignment behind him with such ease. Instead, she said, "Yes, yes. I know. I'm getting there."

"You might want to try and hurry that along."

Since being back, Taylor had spent her nights staring at the ceiling, replaying over and over the events of the ten months she had worked undercover as a buyer for a sex trafficking ring. All for nothing. In the end, they'd come up short. Somehow, the ring had found out there was about to be a bust, and the next day, they'd disappeared. Poof, into the ether. In the seven years she'd been with the FBI, this had been the biggest case she'd worked on and her biggest failure in so many ways.

"I had drinks with the boss last night." Gil crossed his arms over his chest.

"You did?" Taylor forced herself to relax her facial muscles and sound casual. It irked her that Gil and their supervisor, Special Agent in Charge Brett Boyd, had a friendship outside the office. It wreaked of "boys club."

"Yeah. He had a few questions on the paperwork we filed."

*And you didn't think to include me?* Inside, Taylor fumed. Outside, all she said was "Oh?" Hoping it seemed as if it didn't bother her in the least. Any other comment would have made her sound defensive and, well...you know...boys club. The way to get into the inner circle wasn't to complain. She just hadn't figured out what more she could do to break that barrier.

"Anyway. We're meeting with the boss at ten. You ready for re-entry?"

"Don't worry about me. I'm good."

"Like hell. You're still not sleeping?"

Taylor stared at him.

"Sorry. Those dark circles. Dead giveaway."

With her teeth, she pulled off the Velcro on the right glove, held it under her arm, and slipped her hand out. Then, she did the same with the other glove and dropped them both into her gym bag. "I'm going to get cleaned up. Meet you in the office," she said while carefully unwinding the hand wraps one at a time.

"Okay." Gil picked up his towel and headed for the men's lockers.

Taylor watched him walk away, wondering how she was still so wrapped up in their loss when Gil's attitude had been almost flippant, like *you win some, you lose some*. But the months she'd spent undercover had cost her. She'd lost the man she'd loved. And worse, the head of the sex trafficking ring had slipped through her hands. It had cost some women their lives, and that was what really kept her up at night.

She opened her locker, hung up her gloves, and pulled her long red hair out of the tie holding her ponytail. The small mirror hanging inside her locker reflected her current

mood—exhausted and annoyed. She really did need to get some sleep, or she'd be no good for anything.

After their undercover assignment, they spent two weeks handling paperwork. Then, their SAC, Brett Boyd, gave them another two weeks of paid time off to decompress, but he fully expected them to be ready to work when they came back. A part of her wondered if she was still cut out for this. The thought was disheartening. Since she was eighteen, all she'd ever wanted was to be a federal agent. The first six years had been exhilarating. There was nothing like taking criminals off the street, and she'd had a good run until this last job. When it really counted.

She blew out a long breath. "Buck up," Taylor said to her reflection and slammed the locker shut. Grabbing a towel from the shelf, she headed for one of the shower stalls.

While undercover, she'd practiced and perfected how to think of nothing. Because if her mind were blank, she wouldn't react to some of the awful things she'd heard and seen. It was not only a useful skill, but it had saved her life. Since returning to the "real world," it was becoming increasingly difficult to make her mind vacant. Uninvited images invaded her thoughts as if she were scrolling through photos on her phone. These days, a peaceful moment was hard for her to come by.

She stepped into the shower stall and turned on the faucets. The hot water streamed down her back. She took a deep breath and lowered her shoulders.

"Get your head in the game." She whispered that phrase over and over like a mantra, psyching herself up for her meeting with Boyd. In her unit, there was no room for self-doubt, second-guessing, or, least of all, self-pity.

Taylor had been thrilled last year when she had finally been assigned to the Child Exploitation and Human Traf-

ficking Task Force. It was the reason she'd joined the Bureau. It was her way of making up for what had happened to her sister, Emily, who disappeared after being trafficked against her will. When the undercover assignment came up, Taylor had leaped at the chance. No way would she have passed up the opportunity to help someone's sister, daughter, or niece, despite knowing it would require leaving everything and everyone behind without any notice.

She stepped out of the shower, toweled dry, and headed for her locker. Twisting her shoulder-length hair into a bun, she put on her white button-down shirt, dark gray pants, and matching jacket. She stepped into her sensible black pumps, holstered her weapon to the side of her belt, grabbed her phone, wallet, and gym bag, pushed through the swinging doors, and walked down the corridor to the elevators.

The FBI's Albany, New York, headquarters was located off Conrad Street in a five-story modern glass building. Taylor took the elevator from the basement to the second floor, where her unit was located.

As she walked down the corridor, she took a deep breath, trying to get her pulse rate back to normal. When she was undercover, there weren't that many rules, except to succeed at the op and stay alive. Now that she was back, she'd have to follow the rules and protocols expected of an agent. To her mind, that might take some getting used to. The thought required another deep breath.

Her gaze scanned the large open room. It looked as if nothing in the office had changed, and yet everything seemed different. Cubicles with walls made of light gray fabric were positioned in clusters in the center. Several offices ran along the perimeter.

Brett Boyd was in one of those offices, pacing while he talked on the phone, his door wide open. As she passed, she

smiled to herself, remembering what a loud talker he was, even when he was trying not to be overheard.

"These are bad people preying on the innocent," his booming voice pronounced. "It's got to be coming from inside the US. The preliminary reports indicate it's here, and we need to find it. I don't care what they have on their plate…"

Taylor kept walking. On her first day back, it wouldn't do any good to be caught standing at the SAC's door, eavesdropping on his conversation. She turned and smiled. In the corner, diagonally across from the SAC's office, were two cubicles facing each other. There was comfort in knowing she had the same three-walled cubicle across from Gil. The half partition between them allowed for little privacy, but after what they'd been through, it didn't really matter. He knew pretty much everything about her.

Taylor put her gym bag under her desk. "Hey."

Gil rocked back in his chair. "The boss just messaged me—said he'll see us in ten when he gets off his call."

Taylor nodded. Her desk phone rang, and she picked up the receiver and spoke into it. "This is Agent Shore."

"Agent Shore, this is Sam from IT. I'll be down in twenty minutes to hook your laptop back into the system."

"Appreciate it. I've got a meeting, so I'll be out of your hair." Taylor hung up the phone and noticed the fortune-cookie slogan thumbtacked to the wall by the desk phone. She removed the push pin and held it in her hand. *YOUR LIFE IS BETTER TOGETHER.* She closed her eyes, and an achy sadness washed over her. Days before she left on her assignment, she'd been out to dinner with Zack Ramirez at their favorite Chinese restaurant. She'd opened her fortune cookie and smiled at its prediction. That was the night he

said he loved her. Little did she know it would be their last time together.

Even though she thought about him every day and missed him with every breath, since her return, she hadn't dared contact him. Disappearing after he told her he loved her. After the implied promise of a possible future together. After spending the most beautiful night of her life with the man she loved. She couldn't possibly contact him. She had left without a word, torn between her duty and Zack. There really was no going back. *There was no going back.*

*Thwack, Thwack, Thwack.* Zack hustled across the pickleball court, reached out his arm, and slammed the ball straight down the center. "My point. And I win." He raised the paddle over his head in triumph. "Let's go again."

"No way. Not even maybe," Max said from across the net. "Losing two matches in one morning could possibly be hazardous to my ego." He half laughed. "Man, you're on fire. When did you suddenly get game?"

For the last couple of months, on Monday mornings, Zack Ramirez played pickleball with his older brother Max, and this was the first time he'd won. He liked the feeling and wasn't ready for it to end. "Don't be like that. Let's go one more round."

"Nope." Max shook his head. "I'm out." He headed off the court, sat on the side bench, picked up his water bottle, and drank deeply.

"Bro, you are a wuss."

"Nah." Max swallowed. "We played two rounds. You whipped my ass and served it to me hot. What more do you want?"

"Vengeance." Zack plopped down next to his brother on the bench. "Hand me my water bottle." Max passed the tall

blue container, and he took a long gulp. "Ahhh. That hit the spot." He let out a devious chuckle. "You know I usually hate working out. But today was fun."

"This is a game, not a workout."

"Oh, stop with the semantics. I'm moving around a court, using every available muscle in my body, getting my heart rate up. Of course it's a workout." Zack took another chug of water. "Anyway, week after week, you win. It was starting to bother me. The one time you lose you're in a huff? Get over yourself."

"I beat you week after week because you've been lazy, dragging your sagging butt around the court like you were wearing lead boots instead of those two-hundred-dollar kicks." Max pointed at the offending sneakers. "Apart from today, there's been no heart in your game. You were just going through the motions. I was almost ready to tell you I was getting a new partner. But today, man, you were aggressive. What gives?"

"It wasn't so much aggression as nerves."

"You? Nervous?" His brother frowned. "What for?"

"I got a date tonight."

Max turned his body to face Zack fully. "Say what?"

He held up a hand. "Let's not make a big deal of this. Okay? It's just a date."

"Just a date. You've been packed on ice for the last year. What changed your mind? I mean, Rafe and I have been worried about you. Like. For real. We noticed."

"You and Rafe were talking about me?"

"Duh. Yeah. We're your brothers—we love you. We care what happens to you. Outside of work and the occasional Sunday dinners with the family, your interests were solitary. Your social life was…well…it was on mute."

Admittedly, it had been a long time since he'd been out

with anyone, but he had his reasons. And they all began and ended with Taylor Shore. He'd thought they had something special. He'd thought she was the one. She'd gone undercover for a few weeks, and when she came back, everything seemed fine. Three weeks later, she disappeared, and for the past year he hadn't heard from her since. No note, no text, no call. Nothing. He hadn't recalled feeling so lost since his mother passed away. Losing Taylor had taken its toll. It had been eleven months, and only now did he feel he could get out there and explore his options. But he certainly wasn't ready for serious. Just dating.

"So, who'd be brave enough to go out with the likes of you?" Max nudged him with his elbow.

Zack shrugged. "Her name's Diane, and she's an accountant. A nice, safe profession."

Max stared at him.

"What's that look for?"

"Nothing. I got no look. Have a good time. I hope you enjoy the evening."

"It's just a date." Zack's words were said with emphasis. He fiddled with his pickleball paddle. "I'll tell you one thing—I am not ready for anything even vaguely serious. It will be a long time before I lay my heart on the line again." He stared ahead and took a long drink from his water.

"She really crushed you, didn't she?"

Zack flicked his hand. "Enough about me." There was only so much time he could spend feeling sorry for himself. "Tell me about this big party Tía Ellie is throwing for you and Jordan."

Max leaned forward, elbows resting on his thighs. "Jordan's all into it, although she'd be fine if we eloped. And don't get me wrong—I'm fine with a big wedding. But a big engagement party? What is the point?"

"Don't be like that. Tía wants to make it nice for Jordan, officially welcome her into the family before the wedding."

"With a big blowout engagement party?"

"Some of our relatives still haven't met Jordan."

"I'm not sure how many more people she can take. She's just getting used to all of us."

"She'll be fine, and you know from where I sit, she doesn't seem to be too averse to people anymore. It looks like it takes less time for her to warm up. Besides, it's just one party." Zack was thrilled that Max had finally popped the question to Jordan. He not only respected her professional hacking skills, but now that she was working for their cybersecurity company, RMZ Digital, he was really getting to know her and loved her like a sister. So, the marriage just made it formal.

"I guess you're right," Max said. "And now that you're dating again, maybe this... Diane, is it?"

Zack nodded.

"Maybe you can bring Diane to the engagement party."

He stood and stretched. "Get serious. One date. We don't even know each other. I mean, it could all be—"

"Hang on—that's my phone." Max dug into his gym bag and pulled out his mobile. "I should take this."

Zack closed his eyes and shook his head impatiently. He didn't believe in being tethered to one's phone every minute of every day. Day in and day out, he watched people walking around with their necks at a ninety-degree angle, looking at their screens instead of looking up at the world around them. For that reason, whenever he played pickleball with his brother or worked out in the gym, he kept his phone in his locker.

"Yes, uh-huh...Sure thing...tomorrow afternoon, then," Max said, swiping off the phone.

"Who was that?"

"Brett Boyd."

Zack gave his brother an odd look. "From the FBI? That Brett Boyd?"

Max nodded and pursed his lips.

He knew that look. His brother was deep in thought after having a conversation with the Special Agent in Charge. Zack waited a beat, but when Max didn't say anything, he playfully punched him in the arm. "Don't keep me hanging—what did he want?"

Max rubbed at the stubble on the side of his face. "I'm not sure. Some case requiring cybersecurity help. They're pulling all the information together, and he'll send some agents to the office tomorrow."

"That was it?"

"Yeah."

Zack sat back, leaned against the railing, dropped his shoulders, and looked up.

"You okay?"

"Why wouldn't I be." Zack's tone was flat.

"Well…let's see. You're not exactly thrilled with the FBI in general. Not after what you've been through with Taylor. Is this going to be a problem?"

He shrugged. "Maybe."

## Chapter 2

"He's ready for us now." Gil began walking toward Boyd's office.

Taylor stood, tugged on the edges of her suit jacket, and sucked in a breath. She knew Boyd was going to give them a new assignment, and a tiny niggle of worry ricocheted through her mind. She didn't think she could take another failure.

Gil turned toward her. "You coming, or what?"

"Yes." She stepped away from her desk and moved quickly to catch up to him.

He knocked on Boyd's door and leaned in. "Sir. Ready for us?"

Their boss stood, hand out. "Yeah, come in. Good to see you both."

Taylor nodded. She admired Boyd. He'd worked his way up, having been with the Bureau for over twenty years. But he was tough, and she usually gave him a wide berth. She figured he was probably in his early fifties but looked ten years younger. Hovering around five feet eleven, he was still trim, with no tire around the midsection, and his gray hair and round-tortoiseshell glasses gave him a distinguished look.

"Have a seat," Boyd said, pointing to the two chairs in

front of his desk. Behind him, a wall of windows overlooked the building's central courtyard.

Not knowing what to expect, anxiety took over, and Taylor's stomach dropped. The same feeling seemed to swamp her each time she got a new assignment. Only this time, she couldn't fail. Whatever this was, she needed to be successful.

"So, I'll skip the preamble. Are you both ready? Had enough time?" The tone in his voice seemed to be filled with impatience. "What happened in the last op was unfortunate, but sometimes these things get away. I'm hoping… no, I'm insisting that doesn't happen again. Too many man hours were invested in that operation…"

Taylor stopped listening. *Too many man hours? No kidding.* She'd spent months of her life with no payoff. *Is he blaming me for the botched op?* A queasy sensation worked its way to the back of her throat.

"Agent Shore? I asked you a question." Boyd stared at her. "Are you ready, or do you need more time?"

"I'm ready, sir. More than ready." Her voice sounded strong, much stronger than she felt.

"All right, then. Despite the outcome of the last operation, you both worked well together, and that's why I'm putting you together on this one. Gil will take the lead."

Taylor nodded, but something about Gil being assigned the lead irked her. Yes, Gil had been in the Bureau longer, and when he joined, Boyd had been his mentor, cementing a special bond between them that she wasn't a part of. But she didn't understand Boyd's reasoning—she had been lead on several cases. *Boys club* came to mind once again. She shifted in her seat. For now, she'd have to suck it up.

It wasn't that she didn't like working with Gil. They'd covered each other's backs on the last op. Her biggest issue

was that she didn't always agree with his decisions or approach. And he sometimes seemed reticent to listen to her ideas or an alternate way of handling a situation.

With her petite frame and easy smile, Taylor gave the illusion that she was demure. Maybe even weak. And for that reason, she'd spent her life bucking up against people who underestimated her toughness. She hadn't gotten this far by being pushed around or letting barriers stop her. She'd take this assignment and wouldn't let Boyd and Gil's real or imagined bromance get in the way.

"So," Boyd continued, "news reports are picking up that the governor's son was rushed to the hospital in critical condition."

Taylor and Gil exchanged glances. This was the first either of them had heard about it.

"It was attempted suicide."

Her eyes widened.

"The governor's office is working hard to keep *that* piece of information out of the media. The kid slit his wrists. The housekeeper found him. Got there just in time. He nearly bled out. He's in the ICU now and resting."

"What happened?" Taylor asked.

"That's where you two come in. The governor's aide said the boy was being blackmailed." Boyd put a hand up. "Before you ask why or by whom, we're sketchy on the details. What we know is the governor discovered that his son had somehow withdrawn over three thousand dollars from his emergency line of credit."

Gil let out a low whistle.

"This morning, while the doctors were attending to his son, the governor scrolled through his phone. That's where he found text messages between his son, Henry, and an unknown woman. Seems they traded nude pictures of each

other." Boyd adjusted his glasses. "I don't have much information. I'll need you to dig into the money trail. But the nude photos, the kid's large withdrawal…well, it suggests a scam."

"What makes you think that?" Gil asked.

"We've had four other cases this month of teenage boys in similar situations, exchanging nude photos with a woman and then being blackmailed."

"Could this possibly be one of those sextortion scams?" Taylor asked, still amazed at the ugly in the world.

Boyd nodded. "That's what it looks like."

"Are we talking about one individual?" she said, "or some sort of organization?"

"That's what I need you two to find out. But my instinct tells me it's a group, or at least more than one person."

"What makes you think it might be a 'ring'—" Gil used air quotes "—rather than a lone lunatic creep?"

Boyd looked over the top of his glasses at Gil. "Four similar cases all in the same month. I'd say that's a bit busy for one person. Not to mention the fact that there are probably more cases we don't know about. Most victims never report it. They're too embarrassed."

"So you're saying you think there are more than the four reported cases, plus the governor's son?" Taylor said.

"That's exactly what I'm saying."

"Apart from trading nude photos and blackmail, are there any other similarities?" she asked.

"The four boys are between the ages of fourteen and seventeen, and they're all avid gamers. Each was initially contacted in one of the game's chat rooms."

"Were they all playing the same game?" Gil asked.

"I don't have that information yet. The cyber team started working on the case, but they're really backed up." Boyd

took off his glasses. "Between the serial-killer case and the bank-hacking case we've been working on, this office has its hands full. Anyway, the cyber team worked up a very preliminary report based on laptops and mobile phones from the first four victims."

Boyd's phone rang. He held up a finger, indicating he'd be a minute, and picked up the receiver.

While Boyd took the call, Taylor contemplated the case. She was eager to get started. Anyone taking advantage of underage kids, in her mind, was a monster. Images of Emily flooded before her eyes, and a simmering anger rose in the back of her throat.

Boyd hung up the phone. "Okay. Where was I?" He looked off to the corner of the room. "Oh, yes. Now that the governor's son is involved, this case is a major priority. That means you will put your full attention on bringing whoever is behind this to justice." He tapped his finger on the desk. "The governor will tell us when it's okay to question his son. In the meantime, you'll go to the house, pick up his son's phone and laptop from the housekeeper, and see what you can find."

A yellow folder sat in the middle of Boyd's desk, and he slid it forward. "This is the hard copy of what we have so far on the first four vics."

Taylor reached for it and then looked toward Gil, making sure it was okay for her to look through the file first since he was the lead.

He gave a short nod.

Glancing through the few pages in the file, she looked up at Boyd. "Doesn't look like the cyber team did a deep dive."

Their boss raised an eyebrow. "Like I said, they've been backed up."

"Sorry, sir," Taylor said, "but it appears they're saying

the blackmail texts came from the Ivory Coast and the Philippines."

"That's typically where these scammers are located." Boyd tilted his head. "Your point?"

Taylor shifted in her chair. "For some reason, I thought this was a US operation." She fiddled with the file in her hands. How could she tell Boyd she'd overheard him talking about the operation being in the US? "Just a thought," she said, "but maybe we should ask the cyber team to check into any US IP addresses. We might get lucky and get a bite from a computer in the States."

He pointed to the file. "For now, that's all we've got. The cyber team will give us their final report on the four cases in a day or two."

Fingering the file, she pursed her lips. "I know everyone's backed up, and I don't mean to criticize, but it looks kind of thin."

"That's the next thing I was going to talk to you about." Boyd stood and put his suit jacket on. "Walk with me. I'm running late for a meeting upstairs."

Taylor quickly stood and followed Boyd and Gil out the door, and the three agents walked down the corridor to the elevator banks.

Boyd pushed the Up button. "Our cyber team is already working round the clock on other priority cases. Because this is an internet scam, it's going to rely heavily on a cyber team. And the governor has made it crystal clear he wants action."

The elevator doors opened, and Boyd stepped in. "The only way to get this op moving quickly is for you two to work with a freelance group. I've chosen the Ramirez brothers at RMZ Digital." He turned to Gil. "Taylor knows them. Terrific at what they do. I'll email you the details." The elevator doors closed.

\* \* \*

The following day, the elevator doors opened, and Zack stepped out, a to-go coffee cup in one hand, a half-eaten doughnut in the other.

"Good morning, Zack," Brittany, the cheery dark-haired receptionist, said.

"'Morning, Britt."

"A doughnut for breakfast?" She placed a hand on her hip. "Have I taught you nothing? There's yogurt and fresh fruit in the break room."

Brittany Dupont had been RMZ Digital's receptionist and office manager for over four years. Although she was in her mid-twenties, she sometimes acted like an overprotective parent. Despite her very vocal opinions, she was the reason the company ran like a high-performance sports car, rarely needing a tune-up.

She was more like a member of the family than an employee. Brittany knew each of the brothers' likes and dislikes. Max preferred a hot breakfast, and Rafe had recently become a health nut. She tried to provide all options in their break area. But Zack still hadn't given up his doughnuts, chips, and ice cream.

"Britt, you're killing my joy." He smiled and took another bite of the doughnut. "Is Rafe in?"

"Not yet. He just sent me a text. He's dropping Justine off at school. Said he'd be about five minutes late."

"And Max?"

"On his way."

"I'll be waiting in the conference room."

Every Tuesday, the brothers held weekly staff meetings to review caseloads, HR issues, sales, and the company budget.

"I'll let them know. You want me to bring in coffee for the meeting?"

"Nah, you got enough to take care of. They're on their own." Zack headed down the corridor, passing the bullpen area, already buzzing with techies hunched over their computers, bopping to whatever music was pumping through their headphones as their eyes stayed glued to the screens in front of them.

RMZ Digital's offices in Hollow Lake, New York, occupied what was once the post office on Main Street. They'd taken over the building, gutted it, and created a modern look with concrete floors, whitewashed brick walls, exposed-beam ceilings, and massive arched windows along the south wall, where the brothers' offices sat enclosed in glass, allowing natural light to pour into the bullpen area.

The conference room, halfway down the corridor, was also fronted by glass. Inside, there was a long, oval table. The three floor-to-ceiling arched windows looked out over Main Street.

Zack rested his backpack on one of the conference room chairs, pressed a button on the sleek silver box sitting in the middle of the table, and spoke into the AI digital assistant. "Rudy, bring up the news."

The large monitor mounted on the far wall came to life, and an image of an ambulance driving down a busy street appeared. The camera cut to a female reporter standing in front of a hospital entrance. "This morning, the governor's son was rushed to the hospital in critical condition—"

"Rudy, mute, please."

Instantly, the sound was off while the picture remained. Zack lived with the dichotomy of wanting to be informed about what was going on in the world while also wanting to shut it out because he found the news too depressing.

"Hey, I made it." Rafe walked in with a coffee to-go cup and dropped into a chair at the head of the table.

"Man, bro, you're looking a little rough," Zack said. "Didn't get a chance to shave this morning?"

Rafe and Zack were only eighteen months apart and looked more like identical twins. They were both well over six feet, with dark brown eyes, high cheekbones, and dimples in the center of their chins. But where Rafe wore his hair long, hitting the top of his shirt collar, Zack's was short with some length on the top.

His brother rubbed at the stubble on his jaw. "So much sweet talk this early?" Rafe let out a long sigh. "Mallory and I aren't getting much sleep. My son has the unique ability to wail for hours at a time." He sipped his coffee. "I felt so bad for him. But there wasn't anything I could do but hold him, walk around the nursery, and pray to god that he would scream himself to sleep."

"Didn't happen?"

"No. Of course, this morning, before I left to take Justine to school, he conked right out. The little stinker."

*"Pobrecito."*

"Who's the poor boy?" Max asked, stepping into the conference room.

"Lucas is going through a wailing-all-night, not-sleeping phase." Zack laughed.

"Ah. Colic?" He put his coffee cup on the table. "So that means no one is sleeping, right?"

"Yeah, that's right." Rafe tipped his head back, locked his hands behind his head, and closed his eyes.

"Hey, bro. Don't fall asleep yet. Let's get through this meeting. Then you can lie down on the couch in your office. We'll cover for you," Zack said.

"Before we start—" Max gave him a pointed look "—how was the date with Diane?"

Rafe rocked forward in his chair—eyes wide. "What

date? Why am I always the last to know what happens around here?"

"Excuse me," Zack said. "This is my personal life."

"And?" he asked. "What's your point? We have no secrets. What date, with who, where did you go, how long did it last, and did you like her?" The words rolled off his tongue.

"Yeah. What happened?" Max leaned forward.

Zack rolled his eyes. "It wasn't a love match. It wasn't even a 'like' match. I mean, I wouldn't call it a disaster. She was nice and all. But…not for me. Not even a little."

"This was just one date. Why you being so picky?" Max said.

He sighed. "The evening was one long commentary of thoughts in her mind that for some reason she felt compelled to share."

Rafe laughed. "It's called *con-ver-sa-tion*."

"Would that it were. I may have been interested."

"Nah. You've just been away from the dating scene too long," Max added.

"I think I know the difference between *con-ver-sa-tion*—" Zack looked at Rafe as he punctuated back each syllable "—and a running commentary." He leaned back, crossed one leg over the other, looked around the room, and raised his voice two octaves. "'My, this is a lovely place. I like wood paneling—reminds me of libraries. The books in libraries… oh, I could spend hours there. But I guess if I'm being honest, I could spend hours shopping. I do love a good sale. Especially when I get a coupon. It's like double savings. And savings is always good for my investment portfolio. My money managers—'"

"Stop." Max laughed. "That bad?"

"She never came up for air." Zack sat forward. "Listen, I'm sure she's a perfect fit for someone. Just not me."

"This was just one date." His brother wiped the tears from his eyes. "It may not have worked out. But you gotta get back out there."

"Yeah...no." He shook his head and sat back.

"I love you, bro," Rafe said, "but you got to get a life. Please. You cannot spend your free time watching telenovelas and gaming alone every night. It's wrong. It's weird. And we're worried about you."

"Awww, come on, back off. I'm fine. Don't knock it."

Rafe looked over at Max. "He's not over Taylor."

Their brother nodded in agreement. "Yeah. That was a deep cut. We all felt it."

Zack slapped his hands on the table. "Let's get off me and get this weekly meeting started. Rafe needs his beauty rest."

Rafe pressed the button on the console in the middle of the table. "Rudy, pull up today's agenda and the spreadsheet from accounting. And please take notes."

The large monitor at the end of the room came to life. The male voice inside the console said, "Today's agenda, Tuesday the twelfth, for RMZ Digital's weekly meeting."

The digital voice was interrupted by Brittany's over the intercom. "Hey, guys. Two FBI agents are here to see you."

Max frowned at Zack. "Boyd told me they'd be here this afternoon. I wasn't expecting them so soon."

"Fill me in," Rafe said. "What's this about?"

He shrugged. "I was going to bring it up first, but we got sidetracked with Lucas's wailing and Zack's nonexistent love life. You were out yesterday when I got a call from the Special Agent in Charge Brett Boyd up in Albany."

"Name sounds familiar. Have we worked with him before?" Rafe asked.

"Yeah," Max said. "Remember about two years ago, he brought us in to help on that internet scam downstate. But he's in a new unit now." He scrolled through his phone. "His email signature has him in charge of the division that handles Child Exploitation and Human Trafficking."

"Sounds ominous," Rafe said.

He nodded. "I have no idea what they want with us. Boyd just said they wanted our help."

"Well, let's find out," Zack said and pressed the intercom button. "Britt, bring them back."

Less than a minute later, Brittany opened the conference room door and ushered in a tall, lanky man.

"Hi, I'm lead investigator Gil Clancy. Special Agent in Charge Brett Boyd called you about a case we need your help with." He pulled out his ID. "And—" he pointed behind himself "—I believe you know Agent Taylor Shore."

# Chapter 3

Max and Rafe stood to shake the lead investigator's hand and introduce themselves, but Zack could not move. Heat rose from his chest to the tips of his ears, and he gripped the arms of his chair, surprised at the anger coursing through him.

He never thought he'd see her again.

Taylor stepped forward and offered her hand, and Zack watched Rafe hesitate before giving her a hug. Max quickly followed suit.

"That's Zack," Rafe said to Agent Clancy and pointed behind him.

Zack remained seated and raised a hand in greeting, keeping his entire focus on Gil.

"It's good to see you, Taylor," Max said.

"I knew you worked on a case with Agent Shore," Gil said to him, "but I didn't realize you were…friendly."

Rafe looked around. "Uh…it turned out that way. But I think it was more than a year ago. Taylor—I mean, Agent Shore—was instrumental…well, she actually led the investigation when my step-daughter was kidnapped." He nodded. "That's how the family got to know her."

Zack was silently grateful that his brother had left out the personal details. Like the part where he and Taylor dated.

And the part where he fell in love with her. And that she'd practically become a member of the family.

When Taylor finally turned her attention toward him and their gazes locked, he momentarily stopped breathing.

How many months had he wished he could see her? Talk to her? Ask her why she'd just left without a word? If she had to go, if that had been her only choice, all he'd wanted was to know that she was safe. But no message ever came. The FBI refused to give him any information except to tell him not to worry about her. When it came to the Bureau, Zack was far from warm and fuzzy. But this—Taylor being part of the op they needed help with—was beyond what he could deal with.

"I was out on another case at the time, so the details are a little sketchy," Gil said, interrupting Zack's thoughts. "Something about a kidnapping and a wealthy guy selling government secrets. Isn't that right?"

Zack wasn't fully paying attention to what he was saying because the dull buzzing in his head didn't allow any other sound to filter through. He'd been emotionally ambushed and was seconds away from getting up and walking out. Only recently had he been able to think about moving on. The constant feeling of a knife firmly lodged in his chest had finally disappeared. Now he felt the physical pain of abandonment once again and the worry he'd carried for so long returning.

"Yeah. That wasn't a great time for our family," Rafe said. "But we got my step-daughter home safe, and we had a lot of help from Agent Shore and the Bureau." He turned his attention to Taylor. "It's great to see you."

She smiled.

"Let's all sit," Max said.

"Can we offer you anything to drink?" Rafe asked.

Gil and Taylor shook their heads and sat opposite Zack at the table.

He remained in his position, working to keep his expression neutral. With his peripheral vision, he watched Taylor. Her piercing green eyes, petite athletic frame, and flamered hair hadn't changed. His gut twisted. She was still the most beautiful woman he'd ever met. He clenched his jaw, working hard to keep a poker face.

"So. Now that we're all seated," Zack spoke first. He couldn't help himself. He had to know why they were here. "What is it that you need from RMZ? How can we possibly help?"

Gil cleared his throat. "I suppose you've heard about the governor's son?" He looked at Zack and his brothers. They all nodded. "What you don't know is that it was an attempted suicide."

That bit of information threw Zack. He had no children of his own, but watching Rafe with his stepdaughter, Justine, and now with his newborn son, Lucas, he had a deeper understanding of the magnitude of what Agent Clancy had revealed. He wondered what would drive a young kid to want to end his life. He didn't need to wait long for an answer.

Taylor folded her hands on the table and spoke. "Governor Hanson's son, Henry, is seventeen years old. We don't have all the information, but from our very preliminary investigation, we believe he's the victim of a sextortion ring."

Zack sat forward, nearly forgetting Taylor was speaking and only concentrating on the details of the case.

"From what we can tell, he plays a lot of games on his phone and laptop. *Robolo* appears to be where he spends most of his time. You can create your own game on that platform or join in on what others have created."

"I know the game," Zack said.

"Then you know a lot of what attracts kids are the chat rooms. In many cases, it's all about the game where they can discuss strategy." Taylor sat a little straighter. "We got this case yesterday morning, and I've done some research, and both Gil and I have investigated the materials we have." As she spoke, she turned her attention to Zack. "Unfortunately, there are a lot of scammers on these games—all sorts of things happen, things that seem innocent but aren't. Bullying, kids trading items that turn out to be fake, and blackmail. One of these scammers enters a chat room, pretends to be a woman or a girl, and eventually, 'she'—" Taylor used air quotes "—trades a nude photo, asks for some from the target, and bam, they're off and running, threatening to post the pictures all over the kid's social media, sending them to parents, teachers, and classmates unless they're paid."

"I heard about this." Rafe sat forward and shook his head. "Which is why my kids aren't going to have a smartphone until they're eighteen."

"Good luck with that," Max countered.

Rafe gave him a look. "Watch me. I'll be as strict as our father."

"Brutal, man."

"Hey, guys, let's get back to the issues," Zack said. "What makes you think this is a sextortion ring and not just one person?"

"We've had four other cases in the last month," Gil said, "and they appear very similar to this one. All four boys between the ages of fourteen and seventeen."

"The truth is," Taylor said, "we don't know for sure. This could be one person or possibly a ring of sextortionists. Just think of how many cases aren't reported because the victim is too embarrassed and pays the money." She pursed her lips. "Look, we need to find whoever is doing this. We need your

help to determine if our five cases are connected. And if it's one person or a ring. And if it's coming from overseas or inside the US. But there's one issue making it difficult."

"In what way?" Zack asked.

"In all cases, the chats began on the gaming sites. Once the kids sent nude photos, the chats were switched to WhisprApp and we lost the trail."

"Yeah. Good luck with finding anything on WhisprApp. All those messages are end-to-end encrypted," he said. "So, how can we help?"

"I think Boyd explained that our in-house cyber team is jammed," Gil said. "We'll need you to look through all the phones and computers we have from these five cases and see if you get anything in terms of IP addresses." He reached into his briefcase, pulled out a sheet of paper, and slid it across the table. "That's a list of all the devices we'll send over."

Rafe picked up the paper and looked it over. "Well, it's a place to start."

"We'll need your written plan on how you'll gather all the data," Gil said. "And a proposal for tracking down the person or persons behind this."

Max glanced over and pointed at Zack. "He's your man."

"How so?" Gil asked.

"I'm a gamer," he said.

"Seriously?" The agent raised a brow.

"It relaxes me." Zack shrugged. "In all the time I've been playing, I haven't seen or been contacted by any sketchy characters."

"Do they know you're an adult?" Gil asked.

He paused and looked up at the ceiling. "I really don't know. Never came up. I mean, when you sign up, you put your birthday, including your birth year."

"But it's not displayed, is it?" Taylor asked.

"No. But I have to assume one of two things," Zack said. "Either whoever is contacting these kids is hacking into the game or based on their chatter in the chat rooms, they can discern who these kids are and their ages."

"So you want us to find out if this is a sextortion ring and where they're located?" Max asked.

Gil nodded. "That's right. Although, for my money, these scams typically come from the Ivory Coast or the Philippines."

"I think the best way to determine that is for us to set up a sort of game war room here at our offices," Zack said.

His brothers looked at him.

"I know this world and how it works, and if I set up fake profiles on social media, pretending to be boys of different ages and set up gaming accounts, I bet I could attract some of these people."

"I'm not sure who you'll attract, specifically," Rafe said. "But I bet you'll get some scammers."

"That's all well and good," Gil said, "but we're under a lot of pressure to catch whoever is victimizing these kids."

"And with good reason." His brother slapped a hand on the table. "Anyone taking advantage of a minor, especially sexual advantage, should be put away for a long time." Rafe looked around. "I definitely want in on this. And since Zack is the most familiar with this gaming world, he should take the lead from the cybersecurity side of things."

"Like I said, I think we set up a war room right here. If we're going to get this up, we'll need Jordan's help."

"Who's Jordan?" Taylor asked. "Is he here? Can we talk to him?"

"Jordan is a she," Max said, "and she's my fiancée. She's

also a world-class hacker and works with us here at RMZ. She brings special skills to the table."

Gil looked at Taylor, then spoke. "I like the idea of setting up multiple accounts and luring them in. But how would that work?"

"I'll map it all out in the written plan."

"Okay. That's good." Gil turned to Zack. "We'd like to start as soon as possible."

"Is tomorrow soon enough?" The words were out before he could take them back. *Stupid.* He said that to impress Taylor. And what for? His brothers were going to kill him. Being ready by tomorrow would take a herculean effort, so he needed to think quickly and backpedal. "Of course...to have it all up and running, it will take overtime hours from the team to set up the type of war room we need. Is that going to work for your budget?"

"The governor has made this a priority. That means we'll do whatever it takes." Gil glanced over at Taylor. "Oh, one more thing. Taylor will be your day-to-day contact. I'll mostly be working from headquarters and the liaison with our SAC, Brett Boyd. Typically, we work hand in hand with our cyber team. And for this op, that's you. So, I'd like Taylor to stay here in town, make it easier to work with you, and not have to do the drive every day or late at night."

Taylor did a double take, and Zack blanched. When he suggested placing the war room at RMZ offices, he was under the impression he'd handle the entire operation. He wasn't prepared to work so closely with Taylor. The idea made his palms sweat. "That might be difficult. Uh...this is a heavy tourist season. You know...leaves changing, apple picking, parents' weekend at the local colleges. She might not find any available accommodations."

"I thought about that last night, and our office looked

into it. Turns out there was a last-minute cancellation at an Airbnb in Ravena, so we booked it."

"You did?" Taylor's tone was filled with surprise.

"Yeah. I thought you might need to work closely with this group. The pressure on this case won't allow for any time delays. And it's a two-bedroom, in case I need to stay." Gil's words had a finality to them.

The expression on Taylor's face mirrored how Zack felt. Trapped.

"All right. Zack, I'll need you to put your proposed op in writing and list all the people you'll have working on this. I'll need that emailed this afternoon. The Bureau will send over the contract paperwork." Gil took out his phone and began typing with his thumbs. "I'm emailing the office now."

He nodded.

"So, I guess this means we're in business," Gil said.

"I guess it does," Zack agreed.

When Boyd informed Taylor they would be working with RMZ, she automatically assumed she could keep her emotions in check. After all, it had a year since she'd seen Zack. But that turned out not to be the case. Taylor's heart hadn't had a regular beat since she'd arrived. And there was no way Gil hadn't picked up on the tension in the room. Why hadn't she at least prepped him about her relationship with the family?

The op wasn't getting off to a great start. Somehow, she was going to have to defuse the tension and get things back on track.

During the months she spent undercover, she had precious few moments to herself. But late at night, when she was finally alone and could let down her guard, her mind

usually traveled over her time with Zack. She'd been holding on to those memories in the hope that one day she would see him and that maybe they could at least be friends. What she didn't expect when she walked into the conference room was the look in his eyes. He despised her, and it nearly broke her seeing the pain she'd caused him.

While Gil and the brothers discussed the contract, Taylor scanned the room. This was the exact place where she had first met Zack. She'd been the lead on the kidnapping case involving Rafe's stepdaughter.

Taylor and Zack had hit it off almost instantly and began dating once the case ended. It hadn't taken long for them to be nearly inseparable. After that bust, her caseload had become lighter as she wrapped things up and testified at several trials. Looking around the table, Taylor wasn't sure what she missed most—being with Zack or being with his crazy, loving family.

"So, I think that settles it. Anything to add, Taylor?" Gil asked.

She tried to focus on the present. She needed to prove she was worthy of the assignment and again lead an investigation. No matter her feelings for Zack, she would have to push that all aside and put effort into solving this case. "I've got nothing more."

"Well then, I think we'll get back to headquarters while you put together the proposal and set up the war room. Taylor—" He stood.

"Excuse me, I hate to interrupt," Brittany said, walking into the room. "It's time for the conference call with Mr. Antebi. Should I reschedule?"

Max checked his watch. "That's fine, Britt. We're just about done here." He raised his brows in a question to Gil.

"Yes. We're done."

"All right, then. Rafe and I are going to take this call."

"Yeah. We won't keep you." Gil and Taylor left the conference room, headed down the corridor, and entered the elevator. When they reached the lobby and the elevator doors opened, Taylor stopped. "Oh, shoot. I left my phone on the conference table. You go ahead. I'll be right back."

Gil stepped out, and Taylor pressed the button for the second floor. When the doors opened to the reception area, she stepped out and didn't give Brittany a chance for a greeting. With determination, Taylor quickly waved and marched down to Zack's office. Without knocking, she opened the door.

Zack was seated at his desk and swiveled to face her as she stepped in, shock evident by the slack in his jaw. For a moment, no one said anything. Taylor's heart was back to performing sixteenth notes on a snare drum. She tried to slow her breathing.

He opened his mouth to say something, but she couldn't let him have the first word.

"Zack..." That was all that came out of her mouth. She wanted to tell him she was so terribly sorry. She wanted to tell him why he hadn't heard from her in so long. She wanted to tell him how much she had missed him. But she said none of those things. No words came out.

Zack leaned forward. "Yes? Something you wanted to say?"

"Are you going to have a problem working with me on this case?"

"Uh...yeah. Absolutely."

# Chapter 4

"Hey, bro. Can we come in?"

Zack swiveled his chair and turned to his brothers. "Are you asking or telling? 'Cause it looks like you're already in."

Rafe raised a brow. "You're in a mood."

"And it ain't a good one," Max said as he and Rafe sat in the chairs facing his desk.

"If you're here to talk about Taylor, don't bother." Zack rubbed his forehead with the palm of his hand. "I really, *really* do not want to talk about it. We've got a job to do. Some a-hole, or many a-holes, are out there taking advantage of children, and that's what's important. Not my past relationship with a woman who ghosted me." He turned back to his computer screen.

"Hold up. Not so fast," Rafe said. "This is an important case. But no one is invincible, least of all you."

Zack made a face. "I resent that."

"No offense—"

"Oh, I think you definitely meant to offend me." He wasn't in the mood to go fifty rounds with Rafe or Max about how he felt and if he was up to the task. Whatever emotions were bouncing around his head and heart weren't up for discussion. Not even with his brothers.

The shock of seeing Taylor when she walked into the

conference room nearly had Zack's head exploding. He still hadn't fully processed it. Why hadn't she told him she was back? The only thing that made sense was the same painful conclusion he'd reached a month ago. Evidently, she didn't love him—not the way he'd loved her. So, he had no choice but to close his mind and heart where Taylor Shore was concerned. He wasn't up for any more hurt.

"Look," Rafe said. "If you want, we'll just make sure you work on your own, and we'll report to Taylor and Agent Clancy. You don't have to see her or talk to her."

Zack thought about that for a moment. Part of him believed that might be a good compromise. The other half knew this was too important an assignment. Kids' lives were at stake, and he knew he could help.

"I appreciate you both trying to protect my feelings. But I'm a big boy, and we all know I'm the best person for this job. I'm a lawyer, I'm a cybersecurity expert, and I'm a gamer. I have all the qualifications to nab these bad actors. We don't need to waste time with you two acting as the middlemen between me and the FBI. Besides, it will be difficult for me to avoid Taylor if she's going to be here every day. So that means I'm going to have to get a grip, suck it up, and work with her."

Max shifted in his chair. "We don't want to see you hurt."

Zack forced out a one-syllable laugh. "Hurt? That already happened—past tense. So. Let's move forward. I'm turning the page on her. She's an agent with the FBI. And we're simply working on a case together."

Rafe leaned forward. "I know you can do this job. I even know you can work with her. But I also know you. And you have a tendency to hide your emotions."

"You're acting like I'm some sixteen-year-old suffering from their first crush. Would you both get real here? I'm

good." He held up a hand. "I swear." Zack knew his brothers meant well. But this was an important job, and despite the deep ache in his heart, he wasn't going to be the one to ruin it. From now on, he'd have to add *actor* to his list of qualifications. He gave his brothers a tight smile. "It's all good."

"Well...all right," Rafe said. "Let's see how it plays out. But if it gets too—"

"Enough." Zack blew out a breath. "Appreciate the support, but we've spent way too much time on me these last couple of days. I'm bored with it. Aren't you?" He huffed. "Let's move on."

"Okay. Moving on," Rafe said. "Let's discuss the details of the operation."

"I was working up an initial plan before you guys came in. I want to set up several laptops and mobile phones as playing stations with fake usernames and matching social media platforms. I think we'll stick with TikTok, Snapchat, and Discord for now. We'll need Jordan on this one for sure."

"Yeah. I agree." Max pulled out his phone. "I'm sending her a text now. She just finished up the Cassin job."

"Okay, good." Zack sat forward. "Once everything's set up with the gaming stations, my plan is to have you guys work on combing through the victims' hard drives and see what comes up. Jordan can work on tracking IP addresses."

"Makes sense," Rafe said.

"In the meantime," he continued, "I'll finish typing the plan and send it to Agent Clancy and Taylor. Then Jordan and her team can configure the devices, and she can create the fake social media accounts."

"Hey, guys, what's up? You need me?" Jordan walked in and sat on the couch. She crossed her long, lean legs and tossed her auburn hair over one shoulder.

"We've got a new assignment," Max said. "Zack's taking lead on this 'cause it's in his wheelhouse."

"Watching telenovelas?" Jordan smirked.

Rafe laughed. "No, his second obsessive hobby."

"Oh, you mean gaming," she said. "Sounds fun."

"Actually, it's kinda tragic. Some sick people out there are luring kids through games and exploiting them." Zack went on to explain the operation and his plan to lure in the bad actors and track them.

Jordan raised her eyebrows. "Sounds like a challenge. But I'm all in." She uncrossed her legs and sat forward. "Uh, I have to ask—the FBI agent we're working with, Taylor Shore, is *the* Taylor. Your ex? The one who disappeared? She's back?"

He nodded.

"You gonna be okay with that?"

"Appreciate the concern, but Rafe and Max have already thoroughly examined the situation. I'm going to be fine. Let's close the book on my emotions and just catch these scammers fast."

"Whatever you say." She stood. "So, where do you want to start?"

"I've got a few ideas on how I'd like to configure the operation. The Bureau is waiting for us to send over the proposal. Why don't I order us lunch, and I can get your feedback on what I have."

"Works for me," Jordan said.

"Okay, so I think we can take off," Max said, rising from his chair. "See you for dinner?" he asked Jordan.

She looked over at Zack. "I think this may be a late night with the team setting everything up."

"Understood. Keep me posted." Max pulled her into his

arms, kissed her soundly on the lips, and Jordan wrapped her arms around his neck.

"Aw, come on, now. *Este es un lugar de negocios. Deja eso*," Zack said with a smile.

"He keeps forgetting I understand Spanish." Jordan laughed. "Yes, I'm aware this is a place of business. I work here, too. But being engaged to one of the owners has its perks." She winked.

"Jealous?" Max asked.

Zack thought about it for a minute. "Yeah. Kind of." He felt exposed the minute the words were out. "All of you leave. Now. Jordan, meet me in the conference room in ten. Text me what you want for lunch."

The first fifteen minutes of the drive back to Albany were quiet. Taylor stared out the window, replaying Zack's response when she asked him if he'd have a problem working with her.

She closed her eyes for a moment and held in a sigh.

"You going to tell me what that was all about back there?" Gil asked. "I knew you worked on the op that brought down the Wizard of Wall Street, but I had no idea you were so close with the family."

"We're not that close," Taylor lied. "But…it was a tense time. I got to know them."

"Tell me about it."

Taylor knew Gil was too smart an agent not to have recognized something was going on. From the moment they entered the conference room at RMZ Digital, it was clear she had a familiarity with Rafe and Max that went beyond simply working on a case. Not to mention, a person would have to be dead not to notice Zack's reaction and how he'd refused to look at her during the entire meeting.

"The short story," Taylor said, "Mallory Stanton, now Ramirez, married to Rafe, was being hunted by her dead husband, Blake, who wasn't really dead. Unbeknownst to Mallory, she had a computer drive that held the information and whereabouts of dozens and dozens of drug traffickers, arms dealers, and payoffs to government officials. When he couldn't get it back from her, he kidnapped their daughter in exchange for the drive. That's when the Bureau was brought in."

"Wild story."

"It was intense."

"So, how is it that you're so familiar with the family?"

It seemed Gil wasn't going to let this go, but Taylor preferred to end this line of questioning. The last thing she wanted was to be taken off the case for personal reasons. "They're a friendly bunch. We helped save the little girl. So, they're appreciative. Nothing more."

Gill shrugged. "I sense there's something more. So, as the lead, I have to ask. Is this going to be a problem? Do you need to be reassigned to a different case?"

Taylor stiffened. Could he get her reassigned? SAC Boyd picked RMZ, and he'd assigned her to the case. Certainly, he knew about her past relationship. So, if her SAC was okay with it, there was no reason to make a big deal or give Gil any reason to doubt her ability to handle work and put her personal feelings aside.

"No. Why would you think just because I know them, there would be a problem?" After coming up short on her last undercover operation, she refused to let anything interfere with this case. One way or another, she would work to make this operation run smoothly. In order for that to happen, she'd have to clear the air between her and Zack. "It's

all fine. I'll get to my apartment, pack, and come back early evening, and we'll start in the morning."

"Good. That's what I like to hear."

While Gil concentrated on the road, Taylor took out her phone and texted Zack.

Hey. It's me. Taylor. Can we talk? Meet me at the restaurant tonight at 7.

She hit Send, turned to face the window, and hoped he hadn't blocked her number.

When they were dating, their favorite place to eat had been a Chinese restaurant in Ravena. It was in the same town where she was staying. The same place where he'd first told her he loved her.

Taylor closed her eyes for a moment and prayed the tears she was holding back wouldn't fall. She'd made her choice. And for her, it had been the right choice. She was just sorry it had to hurt Zack as much as it hurt her. Her phone vibrated, and she checked the text on the screen.

K

The one-letter response annoyed her. But she supposed that was par for the course. It was his way of letting her know he was pissed off. For now, she'd deal with it. Maybe, just maybe, after all this, they could at least be friends.

Taylor let out a heavy sigh. Who was she kidding? Being friends was the last thing she wanted. She'd pushed her emotions for him into the recesses of her mind for months. Whatever feelings for Zack she'd stifled in order to keep alive while she was undercover were now coming to the surface like water through a broken dam. She'd never felt

so lonely in her life. She'd lost so much—much more than she allowed herself to believe.

They rode the rest of the way in silence. The only sound was the chatter inside her head.

Gil pulled the car up in front of FBI headquarters. "I've got an errand to run. Should be back in an hour. While I'm gone, check on the contract paperwork with RMZ."

"Yeah. Sure thing."

Once at her desk, Taylor put her purse in the bottom drawer, sat, and booted up her laptop. The ding of an incoming message from SAC Boyd had her leaning in. She clicked open the email and quickly scanned the contents. "Damn. Three more cases."

The message from their SAC listed three more parents who reported their teenage sons had been victims. One of the boys hadn't paid his blackmailer, and his nude photos were posted on the internet. He'd been missing for over twenty-four hours. Fortunately, the police found him walking despondently on the interstate, and when questioned, they discovered what happened.

"This has got to stop." She glanced around the bullpen area. Gil wouldn't be back for a while, and she needed to quickly gather as much information as possible. They couldn't let the trail grow cold.

Taylor took the stairs to the third floor to see if the cyber team had an update. Pressing her interoffice badge on the door, she entered the lab and was surprised to see SAC Boyd. "Hey, boss."

He looked up and stepped away from the computer. "Hello, Agent Shore. What brings you here?"

"I got your email and hoped the victim's devices had already been turned in. I wanted to grab them and take them over to RMZ."

"We don't have everything yet, but two have been tagged. Cyber needs to scan them. We should have another laptop and phone by tomorrow." Boyd glanced around. "Where's Gil?"

"Lunch," she said. He didn't need to know he was running an errand on company time.

"All right." He tapped the top of one of the laptops. "Once they're scanned, they're all yours. Keep me posted."

Taylor spoke to the skinny-necked admin on duty in the lab. "I know you guys are swamped, but can you tell me when these will be ready?"

"These should be tagged and scanned and ready in another half hour."

Reluctantly, Taylor stepped away. With this many cases popping up so quickly, it looked increasingly like an organization was behind this. And if that were the situation, she had the chilling feeling there would be more cases soon.

The sense of urgency to find the person or people behind this had Taylor jogging back down the stairs to her desk. She spent the next thirty minutes filling out the requisition to push through the work contract for RMZ Digital.

"Excuse me."

Taylor looked up to find Calvin, the coordinator for the cyber team, wheeling a cart with the tagged devices up to her desk. "Hi."

"Do you want to take these with you, or do you want us to send them to—" he looked at the requisition sheet in his hand "—to RMZ Digital in Hollow Lake?"

"She'll take them with her," Gil said, appearing out of nowhere.

"Oh, you're back." Taylor tilted her head. "I'm not going straight to RMZ tonight."

"If they go by courier, when will they arrive?" Gil asked.

Calvin checked the manifest. "Two days."

"Why so long?" she asked.

"We're really, really backed up," Calvin said. "And we don't have approval for these to be taken by an outside courier service."

"Okay," Taylor let out a huff. "Can you put them in a box? I'll take them with me and bring them to RMZ in the morning."

She needed to get to her apartment, pack, and get this op off the ground. She also wanted to see if it were possible to smooth things over with Zack. If nothing else, it was time to tell him the truth. Or at least as much as she thought necessary.

## Chapter 5

Taylor pulled up to the restaurant five minutes before seven. She reached into her purse and pulled out her favorite lip gloss, a pale nude that complimented her skin tone. Adjusting the rearview mirror, she stilled the slight tremble in her hand and applied the gloss. When done, she turned her face from side to side and brushed a few loose strands of hair back into her bun. "What is wrong with you?" she said to her reflection. "You've faced crazed, murderous, thieving criminals, and you weren't this nervous." Maybe because she'd been playing a role and there were no emotions involved. This was different. This was her real life.

She stepped out of the car, locked the door with the key fob, and hooked her purse strap over her shoulder. The night air had a little chill, and she crossed her arms around her waist.

When she stepped into the restaurant, the familiarity of the place was one more reminder of all she'd lost. The atmosphere was elegant, the aromas inviting. Several round tables were neatly positioned down the center, each able to seat a family of six to eight. Against the walls were tables for two and four people. From the ceiling hung dozens of white rice-paper lanterns, giving off a soft glow and creating an intimate atmosphere. Wall panels featured elegant

floral designs interspersed along the gold-toned walls. In comparison to the calming atmosphere, her heart beat with quick palpitations.

The host smiled at Taylor. "Ah, long time no see."

Heat rose to her cheeks, and she was grateful for the low lighting. Yet another reminder of what she'd lost. Taylor glanced around the nearly full restaurant.

"Mr. Ramirez is already here. I'll take you to your table."

Taylor put on a smile, gripped her purse tightly under her arm, and followed him. Nearly a year had passed since she was last here. She'd dreamed about having a moment alone with Zack, and this was her chance. She swallowed hard.

When they reached the table, she forced herself to relax the muscles in her face and looked him straight in the eyes. He didn't need to know her nerves were on hyperdrive. "Hey."

Zack looked up. He was still strikingly handsome, and her breath caught as she stared into his deep brown eyes.

From the moment she'd met him, she liked being with him. He was smart, kind, thoughtful, and fun. Tonight so much of what she'd loved about him seemed to be missing. His tight smile told her she had her work cut out for her if she ever hoped to rekindle even a friendship.

"Enjoy your evening. I'll send your server over," the host said.

"Thank you." She slid into her seat across from Zack and slipped off her jacket. "I was surprised you agreed to meet me."

"I was surprised you asked."

Taylor took the cloth napkin from the table and placed it on her lap in an effort to give herself a moment to slow her breathing. "Well, I'm glad you agreed. I know I had no right to ask."

"That's right. You didn't."

She'd been here all of two seconds, and already the evening was going sideways. "Can I suggest we order some wine and our dinner first? Then I'd like the chance to tell you what happened."

Zack didn't respond, and his silence only gave way to more anxiety.

"Look," she said, "you're here. I'm here. If nothing else, it's a chance to enjoy some good food. But I would appreciate it if you could maybe keep an open mind."

This time the silence wasn't as long. "Okay. I'm going to give you the benefit of the doubt because, if nothing else, I'm damn curious about what happened to you."

Far from the kumbaya moment she'd hoped for, Taylor sat back and decided to take what she could get. "Great."

Zack lifted his hand and called the server over. He ordered a bottle of their favorite pinot noir.

"Do you know what you'd like?" the server asked.

Zack looked over at Taylor. "How about we go with the usual?"

She half smiled and nodded, hoping this was an attempt to break the ice.

He ordered three of their favorite dishes, and that small gesture put her at ease. "So," Zack said. "What did you want to tell me?"

Taylor stared at her clasped hands in her lap, not knowing where to begin but knowing she needed to start somewhere. "I want you to know I was as surprised as you about this assignment. I didn't expect that the Bureau's cyber team would be booked. I thought about coming up with a story to my SAC about why I couldn't be on this project, but honestly, it wouldn't have gone over well. I need to be seen as a team player, able to make it work wherever they put me."

"I see."

She thought he'd say something else. But no other words followed, and from the harsh look on his face, she realized she'd been wrong. The ice clearly wasn't broken. "You're not going to make this easy, are you?"

"I'm not in a position—"

Taylor turned her attention to the server approaching the table with the wine. They waited as he uncorked the bottle. He was about to pour a taste but Zack put a hand over his glass and pointed at Taylor.

The server nodded and poured a taste into Taylor's glass.

She picked up the glass and, over the rim, watched Zack as she sniffed, swirled, and tasted. She nodded to the server, and he poured the wine.

The moment seemed bittersweet. When they were dating, they wanted to do something fun together. Neither of them was much for hiking or even bike riding. Taylor loved kickboxing. But Zack worked out purely for health reasons. He'd confessed to her that he hated every second of it, and if it weren't for the fact that he needed to stay healthy, he would never go to the gym. So, as an activity they could enjoy together, they decided to take a wine-tasting course. Learning about the different countries and regions where wine was made had been great fun. They'd spend Sunday mornings drinking coffee, reading the paper, and talking about the different countries they'd visit to taste the wines.

Inwardly, she sighed. That was another lifetime ago.

"So. The floor is all yours. You were saying…"

Taylor took another sip of wine before she spoke. "I didn't ask for this assignment, but it's important. There are people out there taking advantage of kids. And that's enough for me to put aside whatever feelings I have and concentrate

on getting this op solved." Before she could continue, the server arrived with their food.

In the center of the table, he placed platters of *moo shu* chicken, Cantonese shrimp in hot sauce, garlic string beans, and a large bowl of steamed rice. "Can I bring you anything else?" he asked.

"Thanks—this is great," Zack said. He picked up a serving spoon and fork and dug into the chicken. "Lift your plate." He proceeded to serve Taylor hefty amounts of everything.

She took a deep breath. The rich aroma of garlic and ginger filled her senses. "This smells as good as I remember," Taylor said.

Zack served himself. "Go ahead...you were saying."

With her chopsticks, Taylor dug into the chicken and put a hefty helping into her mouth. She held up a hand and chewed, indicating he'd have to wait a moment. She looked at Zack and managed a smile while continuing to chew.

Since Zack had made it painfully obvious that he was neither in a friendly nor forgiving mood, Taylor was sure that what she was about to tell him would likely push him over the edge. If that were the case, she thought she might as well enjoy a few moments of eating at her favorite restaurant without the benefit of conversation. She swallowed and took a sip of wine. "I'd like a ten-minute grace period while I inhale this. You good with that?"

He shrugged. "No use letting a good dinner go cold."

"Thanks." She dug in. The meal helped calm her nerves. Her shoulders relaxed, and her stomach seemed to settle, as did her heart rate. She took another swallow of wine, knowing it was time to try and clear the air. If that was even possible. He would understand, or he wouldn't. Either way, at least she'd know she'd tried.

Taylor put her chopsticks down and dabbed her mouth with her napkin. "So. Here we are. First, I want to say I'm sorry. That's how I should have started. It was the first thing I wanted to say when I got back to town."

"How long have you been back?"

"A little over a month," she said and recognized the shocked look on his face.

"Wow. That long?" He looked away. "Where were you before you came back?"

"Undercover."

"I don't understand. When we were together, you went undercover for three weeks. Then you came back. You told me the job was done. Then you disappeared without a word for almost a year. You went undercover again?"

She nodded. "The night after we had dinner here. Remember? I got that fortune cookie, and you told me—"

"Yeah. Yeah." He waved a hand. "Let's not get bogged down in the details of that night. I remember. Go on."

His brusque tone made her pause. She'd never seen this side of him. Taylor took a breath. "So, the next day, after our dinner, my SAC, Brett Boyd, called me into his office to tell me the op was on again. You see, during the first three weeks that I was originally undercover, I worked on infiltrating a sex trafficking ring. My job was to work the streets and find a lead to the head of the ring."

"What do you mean working the streets? Like a sex worker?"

"Please lower your voice." Her gaze scanned the room. "No. I was pretending to be the middle person between the buyer and the seller."

"You mean selling women?"

"Yes, that's exactly what I mean. But I didn't get any

traction the first time I was out there. Then, the night I disappeared, I got a call on my hot phone—"

"Hot phone?"

"The phone I used to contact buyers."

"What took them so long?"

Taylor explained to Zack how the operation went down. Her initial three weeks were spent getting out on the street and gaining a reputation. When she didn't get any bites, they pulled her back to headquarters. "We were after a very specific person. Someone who was not only the mastermind behind this sex trafficking ring but also gun running, drugs, and hits on rival gangs. He's as bad as it gets. His name is Alonzo Piquot. But he disappeared."

"He disappeared the first time you went undercover?"

Taylor nodded. "That's when I came back to Hollow Lake for a couple of weeks. But soon after, he resurfaced, and I was the only one who'd been out there. His crew knew me. I'd gained their trust. So, the SAC sent me back out."

"And you didn't think to let me know?" Zack's voice was threaded with anger.

"I wasn't given a choice."

"What does that even mean?"

"Either I left that night or Boyd would get someone else for the op. And this one was important to me. I couldn't let it go."

"How could they threaten to replace you with someone else if you were the only one who had gained traction with these people?"

Taylor bristled at the question. "It's complicated."

Zack leaned forward. "Uncomplicate it."

"They were willing to start the entire operation all over again if I didn't go—"

"So you didn't have to go, did you?"

His combativeness put her on the defensive. She bit her lower lip, working out how to answer his question. Clearly, he didn't understand her, her work, or how important this was. "Listen, Zack, I had to go on this assignment. And if I didn't go, I was out."

"How is that even fair? Or right?"

"I knew what I was signing up for."

Zack stared and narrowed his eyes. "But what about us? I thought we meant something to each other."

"You meant everything to me." What she didn't say was that she never thought she'd have to choose between her career and the man she loved. Deep down, she thought he'd understand.

"Really? Because it didn't feel like that. I haven't heard from you for months. The Bureau iced me out."

"It was for my safety. The people I was dealing with were bad, and I couldn't take the chance that anything would trace back to my real life or to the people I cared about. It was for your safety, too. That's how these people operate." Taylor tilted her head up, desperately trying to keep the tears from spilling. She sniffed. "I couldn't take the chance they'd find out who I was and then hurt anyone I love. That included you." She paused to find the words to tell him why she took the assignment.

He put his napkin on the table, and Taylor reached for his hand. "Listen, I had to do this for Emily."

"How does your sister figure into all of this?" Zack pulled his hand away.

Taylor sat back. "I've told you about her."

"Just that you didn't keep in touch anymore."

"That's not exactly the truth."

Zack frowned.

"She was sex trafficked."

"Wait. What did you say?" His eyes widened.

Taylor held up a hand to stop Zack from asking any more questions so she could get through this. "Her last year in high school, she started doing drugs. I don't know how she got involved with drugs or who she was mixed up with. Neither did any of her friends. They said she simply stopped coming to school."

"Didn't your parents suspect something was wrong?"

"My parents were useless. It's why I barely speak to them. They were more concerned with building their business, making millions, and traveling in the right social circles. I'd been Emily's surrogate parent since we were kids. But when I went away to college, no one watched out for her."

"How do you know she was a victim of trafficking?"

"About a month after she'd been listed as a missing person, an attendant at a gas station in Texas called the cops about a suspicious van that had pulled into the station."

"Suspicious in what way?"

"For one thing, the windows were blacked out. And when he went to fill the tank, six young girls got out and were ushered into the ladies' room by two guys who looked to be wearing side arms. Five minutes later, the girls were ushered back into the van and drove off. The FBI looked at the CCTV and positively identified one of the girls as my sister." Taylor looked away and tried to hold back the tears. "That was seven years ago." She swiped at her eyes. "My sister was a perfect mark. No parental supervision, was into drugs, cut class, and was a tall, blonde, blue-eyed beauty."

Oddly, Taylor felt a sense of relief knowing she'd finally told him the truth. To her surprise, Zack had a look on his face she'd never seen, and she couldn't imagine what he was thinking. She shifted in her seat. "Well. Aren't you going to say anything? I had to be in on this operation. If

I couldn't help Emily, maybe I could help someone else's sister or daughter or niece."

His mouth was taut. He stared at her for several moments before he spoke in a low tone. "I'm very sorry about your sister. I truly am. But I have no idea who you are. Man." He took a breath. "It seems I never really knew you." Zack rested his forearms on the table and clasped his hands.

"You did know me. I didn't tell you about my sister because…oh hell, I was afraid you'd reject me."

"Reject you? What are you talking about?"

"Come on, Zack. You come from a tight, loving family. I saw that's what you wanted in a relationship. I… I…thought I wouldn't measure up if you knew about my family."

Zack rested his forehead in the palm of his hand. For several moments, he didn't speak. When he finally looked up, she could see the hurt in his eyes. She'd deceived him for so long. She'd held herself back from him.

"I was hurt when you left without a word. I worried about you more nights than I'd care to discuss. My life felt as though it was missing a piece. My family worried about you and about me because I couldn't seem to lift myself out of the depth of sadness I'd never experienced before." He sat back and scoffed. "But what for? Huh? What was it all for? The woman I was mourning and the one sitting in front of me—well, I don't know who you are. I thought we had something. That something includes telling the truth, respecting your partner enough to trust them with the truth. I have no idea why I'm just now finding out the real story of your sister and why you chose to lie to me. I can only think that you never trusted me, didn't love me enough." Zack shook his head.

"Wait. I did love—"

"Listen, Taylor, we'll work this job. It's important on too

many levels. But you and me … I'm not sure we'll ever get back to where we were or even be friends. Too much has happened. Too many secrets."

Taylor felt as if her heart had stopped. She felt lost, staring into his icy eyes. Maybe she had handled it all wrong. But she hadn't expected that reaction. Zack didn't have any right to be angry.

"Well, this is cozy."

Taylor turned to the sound of the voice. "Gil? What are you doing here?"

"I was in the neighborhood. Having a nice dinner?"

She didn't know what to say. "We're discussing…strategy."

"I see. Well, it's lucky I ran into you both." Gil turned to Zack. "I was going to call you. Boyd read through your plan, and now he's asking for the aliases you've created."

"Aliases?" Zack tilted his head. "I don't understand."

"The report says you were creating several fake profiles for each gamer with corresponding social media accounts. He wants all of that information."

"Oh," he said. "Uh… I guess, sure. I'll get that to you in the morning."

"Good." Gil turned to Taylor. "I have some business I need to discuss with you."

"Yes?"

"It's private. Let's take this outside." He nodded in the direction of the front door.

Taylor had the distinct impression Gil was pulling rank, and an uneasy feeling swamped her. Was he annoyed she was having dinner with Zack? He might be the lead on the case, but he had no right to her private life. She placed her napkin onto the table. "I'll be back," she said to Zack and followed Gil.

They left the restaurant and walked to the far end of the parking lot where his black four-door SUV sat. When they reached the car, her nerves were replaced by a frosty annoyance.

Gil leaned against the side of the car and crossed his legs at the ankle. "Wanna tell me what that was all about?"

His attitude irked her, and her back stiffened. After what she'd just been through with Zack, she wasn't in the mood for more testosterone being thrown her way. "Like I told you, we were discussing strategy," she said, refusing to be intimidated or put on the defensive.

"Strategy talks over dinner?"

While she found this inquisition tedious, it wasn't surprising. She'd discovered on the last op that Gil had a tendency to pull rank. Most times, she didn't mind, but only because he'd been there for her when things had gotten rough.

Once while at a bar, looking to begin negotiations with one of Alonzo Piquot's men, another of his lieutenants who'd had too much to drink thought she'd make a good punching bag. Gil deflected the situation by pulling a fight with another drunk patron. He'd gotten a black eye for it, but it saved her. Because he'd had her back on several occasions during that op, she was willing to cut him a little slack.

It didn't mitigate the fact that she was still annoyed. She needed to let him know that while he was the lead on the case, she wasn't going to be pushed around. "I think the better question is what are you doing here? I thought you were staying in Albany?"

Gil folded his arms across his chest. "I wanted to check out the Airbnb."

"You were at the place?"

"Yeah. It's not bad."

"Are you planning on staying tonight?"

"No."

There was something he wasn't saying, and despite the fact that she wanted to get back inside and finish her conversation with Zack, she was willing to wait him out. "All right. What else?"

"The full report from the initial review of the first four sextortion cases by our in-house cyber team is in."

Finally, she thought. Now they were getting somewhere. There had to be some US connection. She was certain. "What's the upshot?"

Gil shook his head. "There's no indication that this is a US operation. It all looks like an overseas deal."

"Really?" Taylor thought that was odd. She couldn't get the conversation she'd heard outside Boyd's office out of her mind. "Did you bring the report with you?"

"Nope. It's on the secure server back in the office."

"Has the boss seen the report?"

"Yeah, he's the one who gave it to me."

The restaurant door opened, and the sound of conversation and dishes clattering filtered out. She turned to see Zack walk out and look around. He nodded toward them, walked in their direction, and stopped in front of her. "Hey," he said. "I gotta be heading out. I need to get back to the office, see how the game war room is going." He held out her purse and sweater. "You left these."

She didn't want him to go, but she was torn in the middle of two incomplete conversations. "Thanks," she said grabbing her things.

"I'll see you in the office in the morning," Zack said, turning to Gil. "Will you be in, too?"

"Not tomorrow," he said.

Zack nodded. "Okay. I'll email you those names. Good night." He turned and walked to his car.

Taylor tried not to react. She hadn't finished her conversation with Zack, but he was clearly done with her. And she didn't understand why Gil was really here.

She watched Zack get into his car and drive away, then turned back to Gil. "So, how'd you know I was here?"

He hesitated. "Oh. I was driving back to Albany and spotted your car. I thought I'd take a chance to see if you were having dinner alone and I'd join you."

Taylor glanced around. Her company car was a three-year-old dark blue Ford Fusion sedan and was the only one of its kind in the lot. On the other hand, Gil was leaning against his brand-new black SUV, and it looked to have all the trimmings. She blew out a breath. *Boys club.* The thought ticked up her annoyance one more notch. "All right, I'll make time to come by the office tomorrow to take a look at the report on the server."

"Do you think that's necessary?"

Taylor gave him a look.

"I mean, you're more than welcome to. It's your case, too. I'm just wondering if that's the best use of your time, considering we only have until Friday to get the governor an update on the case's progress." Gil paused. "I'll tell you what. This is important. So, let me see if I can get approval to print the report and get it to you."

"That would be great," she said. "I guess I'll head back to the Airbnb." She pulled her car keys from her purse. "If there's nothing else, I'll say good-night."

"Nope. Nothing else. Get back safe."

She turned, pressed her key fob, waited for the chirps, and headed to her car. All the while, she couldn't stop one particular thought from roaming around in her mind—the findings of the report that the scammers were overseas were wrong.

## *Chapter 6*

Despite the incessant beeping of her alarm clock, Taylor didn't move a muscle. It wasn't until she heard the sound of bacon frying in the pan that she finally began to move closer to a state of consciousness. With her eyes still closed, she half smiled and took a deep breath, but all she smelled was… nothing. It took a minute for her brain to catch up to the fact that the sound wasn't something frying but rain on the roof.

Rolling over, she punched a button, silenced the alarm clock, and squinted at the digital readout. The digits 4:30 flashed in red, and she groaned. The idea of staying in shape and working out seemed like a fine idea yesterday afternoon. Not so much on a cold rainy morning when it wasn't even light out.

On the drive back to the Airbnb she discovered a small, newly opened gym in a strip mall. She'd taken a photo of the storefront sign and called to see what they offered. To her delight, she learned they had mixed martial arts classes, and they opened at five in the morning. Just enough time for her to get in a decent workout, shower, and get to RMZ. A perfect start to her day, considering she had pent-up anger toward Zack. She'd punch and kick her aggressions out before she saw him at the office. Better for her. Better for him.

Pulling herself out of bed wasn't easy. She'd chosen the

upstairs bedroom with the private bath at the farmhouse-style Airbnb. It had been the right choice because it was the best mattress she'd ever slept on, making it much more difficult to contemplate leaving the coziness and warmth.

Again, she groaned and then dragged the covers off, threw her legs over the edge of the bed, stood, and clumsily stepped into the gym clothes she'd placed by the armchair in the corner. Work out first. Coffee later.

The night before, she'd prepped her clothes for the day, choosing an office casual look to mimic the staff working at RMZ. She placed her neatly folded turtleneck, jeans, and ankle boots into her gym bag, alongside her hand tape and kickboxing gloves. *Workout first. Coffee later*, she thought again, because there had to be some kind of reward waiting for her if she was getting up this early. She could almost smell the rich, chocolaty aroma of the warm brew she'd have after her workout. "Stay on track. Keep moving. Workout first. Then you get a treat."

She grabbed her car keys and stumbled outside into the dreary cold mid-October morning. The rain had turned to a steady drizzle. Once inside the car, she shivered as she waited for the car to warm up and the heat to come on. "You can do this."

Even though it was the ass crack of dawn and the weather sucked, she reminded herself this was for her benefit. Physically and emotionally. This op promised multiple hours of "seat warming" while staring at a computer screen. And that was unhealthy on too many levels. It was what gave her the impetus to get her sorry ass out of bed before the sun rose.

When the car finally warmed up, she turned on her windshield wipers and drove the ten miles to the gym. The traffic was light, and she arrived at the strip mall off the main road within fifteen minutes.

There were only a few cars in the lot at this time, allowing Taylor to pull into a spot directly in front of the door. The painted sign on the wall read *ATLAS*. It was as no-frills as you could get. She pushed open the door and stepped into a small entryway that faced a waist-high counter manned by a middle-aged, bald-headed man wearing a sleeveless T-shirt barely covering his barrel chest. "Can I help you?"

"Uh. Yeah. Hi. I called yesterday about joining on a weekly. I'm, uh, here for the kickboxing."

He pointed his pen at her and smiled wide. "Yeah. Yeah. I took the call. I'm Harry."

She smiled. "Taylor."

"Nice to meet you." Harry reached for something behind him, then turned and handed her a clipboard with a membership application. "Fill this out."

Taylor dropped her bag and took the offered clipboard and pen. "You take credit cards?"

"Sure do."

She handed over her card, and while Harry rung up her weekly dues, she quickly read over the membership application—a standard form pretty much excusing the gym of any liability.

"Here you go," he said, handing her back her card and the receipt.

Taylor signed the membership application and handed back the clipboard.

"There's a womens' locker room around that corner." He nodded toward the right. "The gym's that way." He nodded to his left. "Julius, the owner, is already on the floor. He helps with the boxing, kickboxing, and weights. You know, whatever is needed. Since there's no one sparring this morning, you can work with him."

"Great. Thanks." Taylor headed down the corridor and

pushed open the door featuring a big letter *W*, assuming it was for *women*. She looked around. At least the place was clean.

The oblong room featured five tall lockers, one sink, a toilet, and a shower stall. A long bench was bolted to the gray concrete floor and ran the length of the lockers.

A few minutes later, Taylor walked onto the gym floor and looked around. She guessed it was about fifteen hundred feet—twenty-five feet wide and about sixty feet deep. The wall along the width of the gym was all mirrors. Set up in various stations, like circuit training, were free weights and a few bars for pull-ups and leg raises.

The sound of a heavy weight clanking onto the concrete floor caught her attention. Two men who looked to be in their twenties were spotting each other at the bench press. She watched as one put another twenty pounds on each end of the barbell for an impressive two hundred pounds.

"Hey."

Taylor turned. A wiry, mustached man in his mid-thirties stood inches from her.

"I'm Julius." He stared at her gloves hanging out of her bag. "I'm guessing you're here for some sparring?"

"Kickboxing."

"I'm happy to spar with you, or you can just use the bag where the mat is."

Since this was her first time, she didn't want to offend the owner by declining an offer. "Sure. Thanks. I'll just need fifteen to warm up."

"Cool."

Taylor walked to the corner, put her gym bag down, and grabbed one of the jump ropes hanging on the wall. For several minutes, she worked to get her heart rate up, then did some light jabs and kicks. Taking a couple of dumbbells off

the rack, she worked on her biceps and triceps. When she was done with that, she gently stretched her hamstrings and quads. She grabbed her towel and wiped her forehead, then took tape from her gym bag, wrapped her hands, put on her gloves, and punched the bag for several minutes. When she was fully warmed up, she stepped onto the mat.

"What level are you?" Julius asked, stepping onto the mat and putting on his gloves.

"I'm intermediate. I've been working on some things but mostly trying to improve my power and speed."

"Okay. Let's see what you've got."

As soon as Taylor got into position, he launched a series of quick jabs and several low kicks, forcing her on the defensive. She blocked and sidestepped, but he didn't relent.

"You said you wanted speed. I'm giving it to you," Julius said while moving from side to side.

"You worry about you," Taylor responded, throwing a set of jabs at his core, certain they'd move him off his center. But to her surprise, he held his position.

As she continued to move forward, he swung out his right leg in an arc, sweeping her feet off the mat. Taylor landed on her backside with a thud so hard her jaw rattled. Momentarily stunned, she shook her head.

Julius leaned down and offered to help her up.

Taylor glared at him and knocked his arm out of the way. This was a match, and she intended to prove herself. Quickly jumping to her feet, she assumed a fighting stance and pushed forward.

With controlled aggression, she pursed her lips and moved in with a jab, cross, and a roundhouse kick, landing solidly on his left side.

"Nice," Julius said.

*Nice? That was some of my best.* Taylor couldn't believe

her sparring partner wasn't even breathing hard. With renewed determination, she summoned all her skills to deliver several body shots. This time, he retreated slightly. She had him on the defensive.

Julius raised his hand and let out a whistle. "Hey, let's take a minute."

Taylor frowned. "Something wrong?"

"Nope. All good. In fact, you're really good. Do you mind if I give you some pointers?"

Her immediate reaction was *Hell yeah, I mind*. But she wanted to be able to use this gym, so she decided to be polite and listen to what the owner had to say. "Sure. What's that?"

"Like I said. You're good. You've got some slick moves. But you get tripped up in two places."

She tilted her head, listening.

"You need to practice your breathing. It's got to stay controlled. Or you waste energy, and it lessens your force."

She had, in fact, wondered why he wasn't breathing hard.

"Practice. There are lots of ways. Box with a bag and slow your breathing. Jog and try to keep your breathing even. It will help. And it will also help you not to panic."

"Okay," she nodded. "Good advice. What else?"

"Study your opponent's moves. Find their patterns. Time their openings. That's how you break down their defenses."

Taylor nodded and then checked the clock on the far wall.

"You need to leave?"

"Yeah. Didn't realize it was so late. Got to get to work."

"What do you do?"

Taylor had thought someone might ask her that question. And while she wasn't undercover, she didn't want people to know she was an FBI agent on assignment. "I'm doing some consulting work for a company in the next town."

"Which one?"

*Nosy much?* "Do you know RMZ?"

A huge smile broke out on Julius's face. "Yes, I know Zack. We went to high school together. Now we work out together."

"Zack kickboxes?"

Julius laughed. "No, we do free weights together. He's not big on working out. So, I see him maybe once a week. If he has to work out, he prefers running. And recently, he's been playing pickleball with his brother Max."

"Interesting."

"Yeah, Zack's a great guy."

"Well, I've got to go. I had fun. Thanks for the spar."

"I'm here every morning if you want to practice."

"I'll take you up on that." Taylor hurried into the locker room, showered, dressed, and left.

Outside, the temperature was just above freezing, and the drizzle had ramped up into a full-on downpour. She ran to her car, turned the heater full blast, and flipped on the wipers. She backed out of the parking space and turned the car toward the exit, where a black sedan sat perpendicular to the road, blocking her.

"What the heck? Is he stuck?" Taylor hit her horn, leaned forward, and squinted, trying to see between the swipes of the windshield wipers.

The man sitting on the driver's side turned and faced her. He stared at her for a moment, slowly smiled, and then quickly turned the wheel and sped out of the parking lot.

For a moment, Taylor sat frozen, then noticed the trunk light on her dashboard was blinking. She threw the car in Park, jumped out, and ran to the back of the vehicle. The trunk was slightly open. She lifted it and discovered the box with the laptops was missing.

## Chapter 7

Zack's morning routine hadn't changed in years. He rose early and forced himself to do some sort of workout. Besides his Monday date with Max on the pickleball courts, if the weather was nice, he preferred to run.

This morning, cold rain was coming down in sheets, but he ran five miles anyway, hoping to clear his mind. Dinner with Taylor had left him in emotional tatters. He was furious that she'd never told him the truth about her life. What else was she hiding? How could he have ever thought he could build a life with someone who couldn't even be straight with him, trust him enough to tell the truth? It didn't make any sense.

With anger fueling his run, he was back home sooner than usual. He dropped his keys into the bowl on the table by the front door and looked around. His two-bedroom cottage had once been his sanctuary, a place to relax. After years of being a criminal defense lawyer, then dealing with his mother's death, and finally helping Rafe get out of prison, he wanted his home to be a place of calm and solitude.

Unfortunately, after Taylor's disappearance, his home held memories that were hard for him to deal with. Now that he knew the truth, he wondered if anything they had was real.

Zack headed straight into his bedroom, stripped, and jumped into the shower. He tried not to think about what Taylor had said, but it was nearly impossible. Her words played over and over in his mind. He banged his fist against the tile. *"Basta,"* he commanded himself. "No more. Stop thinking."

When he finished his shower, he went to his closet and began sliding hangers, one by one, inspecting each of his neatly pressed pants.

"Damn, Ramirez, you've lost your mind. What are you doing?" Was he really worried about how he'd look in front of Taylor? He closed his eyes and blew out a breath. The answer was yes. After all this time and the roller coaster he'd been through with her, he still cared what she thought.

He yanked a pair of black jeans off the hanger and grabbed a cream-colored crew-neck cashmere sweater from the drawer, finishing it off with a pair of black Chucks. Then he looked at himself in the mirror and stared, thinking, *Nothing says we're just working together like dressing casually.* He turned on the heel of his sneakers and headed straight for the kitchen.

He poured milk into a saucepan, placed it on the stove over a low flame, hit the Espresso switch, and pulled his *quesito* out of the fridge. When the milk was almost at a boil, he poured it into a cup, added his coffee, and took a long, savory sip of his *café con leche*. He bit into the flaky pastry. Mmm. He savored the sweet taste of the cheese in his *quesito* and smiled for the first time since last night. "At least there's breakfast."

Zack reached over, opened his laptop, and pulled up YouTube TV to his favorite telenovela, *Mi Amor para Siempre*, a multigenerational saga with *muchos* twists and turns. He scrolled through the channel lineup and chose the latest

episode. Besides gaming, this was his way of getting away from the world. Zack still had hopes that one day he'd write a screenplay, and to his mind, there were no better stories than the shockwaves, shake-ups, and game changers of a Spanish soap opera.

He smiled as the opening titles animated across the screen, remembering how he got hooked on these when his *abuela* babysat him and his brothers every afternoon while his parents were at work.

As soon as he stepped off the school bus, he'd run to the kitchen door. His grandmother's smile and a warm embrace greeted each of them. The aromas of garlic, cilantro, onions, and peppers—the basis for whatever that night's dinner would be—filled the room. After washing their hands, they'd sit for an afterschool treat, then go off to do their homework. Only then would she allow them to play while she watched her favorite telenovela.

Often, while Max and Rafe shot hoops over the garage, Zack would sit in the living room with his Nintendo GameCube, one eye on his game, the other watching an evil-twin plot play out on the television. The daily cliffhangers had him coming back for more. It wasn't long before he, too, was hooked. Zack smiled at the memory.

He looked back at the screen just as the opening credits finished. "Okay, Sandra, what have you got up your sleeve today?" He turned up the volume.

*"Miguel, te amo, pero—"*

"You love him, but what? Come on, Sandra, don't be like that. Don't do this man wrong. He has sacrificed everything for you." Zack leaned in closer to the screen. Yelling at the characters was part of the ritual.

*"Miguel, tengo un secreto. Debería habértelo dicho antes."*

"You have a secret you should have told him sooner? Oh, that's rich!" He slammed the lid of his laptop shut. "I can't. That's too freaky. Too close to home."

Zack turned when his doorbell rang. He checked the outside camera on his phone. "Rafe. What are you doing here?" he said, speaking into the mic.

"Open up. It's cold. It's raining."

He laughed as he walked to open the door.

Huddled under an umbrella, Rafe looked up, eyebrow raised. "I need caffeine. Lots and lots. Shoot it in my veins."

"Whoa. No sleep again?"

"Observant." Rafe closed his umbrella and dragged himself over the threshold, across the living room, and into the kitchen area. *"Café con leche, por favor."* He dropped into a chair. "I'm begging you."

"Coming right up." Zack poured milk into the saucepan and turned on the flame.

"When are you going to get yourself a real milk steamer? It's not like you can't afford one."

Zack gave him a death stare. "You want coffee, or you want to criticize? You can't do both."

Rafe made a face. "A little touchy."

"We're not talking about me. We're addressing those big black bags that seem to have become a permanent fixture under your eyes. Lucas still deciding sleep isn't for him?"

"I love my son. But he would try the patience of Job. For real. We have no idea why he won't sleep. Why he cries. We've pretty much tried everything. Mallory says Justine was the perfect baby, so she's just as mystified as I am."

"What does the doctor say?"

"His pediatrician says he's colicky and he'll grow out of it." Rafe rubbed a hand over his face. "But not soon enough."

"Are you planning on keeping that facial hair? 'Cause

yesterday the stubble was kind of manly, but this is…moving over into sloppy."

His brother held up a hand. "I am going to ask you and Max for a grace period. No comments on how I look until my son starts sleeping."

Zack laughed. "Fine. I'll shut up. Here's your coffee." He placed the mug in front of Rafe.

"What's to eat?"

"Hey, if you wanted a full breakfast, you should have gone to Fritz's & Dean's Diner."

"Yeah, but then I wouldn't get to hear what happened last night with you and Taylor."

Zack groaned.

"That bad?"

"Worse."

"Well, feed me. Then fill me in."

He pulled out another *quesito* from the fridge and put it onto a plate.

"Where did you get those? I haven't had one in ages."

The corner of Zack's mouth ticked up in a sly smile. "I found a little Puerto Rican bakery shop in Albany off Highland and Drew, called Delicioso. And man, they ain't kidding—everything in there is delicious. Reminds me of Ma. Even when she had a big caseload, she always baked something amazing after church on Sundays."

Rafe gave a knowing smile, then wiggled his fingers in a *give it here* motion. "You think you could pause your walk down memory lane and hand me what you got in your hands?"

"*¡Ay! ¡Paciencia, mijo!*"

"You're talking to a man who hasn't slept in days. My ears are still ringing from my poor son's crying. Any sem-

blance of patience left days ago. Now, before I strangle you, give me that *quesito*, and tell me what happened."

Zack placed the food in front of Rafe, grabbed his own coffee, and sat across from him. "I don't know where to start." He rubbed the back of his neck.

His brother remained silent, chewing on his pastry.

He took a sip of his coffee. "I found out that I never really knew Taylor."

"How's that even possible?"

"She has secrets. Things—important things—she didn't feel she could share with me. I thought we meant more to each other than that." Zack sat back and relayed the events of his evening with Taylor.

"Wow," Rafe said.

"Don't say anything." He wagged his index finger. "Please. I don't want advice. I don't want your take on this. I want to get through this job and move on."

"I can't keep quiet about this." Rafe put his mug down and leaned forward. "It's not like I know firsthand, but undercover work sounds dangerous. And what happened to her sister was straight-up evil. No wonder she took the sex trafficking case and this sextortion assignment. I give her props."

Zack stared at him.

"Don't tell me you're going to make her wrong," Rafe said. "Man, you knew what she did for a living before you decided to ask her out. From what I can see, this is on you. Not her. Besides, I thought our mother raised us better than that. She had a career, remember?"

Zack shrugged.

"That's not an answer. You know I'm not the guy to give relationship advice—"

"Then don't."

"Sorry, bro. I gotta say this. If Taylor didn't tell you things, maybe there's a reason."

"What possible reason could she have?"

Rafe paused. "Being married to Mallory has taught me a lot about how to make a relationship work. It's not always easy. And I don't want you to bite my head off, but is it possible that Taylor didn't feel she could tell you the truth?"

"Now you're talking psycho-babble."

"Nah, man. Trying to get you to look at the other side. 'Cause that's what being with another person means—looking at their side of things, too. Anyway, she had a job to do. It was important to her. And given what happened to her sister—well, you can't say that's not something we wouldn't do for each other."

Zack didn't answer. He didn't know what to say. Rafe was right. Taylor had gone undercover, and that was part of her job. The truth was he couldn't deal with it. He didn't know why. He didn't know how to make it better. He didn't know where to put his anger, misplaced or not. He just felt the way he felt and couldn't move off it.

"Okay," Rafe said. "I'll drop it. Just one more question. You sure you're going to be able to do this? You're the lead on this assignment, and that means working closely with Taylor."

"I'm good. Swear."

"Okay, but if— Hang on." He pulled his phone out. "It's a text from Max."

"Group text," Zack said, looking at his phone.

Where the hell r you guys. Jordan worked through the night. Almost done setting up.

"Oops. Pity party is over." He slid off his chair. "I'll grab my jacket and follow you."

"Heading out. Thanks for the coffee. Taking the *quesito* to go."

Zack's phone buzzed with another text. "Oh, Max." He groaned. "You don't need to keep sending texts. We'll be there." He swiped open the screen. His pulse sped up. It was from Taylor.

Heading into the office now. We've got a problem.

# Chapter 8

The rain stopped just as Taylor pulled into the lot behind RMZ headquarters. She spotted Zack getting out of his car and gave a short honk.

He turned and walked toward her. "Hey, what's up? What's going on?"

She unfastened her seat belt, hurried out of the car, and pointed to the trunk.

Zack held his hands out to the side. "What am I supposed to be looking at?"

"My trunk." She stomped her foot.

"It looks like it's not closed."

"It's not. Because it's broken."

"Is that the problem?" Zack turned as Rafe drove into the lot. He pulled up beside them and lowered his window. "What's happening?"

Zack scratched the side of his face. "Not sure."

"I was at the gym this morning," Taylor said.

"What gym?" he asked, his tone impatient.

"In Ravena." She blew out an exasperated breath and explained to Zack and Rafe what had happened as she was leaving the gym.

When she finished, Zack took a look inside the trunk. "They left the jack, flashlight, blanket, and jumper cables.

Was there anything else besides these things and the laptops in here?"

"No. That was it."

"Looks like they were definitely after the laptops. How would anyone even know you had them in your trunk?"

Taylor glanced away and pursed her lips. "Yeah, that's a head scratch. Only a few people knew. And none of them are likely to have either stolen them or given the information to someone else."

"Listen, I'm going to park," Rafe said. "Let's take this upstairs. I'll meet you there."

She nodded. "Before too much more time passes, I have to reach Gil." Taylor lowered the hood of the trunk, turned on her heel, and headed toward the building.

Zack jogged up next to her and opened the entrance door. Together, they moved quickly across the lobby toward the elevator. She pressed the Call button and waited. Several seconds passed, and she looked up at the floor indicator panel, which showed the elevator sitting on three. She waited several more seconds before pushing the Call button repeatedly, but the elevator didn't move. "Ah, screw it. Let's take the stairs."

"Follow me," Zack said.

They rushed up the two flights. In the second-floor stairwell, Zack punched in the security code, and Taylor pushed the door open onto the RMZ reception area.

"Hi, Taylor. Good morning, Zack," Brittany said. "Is there something wrong with the elevator?"

"Nothing's wrong," Zack said. "We wanted the exercise." He smiled and caught up to Taylor. "Let's check the conference room first."

She was about to argue that that wasn't a priority but didn't get a chance. Zack took her by the elbow and ushered

her down the hall straight into the conference room, where Jordan and her tech crew were putting the final touches on the gaming stations.

"Good morning, you two," Jordan said. "We're just wrapping up. You ready for a tour?"

Taylor forced a smile and glanced around the room. It was evident that Jordan had put in a great deal of time and effort to set everything up in one day. She and her crew had turned the conference room into what looked like an impressive state-of-the-art gaming station. It put her mind slightly at ease, knowing this part of the op was moving forward.

While she wanted to get a closer look, at the moment reaching Gil was more important. "Would love a tour. But—"

"This looks great," Zack interrupted. "Thanks for working so quickly. Really appreciate it, but something's come up with the assignment. We'll call you when we're ready."

"Totally get it," Jordan said. "I'll wait in the tech room."

When Jordan left, Zack looked at Taylor. "I wanted to make sure we were ready to go on this end, and it looks like we are. Now, let's go into my office, and we can work on the missing laptops."

Once inside his office, Taylor threw her bag onto the couch. "I've left a couple of voice messages and texts for Gil, but he hasn't responded."

"That's troubling," Zack said.

"My messages didn't say what was wrong, just that I needed to speak with him. I don't want to alert Boyd yet. Not until I speak with Gil."

"Can you give me any more information about the laptops?"

"I don't have any more information. All I know is what I told you already. Three new cases came in, and we had lap-

tops from two of the cases. I took those with me so Max and Rafe would have them first thing this morning to see what information they could get off their hard drives."

"And you haven't heard from Gil?"

"No. I'm going to text him again." Taylor pulled out her phone, shot off a message, and waited. She paced back and forth, checking the time every few seconds. Five minutes went by, and still, she didn't get a response.

Max poked his head into the office, with Rafe right behind him. "Jordan said you guys were here but haven't started working in the war room yet. Something wrong?"

Her phone pinged before she had a chance to respond. "Hang on. I need to look at this."

"From Gil?" Zack asked.

She nodded and read the message.

The third laptop and mobile device are in. Scanned and tagged. I'll bring them to RMZ this afternoon.

She pursed her lips before her thumbs raced over the phone's keyboard, informing Gil that the two devices had been stolen from her trunk. She waited for a response, and instead of a text, her phone rang. She looked up. "It's Gil. I'm going to take it."

"I'll be in the war room," Max said.

"Should I leave?" Zack pointed to the door.

Taylor shook her head and swiped open her phone. "Hey."

"Give me all the details," Gil said with no preamble.

Taylor explained what happened, including the car that blocked her exit from the gym's parking lot and then took off. She further explained she didn't get a license plate or what the guy looked like, as there was a deluge of rain and her wipers hadn't been able to keep up.

"Okay," Gil said, "For starters, write up a report. Send it to me, and I'll make sure Boyd sees it. We'll take it from there."

Taylor imagined Boyd wouldn't be pleased to hear about the latest turn of events. The operation wasn't getting off to a great start.

She hung up the phone and found Zack staring at her. "What?"

"You left out the part about being blocked by a car. What happened?" The look of concern on Zack's face was evident, and it confused her. He'd made it clear they were only working together—nothing more.

"It's not information I would share with a civilian."

He took a step back. A slight scowl crossed his face.

"Look, you don't need to be concerned. I can handle myself."

Zack scoffed. "We are working together. Don't I have a right to know if the project is being jeopardized? Which, clearly, it is."

The air seemed to swoosh out of her lungs. His concern wasn't for her. It was for the operation. How could she have thought otherwise? She had to move past her desire to patch things up with Zack. It would only bog the case down and make her more miserable than she already felt. If he wanted a strictly working relationship, she'd give him one. Taylor made the decision she'd work with him the way she worked with the Bureau's in-house cyber team—she'd be clinical and provide all the pertinent information.

"Okay. You're right. From now on, I'll give you all the information. The laptop and phone from the third victim are ready, and Gil's bringing them down this afternoon. And that's it." She held her arms out to the side. "As of this moment, you know everything I do."

Taylor turned and walked to the large arched window. It was raining heavily again. Several people were running down the sidewalk, holding umbrellas against the wind. She rubbed her temples with her index fingers.

"Got a headache?" Zack asked.

She lifted her head to the ceiling. "Lack of caffeine. Didn't get a chance to have my java jolt this morning."

Zack walked to his desk and picked up the phone. "Hey, Britt, would you mind bringing in a cup of black coffee for Taylor? Thanks."

She turned to face him. "That was nice."

"Well, we have a lot of work to do, and I know you cannot function without a cup."

She picked up her bag from the couch and pulled out her laptop. "Before I do anything else, I need a minute to write that report for Gil. Mind if I use your office?"

"No problem. I'm going to the war room and see what Jordan has set up."

As he was leaving, Brittany walked in with a hot, steaming cup of coffee and handed it to Taylor.

"Bless you." Taylor smiled for the first time that day.

She sat at Zack's desk, opened her laptop, and began typing the report.

Twenty minutes later, Zack marched back in.

Taylor looked up. "I just finished the report and hit Send. Now all I have to do is wait and see what Boyd wants to do about it."

"I guess we'll know soon enough. But I've been thinking. You've got a situation with the missing laptops. Even though we don't physically have them, there's a way to get information from them." He plopped into the chair facing her. "I'm not sure exactly how yet, but this is clearly a cy-

her crime, and that's what we excel at. Plus, we have Jordan, who can pretty much find out anything we need to know. So, let's get to work."

Taylor dropped her shoulders, and for the first time today, there was a slight glimmer of hope that she might be able to fix this problem. The fact that Zack and his brothers were at the top of their field of cybersecurity helped put her mind further at ease. They were one of the few outside companies the FBI had vetted and chosen as one of their top vendors.

"Let's start by getting a tour of what Jordan and her team have put together," he said.

"I'll be right there. I want to see if I get a response from Gil."

"Okay. Meet you there in, what, five?"

Taylor nodded. As she stared at her laptop screen, a chat from the Evidence Response Team popped up in a side window. They were on their way to dust for prints on her car.

Well, she thought. Obviously, Gil sent the report to Boyd, and this was the next step. The ease she felt a moment ago was replaced by a cold sensation like icicles dripping down her spine, and she shivered. It was the same sensation she'd been experiencing on and off all morning. Despite Zack's confidence that they could get information from the missing devices, she couldn't ignore her instincts—they told her trouble was close.

While she'd told Zack he knew everything she did, she hadn't mentioned she'd suspected that whoever was behind the sextortion ring also stole those laptops from her trunk. It had been gnawing at her all morning, and as she thought about it, it came into focus. It meant that the ring was closer than anyone thought. Whoever was behind this not only knew about the Bureau's operation to bring them

down, they were also clearly prepared to do anything to sabotage it.

This wasn't information she should keep from the team. And yet she hesitated. Would involving them put their lives in danger?

## *Chapter 9*

Zack paused outside the tech area. The office was buzzing, and every cubicle was occupied with employees working on various projects. The hum of a busy workday began to settle him. The sounds of fingers clicking on keyboards, printers whirring, phones ringing, and intermittent conversations across half-cubicle walls all signaled normal. He liked normal. He craved normal. Months of angst was quite enough for him.

As he passed the tech area, he heard snippets of conversations. Some talked about work, others about the latest true crime podcast. Many of the people who worked for their company had been with them from the beginning. He smiled momentarily, recognizing what he and his brothers had built. Of the thirty or so employees, most were like family. RMZ Digital was recognized as one of the best in the cybersecurity world. They were sought after, and he knew they were exceptionally competent. Despite his mixed emotions concerning Taylor, this job would be no exception. They would do whatever it took to complete the operation successfully.

Zack stopped at the doorway to the conference room. His gaze scanned the space appreciatively as he counted six laptops and six mobile phones spread out like individual stations at the long conference table. This was precisely what

he needed. Concentrating on work would take his mind off his conflicted emotions and put his love life where it needed to be—on the back burner. He stepped inside. "Looks impressive."

"Ah, you're back. Is everything okay?" Jordan plugged a USB cable into a box in the center of the table.

"Not yet, but it will be once we're up and running. I'll fill you in after the tour."

"Give me a minute, and I'll walk you through. I decided to change out one of the ports for better speed." She tugged on the cable, then stood and clapped her hands together. "All right. What we have here, as you can see, are six laptops and six mobile phones. Each device is connected to that main computer." She pointed to a large desktop unit at the head of the table. "It's programmed to record and monitor all gaming and chat activity. We'll keep each day's activities on separate drives so you can go back and review anytime."

Zack smiled as he walked around the table, checking out each station as Jordan spoke.

"I've also set up that large monitor on the wall. You'll be able to see what's happening on all the devices at once, or you can focus on one at a time."

"Wow. Nice job," he said.

"That's not all. You can switch screens and update the social media profiles I've created for each player."

"This is what I call a war room." The setup nearly electrified the gamer in him. The idea of working in this room and catching people preying on kids lifted his mood considerably.

"Glad you like it." Jordan smiled. "Now we need you to test it out. Although I don't think you'll find any problems."

"If this wasn't a job, this could be a gamer's fantasy."

She tilted her head and wrinkled her forehead. "How so?"

"Just look. Gaming, gaming, gaming…" He pointed at each device. "For some people, this would be a dream come true."

"That's just sad." The corners of her mouth folded downward. "You do know there's more to life than games."

"You've been talking to Max about my social life, haven't you?"

"Uh, yeah. We live together." She smirked. "Anyway, take your time and work with each device. Let's make sure everything meets your specs, and if there are any bugs that need—" There was a knock on the glass door, and Jordan stopped talking. She turned toward whoever was walking inside. "Hey, Taylor. You're just in time for the grand tour."

Taylor glanced between them. "Thanks, but I need to meet with all of you. There have been some developments that affect this case."

"Including Rafe and Max?" Jordan asked.

"Yes."

The look on Taylor's face troubled Zack. Only minutes ago, she seemed fine. He couldn't imagine what had happened in that short amount of time. Zack looked around. "It's a bit crowded in here. Let's meet in the smaller conference room."

"I'll get the guys," Jordan said and walked out.

"Everything okay?" Zack asked and was suddenly hit by déjà vu. When Rafe's stepdaughter was kidnapped, they'd set up a war room of a different kind in this same conference room. It was the very first time he'd met Taylor Shore. Somehow, he'd mistaken the look on her face when she walked in just now. She wasn't troubled. She'd had that same determined, *do not mess with me* look then as now. She was onto something, and every fiber of his being said he wanted to be in on it, too.

"Everything will be fine once we have a game plan," Taylor said. "The office is sending a team to dust for prints on my car."

"That was fast."

"Yeah. Well, you know, FBI and all."

"The smaller conference room is on the other side," Zack stood, leading the way across the floor through a maze of techies at their computer stations.

The thirty-by-thirty room had no windows, and unlike the rest of the office, it was sparsely furnished. There wasn't much besides a round glass table and gray cushioned swivel chairs that could comfortably seat six. A plastic potted fern occupied one corner. A large monitor was mounted on the opposite wall. In the center of the table sat a gray box that housed the AI digital assistant.

"Never been in here," Taylor said, sitting in a chair situated at the middle of the table.

"The techs use this room when troubleshooting with clients," Zack said, sitting beside her. She stared intently at him, and he lost his concentration momentarily. He found it slightly unsettling to be so close and gaze into her sparkling green eyes.

"You were saying?"

He cleared his throat. "No windows, no glass wall to look out onto the bullpen area. It's secure, so whatever material they're working on isn't exposed to anyone who may be visiting the office."

Taylor turned when Max, Rafe, and Jordan filed into the room.

"We're here. What's happening?" Max asked as they took their seats.

She absently tapped the pen on the white sheets of paper

she'd positioned in front of herself. Once everyone was settled, she filled the group in on the stolen laptops and their significance.

Max let out a low whistle. "Could this maybe be a random burglary?"

Taylor shook her head. "Don't think so. My car was parked at Atlas Gym. There were four other cars in the lot when I arrived. That accounts for exactly the number of people in the gym. And when I left, those four cars were parked in the same spots, with the addition of the one black SUV blocking the exit."

"Are you thinking someone knew you had the laptops?" Max asked.

Taylor nodded. "I don't think this was random at all." She looked squarely at Jordan. "They tell me you're the best when it comes to hacking. And Zack believes we can still get information from them even though they aren't in our possession. Is that true?"

Jordan's lips curled into a sly smile.

"Is there any possibility you can track the stolen devices if I give you the serial numbers?"

She rocked back and forth in her chair before she answered. "It's challenging. But not impossible. Get me the numbers, and I'll start working on it right away."

"I'll have our cyber team email you the info." Taylor took out her phone, and she continued to speak while emailing the team's coordinator for the serial numbers. "Jordan, do you have any news on the devices from the first four victims?"

"We're working on that."

"Okay. In addition to those, I'm especially interested in Henry, the governor's son. He'll want a report soon."

Jordan sighed. "These bad actors were very clever. They

used multiple networks and bounced their signals from one virtual private network to the next."

Taylor raised her hand and spoke. "Since VPNs are private and impossible to detect, how are you planning to find these locations?"

Jordan raised a brow. "There are always traffic patterns. I monitor the traffic going in and the traffic going out, then analyze those patterns and match the user's activity to their location. It can be a slow process. But we are making progress. I'm hoping we can find the origination point, which will tell us where to look. So far, it is pointing overseas."

That piece of information surprised Taylor. While it corroborated the information Gil brought her last night, the overseas angle still didn't make sense. She had no concrete evidence to the contrary, just raw instinct. The only way to know for sure was to find the origination point. "Do you think the stolen laptops might have provided more information?"

Jordan pressed her lips together. "Might have. Hard to tell. But I see where you're going with this. Why steal them if they didn't contain information someone didn't want us to have?"

"Exactly." Taylor tapped the pen on the table several times. "All right," she said, "we keep working on finding out where these bad actors are located."

"Hold up." Zack raised a hand. "Maybe there's a way to speed this up. We don't have the stolen laptops, but do you have the names of the kids who owned the devices?"

Taylor nodded. "Why?"

"I'll be right back." He sprang up from his chair and ran out of the room.

"What's he getting?" Taylor asked. Her question was met with shrugs. She didn't need to wait long to find out. Within

minutes, Zack returned, placed his laptop on the table, and connected it to the digital assistant. He spoke while it booted up onto the big screen on the far wall. "With the information we had from the first four cases, plus the governor's son, I started a database last night and created several categories."

Zack cleared his throat, moved two fingers on his trackpad, and pulled up the spreadsheet onto the big screen. He reached over and grabbed the laser pen light sitting next to the digital assistant and pointed to the spreadsheet projected on the monitor. "On the left are the obvious categories—name, sex, age, gaming handles, and location." The red light from the laser pen followed the column on the screen as Zack spoke.

"What's that over here?" Taylor pointed to the right side, where the columns were vertical and not horizontal. "Are those the games the vics played?"

He placed the pointer over a list of games. "These are the ten most popular. Two of the ten were found on Henry's computer and phone. Those same two games were also found on the devices from the first set of vics."

"And this helps us how?" she asked.

Zack placed the laser pointer on the table. "We don't have the stolen laptops, but we have the names."

"Yes. That's already been established." Taylor tapped her pen on the table impatiently.

"We need to get information on the games they played, the approximate times they were online, and for how long," Zack said. "If any of the times or games match up, which I think they will—"

"Then we're that much closer to narrowing down what we're looking for." She slammed the pen onto the table. "That could work. We'll have to contact the parents and get permission to talk to the kids."

"When we get that information, putting it into the database will be easy now that it's set up. It will tell us what games we need to concentrate on. It will cut our work in half, and hopefully, we get answers sooner."

"Great." Taylor rose and walked toward the screen. With her hands on her hips, she stared at the information. "Jordan," she said and turned around, "based on the information that exists in the computers we do have, can you pinpoint the exact times the chats occurred and add that information to this database?"

"Yeah. Sure."

"Okay, that might give us a pattern for when we should be online," Taylor said.

"Smart," Zack said.

"Now, about the actual gaming part of this. Is the plan to set up a different handle on each laptop and phone?"

"Yeah. Already done. Each device has a fake name and a social media account associated with that name. Jordan rigged it all up," he said.

"There is one more thing," Jordan spoke up. "The reports you gave me indicate the boys who were targeted had a history of gaming. They'd all been at it anywhere from a year to five years. They were experienced and, I think, a bit addicted."

"In what way?" Taylor said.

"I did an analysis, and between his phone and laptop, the governor's son would spend five to eight hours a night gaming."

"Seriously?"

Jordan nodded. "He must have gotten home from school at, what, three thirty? From what I can see of his activity, he gamed from that time until midnight."

"Wait a minute. That would mean he ate dinner while he was gaming," Taylor said. "Where were his parents?"

Zack shrugged. "That's not for us to examine."

She scoffed. "Well, someone should examine it."

"I don't disagree. But you know as well as I that's not the assignment," he said.

"Anyway," Jordan continued, "my point is these boys are experienced gamers, and that seems to be a beacon for these sextortionists."

"But why not go after an inexperienced gamer?" Taylor said.

"I guess these guys know that a kid who spends that much time online is someone they'll easily be able to reach," Jordan said. "The scam starts with a simple conversation and grows daily. They need the ones who keep coming back."

Taylor stared at the screen. "This is so sad." She shook her head. "If these perpetrators go after seasoned players, how can we hope to lure them as newbies?"

Zack smiled slyly. "This is why we're lucky Jordan works at RMZ. She spent the night creating fake gaming histories for each mock player. The moment we begin playing a game with one of the usernames from our database, it will automatically populate a history containing fictitious scores, prizes we allegedly won, and fake chats."

"That's genius." Taylor nodded at Jordan. "How did you do that?"

She shrugged. "If I revealed all my tricks, I'd be out of a job. And I like working here." Jordan winked at Max.

"Okay. So—" Taylor's phone pinged, and she stopped to look at several messages on her screen. "Uh, sending you the serial numbers now, Jordan. And it looks like the team is here to dust my car." She looked up at Zack. "Why don't you and your guys start working on the games? I'm going

to meet the team in the parking lot. Then, I'm going back to Atlas. Maybe Julius knows something about the car that blocked me."

"Hey. Julius is a solid guy."

Taylor immediately realized her mistake. Zack thought she was accusing the gym's owner of something nefarious. "No, I don't think Julius is involved. But he's probably familiar with who comes and goes in that strip mall. Nothing else was open at that time of the morning. I don't understand how anyone would know I'd be there and that the laptops would be locked in my trunk. Why? Is there a problem?"

Zack looked down at his hands, then looked over at Rafe.

"What is it you're not saying?" Her question was met with silence. "Come on. The clock is ticking on this one. Every minute wasted puts us further away from catching these people."

He cleared his throat. "Julius has a criminal record."

## Chapter 10

Taylor crossed her arms over her chest and sat back. "Uh, could we have the room?"

Max, Jordan, and Rafe looked at each other, seeming to understand she was about to lay down the law. They stood and walked out without a word.

Taylor waited for the door to close before she spoke. "Now who's the one with secrets? You knew about this for over an hour, and you didn't think to tell me that *your* friend—" she pointed at him "—who owns the place where the laptops were stolen had a criminal record. What did he do?"

"It was a long time ago."

"You're not answering the question."

Her phone pinged again. She looked up at Zack. "The techs are in the parking lot waiting for me. We're not done with this conversation." She raised one brow, stood, and marched out, her frustration evident in every step.

Two lab techs from the Evidence Response Team were dusting her trunk for prints when Taylor stepped out of the building and into the parking lot. Ironically, the rain had finally stopped, giving way to a bright, cloudless sky. What had begun as a gray day was now a beautiful fall afternoon. The antithesis of what she was feeling.

"Hey, guys," Taylor called out.

The freckle-faced tech looked up from his crouched position by the trunk. "Oh, hey, Shore."

"Hi, Sam," she said.

The second tech was bent over the passenger-side wheel with his back to Taylor. It wasn't until she saw the shiny patch of bald at the top of his head and heard him grunt that she knew who it was. The surly manager of the cyber tech team, Roger Abbot. He'd been with the Bureau for ages and had never been promoted past manager. He was in a perpetually foul mood. The only way she'd ever been able to deal with him was with forced cheeriness. "Roger, what a surprise. Didn't expect to see you here. I thought you guys were jammed up." Her voice rose another cheery half octave. "What are you doing with the Evidence Response Team?"

"We are jammed up." He straightened, turned to face her, and wiped his nose with the back of his gloved hand. "Boyd personally asked me to check it out since this case is a cybercrime and high profile. And—" he smacked his lips together as if he were enjoying what he was about to say "—it's looking like with all the rain and the way this trunk was opened, we'll need to take it in for a better analysis."

"What do you mean the way the trunk was opened?"

"It doesn't look like someone broke in. It looks like someone used the key to open it and then slid the child-safety anti-lock to keep it from closing all the way." Roger paused. "Who else has keys to your car?"

"No one. Just me."

"Yeah, something doesn't add up," Sam muttered, taking off his rubber gloves.

Taylor thought a lot of things about this case weren't adding up. "Listen, before I bring the car back to headquarters, I need to make a stop."

"No can do." Roger shook his head. "This ride needs to go right back. No stops."

His meaning was clear: The laptops were gone, and she was the only one with the key. If she didn't know any better, she'd think he was pointing the finger at her. The idea was preposterous, but she didn't want to stand there and argue with him. At this point, it was better to avoid any further conversation. "All right. Roger, why don't you drive it back?"

"You want me to give you a lift back to HQ in the van?" Sam offered.

Taylor thought about that for a moment. She really did need to speak with Julius at the gym before going to Albany. "Nah. I need to make one stop. I'll figure out a way back. See you later."

She pulled out her phone and thought about who to call for a ride.

Ten minutes later, Taylor was in the passenger seat of Zack's silver-gray Porsche Boxster as they drove down County Road 385 to Atlas Gym.

The slight hum of the Porsche's engine under her seat was familiar and comforting. Happier times. She thought of all weekend afternoons when she and Zack would drive through the Catskill Mountains with the heat blasting and the top down, enjoying the crisp air and the beauty of the leaves in their autumn splendor. She sighed. The past was the past.

She looked over at Zack, who wore his irritation on his face like a tight ski mask. Clearly, he wasn't thinking about their jaunts through the mountains. "So. You going to tell me what Julius did? Or do I just ask him myself?"

"Damnit!" Zack banged his palm on the steering wheel. "He's one of the good guys."

"That's not helping," she muttered. Taylor wasn't about

to back down, no matter how annoyed he was. Silently, she waited. Several minutes passed before he finally spoke.

"It happened in high school. He played on the junior varsity basketball team. His parents didn't have a lot of money and couldn't afford to get him the letterman jacket everyone else had. So, he took a job working after school and on weekends at Chip's Garage." He paused and took a breath. "One day, some guy rides in needing a tire fixed and strikes up a conversation with Julius. Asks him if he knows anyone who needs to make a quick one hundred and fifty bucks. The exact amount he needs for the jacket. Julius jumps at the chance. The guy tells him to meet him in Albany by this electronics store. Julius gets there, and the guy hands him a phone. Tells him to wait on the corner. If anyone comes by, give him a call."

"And he didn't think that was strange?"

He gave Taylor a quick look. "He was sixteen, desperately wanting a jacket—you know, to fit in. All he thought he had to do was stand on some corner. He had no idea the store was being robbed until six cop cars pulled up with guns aimed at him. That's when he knew he'd messed up."

"That's one way of putting it. How much time did he do?"

"He was in juvie on criminal conspiracy but was out in a couple of weeks, and his record was expunged."

She blew out a breath. "He must have had one helluva lawyer."

"Yeah. He did. My mother. But he was innocent. So it wasn't hard to get him off."

Taylor looked at him, understanding this was one of his good friends. "I get it. You believe he had nothing to do with the robbery—"

"Because he didn't." Zack raised his voice. "And he didn't

have anything to do with this. Nothing to do with it at all. But you do what you have to."

Taylor remained silent. She fully planned to do her job and check every lead, regardless of Zack's feelings.

When they reached the gym, Zack zipped into a spot at the far end of the rectangular-shaped lot. Taylor got out and looked around. The gym shared the strip mall with Missy's House of Hands Nail Salon, Weight Watchers, and a Suds-n-Wash laundromat.

Earlier in the morning, when she'd come for her workout, none of the other businesses had been open, but there were at least a dozen other cars at this hour.

Together, they crossed the lot and headed into Atlas. The same barrel-chested man was behind the reception desk.

"Hi, Harry."

"Oh, hey, Zack. This is a surprise." Harry looked at Taylor. "Do you two know each other?"

"Yes, we do," she answered.

"Is Julius expecting you?" Harry asked.

"Yeah. I sent him a text," Zack said.

"He may not have seen it. He's been with clients all morning. And you know he's like you—doesn't keep his phone on him while he's working in the gym." Harry turned to check the time. "He's done in five minutes."

Taylor nodded. The reception area was tiny, and she felt claustrophobic. Until Julius was ready, she'd check out the cars in the lot. "Thanks. We'll wait outside."

Of the more than a dozen cars, only two were black SUVs. Taylor headed to the first one and checked out the rear window. The attached decal said *Rollin' with my squad #MomLife*. She shook her head and muttered, "Yeah. That's not it."

"What are you looking for?" Zack asked as he stepped up beside her.

"The car that blocked me this morning had a gray decal with a drawing in black ink of an eagle. There are two similar SUVs in this lot. This one—" she pointed to the hashtag-mom decal "—isn't it. And I can see from here that one across the lot doesn't have a decal."

"Hey, you looking for me?" Julius called from the front door of the gym.

"Hi," Zack said. "You got a minute?"

"For you? Anytime. Let's go to my office."

Taylor followed them past the reception desk and down the hall until they were two doors from the women's lockers. He held open his office door open, and Zack and Taylor stepped inside. A large metal desk dwarfed the space. Curled in the corner on top of several mats was a black cat with a patch of white across the right eye. A small window behind the desk looked out into an alley. Taylor wished it was open. The smell of wet cat filled the cramped room. She wrinkled her nose and took a seat across from Julius.

"This looks serious. What's up?" He sat and folded his hands on top of the desk.

Zack looked at Taylor. "Sorry to be so mysterious." She pulled out her badge and showed it to him.

Julius raised a brow. "FBI? Am I in some sort of trouble I'm not aware of?"

Taylor clipped her badge back onto the waistband of her jeans. "My car was vandalized outside the gym this morning, and important evidence is missing."

"In the lot outside?" Julius pointed past them. "While you were in here working out?"

"Yeah." Taylor went on to explain as best she could the make of the car and the decal as the only distinguishing

mark. As she spoke, she watched Julius's face. Either he was a damn good actor or he really was shocked to hear that her car had been broken into. The more she thought about it, the more it seemed as if he wasn't a viable suspect. They'd never met until they sparred this morning, and he had no idea she worked for the FBI.

"Well, we may be able to get more information," Julius volunteered. "We can check the CCTV."

"You put in cameras?" Zack asked.

"Yeah. The nail salon next door has been having some sketchy characters coming in and out. Sometimes after hours."

"Sketchy?" Taylor asked.

Julius rubbed the back of his head. "Guys looked like they're in their late twenties. Tattoos, earrings." He held up his hand. "Nothing wrong with ink and bling, but some facial scars, just a... I don't know, a general feeling. These guys coming in and out of a nail salon? Didn't make sense to me. So I just wanted to be safe and not sorry."

"Why didn't you tell me?"

"Aw, Zack, you've already done too much to help me get this place started. I didn't want to bother you."

"It's not a bother. I mean, you do know we run a cybersecurity company. We could hook you up with the latest." Zack paused. "In fact, let's check out what you have. If it's not satisfactory, I'm going to have it upgraded."

"I do not want you to go through any—"

"Stop yourself. Don't say another word. It's no trouble." He stood. "Where's the feed?"

Julius rose and walked around his desk. Taylor and Zack followed. At the end of the hall was a small closet. When Julius opened the door, Zack sighed.

"Hey, don't give me that pitiful look," Julius said. "At least I got cameras."

"The both of you can work this out later," Taylor interrupted. "Can you eject the microSD card so we can take a look?"

Julius took the card out of the recorder and placed it into the port of the laptop that was part of the CCTV system. "What time did you leave the gym this morning?"

"Around six twenty," Taylor said. "Let's look at the hours between five fifteen and six forty."

Julius scrolled through the disc to the date and approximate time. "Here we are—it's about five." The image on the screen was split in half. The two cameras above the gym's entrance showed a view of the lot and one of the front door.

Taylor watched as the cameras captured Julius and Harry arriving separately and heading into the gym. Several moments later, the image of the two men working out this morning entered. And finally, Taylor's Ford Fusion parked and she entered. They continued monitoring the feed.

"Wait. Stop," Taylor called out. "Did you see that?" She looked at Zack. "Something moved the cameras."

Julius inched the footage backward.

"There. Right there." She held up a hand.

The three watched the screen as the camera angles were redirected from the parking lot and the front entrance to a view of the sky. The cameras' lenses showed nothing but raindrops.

"Wow," Julius said.

Taylor stepped back, noting that at no time did either Julius or Harry step outside. It appeared as if someone was standing to the left of the cameras, away from the front door.

"Whoever did this knew exactly where to stand so they'd be out of sight when they re-aimed the cameras."

"But I don't understand how they were moved. They're mounted so high that I need a stool to reach them."

"Probably some sort of stick or pole," Taylor said as her phone rang. She slipped it out of her back pocket and checked the screen. "It's Gil," she said to Zack. "I need to take this."

She stepped out of the closet and swiped open her phone. "Hey," she said, walking down the hall and out of the gym. "What's up?"

"The boss read your report on the stolen devices and wants to talk to you," Gil said.

"Now? Should I call him?"

"No, he wants you here in the office."

Taylor's heart picked up speed, and she sensed something was off. "Gil, just tell me what's going on." There was silence on the other end. "Gil!"

"Look, I'm not supposed to say anything until the lab writes it up, but Roger spoke with Boyd and gave his initial findings. We know there's more analysis to do, but the boss wanted whatever they had now. At this point, the only prints on or in the trunk of your car are yours."

"Of course my prints are there. It's my car. Obviously, whoever stole the laptops used gloves, or maybe the rain washed them away."

"Well, that's the question, isn't it? Because your prints didn't wash away in the rain. And there's the question of the trunk being opened with a key."

"Meaning what?" Taylor knew what he meant, but she wanted to hear him say it.

Instead, Gil didn't answer her question. "Anyway. I'm not your judge and jury. Did you get anything from the gym?"

"No. They have CCTV, but the cameras were moved." She turned to look at the other storefronts. "Hang on." Taylor's gaze quickly scanned the other establishments. Other than the cameras for the gym, there didn't appear to be any security for the other storefronts. "Sorry—just checking if anyone else might have cameras at this strip mall."

"And?"

"And nothing."

"Anyway, like I said, Boyd wants to talk to you. In person."

"I'll get there as soon as I can. They were supposed to drop off a car for me this afternoon. Not sure when it will get here."

"It wasn't a get-here-when-you-can invitation. Figure it out and get here within the hour."

The call ended, and Taylor stared at her blank phone screen.

"Hey, you coming back in?" Zack called from the doorway.

"I think we're done here." She tucked her hair behind her ears. "I have to get back to headquarters."

"Now?"

"Yes, I'm being summoned by my boss."

"But you don't have a car."

"That's who I'm calling now—the transport team to see if they're on their way. I have one hour to get to a meeting with Boyd." Taylor put the phone to her ear and waited for what seemed like an eternity for someone to answer.

"Transport. Liam speaking," said the tiny voice on the other end.

"Hey, Liam, it's Taylor Shore. Do you know if my ride is ready?"

"Hang on."

Taylor heard him put the phone down. She leaned against the outside wall of the gym and tapped her foot. What did the SAC want to see her about? This assignment was stalling out, and she needed to get it on the right track.

"Agent Shore, sorry, but we won't be ready for you until maybe four this afternoon."

"Seriously? I'm on assignment and without wheels—that makes it difficult for me to do my job. There's nothing in the garage?"

"The work order here says 'Ready after seven.' We're already rushing it by having it to you by four."

Taylor stamped her foot and looked up at the sky. "Okay. Thanks." She swiped off the call. "Damn it!"

"I can drive you to Albany," Zack offered.

"I really wanted you to start in on the games. It feels like too much time is slipping by, and I'm concerned."

"We have a team back at the office that has already started on the games. But it's your op. You tell me what you need and want from me, and I'm there."

Taylor thought for a moment. Between the stolen laptops, the unusable CCTV footage, and Boyd's desire to see her, she needed to move this op into overdrive if she had any hope of solving this case. It sure as hell felt like she was being purposefully thwarted.

"Thanks, Zack. I'll take that ride."

"Okay. I'll be right back. I'm going to let Julius know we're leaving."

She paced back and forth in front of the gym, her mind turning to her next moves. When her phone pinged, she thought it was Gil, wondering if she was on her way. Instead,

it was a text with a picture. Taylor clicked on the image, and a photo of her empty trunk appeared. She opened the message to get the phone number of the sender, and the image disappeared as if it had never been sent. "What the—"

## Chapter 11

Before Zack left the gym, he spent a few minutes with Julius discussing the new security system he would install, refusing to listen to any of Julius's protests. "Two techies will be here on Friday, and they'll put in the new equipment." He put up his hand. "The discussion is closed. And I've gotta go—Taylor's waiting."

Julius stuck out his hand, and they shook. "You don't have to do this, but I really appreciate it, man."

Zack patted him on the shoulder. "It's a nonissue. I'll see you next week for a workout."

As soon as he stepped outside, he spotted Taylor leaning on the side of his car, her attention entirely focused on her phone. "Hey," he called out. When she looked up, the expression on her face telegraphed something was wrong. "What's the matter?"

"Nothing. Why?"

"You look—I don't know—like you're angry."

"Yeah. I'm a little pissed off. Can you blame me?" She paused and took a breath. "A lot's going wrong with this case, and it's only day one. Man—" she slapped her thigh "—talk about being on the struggle bus express. It seems every other minute, there's something new I need to deal

with. It's like someone is purposefully throwing concrete roadblocks in front of me."

Zack had never seen her this frustrated, and he couldn't blame her for being upset. She had a lot on her plate.

"Why are you staring at me?" Taylor pulled on the car's door handle. "Come on. We've gotta go."

Zack unlocked the car before walking to the driver's side and getting in. He wasn't about to press the issue if she didn't want to talk about it. At least not at the moment.

As far as he could tell, things seemed to be going south rapidly, and they hadn't even started the operation. He imagined the fact that her boss was demanding to see her wasn't a good sign. She had to be feeling the pressure.

He pulled the Porsche out onto the county road. They drove in silence, but the quiet fury radiating off Taylor was palpable, and his instincts told him it was more than just the stolen laptops or the meeting with Boyd. From what he knew of Taylor Shore, she wasn't the type to let a difficult case upset her this much. He had first-hand experience watching her in action when she led Rafe's stepdaughter's kidnapping case. And throughout those complex negotiations, she'd remained calm and in control. This situation seemed different, as if the stakes had been taken up several notches. Whatever she was chewing on, he had a sudden and undeniable urge to help. Regardless of his conflicted feelings for her, he didn't want to see her fail. And he didn't want to see her get hurt.

Within ten minutes, they were on the thruway heading toward Albany. While Taylor silently stared out the passenger window, Zack's mind went over everything that had happened since meeting her in the parking lot at RMZ offices earlier. It was a lot to take in, and it gave him a little insight into the types of things she had to deal with as an

FBI agent. He'd have to be an emotional black hole not to recognize she didn't have an easy job and that there were things she couldn't and wouldn't tell him.

Reluctant as he was to admit it, he was beginning to understand that maybe it wasn't so much about secrets as it was information she either wasn't yet ready to share or wasn't able to share. That realization shifted something inside him. The anger he'd been holding on to seemed to release a little, and his muscles relaxed. However, it would take another minute for him to wrap his mind around why Taylor kept her sister's disappearance from him.

Zack shook his head. Now was not the time to get into that. He was sensitive enough to know she didn't need his anger or his questions. She needed his help.

"Anything you want to talk about?" Zack asked, knowing his help might be rejected. And for the first time, that was okay with him.

Taylor turned toward him. "I'm thinking through a few things."

"Want to think out loud?"

"I do." She turned in her seat to face him. "Listen, Zack. I'm sitting here, and my mind is buzzing. There's a lot going on. Some things I can't say. And it's not because I don't want to—"

"I get it. They're privileged."

She waved a hand. "That's not it. It's because I haven't fully formulated what I'm thinking. And I don't want to jump to any conclusions. But the things that I can say for sure right now, I will."

"I'm listening." Zack stole a quick glance at her, then focused back on the road.

"Back there, when you came out of Atlas Gym, I was looking at my phone."

"Intently, I might add."

"Yeah. You could say that." She tilted her head to one side. "While I was waiting for you, I got a text. No words, just an image."

"An image?"

"Yeah, a photo. Someone sent me a photo of the inside of my trunk with the box of laptops. From the way the image was captured, I could see it was dark and raining."

"That's great. Maybe there's metadata on the pic to tell us when and where it was taken."

"That's the problem. I clicked open the photo, and it was on my screen for maybe five seconds, but then it disappeared."

Zack wasn't sure he had heard her correctly. "Did you say disappeared? How?"

"That's the question I don't have an answer for. I mean, one second I was looking at it, and the next second it was gone. I couldn't find the number it came from—it's as if I never received the text." Taylor scoffed. "I know I didn't hallucinate that photo. It was there."

"How long do you think you'll be at headquarters?" he asked.

"Hard to say. Either way, my car won't be ready until four this afternoon. So I'll be there until at least then. Why?"

"I think we need to have Jordan look at the phone. See if there's a ghost or some way to trace that disappearing message."

"I'm no cyber expert, but do you think that's even possible?"

Zack smiled. "If there's one thing I've learned since meeting Jordan, her hacking skills are undeniable. And she has ways with technology that we mere mortals know nothing of. I'd say there's a fifty-fifty chance."

"Great—I'll text her now."

"Hold up." He shook his head. "I wouldn't do that. Whoever sent you that text and made it disappear is tech-savvy. We have no idea if they have access to your phone. I'd say we have Jordan do a full sweep when you get back to the office."

Taylor sat back in her seat. "That makes sense. In fact, I'll give you my phone. Take it to Jordan so she can start working on it right away. I'll call you from my desk phone when I'm leaving."

"Good deal," Zack said.

"We need to move fast. Once you drop me off, what's your plan?"

"I'll take your lead on this. But I'm assuming I join the team and start playing games right away."

"Yeah. That's as good a plan as any for right now. I'll drive back to Hollow Lake as soon as I can." Before she got out of the car, she turned to Zack. "If Jordan comes up with anything, anything at all, on the missing laptops or my phone, call the Bureau and ask for me."

"Will do."

Taylor headed straight into headquarters and took the elevator to the second floor. Walking directly to her desk, she passed Brett Boyd's office. The door was slightly ajar and revealed he was sitting with Roger, the manager of the cyber tech team, and Gil. That didn't bode well, she thought. From her desktop computer, she sent an interoffice message to Boyd's assistant, letting him know she was here and ready to meet whenever he was free. She assumed she'd be ushered into the current meeting.

A message came back within seconds.

He'll call you when he's ready.

Taylor sat back, tapped her fingers on her desk, and looked around impatiently. While waiting, she thought she might as well get the reports from the cyber team that Boyd uploaded. She sent an email to the cybercrime unit requesting the report.

The return message was swift: These documents were already requested. You should have received them two hours ago.

Taylor squinted at the email. What the heck? She hadn't put in any request. This had to be a mistake. Her computer pinged with an incoming interoffice message—Boyd was ready for her.

Taking a deep breath, she stood and, with her fingers, combed her hair away from her face. She'd deal with that missing report later. Squaring her shoulders, she headed for his office. She knocked lightly on the door jamb, and Boyd motioned her in. As she entered, Roger exited, giving her a cursory nod.

"Have a seat, Shore." Boyd's tone was sharp.

The air in the room was close, and she took the still-warm seat Roger had vacated.

Boyd lifted a piece of paper from his desk. "This is the report from the lab techs."

She nodded.

"There's no evidence to indicate the car was broken into—"

"But—"

He held up a hand. "Shore, you'll have your chance to speak. Let me finish."

Taylor nodded and sat back in her chair. A trickle of sweat ran down her back. The uneasy feeling in the pit of her stomach intensified. She looked over at Gil. He had a look she hadn't seen before, like he was distancing him-

self from her, and she wondered how she'd gotten herself into this position. It was as if she were on the wrong side of things and on her own.

Boyd continued explaining that the only prints on the car were hers—inside and outside of the trunk—just as the lab techs had initially informed her. Additionally, it had been verified that a key had been used to open the trunk. Then, the child-proof safety feature, a small button on the inside of the trunk, was slipped into the active position, preventing it from being closed. This was a feature Taylor was unaware of.

However, in this case, with the only viable prints being hers and the fact that the trunk was opened using a key, Boyd explained the theft of the computers looked suspicious. He spoke with simmering fury. "Damnit, Shore, this isn't going as I thought."

"Sir? Are you accusing me of something?"

Boyd turned. His dark eyes glared at her. "No. Just… some things aren't adding up. It's up to you to untangle this mess. You were the last one to have the box with the laptops."

She stared at him, keeping her face expressionless. She couldn't believe anyone would even think she had something to do with the stolen laptops. But it certainly felt as if that was exactly what was happening. Her mind raced over the last twenty-four hours. Too many things weren't adding up. Instinctively, she knew she couldn't tell them about the disappearing text. She'd look like a fool. For right now, she'd wait to see if she was still even on this case.

She watched Boyd as he stood and began to pace behind his desk.

"As you can see, this puts me in a very awkward position." He rubbed his jaw. Stopped. Then stared down at her.

"I happen to think you're a good agent. I happen to think this may be, just *may be*, a horrible set of circumstances." He spread his arms out. "But as you can see, the evidence is contrary." He raised his hand again. "Don't speak yet."

He paced for several more seconds. "So. If I go strictly by your record, up until the last operation, there's no reason to believe you're anything but a good, solid, loyal FBI agent. Needless to say, there is some concern that the last op failed, and this incident is a black mark. But I know you, and I know your work. So. For now, I'm tabling this and giving you the benefit of the doubt."

Taylor's mind was on hyperdrive. All she ever wanted was to be an FBI agent. There wasn't a single possibility that she would ever betray the agency or go rogue.

It made her nervous that Boyd continued to pace and that Gil hadn't said one single word in her defense. Taylor wondered if he was suspicious of her, too, or if he didn't want to go up against his mentor in her defense. The current situation was only going to make it more difficult for them to work together on this assignment. He'd end up questioning her every move. She needed Gil to believe she had nothing to do with this. Her only hope was that Jordan was able to track those stolen computers.

"We're moving on. This case is important. And the department is stretched. If I had someone else to put on the case, I'd strongly consider it." Boyd stopped pacing and stood behind his desk. "But let me make this perfectly clear." He put both hands on his desk and leaned forward. "If you thought I had eyes on it before, you better know I'm hyperfocused now." He glanced at both of them. "Understood?"

"Yes, sir," Taylor said. But a part of her wondered if he thought she might be capable of bad acts if the evidence of the stolen computers pointed to her—why would he be

keeping her on the job? There was more to this than what was on the surface.

"From what Gil tells me, you're nowhere in the investigation." Boyd's eyes were stern and seemed to stare directly into her soul.

Taylor glanced over at Gil, feeling increasingly like he was playing politics and she was sure to be on the losing end. "We just started, sir. The game war room at RMZ Digital is set up, and we're going fishing, working on how to snag a bad actor. That's step number one. We're also working on finding and retrieving any metadata from the victims' devices. We're hoping that will give us a clue to the location."

"So what you're saying is right now you have nothing?" Boyd demanded.

"We're working on it," Taylor said, annoyed that Gil remained silent.

"Give me something." Boyd slammed his fist on the desk. "I'm scheduled to meet the governor on Friday afternoon at three sharp. I'm not going into that meeting with nothing. You can damn well be sure of that. So get me something fast." He sat and leaned back in his chair.

"Moving forward, this is how it's going to go. Gil is still lead in the investigation. Right now, Agent Shore, your only job is to work with RMZ and flush out the bad actors. Whatever information you get, and I mean any lead, you turn it right over to Gil. I want you reporting to him every single evening. You are not to take matters into your own hands. You are not to make any decisions."

"But, sir—"

"No." He slapped a hand on the desk. "That's how we're going to play this. I don't have any evidence to put you on administrative leave. But the situation doesn't look good. So no more mistakes. Is that understood?"

"Yes, sir." Taylor rose and looked at Gil, but he remained seated. Clearly, she was meant to leave alone. She stiffened her back and walked out.

The air outside his office seemed cooler, and she took a deep, relieved breath. Boyd was being pressed, so he had to press her. But so many things didn't make sense.

She sat at her desk, and a chat popped up from the Transport Department. They had a car ready for her. Great, she thought. She'd drive back to Hollow Lake tonight, and on the way, she'd process everything that happened since five o'clock that morning, starting with what the heck was going on—the missing computers, the disappearing text, and the missing report that she supposedly had already received.

Looking up, she spotted Boyd and Gil coming out of his office.

"We're going to dinner," Boyd said to his assistant.

As the two walked out of the cubicle area and toward the elevator, they had their heads together and spoke in low tones. The passing thought in her mind was scary. Was she being set up? And why?

The entire situation was exhausting, but she couldn't give in. The idea that someone was trying to get her off the case not only pissed her off but fueled her with the necessary adrenaline to keep going. "You have no idea who you're dealing with. I do not scare easily. There's a change in plans," she said under her breath. She wanted answers, and she was determined to get them.

The first order of business was to get that report she supposedly already requested. Then she'd drive back to Hollow Lake and meet with Zack.

Taylor sat at her desk and sent a message to the head of Cybercrime. Sorry didn't get the report. Can you please resend. I'm in the office now.

A few minutes later, her desk phone rang. "This is Agent Shore."

"Shore. This is Camille in Cybercrime. I sent you that report hours ago."

"Really? I didn't get it. Wait. Hang on." Taylor quickly looked through her email and interoffice chat and saw nothing. "You sure you sent it?"

The only response on the other end was a huff.

"Listen, let me come see you." Taylor didn't wait for a response. She hung up the phone and marched down one flight of stairs to the cybercrime unit. She heard Camille before she spotted her behind the reception desk. Her low-toned, smoky voice was handling a call. Taylor would wait. She needed to clear up who exactly got the report because she sure as hell didn't have it.

Camille finished her call and pushed her black-framed cat-eye glasses up the bridge of her nose. "I told you I sent you that report."

"Yeah, I know, Camille. I'm sure you did. And I'll get IT to look into it. But for whatever reason, I never got it."

She let out a long-suffering breath. "I wish you people would keep track of your incoming traffic. You should know better. This stuff is confidential. Good thing I like and trust you, kid, but I've got better things to do than send you reports multiple times." Her long red nails clicked on several keys as she stared at her monitor. "Here it is." She looked over at Taylor. "Make sure you check with IT as to why you didn't get it the first time I sent it." She put her hand on her hip. "You need me to print this out?"

"Yes. Please."

Within minutes, Taylor was jogging back up the stairs to her cubicle—report in hand. Reaching down for her purse, she picked up her desk phone, called Zack, and let him know

she'd be in Hollow Lake within the hour. They agreed to meet at Fritz's Diner for a quick bite.

She headed for the garage and picked up her car from the transport team. The drive back gave Taylor time to think about everything that had transpired since she started this op. As far as Boyd was concerned, she was walking on eggshells until she could find those missing laptops. Gil seemed to be playing politics by keeping his distance. With so many things going wrong, her gut told her she was on her own.

She drummed her fingers on the steering wheel. Was there really no one she could trust? She raised an eyebrow and drummed her fingers harder. "Well, there is one person," she said out loud to no one. "Zack."

There was only one problem with that. Would he be willing to help her?

# Chapter 12

Fritz's Diner was busy with an early dinner crowd. The smell of roast chicken and mashed potatoes filled his nostrils. Zack hadn't eaten lunch, and he found himself slightly salivating.

A young man with broad shoulders and short-cropped, curly black hair approached. "Hey, Zack."

"Hey, Leon. How's school?"

"Oh, you know. My senior year of college. After that, I'll be out there pounding the pavement for a real job."

"Yeah. Sadly, it's called life." Zack chuckled.

"Just you tonight?"

"No. I'm meeting someone." He pointed toward the back. "How about that booth over there?"

"Sure, let me just clean it off first."

Zack waited while Leon cleared the table and thought about the countless meals he and Taylor had eaten at this diner. The last time they were here, she'd said there wasn't a place in the United States that made french fries and onion rings like Fritz's.

"Table's all ready," Leon called out.

Just as Zack slid into the booth, Leon placed menus on the table.

"We won't need those." He pointed to the menus. "I think

my friend will be hungry when she gets here, and I know what she wants, so I'll order for both of us."

"Sure thing." Leon took out a pad and pen from his apron and wrote down the order.

Ten minutes later, Taylor entered, and Zack instantly spotted the concerned look, a look he'd seen more and more on her face. He waved her over.

She unbuttoned her jacket, placed it on an overhead hook, and slid into the booth opposite Zack.

"Hey. You okay?"

"I don't even know where to start."

"What did Boyd say?"

Taylor blew out a long breath. "Let's just say no one at the Bureau is too thrilled with me. It's not like they're directly saying I stole the laptops, but they blame me for the fact that they were stolen." She pursed her lips. "Obviously, I was responsible for them. I shouldn't have left them in the car while I went to the gym. Better yet, I should've gone straight to your offices and skipped the gym."

"Don't beat yourself up. You had no idea they'd be stolen."

"I'm an agent for the FBI, and I'm trained to take all considerations into account." She shook her head. "But that's not the point. It's not that I'm being blamed so much as several times, there was some underlying, unspoken suggestion that I might have something to do with the fact that they went missing because the car wasn't broken into. The child safety lock was undone."

"That's crazy. You had nothing to do with it."

"You know that. And I know that. For the time being, Boyd's giving me the benefit of the doubt, but moving forward, I have to run everything by Gil. It's like I'm an agent in training."

"Here's your order." Leon stepped up to the booth, took several dishes off the round stainless-steel platter, and placed them on the table.

"Thanks," Zack said.

Taylor smiled. "You ordered all my favorites."

"Comfort food," they both said simultaneously.

"I figured you could use some comfort about now."

"Appreciate it." Without waiting a beat, Taylor grabbed the ketchup, mayo, and mustard jars from the condiment caddy and placed a dollop of each on a corner of her plate. Zack watched in fascination as she performed a ritual he'd seen dozens of times. And it made him smile.

Taylor mixed all three with her fork until she seemed happy with the consistency. Then she grabbed a fry and dragged it through her homemade dressing. "Mmm. Just what I needed," she said while chewing.

She bit into her grilled Swiss with tomato. "I haven't had one of these in forever. What made you order this for me?"

"I remembered it was one of your go-tos when you had a rough day at work."

She took another bite, closed her eyes, moaned, and chewed at the same time. "This has to be the bright spot of my day." Taylor wiped her mouth with her napkin.

The contented look on her face reminded Zack of their weeknight ritual of cooking dinner at his house. He had looked forward to those evenings. Each night, they seamlessly moved about the kitchen as if they were choreographed, preparing whatever new meal they were anxious to try. He could almost smell the exotic aromas and hear the beats of the music that would fill the room from their combined playlists. Sometimes, while they waited for a pot to boil or the oven timer to go off, they would hold each other tight and sway to the music.

Inwardly, he smiled. It was a memory he hadn't allowed himself to look at until now. He supposed it was spending so much time with Taylor that old feelings were bound to push through. He wasn't sure if they would ever be able to get back to that. The fear of being hurt again was real. So, for now, being friends was a big enough step.

Zack kept his eyes on Taylor as they ate their dinner, noticing the look of contentment turning into something else as the furrow in her brow grew deeper. "Besides your sandwich, what are you chewing on? You look like you're working out yet another problem."

Taylor put her half-eaten sandwich on the plate, grabbed another fry, dipped, and chewed. "I'm gonna tell you something... I'm not even sure I should." She held up a hand. "It's not for security reasons. It's because it's...it's not based on any facts—it's just what I think, and I could be—no, I hope like hell I'm wrong."

"Now you're making me worried. Just spit it out. You've always had good instincts." Zack leaned forward and grabbed her hand. "Whatever it is, we'll work it out." He surprised himself with that statement because he meant it. While he knew she was perfectly capable of taking care of herself, he wanted to help her.

"I think Boyd's dirty."

"Dirty?" He frowned. "What do you mean?"

"Yeah, see, even when I say it, it sounds off. But there are too many things that do not add up. I mean, I cannot make them make sense." Taylor began to spell out her reasoning. "Just before we were given this assignment, I overheard Boyd in his office, and he specifically stated that the people behind this were located in the US. I mean, those weren't his exact words, but that's what I gathered."

"Is it possible he was talking about another op?"

"Possible, but not likely, since the entire situation with the governor's son was blowing up that morning, and it had become a high priority for Boyd. We were scheduled to meet with him after that call." She looked out the large glass window. "So, no, I don't think so. But we can table that for the moment."

"Okay. What else?"

"When the two of three additional laptops arrived at the office, Boyd was in the Cybercrime lab talking to the tech."

"What's unusual about that?"

"Boyd never goes down there. He waits for his agents to get all the prelim, then download the information to him in a report." She shrugged. "It's just unusual. Unusual enough so that I noticed."

"Al-l-l-righty. I'll give you that. Especially if it's not protocol."

"The Cybercrime lab performed the initial report on the first four laptops. They didn't get too far because they were jammed with other cases, and Boyd told them to stop working on it because he had planned on turning the case over to you. But they did have some information they were waiting on, and they planned to forward the last bit of information to Gil and me. Only Boyd picked it up and uploaded it to the portal himself. Again, not protocol."

"Hmm." Zack frowned again. He was beginning to get the creeps and, without realizing it, checked their surroundings. It almost had a cloak-and-dagger feel.

"I was tempted to talk to Gil about it, but he'd never believe me."

"Why not?"

"Because Boyd's his mentor. They have a very tight bond. In fact, after Boyd gave me a dressing down tonight, he and Gil went off to dinner—*together*. Gil would never think

anything bad about Boyd." Taylor blew out a breath. "Hell, I'm not sure I totally believe it. I mean, Boyd's been with the Bureau forever. He's got a slew of commendations." She threw up a hand. "I don't even know what to think anymore." Taylor put her chin in her hand and, with the other, drummed her fingers on the table.

"But the facts are the facts," she continued. "Tonight when I asked for the report, the lab said I'd already asked for it. They sent it. Only until that moment, I hadn't asked for it, and I never got what they initially sent." Her bag sat beside her, and she reached over and pulled out the file. "I finally went down to the lab and got this before I came here." She put the file on the table. "I haven't looked at it yet."

Pushing her plate to the side, she opened the folder and scanned the contents. She raised a brow and tsked.

"What?"

"This says there might be a possible connection to the US but there wasn't any time to pursue it."

"That's unusual because why?"

"Gil told me that Boyd said everything was overseas." She slammed the folder shut. "None of this makes sense."

"It looks like we're back to where we started."

"How so?"

"We need to start our own investigation. Simple as that. And the good news is we're set up for it," Zack said. "And here—" he reached into his pocket and pulled out her mobile "—Jordan got a hit off the disappearing photo and is tracing the metadata."

"Seriously? That's amazing."

"Yeah. Told you she's good." He looked at her half-eaten food. "You done?"

"Yeah. Seemed to have lost my appetite along the way."

"I'll get the check, and we'll head back to the office. The

war room is up and running, and we have six techies playing games under the made-up aliases."

As Zack raised his hand for the check, his phone pinged, and he checked the screen. "It's a text from Jordan. One of the techs got a scammer on the line, and it looks like the signal is coming from Albany."

Taylor stood, put her jacket on, and grabbed the file. "Maybe my luck is finally turning."

## *Chapter 13*

Taylor and Zack entered the war room at RMZ Digital offices. The overhead lights were off, and the glow of six computer screens flickered in the darkened room.

At each station, a member of Jordan's tech team wore a pair of headsets as they either concentrated on playing a game or were lost in a chat room. Except for the clacking of the keyboards, the room was silent. The headsets filtered out the sounds of laser guns being fired, planets being blown up, and zombies chopping up bodies.

At the station farthest from the door, Jordan huddled with one of the techies and looked up. "Hey," she called out. "Over here."

They made their way to the other side of the room.

"This is Fred," Jordan said. "His handle is MidasX."

Fred didn't look up from his screen, blue light flickering across his pale face. He brushed a dark lock from his forehead.

"Looks like he has a bad actor on the hook." She pointed to the screen on the far wall. "See for yourself. I'll put up their chat from the last twenty minutes."

Taylor and Zack moved toward the screen to read the chat transcript between the RMZ techie, MidasX, and a

player called Julie84. For several minutes, their attention was glued to the screen.

"Wow," Taylor said. "Whoever this is, they're moving fast. This Julie84 character went from gaming to intimacy in what looks like an hour. Could be a trap."

"Could be. But they've been playing for the last four hours," Jordan said. "And Fred's profile indicates he's a long-time gamer who likes sharing new games and trading prizes. The research on the computers you brought in shows they definitely target someone with the profile we created." She shrugged. "Maybe we're just catching a break."

Was it a coincidence they were getting a bite so soon, or was this a setup? Did whoever, or whatever organization, they were after know they were on to them? Taylor thought as she walked around the table where the other RMZ tech nerds were hunched over gaming stations playing various games and pondered her next move. She couldn't stop the niggling sensation that tickled at the back of her mind that maybe this was all happening too soon. The war room hadn't been up for more than twelve hours. On the other hand, maybe the organization behind these sextortions was getting more aggressive. Bolder. Maybe they knew someone was on to them and were going after whatever they could get before they folded up their operation. In which case, she'd need to move quickly.

She turned abruptly to face Jordan. "Do you have an address for Julie84?"

"That's what I'm working on now—trying to get a lock on an exact location. I had it pinned to downtown Albany, but now the VPN traffic is bouncing all over upstate New York."

Taylor rushed over to where Jordan was working on locking down the exact location.

"Fred, whatever you do, keep that chat going until we get the location locked," Zack called out.

"She wants me to send her my picture," Fred said.

"Keep her dangling," he said, heading for an empty laptop station at the table.

"How?"

"Ask…ask what kind of pic 'she' wants."

Taylor stepped toward Zack. "Do we have a solve for this?"

He nodded. "Yeah. I can quickly put together an AI-generated composite of a face that will hopefully resemble an amalgamation of people and no one in particular. But I'd rather we didn't have to send it if Fred can string her along." He looked over at Fred. "Have you described yourself yet?" Zack asked as he swung a chair around and sat in front of the laptop, his fingers flying over the screen.

"I'm tall, with brown hair and dark eyes," Fred said as he continued to chat on screen with whoever was on the other end.

"She just sent me a photo. Just a headshot. Brunette in her late twenties," Fred called out. "She's insisting I send her one."

Taylor walked to the back of the room and read the real-time chat from the large wall screen monitor. "Jordan, how are we coming with the VPN address?"

"I'm not there yet. Soon."

"What's taking so long?"

Jordan sighed. "It takes a minute to monitor the traffic in and out of the VPN. Then I need to analyze the pattern and match their activity to get to their real location."

"Sorry I asked." Taylor paced.

The room was electric with energy. Each working to get an answer as to who was on the other end of this chat. She

could feel they were onto something if Fred could hold off the person on the other end long enough for Jordan to get a location.

"Fred, I'm sending you a headshot now," Zack said.

Fred's screen dinged, and he pulled up the AI-manufactured photo and uploaded it into the chat.

Taylor read the simultaneous transcript of the chat on the big screen.

Julie84: Your look is doing things to me

Taylor let out a groan. *Is this for real?*

MidasX: Cool

Julie84: I got something else to show you

MidasX: Like what?

A photo of her looking straight into the camera, hair carefully tousled, lips puckered, wearing a lace bra and underwear.

MidasX: Very Cool

Julie84: Want to see more?

MidasX: What you got?

"I got it!" Jordan exclaimed.

Taylor rushed over, abandoning the transcript. "Where are they?"

"I got a lock on the incoming and outgoing traffic, and

it looks like a warehouse in Albany. Uh… Twelfth Street and Cornelius."

Taylor stood over the other woman's shoulders. "Show me," she said.

Jordan pulled up the traffic patterns. She was correct. There was a clear signal coming and going from that location.

"Fred, keep it up. Don't stop the chat. I'll make up some images that aren't nudes," Zack said. "We need to keep them on the line."

Taylor whipped out her phone and called Gil. It took all of three minutes to tell him what was happening and the location of the sextortionist. "I'm in Hollow Lake. I'll meet you there."

"This is too hot. We can't wait for you," Gil said. "I'll text Boyd. He'll dispatch a crew. I'll see you when you get there." He ended the call without saying another word.

"Zack, I have to go. Keep that person on the other end. If anything changes, call me."

Taylor sprinted out of the war room, took the stairs, and headed for the parking lot in the back.

Forty minutes later, she exited the thruway, heading for downtown Albany. It took another ten minutes for her to arrive at the warehouse, where there were at least a dozen unmarked cars, SUVs, and agents with their FBI shields in plain view surrounding the warehouse. From where she sat, she could see SAC Boyd and Gil standing at the entrance.

Taylor threw the gear shift into Park, unclicked her seat belt, threw on her FBI jacket, and bolted out of her vehicle. She jogged over to Boyd and Gil, nearly stopping dead in her tracks when she saw the looks on their faces. Even in the dim light, their displeasure was evident.

"What?" she said.

"That's what I'd like to know," Boyd said, his tone full of anger.

Taylor furrowed her brow and looked at Gil, her hands to her side, palms up, in the universal *what is going on?* sign.

"Empty," was Gil's only word.

"Empty?" She looked from one to the other. "I don't understand."

"Empty, as in no one is there. Nothing is there. It's a vacant warehouse. Apparently, it has been since the last tenant, a paper company, moved out twelve months ago," Boyd said and held up a hand. "Before you say anything, we checked it out. This place hasn't been used for anything in months. Not even squatters."

Taylor took a step back. She was certain this was the correct address. She'd followed the VPN signal right alongside Jordan. How could they both get it so wrong?

"The intel didn't check out—seems like we were sent on a wild-goose chase," Boyd said and brushed past her. "I'll expect a report from you in the morning." He got into his vehicle, and Taylor watched as he took off.

She waited a moment, then turned to Gil. "That lead was solid. I was there. I saw where the signal was coming from."

"How solid could it be? Look. Nothing here."

"I don't understand."

"Neither do I," Gil said. "If we have any hope of solving this case, you need to concentrate on overseas and stop chasing any leads inside the US. It's clearly the wrong target."

Taylor shoved her hands inside her pockets, wondering if he was right or if Boyd had something to do with the false lead. She wasn't sure. But it was late, and she was running past empty and couldn't think how to fix this.

"Look, go back to the Airbnb and get some rest," Gil said. "In the morning, work with RMZ on putting together

a report of how you got the intel, and I'll meet you at the office around noon. Okay?"

Taylor barely registered what he was saying. She felt as if she'd been punched in the gut. How did she get this so wrong? She was there, in the war room. She saw the VPN traffic signals. She didn't know how those could be faked.

"Hey. Are you hearing me?" Gil put his hand on her shoulder.

Taylor nodded. "Yeah. I heard you." She rubbed at the side of her face. "Maybe you're right. I'll get some sleep and work out how we got here." She chewed on her bottom lip, not totally buying that she'd been the one to make the mistake. Something was here. Something was in this warehouse. "I just want to go inside for a minute, see for myself."

"Forensics is in there. Let them do their job."

"I just want to see inside."

Gil shrugged. "If you have to. I'll go with you."

They stepped inside the large, empty warehouse. If she had to guess, it was about fifty thousand square feet, with twenty-foot ceilings. The forensic team set up night lights every several hundred feet as they dusted for prints and looked for any possible evidence.

From what Taylor could see, there wasn't anything for them to find. It was as Boyd had said—empty.

Her shoulders slumped. How had she gotten this so wrong?

"Don't worry. We'll get this case back on track." Gil patted her on the back.

She bristled under his touch. *Patronizing much?*

"I'm not blaming myself. And I don't think we got faulty intel. Something isn't right, and I'm going to find out what it is." She stomped out of the warehouse.

"You should get some rest," Gil called after her.

She held up her hand, never turning around. "Heading back now. See you tomorrow."

Taylor drove on the thruway, lost in thought. A few miles from her exit, she pressed the button on the steering wheel and spoke into the microphone, "Call Zack."

The phone barely rang before he picked it up.

"Are you okay? What happened?" Zack said.

"Yes. I'm okay. The op, not so much."

"What do you mean?"

"The warehouse was empty. The location we got was wrong." Taylor explained what she saw and how both Boyd and Gil reacted. "I'm not sure what the next move is."

"We'll talk to Jordan in the morning. Sounds to me like someone played us. And we need to find out who that is."

"I thought the same thing." She flipped on her blinker. "I'm at my exit. I need a hot bath and a good night's sleep. Why don't I meet you in the office at, say, seven?"

"Works for me."

"Okay, then. Good night."

"Hey, Taylor."

"Yeah?"

"Take care of yourself."

"Stop worrying, Zack. I'll see you in the morning." She exited the thruway and headed down County Road 385 to her Airbnb.

The house was slightly chilly when she entered. She checked the thermostat, and it was set at sixty-two degrees. But the outside temperature was in the low forties, so she thought she'd get the house a little warm and take a nice hot bath before she went to bed.

Taylor headed straight upstairs and into the bathroom. She turned on the faucets and sprinkled in some of her lavender bath salts. She smiled at the scent. Oh, yeah, this

was going to get her into a sleepy-time mood. And what she wanted now, more than anything, was a good night's sleep. Her mind needed a reset to tackle the problem with a fresh perspective.

Twenty minutes later, she was soaking in the warmth of a deep tub immersed in her delicious-smelling salts. She leaned back, closed her eyes, and tried to make her mind blank. But after several attempts, her mind wouldn't settle. For some reason, when she closed her eyes, images of her sister, Emily, danced in her head. They'd always been there for each other, and she could have used her tonight to talk things through and help her make sense of what was happening.

Taylor closed her eyes again in a vain attempt to relax. She blew out several breaths, repositioned her head against the foam pillow at the edge of the tub, and told herself to chill out.

Several minutes passed before she slapped a hand in the water. It was no use—no way could she relax tonight. She was jacked up, alone, and out of sorts. The man she loved wasn't hers anymore, and now for a reason she didn't understand, she was focused on her sister. She missed Emily more than she could say.

Taylor thought about how quickly her parents moved on with their lives after Emily disappeared. It was one of the many reasons she never spoke to them. She'd always known they differed from her friends' parents, but she'd never realized how utterly selfish they were. The mystery she was never able to figure out was why they had kids in the first place. They were never home and left the raising of her and her sister to a parade of nannies who came and went and, most times, didn't care enough about her or Emily. When Taylor was ten, she made the decision she'd make sure her

sister was cared for since the nannies were mostly useless and her parents were clearly either not capable or didn't care enough. And for years, that was how it stayed. Taylor made sure Emily had enough to eat, demanded she get new clothes when she needed them, and helped her study, so she'd get good grades. She was Emily's surrogate mother. Taylor wiped the tears that were now flowing.

Taylor would never forgive herself for going away to college. At first, she had rejected the idea, not wanting to leave her sister alone. But Emily was fifteen and insisted Taylor not give up her dream. She promised to maintain her grade point average, eat right, and stay out of trouble. Taylor finally reasoned she'd be able to check up on Emily through FaceTime and come home whenever she could. She even had a false hope that her parents would take an interest and wouldn't constantly be jet-setting or throwing parties. But that never happened, and Taylor got so wrapped up in her new life that she hadn't noticed the subtle and not-so-subtle changes in her sister.

She slapped at the water again. "Damnit!" If only she'd paid more attention. Emily had been missing for seven years now, but it felt like yesterday.

There was no way she could let whoever was behind this sextortion ring get away. She wasn't prepared to lose. Not again.

Dragging herself out of the lukewarm tub, she dried off and put on a T-shirt and her comfy pajama bottoms. She sat at the edge of the bed and cried for a good long while. With the last tear shed, she blew her nose and exhaled. Mentally, emotionally, and physically exhausted, she crawled under the covers and was asleep within minutes.

Taylor woke with a tickle in the back of her throat and a cough. *I don't have time to be sick.* She checked the bed-

side clock. The red digital numbers were illuminated at 3:05. Taylor groaned, lifted herself onto her elbows, and coughed again. She scanned the room. Something was off. Although it was dark, she not only sensed smoke but smelled it, and she began to cough in earnest. It took another few seconds for her mind to register that something was burning.

Leaping from the bed, she shoved her feet into her nearby sneakers and ran to open the door but jerked her hand back. The doorknob was scorching hot. "Damn. It's a fire." She looked around as smoke continued to seep into the room from the crack under the door.

Taylor ran to the bedside table, reached for her phone, and called for help.

"Nine-one-one. What's your emergency?"

"Hurry." She coughed. "Fire. There's a fire in the house. I'm at 289 Crossgates Road. I need to find a way out." Without waiting for a response, Taylor swiped off the phone and shoved it into her pajamas pocket and grabbed her purse from the nightstand.

She ran into the bathroom, grabbed a bath towel and a washcloth, dumped them into the sink, and soaked them both with cold water. Taylor put the towel over her head and, with the washcloth, took hold of the doorknob, but it wouldn't turn. "Come on. Come on." She planted her feet firmly on the ground and pulled with all her might, but the door wouldn't budge. It was as if something was wedged under the doorknob from the other side.

Smoke billowed into the room from beneath the door, and she was having difficulty breathing. Taylor ran to the window, threw it open, stuck her head out, and took in great big gulps of air. She looked down and saw nothing to grab onto

and nothing to break her fall. There was no way for her to jump without breaking at least one of her legs.

She turned to find the room filling up with smoke. *Where the hell is the fire truck?* Taylor began to wonder if she'd get out of this alive. With no more time to wait for help or think this through, her only option was to go through the fire. She took ten steps back and charged at the door, and with her right leg arcing into a roundhouse, she kicked once, then rounded again and kicked a second time. Through the smoke, she could see the splintered wood around the door frame. "Come on, you piece of crap." She took several steps back and, with a running jump, thrust her leg out and planted her foot in the center of the door, finally forcing it open.

With the wet towel over her head, she stepped into the smoke-filled hallway. She peeked over the railing and saw the living room in flames. There was one small path behind the sofa. Registering she had moments to get to the front door, she charged down the stairs and, with the wet towel over her head, ran in a zigzag pattern to avoid the flames through the living room and out the front door.

Just as she collapsed on the front lawn, coughing and taking in large gulps of air. She heard sirens and looked up to find two fire trucks and a police car roaring down the road.

The trucks pulled up at the front of the house, and several firefighters rushed off the truck, surrounding the front yard. One rushed toward her and squatted beside her. "Hey, there, anyone else inside?"

Taylor got up onto her forearms and, between coughs, shook her head. She'd swallowed so much smoke it hurt to breathe.

"I'll be right back. I'm going to get you some water,"

the firefighter said. Or at least that was what she thought he said. Despite being disoriented and frankly scared out of her mind, there was one thought that wouldn't leave her: *Someone tried to kill me.*

## Chapter 14

The Airbnb was nestled on a quiet road, along with three other homes that were a good distance apart. Tonight all the residents were out in pajamas and jackets, watching the firefighters put out the blaze. Within an hour, the fire was under control, but much of the lower level of the house had been destroyed.

Taylor sat in Zack's car with a blanket wrapped around her shoulders. He was the first person she thought to call the moment she'd had a coherent thought. Within fifteen minutes, he'd arrived. Now they sat, not so patiently, waiting for the fire inspector, who had questions for Taylor.

At first, Zack insisted he take her to the emergency room, but Taylor refused, saying she was okay. She knew if she went, they'd want to keep her for observation, and the only thing she wanted was to find out who the hell did this. If she hadn't been sure before, she was certain now that someone, or several people, were trying to not only sabotage the case but get rid of her altogether. Whoever did this had no idea what they were up against. She had no intentions of backing down.

The inspector approached Zack's car, and Taylor tightened the blanket around her shoulders and slipped out of the passenger seat.

"Hi. I'm Fire Inspector Troy. Are you the homeowner?" he asked.

Even in the dark, she noticed the prominently displayed badge on his fire-retardant jacket. He was as tall as Zack and had a long face and thin lips.

"No. It's an Airbnb." She looked at Zack. "I actually don't know who owns it. I'm FBI, and my Bureau in Albany rented it."

"Have you contacted them?"

"Not yet."

He gave her a quizzical look.

"It's the middle of the night. I thought I'd wait until first thing in the morning."

"The homeowners have a right to know. They'll need to get in touch with their insurance company."

"Right. Sorry. I'll call the Bureau."

He held up a hand. "Before you do that, can you tell me what happened? Give me the details of what you did last night."

She shook her head, not knowing what to say. "I… I… I honestly don't know. I got here a little after ten. I turned up the thermostat to about sixty-eight—"

"Gas or oil?"

"Gas or what?" She tilted her head.

"The furnace."

She shrugged. "I have no clue."

The inspector made a note on his pad. "Okay, then what?"

"I went upstairs, took a bath, and was in bed before midnight."

"Did you go back downstairs for any reason?"

"No." She shivered and pulled the blanket tighter. "I'd locked up before I went upstairs. There was no reason to go back down. Besides, I was exhausted."

Zack moved in close and put an arm around her shoulder.

"I was sound asleep," she continued, "but at five minutes after three, I woke up coughing."

"That's a pretty specific time."

"Yeah, I checked the clock on the bedside table. At first, I thought I was coming down with something. But then I noticed there was smoke in the room. Anyway, I tried to get out, but the door was stuck."

"Stuck?"

"Yeah, like something was jammed underneath the doorknob."

"Are you sure?"

She gave him a withering look. Taylor felt she'd endured quite enough tonight. She didn't want to be questioned or second-guessed. "Positive. I ended up kickboxing my way out. I'm sure the door is splintered." Her tone was emphatic.

"Wait here a moment." The inspector walked over to three firefighters who were exiting the house. They spoke briefly. One of the firefighters pointed to the second floor.

Zack pulled her into a fierce hug. "You didn't tell me the door was jammed. Oh, my God. I can't even think of what would have happened if you hadn't ninja'd your way out of there."

Taylor remained quiet and leaned into him, soaking up his warmth. Within a few minutes, the front yard was being cordoned off with red tape.

"What's going on?" she murmured.

"Looks like they think this is a crime scene."

Taylor pulled back and looked at Zack. "I could have told them that."

Inspector Troy walked toward them. "There is the possibility that this fire is suspicious, so once it's safe to go back inside, we'll conduct a thorough investigation."

"Arson?" Zack asked.

"We can't be sure. And it doesn't do anyone any good to jump to conclusions. We'll conduct a standard inspection, and then we'll know one way or the other." He made another note on his pad. "And it turns out the local police are notifying the homeowners. Do you have a place to stay?" the inspector asked Taylor.

"She does," Zack rushed to answer, which surprised Taylor and, if she were being honest, pleased her.

"All right. If we have questions, is this the best number at which to reach you?" He turned his pad toward her and tapped it next to her mobile number.

"Yes."

"Good. We'll be in touch when we finish the investigation."

"Thank you."

"Here's my card if you think of anything else." He turned and walked back to his vehicle.

Zack's phone pinged. He pulled it out of his back pocket and swiped it open. "It's Rafe. He wants to know if you're okay and what's happening."

Taylor pulled her phone from her pajama bottoms pocket. "It's almost five. What's he doing up? And how does he know?"

"I sent a text to him and Max. When you called, it just seemed like one more bad thing happening, and it didn't feel like a coincidence. Anyway, he's up, and he wants us to come over. Mallory's got the coffee on."

Taylor pursed her lips. "I don't want to impose. Maybe I can find a hotel."

"Stop. Just stop." Zack pulled her back into a hug, resting his chin on the top of her head. "I think we can put aside our past upsets right now." He took in a deep breath. "I swear

when you called me and told me the house was on fire, I nearly had heart failure. The idea of anything happening to you… I can't even think about it." He pulled away and gave her a gentle kiss on the lips.

Taylor couldn't believe how much she'd missed this. It felt right, and she needed Zack's support. It didn't seem like she could rely on anyone else, including her partner, Gil.

For now, a strong cup of coffee and a minute to sort through what just happened would help her determine her next move. She leaned into Zack. "Okay. Let's get coffee. I could use some of your family's smothering."

He gave her a smirk. "Yeah, let's go."

"Wait. What about my car?"

"We'll pick it up later." Zack pulled her by the arm. "It's not going anywhere."

They pulled up to the yellow Victorian house sitting on a slight hill. Their widowed aunt, Ellie, had given Rafe and Mallory the house when she decided to live with her sister, Claudia, in Saratoga. It fit Rafe and his growing family, and Tía Ellie was never far away, always volunteering to come down and babysit.

"Oh, look. The whole family's here," Zack said, pointing out Max's silver-gray BMW parked out front.

Taylor laughed for the first time that day. "It wouldn't be a Ramirez meal without everyone. I'm surprised your father and aunt aren't here."

Zack cocked his head. "Shh. You might bring them with your thoughts."

"Are we going to sit here all morning, or can I get a cup of coffee?" She let out a breath, released the seat belt, and got out of the car.

They climbed the steps to the porch, and Zack pushed

the front door open. He turned to Taylor and, with an index finger over his mouth, signaled they should be quiet. He mouthed the words, *Lucas may be sleeping.*

Taylor heard voices coming from the kitchen in the back of the house and the sound of a baby laughing. "I think they're all up and about."

"Well, in that case, we don't need to be quiet." Zack grabbed her by the hand and marched down the hall and into the kitchen.

Mallory and Rafe were at the stove. Max had his nephew, Lucas, in his lap, and Jordan was coloring with Mallory's daughter, Justine.

Rafe turned. "There you are." His eyes went wide. "Jeez, Taylor, are you all right?" He rushed toward her and took her by the shoulders, holding her at arm's length, looking her up and down. The rest of the room stared.

"What?" she said, not knowing what had them all so bug-eyed.

"Have you seen yourself?" Jordan asked.

"You look like you've been in a fire," Mallory said.

"Well, yeah... I have been."

"We know—we just hadn't realized how close it was. Here..." Mallory turned Taylor to face a gold-framed mirror hanging on the far wall by the telephone.

Her mouth fell open. "Zack, why didn't you tell me?"

"I think we were busy with some other more pressing matters."

She looked back at her reflection. Soot streaked across her forehead, the side of her face, and down her neck. Her pajama top looked slightly charred. Taylor folded her lips together. "I guess it was a lot closer than I remember. I was trying to get the hell out of there."

"Is Taylor going to be all right?" Justine asked, her lips trembling.

"Oh, Punkie, she'll be fine." Mallory lifted her daughter out of the chair and wrapped her in a hug. "Just a close call." She turned to Taylor. "Look, we're making breakfast for everyone, but first, you are going to take a shower. You've gotta get out of those things." She stared at Taylor for a moment. "We're about the same size. I'll give you something to wear for today."

Mallory handed Justine to Rafe and took Taylor by the hand. "Come on." She led her out of the kitchen and up the stairs to the guest bedroom.

Thirty minutes later, Taylor came back down, hair wet in a high ponytail, wearing a black crew-neck sweater, jeans, and sneakers. Lucas was sleeping in a bassinet, and Justine was in the living room watching cartoons. The brothers, Mallory, and Jordan were at the large kitchen table.

Zack rose and went to Taylor. "How are you feeling?"

"Truth?"

"Yeah."

"A little shaky. I've had time to recognize what I'd been through." She took a seat at the table. All eyes were on her. Zack took her hand under the table and squeezed. Electricity shot through her. She squeezed back, and her shoulders relaxed. With Zack sitting beside her, her mind settled.

When they'd stood together outside the burning house, he'd said that what was past was past. She sure hoped that was true because being with him, being with his family, even after everything she'd been through and was about to go through, gave her the confidence to move forward.

Looking around the kitchen, she saw the strength of this family. They'd always been there for one another, and they'd do anything for each other. The thought saddened her, real-

izing she didn't have a family and hadn't had a normal childhood. Her parents weren't loving or caring or even present. They'd made her the surrogate parent for her younger sister when she was just a kid herself. Looking back, she realized it was a form of child abuse.

For years, her only thought was to care for herself and her sister. But when she'd lost Emily, she blamed herself for not doing a good enough job. After that, she'd closed a piece of herself off because the pain of losing someone you loved was too deep a hurt, and that was something she didn't want to experience again. She was better off being on her own.

Suddenly, she realized that was how she'd approached her relationship with Zack—always holding a piece of herself back so she wouldn't be hurt. She supposed that was what made it possible for her to walk away and go undercover without so much as a goodbye. Taylor wondered if she'd ever be able to fully give herself to someone again.

"Coffee?" Rafe asked, interrupting her thoughts.

She nodded.

"How about something to eat? I think we could all use a little breakfast, and the bacon's already in the oven," Mallory said.

"Believe it or not, I am kinda hungry." Taylor patted her stomach. "Must be the adrenaline leaving my body."

"I could go for something, too." Zack rose to refill his coffee cup. "Then we need to discuss what's been happening with this job. Since it started, there have been too many incidents." He pointed at Taylor. "This last one nearly killed you. We're in the middle of something, and we need to figure it out fast."

Rafe stood and walked to the stove. "Don't disagree, bro. We'll all think better once we're fed."

Mallory rose and gathered the ingredients for the waffle

batter. After Rafe checked the bacon in the oven, he whisked eggs in a bowl.

Max put out plates, cutlery, napkins, and maple syrup.

"With everything that's happened," Rafe said, "I have to admit—something's sketchy." He dropped the butter into the hot fry pan.

"Shady, for sure," Jordan said.

"Doesn't pass the smell test," Max said and sat at the table.

"Well, now that we all agree that something is terribly off, let's figure out how we make this right before Boyd kicks me off the case." Taylor took a sip of her coffee and stared off.

The kitchen began to fill with the smells of breakfast. The eggs hit the pan, and the batter was ladled into the waffle iron. The sweet, creamy scent of butter and vanilla filled the room and made her stomach growl.

"Taylor, was there anything else you noticed when you discovered the laptops missing from your trunk?" Max asked. "Anything at all? See anyone?"

She put her hand under her chin and thought about it for a moment, trying to recall if she'd missed anything. "I can't think of a thing I haven't already said. But wait—" she pointed at Jordan "—what about the metadata trace on that disappearing image on my phone? That was definitely a photo of my trunk, open in the rain, with the devices in a box."

Jordan shook her head. "I was lucky enough to get the metadata, but I was only able to get a ghost of a trace, which I haven't been able to track." She lifted her index finger. "Not yet anyway. And I'm not giving up."

"Appreciate it." Taylor gave a half smile.

"And there's one more possibility," she said. "I set up a

trace on the stolen computers. I have the serial numbers, and if one of them gets turned on, I'll be able to track it."

"Let's take a minute. Time to eat." Rafe put a large platter of scrambled eggs with a side of bacon on the table, and Mallory followed with a stack of waffles.

"Looks terrific," Jordan said.

"Thanks." Mallory went back to the stove and put waffles on a small plate. "I'm going to take this to Justine."

They passed the platter around and began to eat.

Max smothered his waffles with syrup and took a big forkful. "Mmm. So good."

Rafe checked on Lucas in his bassinet. He was still sound asleep. "Justine okay?" he asked when his wife stepped back into the kitchen.

"She's in heaven. We're letting her watch cartoons and eat in the living room." Mallory took her place at the table.

"While you were upstairs showering, Zack filled us in on what's happened so far. But just so I'm clear—" Max pointed his fork toward Taylor "—we've got missing laptops, reports you requested but didn't get, an incorrect VPN—"

"Hold up, Max." Jordan's tone was harsh. "That VPN was correct. It definitely came from a warehouse on Twelfth Street in Albany. Someone is messing with us."

"Okay," he said. "Let's say they did mess with us. To what end?"

"To keep us running in circles." Taylor took a bite of a waffle. "And my gut tells me it's got to be the same person or persons who sent the disappearing text and who started the fire."

"It doesn't make sense that whoever is doing this would be overseas since it's all happening in real-time, right here in Hollow Lake." Zack chewed on a piece of bacon.

"That's exactly what I was thinking," Taylor said. "I

thought from the beginning this was a US operation. And nothing that's happened so far has changed my mind." She fiddled with her fork. "I need to go back to the Bureau. If I can somehow find out who requested the report using my ID, it will tell me what terminal the request was sent from. And that will tell me who's behind this."

"Whoa, whoa. That's a big leap," Zack said.

"Not really. It's the first tangible lead. It's something I can actually investigate and get some answers."

"It's a start," Rafe said.

"Someone was trying to make it look like I requested a copy of the report when I hadn't had a chance to ask for it yet. Why would they do that?" Taylor put her fork down. "Or maybe they wanted to see what was in the report and used my ID to request it."

"I don't see the problem," Mallory said. "You ended up with the report anyway."

Taylor tilted her head toward the ceiling. "Yes. That's true, I did." She looked at Mallory. "But there are way too many inconsistencies surrounding that report."

"In what way?" Zack asked.

"Gil told me the report indicated there was no US connection. But the report clearly states there were a couple of pings in the US."

"Well, I'd say that indicates a definite inconsistency," Rafe said.

"Then there's the little matter of the information in that report happens to be classified. Someone used my ID to request the report. I don't know how they did it, but they did. And the Bureau doesn't take kindly to losing information. Typically, I would have had to fill out a requisition stating I lost the original file—"

"Once again, making you look bad," Rafe offered.

"Exactly," she said. "Anyway, by the time I got to the cybercrime unit to find out what happened, it was late, and Camille, the head of the unit, wanted to shut down and pack it in for the night. She trusted me and made me promise I'd check into the mix-up with IT. That's the only reason she gave me the report for a quote, unquote second time.

"But the biggest issue is that I keep being told to concentrate only on overseas scammers. I mean, they said there is no US connection. But it's not what they're saying—it's the way they are saying it. Like, don't look…nothing to see over there."

"But who is 'they'?" Jordan asked.

"Boyd," Taylor said. "Especially after the empty warehouse raid. He's convinced it's got nothing to do with the United States."

"Speaking of which, have you even called Gil or Boyd to tell them what happened with the fire?" Zack asked.

"I just sent them a text."

"You didn't call them?" he asked.

"I didn't want to talk to either of them. I'm still working things out in my mind." She paused. "That fire was deliberate. Someone set it."

"You know this for a fact?" Jordan leaned forward.

"The door to my bedroom was jammed. Something was stuck underneath the doorknob. I couldn't get the door open. I literally had to kickbox my way out."

"That's scary," Mallory said.

"Wait." Jordan held up a hand. "Do you think someone at the Bureau is involved?"

Taylor wiped her mouth with her napkin. "I'm not ruling it out."

"Holy crap." Max whistled. "So, what are we working with here?"

She huffed. "Someone wanted me dead. And I intend to find out who. Right now, as far as I'm concerned, everyone is a suspect. And that includes Boyd."

The looks of shock from the faces staring back at her told Taylor they weren't totally behind her assumption that someone on the inside was involved. It didn't matter. She knew better.

Taylor's phone pinged. She retrieved it from her back pocket, placed it on the table, and swiped it open. It was a text containing a photo of her lying on the ground in front of the fire.

Zack leaned over her shoulder. "What the hell?"

Before either of them could say another word, the photo disappeared.

# Chapter 15

Zack picked up Taylor's phone and stared. "Okay, that's twice now. Time for a new game plan."

"What's going on?" Max asked.

Zack tossed the phone to Jordan. "Another disappearing text."

"What did you see?" she asked.

"It was a pic of me lying on the grass outside the Airbnb before the fire engines arrived."

"Holy crap," Rafe said.

"It was on the screen for less than thirty seconds before it vanished." Taylor shivered.

"Rafe, do you have your laptop here, and does it have any forensic tools on it?" Jordan asked.

"I'll go get it." He jogged out of the kitchen and up the stairs. Lucas began to fuss and let out a small cry, building to something bigger.

"Someone's hungry." Mallory went to the bassinet in the corner and lifted her fussy infant. "Come on, sweetie, let's get your big sister and get you fed." With Lucas draped over her shoulder, she turned to the group. "I'll be back."

As she exited, Rafe entered with his laptop. He stopped to put his hand on his son's head. "Everything okay?"

Mallory nodded. "He's hungry. I'll feed him and be back."

Jordan took the laptop, and Rafe leaned against the kitchen counter behind her. He gave her the password and watched as she booted up the program.

"That photo was clear evidence someone's watching you. That much is obvious." Zack turned to face Taylor. "Look, I know you're an FBI agent. I know you know how to take care of yourself. Hell, most people would not have been able to get out of a burning building by kicking down a door. But you did. So it's not that I'm trying to be all alpha macho. But I sure would feel extra relaxed if you agreed to stay at my house." He stared at her.

"I'd feel better, too," Max said, "knowing you were near and safe."

"I'm going jump in on this one." Rafe pushed off the counter. "Zack's right. Stay with him. Don't stay in your apartment in Albany or at a hotel where you could be an easy target."

Taylor looked at Zack. "Okay. But only until we figure out who's behind this."

He squeezed her shoulder.

"Hey, Zack, I think it would be a good idea if I have the tech team rig some extra security around your house," Jordan said, looking up from the laptop screen.

"Good thinking. Thanks." Zack turned to stare at Taylor, surprised at how quickly the old feelings he had for her came to the surface. The anger and resentment he'd harbored seemed to have simmered. In all the time he'd known her, she'd never seemed vulnerable. But when he saw her lying on the front lawn of the Airbnb, his heart cracked a little. It was then that he realized he'd never stopped loving her. No matter how pissed off he was. He wanted to be with her, be by her side. But there was still something holding him back. She worked in a dangerous profession, and that was some-

thing he still couldn't quite get his mind around. He didn't know how to deal with it—and wondered if he ever would.

"Hey, listen," Jordan said without taking her eyes off the laptop screen. "I got something."

"What?" Zack asked.

"This is some very sophisticated maneuvering. Whoever sent that disappearing photo knows what they are doing."

He and Taylor stood and leaned over Jordan's shoulder.

Using the trackpad, she pointed out the various connections from which the signal bounced. "Look, it begins in Sydney, goes to Wales, bounces to Cape Town, then onto Greenland, and then back here to Hollow Lake."

"So you think the perp is from Australia?" Taylor asked.

Jordan looked over her shoulder at Taylor and raised a brow. "That's what they want us to believe. But look at this." She continued with the trackpad pointer. "This origination point is a ghost."

"A ghost?" Zack furrowed his brow.

"Yeah. It's not really there."

"How do you know that?"

"The metadata doesn't match up." She continued punching keys on the keyboard and making concerned faces at the screen.

Zack and the others stared at her, waiting for some pronouncement, hoping she was onto something that would give them a clue of where to start.

"I feel all eyes on me, and it's not helping," Jordan muttered. She tapped a few more keystrokes, then looked up. "It's definitely a false origination point." By the time she finished explaining how that was possible, they were all seated at the kitchen table.

"So," Taylor said, "someone's jerking us around and keeping us from getting to them. I mean, first they sent

us to the wrong warehouse location. Now the disappearing photo allegedly coming from Australia, but not really."

"I'm convinced that's the case," Jordan said.

"And I'm convinced we've somehow rattled some cages," she said.

"Who rattled what cage?" Mallory asked as she stepped back into the kitchen.

"We seem to have upset whoever is behind this sextortion ring."

"How so?" she asked.

"Think about it. Ever since Zack sent Gil his report on how RMZ planned to capture the sextortionists, things have gone wrong. That leads me to two conclusions. One—" Taylor held up her index finger "—the report somehow got into the wrong hands, and the bad actors know our every move where the gaming war room is concerned. And two—" she added her second finger "—someone inside the Bureau is involved."

"Whoa, that's scary," Jordan said.

"You're all looking at me like I've grown two heads."

"It's a serious accusation," Rafe said.

Taylor sat back. "You're right. It's a serious accusation, but hear me out. We were all surprised when the warehouse location was a bust. Right?"

Everyone at the table nodded.

"Before Jordan traced the VPN to the warehouse, I had thought the chat between Fred and the mysterious Julie84 had progressed rather rapidly. In fact, afterward, when I thought about other transcripts I'd read from some of our victims, I realized that in most cases, it would take a few days before they asked to swap nude photos." Taylor stood and began to pace. "At the time, I second-guessed myself and thought maybe after all that happened, we were catch-

ing a break. I convinced myself not to look too closely, to look at the situation as a gift after such a rough start."

She put her hands on the back of her chair and leaned forward. "That wasn't the case. We were purposefully led to that empty warehouse."

"What makes you think that?" Max asked.

"First, it was too easy. Second, the only people who had the names of the players we were using and their social media accounts—"

Zack snapped his fingers. "Gil and Boyd."

"Bingo," Taylor said. "I think someone in the Bureau—I'm not saying who—targeted our players."

"You mean like specifically sought them out to trap us?" Jordan asked.

"That's exactly what I'm saying." Taylor sat.

"Are you sure it was Gil or Boyd?" Rafe asked.

"No." She shook her head. "I know they got the information from Zack, but I don't know who else had access to the list."

"So whoever is behind this purposefully sent us to the wrong location," Jordan said.

"How is that even possible?" Max asked.

"That's what we need to find out." Taylor placed her forearms on the table and leaned forward. "More importantly, in order to get to the real sextortionists, we are going to have to come up with a new plan that flushes them out."

For the next hour, they discussed, argued, and mapped out various scenarios. They punched holes in every idea until they came up with one they all agreed could work.

Zack stood, poured himself another cup of coffee, and leaned against the counter facing the group. "I'm going to repeat the plan one more time so that we're all clear. If what I'm saying isn't correct, now is the time to speak up."

Everyone nodded.

"We're going to increase the number of stations and techies playing in the war room. They will continue to play games day and night with the intent of catching the bad actors. Jordan will be in charge of that part of the operation."

"That's the plan," Jordan said.

"Taylor will report to the Bureau and give Boyd and Gil a full report on the fire. Meanwhile, you two—" he pointed at Rafe and Max "—are going to come up with a report for Boyd to give to the governor. Just enough information that shows we've made some progress and keeps us on the case."

"I'll give them what we have, but it's not much information," Max said.

"Not true. We have enough to make them think we're on the right track," Rafe said and lightly punched him in the arm.

"Ow." Max rubbed his arm. "What was that for?"

"For that bit of negativity. We'll need to present a positive outlook to Gil Clancy. Let him think we are gaining traction on this case by working the overseas connection. We need to do that if we're going to find out who is behind the sextortion ring and behind trying to kill Taylor."

Zack stiffened. Rafe's words, *trying to kill Taylor*, when said out loud, rattled him. He looked at her. It was hard to admit to himself, but the thought of anything happening to her wasn't something he wanted to contemplate. "Okay, okay. What else do we need to review?"

Jordan raised her hand. "I'll keep working on getting a signal from the stolen computers. And I'll also work on getting the exact location of where those disappearing texts came from."

"Are we leaving anything out?" Zack asked.

"One more thing," Max said. "Me and Rafe will prepare

a report on the warehouse debacle for Taylor to present to Boyd and Gil." He shook his head. "Damn, you bureaucrats require a lot of paperwork."

"Welcome to the FBI," Taylor said and checked the wall clock. "It's getting late. I'll put the rest of the plan into action when I get to the Bureau. I'll keep Zack posted, but we're not going to give the rest of you any updates. We need to keep any chatter about what we're really doing to a bare minimum. We don't know who's watching. For now, the fact that Zack and I are running a separate operation stays between us and only us."

"It's nearly nine o'clock." Zack stood and stretched his arms over his head. "What time does the next shift take over in the gaming war room?"

"In a few minutes," Jordan said, pulled out her phone, and stared at the screen. "I should have a progress report on how things went overnight." She paused. "Yup, here it is. So far, no unusual activity. Nothing suspicious in the chats, just the usual stuff between gamers—strategy discussions, token trades, and new ways to level up."

Taylor scoffed. "It was probably quiet last night in the game chats because whoever is behind this was too busy setting the fire at my Airbnb."

"We'll find out soon enough," Zack said. "But right now, it's time for all of us to get to work."

The day turned out to be gray and overcast. Zack pulled up to the Airbnb. In the dim light, Taylor couldn't believe what she was seeing.

Red tape surrounded the front yard of what used to be a house and was now only a hollowed-out shell. The large picture window on the first floor had shattered from the heat, which gave her a perfect view of the extensive dam-

age inside. The wall that had been on the right side of the living room was completely disintegrated. Electrical wires dangled from the ceiling, and only charred pieces of chairs, tables, and a sofa remained.

Taylor pushed a button on the car's middle console, and the window rolled down. The acrid smell of smoke filled her lungs. She coughed and quickly rolled the window back up.

She shook her head. "Holy crap." Her mind tried to adjust to the fact that she'd narrowly escaped the blaze and instead could've been lying among the ruins. Her shock quickly melded into anger, knowing the fire had been deliberately set.

"Son of a bitch. Someone really wants me off this." She spat the words out. "Well, not going to happen. *Not going to happen.*"

Zack reached over and squeezed her hand.

"I'm all right. If anything, I'm super pissed off. And that's a good thing."

He turned to face her. "You still want to go through with your plan?"

"Hell to the yes. I'm ready." She unclipped her seat belt and looked at Zack. "I'll see you later." She got out of the car, marched over to her car, and climbed in.

Zack gave her a quick honk and pulled out. For several more minutes, she sat mesmerized by the destruction. Taylor had spent the past seven years dealing with the criminal element, but it still surprised her what an evil person was capable of. And this was the work of evil. She gripped the gear stick, shoved it into Reverse, backed out of the drive, and headed for the thruway.

Boyd had given Taylor the morning off, and she planned on seeing him once she got to the office. Before heading into the Bureau, she made a stop at her apartment to pack.

Zack was right. It wasn't smart for her to stay at her place or even at a hotel in Hollow Lake by herself. That, she had to admit, was inviting trouble. Taylor took one more look around her apartment, satisfied that she had packed what she would need for a week, closed her suitcase, and left.

It was a few minutes before noon when Taylor slipped into her cubicle. She glanced around and saw no signs of Gil. When she spoke to him earlier, she told him she'd meet him in the office. Boyd had made it clear she was to let him know the moment she arrived.

She put her purse in the bottom desk drawer, booted up her computer, and sent a message to Boyd's admin that she had arrived.

The response came back that he'd meet with her in fifteen minutes.

In the meantime, Taylor filled out the necessary paperwork for her lost badge, gun, and her ID. She had no idea if any of it had survived the fire, but she hadn't been allowed inside to find out. For now, she needed replacements.

"There you are!" Gil exclaimed and sat at the edge of her desk, facing her. "Are you all right? I was seriously worried about you. And why didn't you call me last night?"

Taylor looked up at him. "It all happened so fast. I mean, one minute I was sleeping, and the next minute I was kicking my way out of the bedroom, running for my life."

"I read the inspector's report."

She furrowed her brow. "You did? How did you get a hold of it?"

"As soon as I finished talking to you, I called Boyd, and he requested the report from the firehouse."

Of course the head of her department would want an official report.

The chat box on her computer dinged, and she read the message. "Boyd's ready now."

She straightened, pushed back her shoulders, and marched into his office ahead of Gil. This time, she wanted to be thrown off the case.

## Chapter 16

"There you are, Agent Shore." Boyd's voice was full of concern. "Are you okay?"

"Sir, I'm fine." She slipped into the chair opposite his desk.

"What in the world happened?"

"I believe the fire inspector is looking into that now. But from where I sit, it was a deliberate fire. It was set with the knowledge I was in the house sleeping."

Boyd smacked his hand on the desk. "Damn! That's what the initial report is looking like." He stood and began to pace. "I don't like this. I don't like this at all." He stopped and turned to face her. "Since you started on this case, it's been one thing after another. And I don't believe in coincidences." He shook his head. "I don't like what I'm about to say, but I think it's for your own safety. I'm going to need you to stand back for a few days."

"Wait a minute, sir." Gil rose. "Is that really necessary?"

Taylor hoped he would drop it. She wanted off. She and Zack had other plans.

"I've made up my mind," Boyd said. "This last incident was too close, and I will not knowingly put any of my agents in danger. It's evident Taylor was a target, and for now, I'm

putting her on desk duty." He held up a hand. "But first I want you to take a couple of days' rest. You deserve it."

Taylor nodded.

"In the meantime," Boyd continued, "I still have a meeting with the governor tomorrow, and I need to give him some answers." He pointed at Gil. "You'll work with RMZ and get me those answers. I don't care what you have to do, but I want to show the governor we are making headway. Do I make myself clear?"

"Yes, sir," Gil said.

"Okay. That's all for now."

"Thank you, sir," Taylor said. Hiding her smile, she stood and headed for the door. This was precisely what she'd hoped for—a way to pursue the case without being on the case. Admittedly, Boyd's concern seemed genuine, and that shocked her. What game was he playing? That was what she couldn't figure out. Maybe he was trying to put her off her guard. That wasn't going to happen. She was getting to the bottom of this and exposing this sextortion ring if it was the last thing she did.

"Oh, Taylor," Boyd said, "I've rushed through your paperwork for your new gun, badge, and ID. You know the procedure. Let me know if you run into any snags."

It was almost too perfect, as if everything was suddenly going the way she wanted. She turned to face him. "Thanks again."

Taylor walked out of the office with Gil close behind. He tapped her on the shoulder. "I'm sorry you're off the case. But it's probably for the best." He ran his hand through his hair. "This last brush with death. I mean, jeez, you had me worried." He put a hand on her shoulder. "I'm really glad you're all right."

"Thanks. I'm going to be fine."

Gil turned and glanced over his shoulder, then lowered his voice. "Listen, I think this is more your case than anybody else's. I'll give Boyd a day or two to cool off, and then I'll talk to him about getting you back on."

Taylor glanced up at him. The sincerity in his eyes touched her. The distance he'd been putting between them suddenly seemed to narrow. She remembered how much he'd watched her back on the last op and how he'd quite literally saved her from getting the crap beat out of her. He'd been a real partner. Leaving him out suddenly didn't seem right. "Listen, Gil...if you've got a minute, there's something—"

"Agent Clancy, in my office now," Boyd yelled.

"I've gotta go," Gil said. "Maybe we could catch up later?"

"Yeah. Sure." Taylor took a deep breath and watched him hurry into Boyd's office—another reminder of how close they were. It wasn't that she couldn't trust Gil, but where Boyd was concerned, she needed to tread very lightly. She shook her head and told herself to stop second-guessing what she'd already decided. And the first order of business was a stop at the firearms department for a new gun.

By the time she'd gotten through the various departments and the paperwork, it was after four. Her next stop was to see Camille in Cybercrime. Taylor still needed to figure out who used her credentials to request the first Cybercrime report.

"Hey, you," Camille said, looking up. "Don't tell me you need the report again."

"No, I'm good. Got it." Taylor leaned against the counter. "I went to IT to have them sort out the mix-up with the first report, but they are slammed. And Boyd put me on administrative leave for a couple of days."

"I heard. Are you okay?"

"Yeah, thanks. I wasn't hurt." Taylor waved a hand. "But

I would like to solve the mystery on that report before I take off for two days."

Camille raised a brow.

"I think if you pull up the initial request, it will tell you what terminal it came from. Then I can sort it from there." Taylor smiled, trying hard to appear calm and nonchalant.

"I suppose I could do that." Camille pushed her glasses further up the bridge of her nose. "Hang on." She typed in a few keystrokes. "Looks like it came from a terminal on the fifth floor."

"Is there a cubicle number?"

"Nope, looks like it's an office. Room 515."

"Great. Thanks. I'll report what I find to IT." Taylor turned on her heel and hurried back to her cubicle. Grabbing some file folders, she headed for the elevators and pressed the button for the fifth floor. When the doors opened, she stepped out onto the landing. To the right was a set of glass doors that required a badge to gain entrance onto the floor. Her temporary badge had the same access as her regulation badge—and neither had the required access.

Holding the file folders close to her chest, she waited at the door as if she had an appointment and someone was about to escort her to a meeting. When a stout woman in her fifties pushed the door open, Taylor acted as if she were about to swipe her badge. Instead, she looked up, smiled, and said, "Hello."

The woman held the door for her, and Taylor nodded and waltzed in.

Taylor glanced around. In seven years, she'd never been on this floor. Never had a reason. The layout was similar to her floor, with offices situated all along the outer perimeter and partitioned gray-colored cubicles in a neat maze in the center of the room where the Bureau's administrative

personnel worked. It was close to five, and many cubicles were already empty.

She headed down the south wall before realizing the office numbers were going in the wrong direction. She turned around and retraced her steps, passed the glass entrance doors, and walked several feet before she found room 515. "What?" she said under her breath and took a step back. The room number was correct, but the sign on the door read JANITORIAL CLOSET.

Taylor took a quick look around. Of the few staff that remained, no one was paying attention to her. Without hesitation, she opened the closet and stepped in. It couldn't have been more than twelve feet by eight feet. Stacks of toilet paper, soap, and paper towels lined metal shelving to her left, and on the right stood another shelf with cleaning supplies. In the corner, leaning against the wall, was an industrial bucket and mop.

She blew out a breath. It all seemed normal, what you'd expect in a janitorial closet.

How did someone send a request from here? There wasn't even a computer terminal. Maybe Camille had given her the wrong information.

Taylor scanned every inch of the room. Twice. She found nothing. Placing her hands on her hips, she threw her head back in frustration. That was when she saw it: A ceiling tile that was slightly crooked. As if it had been moved.

Standing on the bottom of one of the metal shelves, she stretched her arm up but couldn't quite reach it. She looked around and decided to use the industrial-size bucket. Wheeling it directly under the crooked tile, she turned the bucket over and heaved herself on top. It gave her just enough height to reach the tile, and when she pushed it aside, computer cables came dangling out.

Taylor squinted, not believing what she was seeing. She reached over to the next ceiling tile and pushed up. The tile was heavier than it needed to be. Something was sitting on top of it. Bracing herself with one hand against the metal shelf on her left, she stood on the tips of her toes and, with her right hand, pushed the tile slightly to the side, revealing a small black laptop.

## Chapter 17

Zack hit Enter on his computer keyboard and pushed away from his desk.

"You done?" Max asked, entering the office.

"Yeah, just put the finishing touches on the report. I'll print it for you." Within seconds, several sheets of paper whooshed out of the printer. Zack reached over, gave the pages a cursory glance, and handed them to Max.

"Well?" Rafe poked his head into Zack's office.

"Fresh off the printer." Zack pointed to the pages in Max's hand.

"Summarize it for me," Rafe said.

*"Calmaté, mijo,"* Max said. "I'm reading."

"I can't be calm. Gil Clancy is on his way over, and I want to make sure we're ready." Rafe sat in the chair next to him.

Zack's gaze went to his brother's foot. It jiggled like it was waiting for someone to ask it to dance. "Rafe. Seriously, take a chill pill."

Rafe blew out a breath. "You mean to tell me the two of you aren't just a little concerned that we are going around the FBI's back?"

The last thing Zack needed was for him to backpedal. They'd all agreed to go along with Taylor's plan. They would continue with the RMZ gaming war room, with techies

working to lure bad actors and reporting to Gil Clancy daily while secretly working another game room that the FBI would know nothing about.

Zack didn't care if what they were doing was sketchy. He wanted to catch these sextortionists, and more than that, he wanted to keep Taylor safe. If this was the only way to do it, he was all in.

It had been Taylor's idea, and no matter how much he was behind it, his stomach was performing acrobatics, and he had to keep wiping at the sweat on his upper lip. It wasn't every day you deceived the FBI and got away with it. But Taylor's gut instinct was that someone within the Bureau was behind all the foul-ups, and she needed time to find out who and why. The fact that she'd pointed a finger at Boyd made Zack doubly nervous.

"This report looks good," Max said. "There's just enough information to make it look like we're onto something and the bad actors are in the Philippines."

"Yeah. And for good measure, on the last page, I explain how we got the wrong VPN location for the Albany warehouse."

"Zack, do not let Jordan hear you say that." Max looked toward the door to make sure she wasn't anywhere nearby.

He gave Max the side-eye. "We both know she's the Jedi master when it comes to tracking. But if this plan is going to work, we have to eat a little crow and act like we made a mistake."

"Don't love it," Rafe said.

The phone on Zack's desk rang, and he pushed the speaker button. "Yeah?"

"Agent Gil Clancy is here," Brittany said.

"Send him to my office." He clicked off the speaker

and, with the back of his hand, wiped the sweat from his upper lip.

"Gentlemen, good to see you," Gil said as he entered the office.

Zack stood, and they shook hands. "Can we get you anything? Coffee, water?"

"Nah, I'm good."

Rafe stood. "Please, have a seat." He walked over to the side of the window, crossed his arms, and leaned against the wall.

"I'm assuming you've heard Taylor's off the case." Gil crossed one leg over the other. "Shame. She's a great agent. I hope we can get closer to zeroing in on who's behind this. I think once that happens, I can convince Boyd to let her back on."

"It is a shame," Zack said. Inside, his stomach was doing a little flip, worried for Taylor. She had phoned him earlier to let him know she was officially off the case and that their plan was moving forward. He sure hoped she knew what she was doing because Gil was their only point of contact, and he wasn't sure how much he could hide from him.

"As you know, Boyd is meeting with the governor tomorrow, and we need to present him with evidence that we are close to or at least somewhere in the vicinity of catching the sextortionist."

"Yes, we know—" Zack leaned forward "—and we're also happy to hear that his son is out of the woods and will make a full recovery."

"Yes. That is lucky." Gil shifted in his seat. "So, what have you got for me?"

"This." Max handed the report to him. "This report outlines the games we play, the number of hours, and who has contacted our players and where they come from."

"And we added a brief report on the foul-up at the Albany warehouse."

Gil looked at Rafe. "So you agree you got the wrong information?"

"It doesn't happen often—" Rafe rubbed his chin "—but even the great RMZ Digital makes a mistake once in a while."

Gil smiled. "It's okay, as long as the information is correct now."

"After the mishap at the warehouse, we immediately doubled our efforts," Zack said.

"Specifics?" Gil arched a brow.

"We've had our team playing for the last seventeen hours. And we got lucky," he said. "We got two hits and traced them back to the Philippines."

Gil slapped the arm of the chair. "I knew it. What specifics do you have?"

Zack shook his head. "The specific location keeps changing, but it's in the same general area—"

"Hold on. Let's not get too excited too soon," Rafe interrupted, "No photos have been traded. No one has asked for money. There's no concrete evidence to make a move. But we have someone on the hook, and we have a good hit on a general location."

Gil looked at Zack. "At least you have a location. How do you plan to handle the rest?"

"Our team will keep playing and chatting in the game rooms, and I hope they make a connection they can develop. Once they start trading nude photos, which we're fairly certain will happen soon, we'll have evidence, and by then, we'll have nailed down the exact location."

"How can you be so certain?" Gil asked.

"We are working on an established pattern based on the

previous cases." Zack shrugged. "It's all we have to go on, but we believe it's a solid way to go."

"To that end," Max said, "over the next two days, we're upping the six-man team to a ten-man team working around the clock."

"With that much manpower, we'll have the advantage," Rafe said.

"How so?" Gil asked.

"We are only concentrating on those games that bad actors go after. With more players playing from our side, we've almost doubled our chances of attracting them. We'll get a sense if this is one, two, or more sextortionists," Rafe said.

"What Rafe is saying is that it will give us insight as to whether this is a lone creep or an actual sextortion ring."

Gil nodded. "That's good." He flipped through the report's pages and stopped at a spreadsheet. "What's this? I thought we had all the fake names, backgrounds, and social media accounts of the players you created."

"Those haven't changed. It's the same list I've already provided," Zack said. "But since we've added people to the team, we're providing those aliases as well."

Gil nodded. "For the purposes of a report to the governor, I don't imagine he needs to be bogged down in every detail of our operation. He simply wants to know that we're onto something. And from what I see on these pages, all indications point to the Philippines. And that means there will be extraditions and arrests. I think this will put his mind at ease for the time being."

"Should I take the spreadsheet from the report and reprint it for you?" Zack asked.

"No." Gil scratched the back of his head. "Why don't you email me exactly what you have, and I'll make sure Boyd gets it. He can decide what he wants to put in or leave out."

"Sounds good. In the meantime, we proceed as planned," Zack said.

The agent nodded. "And I expect a nightly report with a transcript of any chats that happen in the game rooms."

"Of course," Max said.

Gil uncrossed his legs and stood. "Okay. I'll take this report, and if anything comes up before you send me your nightly report, call me."

"Fair enough." Zack nodded. "So, are you staying to watch the war room in action?"

"Can't—have another meeting."

"I'll walk you out." Max stood, and together, he and Gil left the office.

Zack blew out a breath and sat back. Rafe sat in the chair Gil just vacated. They remained silent, waiting for Max to return.

They didn't have long before he strode through the door and closed it behind him with the flick of his foot. He plopped into the chair next to Rafe. "You think he bought it?"

"Yup," Rafe said.

Zack held up his hands. "The guy fell for it. And that means the first part of Taylor's plan is in operation."

Max leaned forward. "He now has the aliases, backgrounds, and social media profiles of every pretend player in the gaming war room."

"And he's going to give it to Boyd," Rafe said. "I hope this doesn't blow up in our faces."

Zack put his feet up on the desk. "Chill, bro. If what Taylor suspects is happening, we should probably be seeing a spike in chatting activity, all coming from overseas."

Rafe got to his feet and walked around Zack's office.

"What if Taylor's wrong? We could be in a world of hurt for lying to federal officials."

"Hey, bro. Sit. Take a load off." Zack took his feet off his desk and leaned forward. "What happened? This morning you were all on board with Taylor's plan. What changed?"

"I know you got a thing for Taylor—"

"Rafe, it's more than a thing, but that is so beside the point."

His brother waved a hand. "I get it. But this kinda puts us all in jeopardy."

"Maybe Rafe's right," Max said.

Zack stood. "The two of you are something else. You want to talk about jeopardy? Come on." He pointed at Rafe. "We were right beside you, ready to do anything when Justine was kidnapped by a supposedly dead lunatic who was her father." He turned to Max. "And we stood by you when Jordan was not only in trouble with a madman working to take out the entire global-transportation system but also had the entire family on the run. How in the world is this different?" He began to pace and mutter to himself. *Paciencia. Paciencia.* "I'm trying to muster up some patience for you two because I love you. But what in the heck is your problem? Taylor was nearly killed. And if this an inside job, she has no one else to help her."

Both of his brothers looked down.

"Maybe one day this family can stop dealing with lunatics and madmen. But guess what—" he stretched his hands out to the side, palms up "—we work in cybersecurity. It's the freaking Wild West, and we're the gatekeepers. We didn't pick an easy profession, but we're good at it. So let's do this."

Zack sat back in his seat. "Taylor needs our help, and she's outlined a plan." He tapped his index finger on the

desk. "A plan, I might add, that we all agreed to. So, there is no going back." He waited for his brothers to say something, but the room remained quiet.

"I'm going to assume your silence is an agreement and we're full steam ahead. Correct?"

"I'm in," Rafe said.

Max nodded. "Me, too."

"All right, then. I'd better be getting out of here." Zack checked the time on his phone. "I promised to meet Jordan at my house in twenty minutes to set up phase two of this op."

"I'll check on what's happening in the war room." Rafe stood and headed for the door but turned before opening it. "Zack. Be careful."

## Chapter 18

When Zack arrived at his cottage, he found Jordan's two-man tech team putting the finishing touches on the additional security around his house.

He rolled down the car window and leaned out. "Hey, Gene," he called to the tall, lean man in jeans and a jacket on the ladder.

Gene turned his head. "Oh, hey, Zack. We're nearly done. If you wait a minute, I can show you what all we've got going on here."

"Be right there." Zack turned off the ignition, jumped out of the car, and strode to the front door just as Gene descended the ladder. "Hey, Bruce," he called to the heavyset, tattooed man holding the ladder.

"Hi, Zack."

"So, where do we start?" he said.

"Jordan's inside with the rest of the team setting up your stations," Gene said. "In the meantime, let me show you your enhanced security system." He waved a hand. "Follow me."

Zack walked with Gene and Bruce to the back of the house. Over the summer, Zack had installed a slate patio and purchased all new backyard furniture. It had become a refuge for him, a part of the day where he could relax. He'd sit out here on a warm evening, drink a beer, and watch the

sun setting over the trees. So many evenings, he'd wished Taylor were sitting beside him, enjoying the breeze and a cold drink, talking about their future.

For a brief moment, he closed his eyes, willing away the thought. Now wasn't the time for thinking about what hadn't been or could never be. This morning he realized his love for Taylor hadn't changed, but he had yet to reconcile how he could cope with a woman whose job was not only dangerous but required her to keep secrets. For now, his main goal was to keep Taylor safe and take this operation to a successful conclusion. He'd worry about what came next when this was over.

"So what do you think?" Gene asked.

"Hmm? What? Sorry—my mind drifted."

"We've added three infrared cameras out here. If a two-legged anything comes within seventy-five feet, you'll get an alert on your phone and laptop."

"Cool."

"We've got the same thing going on the front and the sides of the house. All three-hundred-sixty degrees of this house are covered. We've also added an additional lock on the back and front doors." Gene patted his pocket. "Here are the keys." He dropped them into Zack's hand.

"Great work. We'll test it out in a minute." Zack smiled. "I'm going to go inside and see what Jordan's rigged up."

He walked around the front and, using the new key, opened the door and dropped the keys into the bowl on the table. "Hello? I'm here."

"Back here," Jordan called out.

Zack headed for the guest room and was surprised when he crossed the threshold. "Whoa. Where did the bed go?"

She looked up from the keyboard she was working on. "Hang on. I'll explain everything. Just need a sec."

"Sure." Zack's gaze scanned his once very functional guest room. As of this morning, there had been a queen-sized bed, two side tables, a cozy reading chair, and a dresser. Now in their place were three folding tables situated in a U-shape. Each held a laptop and a large monitor. In the corner were wires, cables, and a television screen hooked onto the wall. Essentially, it was a mini version of the gaming war room at RMZ Digital.

Taylor's plan had been clever and slightly complicated. But when they'd all put their heads together, they'd manage to come up with the proper execution.

The first part of the plan had already been implemented. By now, Gil had given Boyd the information on the new aliases of the additional tech team members who were playing games at the RMZ gaming war room. If there was a sudden spike in activity in the chat rooms and those signals could be traced overseas, then Taylor was certain they were not only false locations designed to put RMZ on a wild-goose chase but also that the information they'd provided Gil had somehow gotten into the wrong hands.

Taylor believed Boyd was at the bottom of this, and she was determined to prove it.

While the RMZ Digital team worked with the FBI, the next step was to create new player aliases to which the FBI wasn't privy. Playing several different games from his home, Zack would use the new aliases in the hopes of snagging who was actually behind the sextortionist scheme. The only way for them to do that was to create a similar setup and go fishing. After much discussion, they'd decided to set it up at Zack's place and have him play the games, since he was the official gamer in the group.

The final step came from Jordan. She would rig the computers so the signal would show each of the three computers

at different locations. New York City, Miami, and Denver. Nothing would be traced back to Hollow Lake.

"Okay. We are all set." Jordan stood, shoved her hands in the pockets of her jeans, and rocked on the heels of her sneakers. "Don't worry—we moved all your furniture to the basement, sealed it in plastic. Once this op is over, we will return this room to its original state." With her index finger, she made a cross over her heart. "I promise."

"Thanks, Jordan." He stepped further into the room. "I'm over my initial shock. But seriously, this all looks great. Is it ready now?"

"Yeah. But let me show you a few things." Grabbing his elbow, she pulled him further into the room. "Let's start here." She moved them to the computer furthest from the door. "Here's the playbook." Next to the keyboard was a black loose-leaf binder, and she flipped it open to the first tab. The heading read *Computer One*. Jordan rested her hand on the monitor. "This is Computer One. And these—" she pointed to the following pages in the loose-leaf binder "—are the aliases. The players' names, what they look like, their ages, their social media handles, and all the rest of the information you'll need to carry this off."

"Impressive. Jordan strikes again." Zack smiled.

"Each computer has two aliases. And each time you use a new alias, you'll need to log out and log back in with the appropriate username and password. That tells the computer to switch its routing so the signal comes from a different city."

"Very, very cool."

"We'll see about that," Jordan said. "Why don't you start playing, and I'll stick around to make sure there aren't any snags."

Zack unbuttoned his shirt sleeves and rolled them up to his elbow. "Here I go."

Sitting in the ergonomic chair that seemed to mold to his body, he smiled. He pulled the binder closer and spent a few minutes leafing through it. He nodded as he went through, making cursory hmms and ahhs. When he had a good sense of each alias, he flipped back to page one, found the username and password for the first player, typed the information into the game, and began to play.

It was six thirty when he heard the doorbell. He looked around. Jordan and her team were gone, and he vaguely remembered saying goodbye. He had been so caught up in playing a couple of different games he barely noticed when they left. While he enjoyed gaming, what he was doing now was different—it was helping keep young people safe.

He checked the doorbell camera on his phone and smiled when he saw Taylor. "Coming," he called out and rushed to open the door.

"Hey," Zack said. "I didn't realize it was so late."

"I figured you got caught up." Taylor walked in holding a pizza box. "I got dinner. I hope you still like pepperoni."

"Oh, yeah."

"Listen, my bags are in the car. We can get them after we eat. I'm starving, and I have a lot to catch you up on what happened today."

"Throw me your keys," Zack said, "and I'll grab your bags now."

Taylor put the pizza box on the kitchen island, dug into her pocket, and fished out her car keys. "Catch." She gave an underhand toss, and Zack caught them in one smooth move.

"I'll be right back."

"And I'll be right here, getting it all ready. You want a salad?"

"Yes," Zack called out as he walked out the front door.

Within minutes, Zack returned with one suitcase on

wheels. He locked the door and wheeled her suitcase into the bedroom. When he walked into the kitchen area, Taylor had a strange look on her face. "Everything okay?"

"Hmm." Taylor reached for the plates in the glass front cabinet above the sink, placing them on the island with a bit of force.

"Anything wrong?"

"No." Taylor shook her head.

Despite her verbal denials, Zack sensed something was off but couldn't imagine what. Maybe it was the stress of everything that happened. He didn't want to push, so he decided to wait until she was ready to tell him. He cleared his throat and leaned against the kitchen island. "What do you want to drink?"

Taylor shrugged. "Whatever. Doesn't matter."

"This is familiar. I know this." Zack pointed to her, then to himself. "This is you being pissed off at me. But I don't understand why."

She looked straight at him. "Don't you?"

Zack put his hands to his chest. "I don't have a clue. Tell me what I did. I'll make it right."

"You can start by removing my suitcase from your bedroom and putting it in the guest room." She crossed her arms over her chest. "I mean, you and I, we're in a better place than we were at the beginning of the week, but we're...we're...not in *that* place." She pointed toward the bedroom. "And who knows if we'll ever get there again. I mean, you don't even agree with what I do for a living." She let out a huff.

"I agree with you."

"You do?"

"Yes. That's why you'll sleep in my room. I've got the couch."

"The couch?"

"Yeah. Jordan has set up a mini gaming war room in the guest room. All the furniture is in the basement. No more guest room. At least for the time being." Zack watched as the color in her cheeks rose.

Taylor's gaze was downcast. "Sorry. I misjudged."

"No problem." He went to the fridge. "Want a beer?"

"Yeah. Sure. Thanks."

"And, Taylor, there will be time when we can talk and figure us out."

Taylor took a long swig of her beer and placed the bottle on the counter. "Why don't you make the salad? I'll doctor the pizza."

"Works for me."

Taylor opened the refrigerator and took out the lettuce, onion, and cucumbers and handed them to Zack. "Do you have tomatoes?"

"Yeah. As a matter of fact, they're the last of my harvest. They're in the bowl by the toaster. I'll get them."

"Your harvest?"

Zack smiled. "Remember how I always wanted a vegetable garden? Well, I started one this summer." He washed the tomatoes in the sink. "There were a few failures. My broccoli was a total disaster. But my peppers, cucumbers, and tomatoes were farmers' market worthy."

"I'm impressed."

"Don't be. It gave me an outdoor activity. I needed one of those."

"Still, it's impressive." Taylor opened the refrigerator again and looked around. "Hey, I don't see the honey-balsamic glaze."

"It's in there. It might be hiding behind the milk."

"Oh, yeah. I see it." She grabbed the bottle and turned to Zack. "Light, medium, or heavy drizzle?"

He busied himself, chopping the cucumbers and onions. "I say we go crazy with a heavy drizzle. What the heck."

Taylor opened the pizza box, drizzled the sauce over the pie, and waited for the oven to warm up. "Do you need help with the salad?"

"If you could wash the lettuce, that would be great."

"Sure thing." Taylor opened the cabinet door next to the dishwasher and grabbed the salad spinner, another cutting board, and a kitchen knife. She set up next to Zack and began chopping the lettuce.

Nothing in the kitchen had changed, and she reached for things by memory. They moved around each other with familiar ease, as if no time had passed.

She went to the sink, washed the lettuce, spun it dry, and handed it to Zack. When the oven timer went off, indicating it had reached the right temperature, she opened the oven door and slid the pizza inside.

"Salad's ready," Zack said. "I'll set the table."

They took their time with dinner while Taylor explained what she'd discovered in the janitorial closet on the fifth floor of the Bureau.

"The laptop is password protected, so I couldn't get into it. I brought it over to Jordan before I came here," she said. "I figured if anyone could hack into it, it would be her. I'm hoping whatever is on there will lead us to whoever is behind this."

For several moments after she spoke, Zack didn't say anything. It was as if he were trying to process what she'd just told him.

"Zack? You're not speaking. I thought for sure you'd have

something to say about all this. You mind telling me what you're thinking?"

"My mind's buzzing. I'm not sure what I think yet." He looked away. "Just so I'm clear, what you're saying is that someone with access to the building used a janitorial closet to send an email, using *your* ID, requesting the Cybercrime report," Zack said. "All in the hopes of getting you…what? Thrown off the case?"

"Looks like it." She pointed her fork at him. "But there's a deeper meaning here."

"Deeper than that?"

"Whoever did this has FBI credentials. That's the only way they could get inside the building, let alone gain access to any floor or room. Secondly, it has to be someone with a level of IT experience."

"Back up on that access part. You need ID to gain access to the different floors?"

"Yes. That's what I'm saying. I had to wait for someone to let me into the fifth floor because my badge didn't grant me access to that floor."

"Are you certain about that? I mean, couldn't someone with serious tech know-how gain access to the building and not be with the FBI?"

"Absolutely not. That place has security upon security upon security." She speared a cucumber. "Nah. I don't see how they could have gotten in." She popped the cucumber into her mouth.

"Maybe they had help," Zack offered.

"That's a scary thought."

"It could be one person on the inside getting help from people who are part of this sextortion ring." He took a swig of beer. "The more I think about it, the more I'm convinced this is a group of people. Too many things have happened

in an effort to disrupt the case for it to be the work of one lone sextortionist."

"I agree with you."

"For now, let's assume whoever used your ID to get that Cybercrime report is an inside person and, with the help of the sextortion ring, had enough tech or hacking power to get access to your ID."

"Yeah, and if that's the case, I need to find out who the inside person is."

"Are you still going with Boyd?"

"He's the only one with security clearance to not only get inside the building but gain access to every room and floor."

"So, what's the plan?"

"That's what I'll be working on tonight."

Zack rose and began cleaning off the dishes from the table. "All right, then we'd better get going. But first, let's clear this up, and then I'll show you my new war room."

Taylor took the glass from his hand, grabbed him by the shoulders, and steered him toward the war room. "You go. I know you're anxious to get back in there. I can see your fingers twitching. I'll clear this up, unpack, and then I'll meet you in there."

"You're right—" he rubbed his hands together "—I am anxious to nail these bastards."

"You do that. I'm going to get with Jordan and figure out a way to nail down who used my ID and what's on that laptop. Now go." She made a shooing motion.

He stopped at the door to the guest room. "I cleared out the top drawer in the dresser for you and made room for you in the closet to hang your clothes. And the bathroom's all yours. I'll use the one down the hall."

"Thanks, Zack." Taylor watched him head into the guest room. A heaviness settled in her chest, and she began load-

ing the few dishes into the dishwasher. On top of everything that was going on and the fact that her SAC might be involved, staying here was a little weird. It was bringing up emotions she'd kept at bay for months.

She'd spent so many nights and weekends in this cottage. Looking back, she knew what she and Zack had was special until she just walked away from it. Taylor shook her head. Of course, she'd justified it like she had so many other things in her life, mostly blaming her parents for everything that has ever happened to her or Emily.

At one point during her undercover assignment, she decided she didn't need anyone anymore. When the undercover op was over, she'd even planned never to contact Zack again. It was safer that way. Attaching yourself to another person only meant you got hurt. But now, here in his kitchen, memories of their time together flooded back. Even though she'd held a piece of herself back when they were together, when she was with him, she'd been her happiest. It had been the only time she'd allowed herself to plan for any kind of future. He had made her want something she hadn't dared to dream of since her sister's disappearance. What would have happened if she'd stayed and not taken the assignment?

She blew out a breath. No sense in wondering about what might have been. The truth was she still hadn't forgiven herself for what happened to Emily. And if she were being honest, deep down, Taylor didn't feel she deserved to be happy.

Taylor placed the last glass in the dishwasher, broke up the pizza box, put it in the recycle bin, and wiped down the counter. Dwelling on the past wouldn't get her anywhere, so she took a breath and tried to focus on the present.

Taylor sighed. She gave all this up for what? Her career was important. Being happy was important, too. She wasn't sure how to reconcile the two. And she sure as hell wasn't

going to figure it out tonight. Folding the dish towel, she placed it on the counter. "Time to unpack."

When she entered Zack's guest room, she took a step back. The change was remarkable. "Wow, you weren't kidding. This is a mini RMZ. Jordan did a great job."

He looked up from the screen. "She sure did."

Taylor walked around the room. "Are you playing at two computer stations at once?"

"Yeah. I'm trying to get some traction here. Each of the three computers has a different IP address, bouncing off different satellites to make it look like I'm different teenage boys located in different parts of the United States."

"Clever." Taylor continued her tour of the room, stopping at each console. "Maybe I could learn to play one of these, speed up the process. I mean, how hard could it be?"

Zack slowly turned in his chair. "That's not the plan we all agreed on. And we need to stick to the plan." He raised an eyebrow.

"Boyd gave me the rest of the day and tomorrow off. Then we have two days on the weekend. Until I have to go back, I could help."

Zack shook his head.

Taylor stared at him, but she knew he was right. Sticking to the plan was essential. They had to avoid any mistakes. What was she thinking? She prided herself on being a calm, steady agent who followed through on a plan. But for some reason, tonight nervous energy flowed through her like water from a faucet. It had to be Zack, the familiar surroundings, and the unresolved issues between them.

"Okay. You're right. We stay the course."

Zack returned to the gaming console, and Taylor watched from behind as he worked the keyboard and played a game

with lifelike animation featuring jets flying over desert terrain with rapid-fire ammunition cascading from what looked like the plane's fuselage. She raised a brow, failing to understand how anyone found this entertaining.

She rubbed the back of her neck, looked around the room, and let her mind drift. Two weeks ago, if you'd have told her she'd be back in Zack's cottage, she would have thought you were out of your mind. When she met him for dinner a few nights ago, she was the last person he'd wanted to see. She'd hurt him badly. But as more problems with the op arose, the frosty exterior Zack had been holding in place when she first arrived seemed to be melting. Maybe he'd forgiven her for ghosting him. Maybe he hadn't.

The one thing she did know was that Zack was not only a decent person, he was one of the kindest people she'd ever met. And if there was one thing that made him stand out, it was his willingness to help others. So maybe this was just Zack being Zack. He knew she had troubles, and he was being kind and helpful.

Deep down, she'd hoped that maybe this was the start of getting back to a friendship—at the very least. Taylor stared at Zack while his focus remained on the screen. He was as handsome as ever. Being here with him, working together, she realized she wanted more. She wanted—dare she think it—what they had. At the thought, her stomach flipped. Maybe staying here, being this close was a mistake. *Keep your eye on the prize. The target here is getting the sextortion ring. Nothing else is on the table.* If for no other reason, getting whoever was behind this would maybe help close the hole in her heart that Emily left.

"You're right, Zack. Stick to the plan." She gave him a tight smile. "I'll go work at the kitchen table. I'll give Jordan

a call and see what's happening at the RMZ gaming room and if she's managed to get into that laptop."

"Hey, wait." He walked over to the far computer station. "Here's a phone for you to use."

Taylor gave him a quizzical look. "This is a burner phone."

"To be on the safe side, Jordan thought it best not to use your phone from here."

## *Chapter 19*

The minute Taylor set up her laptop on Zack's kitchen table, the burner phone rang. She didn't recognize the caller ID but answered anyway.

"Hello?"

"Hey, it's me, Jordan."

"I didn't recognize the number."

"I'm calling you from a burner. Since you've been getting those strange disappearing photos, I figured it was better if we communicate this way."

"Smart."

"Safe," Jordan said. "I haven't hacked into the laptop, but I'm getting close."

"Let me know the minute you do."

"Copy that," she said. "Now, as for what's happening at the RMZ gaming war room. First, as you suspected, now that we've given Gil the quote, unquote identities of all our players, their gaming stations are being lit up like Christmas trees. This war room is practically radioactive."

"Really?"

"Yeah. There's always quite a bit of chatter in the chat rooms, but as of today, it's on fire."

"In what way?"

"The chats are typically all about the game, you know,

strategy, new ways to play or beat your opponent, or about the different characters and leveling up."

"And today was different?"

"Yeah. Different like chocolate and broccoli are different. The chats start out like normal teenagers, but within an hour, they move on to personal stuff. The person on the other end is asking about family, school, and what they do besides gaming. They're even following these identities we created on social media."

"So they're moving in fast?"

"I'd say so. Of the seven techies we had gaming today, five of them are in the middle of personal chats. But whoever is behind this—and believe me, this is a definite setup—is taking a little bit more time so they don't seem as obvious as the one that sent us to the Twelfth Street warehouse in Albany."

Taylor was silent, trying to work out the next moves.

"Oh," Jordan said, interrupting her thoughts, "I almost forgot the most important part. All of these chats are easily traceable to the Philippines. They aren't even trying to mask their location."

"We're being set up. Or, at the very least, we're purposefully being pointed in the wrong direction."

"It sure looks like that."

"All that needs to happen now is the trading of nude photos and the demand for money." Taylor looked out the window and tried to think.

"You still there?" Jordan asked.

"Sorry. Thinking."

"There's a lot to chew on. But this is what you wanted to have happen. Right?"

"Yes. It was a test to see if someone inside the Bureau

was leaking the information we gave Gil. And it seems they have and are using it to throw us off."

"But Zack's working on trying to find out who the real sextortionists are?"

"He's in there right now playing his heart out." Taylor got up, walked down the hallway toward the guest room, and peeked in. Zack was hunched over, completely oblivious to anything but the screen he was fixated on.

"Listen," Taylor continued, "I think your war room is going to get requests for nudes very soon."

"You're probably right."

"Because whoever is behind this knows you'll have to report it to the Bureau, and it will all trace it back to the Philippines. The FBI will have to spend time and resources tracking down the person or people. It could take months. Meanwhile, the real sextortionists lie low until they feel safe enough to start their operation all over again."

She walked back into the kitchen and paced. "Zack is really going to have to pick up the pace...unless...can we get someone else over here tomorrow? I think we need to be aggressive on this end."

"It's not a bad idea. But we'll need to run it by Zack first. You know that."

Taylor huffed. "That's what I was afraid of. He'll think it's a bad idea. But he's got to know we are seriously under a time pressure. Once it's confirmed from your end that it's an overseas operation, they won't need your game room any more. RMZ's portion of the op will be over, and the bad guys get away."

"Then you'd better talk to Zack tonight. I can have one of my guys over there in the morning. But only if Zack agrees."

"Got it."

"I'm still working on those missing laptops and the disappearing photos on your phone."

"Great. Keep me posted."

"Will do."

Taylor swiped off the phone, went to the kitchen window, and stared out. She found herself smiling when she looked down and saw what remained of Zack's summer vegetable garden. Everything had been picked. The indentations in the now barren ground remained where he'd created separate beds for the different vegetables. And in the far right corner, several lone tomato spikes were still in the ground.

So much had happened since she'd been gone. He was living his life.

Her career was important, but she wondered if she'd ever have a normal life. Until now, it wasn't something she'd thought about. But working with Zack, being with him and his family again, and seeing that he was moving on with his life made her want a piece of this.

Taylor had never thought this way before. Why now? It had to be this assignment and the idea that if she somehow caught these bastards, it would help Emily.

She turned away from the window. What felt like a dark cloud passed over her mind. Emily was gone, and nothing she did would ever bring her back. Taylor sat at the kitchen table, put her head in her hands, and wept.

The gentle rubbing on her shoulder woke her. At first she had no idea where she was. Then she heard his voice and smiled. It was Zack calling her name. She'd fallen asleep with her face on the kitchen table. Taylor sat up and rubbed the crick in the back of her neck.

"You fell asleep." Zack's voice was soft and comforting.

He sat in the chair next to her and kept his hand on her arm. "Are you all right?"

"What time is it?"

"One thirty. You should go to bed. You need rest."

"What about you? Are you still playing?"

"Just for another hour. Don't worry about me. Let me get you some water. Then you should get some sleep."

"Hey, listen. Jordan and I think we should get another tech over here. Help you in the morning with the games. Speed up the progress. I mean, it couldn't hurt."

Zack shrugged. "Let me think about it. It may not be a bad idea. I'll get you that water."

Taylor didn't want him to go. She didn't want him to take his hand away. It soothed her.

He brought her a glass of water and insisted she drink. "You look a little disoriented. Let me help you up."

Taylor wanted to resist, but she couldn't. She did feel out of sorts.

Zack lifted her from beneath her arms until she was standing upright. "The bedroom's this way."

"I remember."

He walked beside her until she made it into the bedroom. "You gonna be okay?"

"Yeah. Just a little out of it from sleeping in a chair with my face planted on the kitchen table, but I'll be fine."

"Okay. I'm going to finish up in the game room, and then I'll be on the couch if you need me. Good night." Zack gently closed the door.

Taylor turned on the bedside lamp and began to get ready for bed. She pulled out her camisole and matching silk shorts and went into the bathroom to wash up and change. Within fifteen minutes, she was under the covers and wide awake with thoughts of Zack.

She punched the pillow a few times to try and get comfortable. She turned on her right side. But that didn't feel comfortable, so she turned to her left, with the same result. She flipped onto her stomach and stared at the wall in the dark.

"Come on. You need to sleep," she whispered to herself. It didn't help that she was in Zack's bedroom, a room in which she'd spent many nights. A room where they'd made passionate love. "Oh, this isn't working," she said.

Taylor tried to think about the operation and what needed to be done. But her mind kept going back to Zack. In frustration, she slapped at the mattress and decided to get a glass of water from the bathroom. She dragged one leg over the side of the bed, followed by the other, but Taylor hadn't realized her legs were tangled up in the sheets and cover from all the flipping and flopping she'd done while trying to get into a comfortable sleeping position. The moment she tried to stand, she found herself unable to extricate herself from the covers and began flailing her arms as she lost her balance and fell flat on her face.

"Oh, man, that hurts," Taylor said, still tangled up in the sheets. Before she could stand, the bedroom door flew open, and Zack was in the room standing over her.

"Taylor, are you all right? Are you hurt?" He knelt beside her.

"I'm fine. My pride is hurt. But I'm fine."

"Looks like you got caught up in the sheets." He kneeled beside her and freed her legs from the covers. "Do you need help getting up?"

She shook her head. "I think I've got it." Taylor lifted herself on her elbows but was having difficulty getting up off the floor. She'd fallen harder than she thought.

"Here. Let me." Zack put his hand under her back and

legs, lifted her in his arms, and then placed her on the bed. He reached over and turned on the bedside light. "Let me get a look at you." He put his hand under her chin and lifted her face toward him. Taylor squinted.

"Looks like you're going to have a bump on your forehead. I'm going to go get some ice."

Zack left the room, and humiliation washed over her. The last thing she wanted was to create a scene. And this was most certainly falling into the "scene" category. If only this night would instantly turn to morning and they could skip over whatever this was. They had work to do, and none of it included her falling out of bed and bumping her head.

Before she had any more time to dwell on her ridiculous situation, Zack was back with a small Ziploc bag filled with ice wrapped in a dishtowel.

He sat on the bed facing Taylor, who was sitting up, her back resting against the headboard. He gently pressed the ice against her forehead. She reached for the bag, taking it from his hands. "I've got it. Thanks."

"How are you feeling?"

"Like I said, my pride's hurt. But everything else is fine."

"You startled me. I was in the kitchen when I heard the crash. I couldn't imagine what was going on. I thought it was someone trying to break into the room."

"Nope. Just clumsy me, trying to get to the bathroom for a glass of water."

"Oh, are you thirsty? I'll get you some from the kitchen." Once again, Zack was out of the room, and Taylor didn't know what to do with herself. She gave up holding the bag to her forehead. If she had a bump in the morning, so be it.

Zack rushed in with the water and handed it to her. She drank deeply and then put the glass on the bedside table.

"Where's the ice?" he asked.

Taylor lifted the bag lying beside her. "Here."

"It belongs on your head."

"I think I should go to bed and forget about everything."

"Maybe that's for the best. Let me just get another look at your forehead." Zack leaned in close. Taylor lowered her gaze. As he came closer, she could feel his warm, sweet breath on her cheek. She closed her eyes as she took in a breath and savored his musky scent. She'd missed the familiar smell.

"It looks like it may turn a bit purple, but the swelling's not too bad," he said as he sat back.

"Zack." Taylor whispered his name but said nothing more.

"What is it?"

She shook her head. Every fiber of her being wanted to reach out and kiss him, but she held back. Clearly, he wasn't interested. Zack was just being his usual kind self.

"Is something wrong?" he asked.

"No." She looked up and gazed into his warm, dark brown eyes. Without knowing what she was doing, she touched his cheek.

Zack frowned.

She didn't care. She lifted her hand, cradled his face, leaned in, and softly pressed her lips against his.

"Taylor. We shouldn't."

She heard his words and waited for him to move away. When he didn't, she opened her eyes and pressed her lips to his again. He put his hand on her arm, and its warmth made her breath hitch. His hand slowly worked its way up to caress the back of her neck, pulling her closer to him.

Taylor's mouth parted, and he slipped his tongue in. Her hands wrapped around his back. She slid down and pulled him on top of her, their lips never parting, his hands touch-

ing every part of her until her skin felt like it was on fire. She pressed her body against his until they were practically one.

When he abruptly stopped, she opened her eyes. Zack raised himself onto his elbows and looked into her eyes. "Taylor, I'm not sure this is a great idea."

"Why?" She was breathless and confused.

"You and I have...unresolved issues."

"What?"

Zack looked away. "It's not that I don't want you and haven't wanted you every day since you left, but...but... how do I know you won't leave again?"

Taylor couldn't believe what she was hearing. Was this about her job? "Are you asking me to choose between you and my job? My career?"

Zack didn't answer. Instead, he sat up, put his legs over the side of the bed, and rubbed the back of his neck. "I don't know what I'm saying."

She turned to her side and placed her hand on his back. "It sounds like you're asking me to make a choice. Zack, I care about you. I'd like to be with you again and see where we could take this relationship, but I can't choose, and you shouldn't be asking me to."

"You're right. I shouldn't. I'm sorry." He got up and walked out of the room.

Taylor stared at the closed door in disbelief. How had she not realized that Zack was so selfish? This was all about him and what he needed. What about her and her needs? She had a job to do. More importantly, she was doing this for Emily. Why couldn't he see that this was her priority? Obviously, he didn't understand her. Never had. Never would.

Taylor swiped the tear from her cheek. "No! You will not cry. He doesn't deserve it." She stood and stomped into the bathroom. She opened up her cosmetics case, got two

aspirins, and swallowed them. She looked at her reflection in the mirror. "You need to get this job done and move on."

She flicked off the light, stomped back into bed, and pulled the covers over her head.

# *Chapter 20*

Zack marched into the kitchen, opened the refrigerator, stared inside, slammed the door shut, and then paced around the island.

*"¿Qué te pasa?"* he said out loud as he continued to pace. "Like, what is wrong with you?" Zack shivered at the memory of pushing Taylor away. What had he done? He'd pushed away the only woman he'd ever loved. Did he really think he couldn't cope with her work? Was he really afraid she'd ghost him again? And if that was the case, why didn't he talk to her? Why hadn't he acted like the man his parents raised and had an honest conversation with her instead of walking out?

Zack stopped in front of the kitchen window and stared out into the darkness. He thought about when Taylor disappeared and how he'd spent months agonizing over her, worried out of his mind. When she finally returned, instead of being happy, he was furious and practically ignored her, even after she told him about her sister. Zack balled his fists. An emotional war raged inside him, and it all had to do with Taylor.

She had disappeared without a word, and he'd nearly gone insane with worry. "Who does that to someone they love?" Zack pursed his lips and raised a brow.

On the other hand, she did what she did to vindicate her sister. Taylor had been fighting for those who couldn't fight for themselves. How could that be a bad thing? How could he blame her for leaving?

Zack pressed his forehead against the window pane. He closed his eyes against the cool glass. "What kind of person are you?" he said to himself. He'd been so unforgiving. Still, a part of him justified his anger. She'd disappeared without a word. She had a career that was dangerous. Why was this so difficult for him to understand and accept?

He stomped to the refrigerator, took out a bottle of water, unscrewed the cap, and drank deeply. Rafe's words came back to him. He was being stubborn, and that never served anyone. It certainly wasn't going to help in this situation. He'd loved Taylor once. He probably still did. "Ah, hell."

Zack slammed the bottle onto the counter and marched toward the bedroom. He gave one loud, quick knock and opened the door. Light from the hallway flooded in, and he saw Taylor leaning on one elbow, squinting at him, and then she jumped out of bed. "What happened? Is everything all right?"

Zack marched right up to her until they were a breath apart. "Listen to me. I'm never gonna stop worrying about you and what you do for a living. But I believe in you. And I'm going to keep that closer to me than the worry because I love you, and I know how much strength you have. And your unlimited capacity to want to help others. But if we're going to have any hope of a future, we need to trust each other."

He cradled her face and kissed her hard and deep. Taylor put her arms around him, and they fell onto the bed. His hand traveled up her leg, past her waist, and caressed her breast. Her nipple was hard, and he pushed away her cami-

sole and took her breast into his mouth. Taylor moaned and dug her nails into his back.

Zack had never been so hard, and he wanted to take her right then, but he wanted this to last, so he slowed his breathing. He licked and sucked at her nipple until she called out his name. Then he started on her other breast while his hand reached between her legs and massaged her.

Taylor moaned and moved underneath him, and he smiled at how wet she was.

"Please, Zack. I need you inside me now."

He kissed her lips. "Soon," he said as he continued to use his fingers to make her wetter. "Soon."

Taylor grabbed the headboard and began to breathe faster. All Zack wanted to do was give her pleasure. He gently used his teeth on her nipple while his fingers played with her pleasure point.

It wasn't long before she cried out, and her hips moved up and down while she orgasmed.

Zack stared at her green eyes, then smiled. He kissed her softly as he took off his T-shirt. He stood, opened the drawer on the side table, took out a condom, and handed it to Taylor. He sat on the side of the bed, pulled off his jeans and shorts, and faced her.

Taylor tore open the condom wrapper and slid it over him, making him that much harder. She smiled and laid back. Zack straddled her, and when he entered her, an electric jolt shot through him. It was familiar yet exhilarating and sexy. Together, they moved in a slow, undulating rhythm as they stared into each other's eyes. He was mesmerized by her beauty and the sensations that shot through him. He wanted to take this slow, but it was becoming increasingly difficult. It had been too long since he'd been with her. "You're so beautiful," he whispered. Then kissed her softly. Slowly.

"I'm not sure I can keep this up," he said.

Taylor laughed. "Don't worry. It's all good."

Zack lifted himself up onto his elbows and smiled. Next time, he'd take it slow. His hips began to move faster. His thrusts were deeper. Taylor seemed to match him stroke for stroke until they both cried out together.

Taylor lay cradled under his arm, her hand on his waist. She sighed. "That was amazing."

Zack kissed the top of her head. "It was."

"I missed that," she said and inched closer to him.

They remained wrapped around each other in companionable silence. Taylor's eyes fluttered, and she yawned. "I'm getting sleepy."

Zack looked over at the alarm clock on the side table. It was past three in the morning. "You should get some sleep."

"What about you?" she asked. "You need sleep, too."

He stretched. "I do, but before I burst in here because I thought you'd hurt yourself, I was onto something in the gaming war room."

"Really? What?"

"I just started up a chat with someone who was playing the same game I was—*Lethal Weapons*. It seemed like a genuine teenage gaming conversation. You know, we chatted about the different animated characters in the game we were both playing. And the person on the other end, CodeSniper, was giving me some expert advice on how to level up." Zack pulled Taylor closer. "I consider myself a very good player, but playing against CodeSniper, I had to really concentrate. He had tricks I'd never seen before. And we started leveling up. It was exciting."

Taylor rolled her eyes. "Oh, my god. You really have turned into a gamer."

"Well, not to cast aspersions, but you weren't around. I had to do something with my nights."

"Sorry, buddy. But I'm not taking the blame for your addiction." She laughed.

"Anyway, for about two hours, I was getting a serious tutorial on how to get to the highest level."

"Sounds like there's a *but* coming."

"Oh, yeah. There's a *but*. You see, we're playing, shooting flares, guns, ammunition flying all over the screen. We're taking down the enemy. In the midst of all that, we're text chatting back and forth. He's telling me which keys to press. He's warning me what's coming next. I mean, this guy clearly knew this game cold. Then suddenly—and it felt like out of nowhere—CodeSniper types in the chat box, *Hey how old are you?*"

Taylor blinked and raised herself up on one shoulder to face it. "That sounds weird. Was it weird?"

Zack nodded. "Yeah. I mean, I'm thinking I'm playing some teenage boy. What teenage boy asks another how old they are? I went on high alert. Figured maybe CodeSniper wasn't who he claimed to be."

"How did you respond?"

"I said I was old enough. And then the strangest thing happened. CodeSniper disconnected. They just left the game."

She lay back. "That is strange. Now what?"

"I was going to keep playing and see if I could get him back, but then I heard you in here falling, and, well, I haven't been back online since then."

"You think you can get him back now?"

"I think CodeSniper is a scammer. So yes, I think he'll get back online. Whether he's a sextortionist or not is another matter. I need to keep going in order to find out."

"I get the sense you want to go back in right now. Am I right?"

Zack blew out a breath. "As lovely as it is to be lying here with you, we have a job to do. The sooner we do it, the sooner we can move on and do more of this." He turned to her and smiled.

Taylor reached up and gave him a long, slow kiss. Zack wrapped his arms around her and pulled her on top of him.

"Oh, no," she said. "That was a goodbye kiss. That was meant to get you back into the game war room so we can put this op to bed." She pushed him away and got off the bed.

"You know, with you standing there, naked and gorgeous, it doesn't really make me want to go back to the cold computer and play make-believe killer pilot."

Taylor laughed. "You go. I'll be here when you're done." She walked into the bathroom and closed the door.

When Taylor came out of the bathroom, Zack was gone. She slipped back into bed and was asleep within minutes.

The chime from an incoming text woke her. She looked around. Zack hadn't come back to bed. She checked the time on the alarm, and it was barely five in the morning. Reaching for her phone, she saw a text from Jordan.

Got a signal from one of the stolen laptops. I've got the location.

Taylor blinked at her phone screen, reread the message, and was instantly awake.

What are you doing awake? How did you get the signal?

I rigged an alert on my phone so I wouldn't miss it.

Taylor smiled. Jordan was two steps ahead of the crowd. No wonder RMZ Digital put so much faith in her.

Spent last hour tracking the signal. But I think it's a setup.

Set up?

Yeah. The signal's coming from 12th St warehouse Albany.

## *Chapter 21*

Taylor hesitated. She sat up, pulled her knees in close, and studied the text on the screen. This could, in fact, be a setup. Why else would the signal be coming from that same abandoned warehouse? If she called Gil or alerted the Bureau, there was a strong possibility they'd arrive, but there would be nothing. Just an empty building, like before.

She couldn't risk putting her career on the line.

Taylor pursed her lips and thought about her options. Her phone pinged again.

You there?

Yeah. Thinking next moves.

You gonna call the Bureau?

No.

WHY?

I trust that you got the right signal but—

Taylor's phone rang before she could finish typing the text. It was Jordan.

"You need to alert the Bureau or, at the very least, Gil."

"I thought of that, but the last time I did, they arrived at an empty warehouse. I can't get it wrong again. My career is on the line."

"Your life is on the line if you go there alone."

"Jordan, I'm a big girl. This is what I do for a living." Taylor pushed out a breath. "Look, I'll let Zack know where I am. And you know that I'm going. If you don't hear from me in an hour, then give Gil a call."

There was silence on the other line.

"Jordan?"

"I don't like this one bit."

"Don't worry. I know what I'm doing. I repeat, if you don't hear from me in an hour, call Gil. I gotta go." Taylor swiped off the call and, with adrenaline coursing through her body, shot out of bed. She threw on her jeans, a sweater, and sneakers. She grabbed her gun and jacket and rushed out of the bedroom into the gaming war room.

Zack was fast asleep, his head slumped over the keyboard. She called his name, but he didn't move. She needed to get a move on. In that moment, she made the decision to leave him a note and head out to the warehouse. She knew he'd only try to stop her by having her alert Gil. Her instincts told her that she needed to check the warehouse first before anyone from the Bureau got there. She didn't want another false alarm situation.

Taylor went into the kitchen, fished out a notepad and pen from a kitchen drawer, and hastily scribbled a note to Zack saying she'd gone to check out a lead and if he had questions, to call Jordan.

She slipped into her leather jacket and left.

Zack opened his eyes and tried to lift his head, but a sharp pain stabbed at the back of his neck. Disoriented, he

looked around and realized he'd fallen asleep on his keyboard with his head in an awkward position. He tried to rub the stiffness out of his neck and slowly blinked himself awake. He squinted at the top right corner of the computer screen. Almost six.

His mouth was dry, and as he moved, he realized his neck wasn't the only part of his body that ached. He should have gone back into the warm bed with Taylor instead of trying to play through the night. Making progress on this op was important, but so was being sensible and getting some sleep.

Zack sat back, lifted his arms over his head, and stretched, trying to get some of the kinks out. Then he smiled when an image of him and Taylor from the night before flashed in his mind. She was probably sleeping. She never did like waking up early. But she did love big breakfasts in bed, and since today was her day off, and she didn't have to be anywhere, he would make her a perfect breakfast. First, he needed a shower.

As he stood, he soon realized how many parts of his body ached from sleeping in the chair. He limped down the hallway, trying to work the stiffness out of his legs. Not wanting to wake Taylor, he headed for the guest shower.

Within thirty minutes, he was in the kitchen fixing a western omelet with toast and home fries. The coffee was going, and fresh orange juice was already on the tray. Zack buttered the toast, placed it on the plate, lifted the tray, and headed to the bedroom.

The door was slightly ajar, and he pushed it open with his foot. "Good morning, sleepy head—" He stopped in his tracks when he realized the bed was empty. "Hey, Taylor, are you in there?" he called, thinking she was in the bathroom. But he didn't get an answer.

Zack placed the tray on the bed and went to the bath-

room door. He knocked, and the door slowly opened. The bathroom was empty.

He didn't know what to think, but he knew he needed to remain calm, even while his breathing was picking up speed. *Where would she have gone?* Racing into the kitchen, he looked around, almost in a daze. "Taylor?" he called out as he went to the front door. That was when he saw that her car was gone. "Where did you go?"

Zack grabbed his phone and called her, but he was sent straight to voicemail. He was becoming infuriated with the situation. He quickly sent her a text.

Where are you? How come you left?

He waited for the three-dot bubble to appear but saw nothing. He sent another text.

I just need to know you're okay. Where the hell are you?

The message might have been a little forceful, but now he was worried. He stepped outside. The air was fresh but frigid. Zack didn't feel the cold. He was too worried. He decided to walk the perimeter of the house. Maybe he'd find some clue as to where she went. He knew he was grasping, but he didn't know what to do with the worry that seemed to have settled in the pit of his stomach. Something wasn't right. That's when he remembered there were new security cameras around his house, and he could take a look to see what time she'd left. Maybe that would give him a clue as to where she was and why she left.

Hurrying into the house, he grabbed his laptop and placed it on the kitchen island. He brought up the feed and began scrolling backward until he saw Taylor leave the house and

get in her car. There was no one else around, and it looked as if she had left of her own free will. The time stamp on the recording read five thirty. That was an hour ago.

This wasn't good. Zack slammed the laptop shut and leaned against the kitchen island. She had left without telling him, and she wasn't answering her phone or responding to his text messages.

Zack's phone rang. He checked the caller ID. It was Max. He swiped open the phone. "Hey, bro."

"You know about Taylor?"

"What do you know about Taylor? All I know is that she's not here, and according to the security cameras, she left here over an hour ago." Zack bowed his head and rubbed at the back of his neck.

That was when he saw a piece of paper on the floor. He picked it up. "Hey, hold up, here's a note from her." He paused. "What the hell? Max, according to this note, I'm supposed to call Jordan to find out what's going on. So what the hell is going on!"

"That's why I'm calling. Jordan just told me she got a trace on one of the stolen laptops. She tracked the signal for over an hour and was certain it was coming from the Twelfth Street abandoned warehouse in Albany."

"The one they already investigated?"

"Yes. Anyway, let me finish. She gave Taylor the information and told her to get in touch with Gil, but she didn't want to in case it was another wild-goose chase."

"What? She didn't tell anyone at the Bureau?"

"No. But she told Jordan she would contact her within the hour. It's been over an hour, and we can't reach her."

"Damn it. Neither can I."

# Chapter 22

Taylor pulled off the thruway and made her way to downtown Albany. The sun was almost cresting over the horizon, making the already sketchy neighborhood seem even seedier. While there were no people on the streets, there were remnants of broken lives all around. Empty bottles, pieces of newspaper, used condoms, drug paraphernalia, and a shoe were all strewn about.

Not wanting to alert whoever was in the warehouse that she was there, Taylor parked several blocks away. She put the car in Park, turned off the ignition, looked around, and then got out.

Taking her weapon from her waistband, she held it low by her side and walked toward the warehouse, keeping her eyes peeled for any movement. The only sound was her breathing and her rapidly beating heart.

When she was within a block from the warehouse, she hovered low and close to the buildings to her left. From what she could see, the warehouse looked dark. She waited several minutes, but there didn't appear to be any activity inside. Taylor was beginning to think this was another false alarm.

Before crossing the street, she looked both ways. The street was deserted. Not a car or a pedestrian in sight. Cau-

tiously, she crossed and walked to the back of the warehouse. She spied a door at the far end and ran toward it. She pulled on the handle, and to her surprise, the door was open. She slipped inside, closing the door behind her.

Once she adjusted her eyes to the dark, Taylor could see it looked very much as it did the last time she was here—an empty, cavernous room with twenty-foot ceilings, with one exception. A light seemed to be coming from beneath a door from the other end. A door she hadn't noticed the last time.

As quietly as she could, Taylor made her way to the far end of the warehouse, keeping her gun out in front at all times. When she was several feet away from the door, she heard a sound, as if someone were typing on a keyboard. Without waiting, she grabbed the door handle, pulled the door open, and shouted, "Freeze, FBI."

The room was no bigger than a closet. Whoever was in there had their back to her. He was facing a computer screen that featured a video game.

"Turn around slowly. Very slowly."

The man, sitting on a swivel stool, turned and then began to clap slowly. "Brava, Agent Shore. You caught me."

Taylor couldn't believe her eyes. The sneer on his face was unmistakable. It was Alonzo Piquot, the leader of the sex trafficking ring that went bust. She kept her hands steady, with the gun pointing straight at his chest. "It's you. You're behind this sextortion ring?"

"Aren't you the clever one?"

"Shut up. I want you to stand very slowly. Then, I want you to turn around, and I'm going to handcuff you."

"What? You're not going to ask me what I'm doing here? Read me my rights? That seems awfully rude, Agent Shore."

"I said shut up. Now stand and turn around."

"If that's the way you want it." He stood.

"I said slowly!"

Alonzo put his hands behind his back and slowly turned.

With one hand, Taylor grabbed the handcuffs from her waistband and walked toward Alonzo. Yanking his hands together, she placed the cuffs on him and backed out of the closet, holding her gun on him. "Now step out."

"I'm surprised. You haven't asked me a single question."

"There'll be time for that once we get you to headquarters." With one hand, she pulled her phone from inside her jacket pocket.

"I wouldn't make that call if I were you."

Taylor frowned. "And why is that?"

"Do you even know who you can trust at your precious FBI?"

The words stung, and they hit a nerve. She really didn't know who she could trust. She must have hesitated too long because, out of nowhere, she was grabbed from behind. Her gun fell to the ground, and Taylor immediately went into fight mode.

She completely relaxed her body and slammed her heel on her assailant's foot, causing just enough damage that he dropped his arms. Bending down low, she turned her body, stood, jutted out her left leg, and kicked him in the face. He stumbled back, and Taylor moved forward. The man was over six feet tall, dressed all in leather, and wore his hair in a ponytail.

His fist came toward her face, and she blocked it with her left arm. She felt the impact all the way into her shoulder, and it put her off balance, but she quickly recovered, feinting a jab before kicking him in the sternum. Her opponent again stumbled back, and this time, she didn't give him a chance to recover. She came at him with a roundhouse kick to the shins. The impact was hard, and he fell to one knee.

"Enough. Stop!" Alonzo called out.

Taylor had no intentions of stopping. She wanted to make sure whoever this was stayed down and wouldn't come at her again. Remaining in a sparring position, she was thrown off balance by the sound of doors opening, a loud engine, and tires screeching. From her peripheral vision, she saw cargo doors opening and a black van speeding into the warehouse and pulling up next to her. Two men jumped out and grabbed her from behind. Before she could make a move, they threw her inside the van.

Taylor hit the metal floor of the van hard and was instantly disoriented. The door slid shut and the van took off. Someone she couldn't see was tying her hands and feet with what felt like electrical tape.

"Search her. Make sure you get any weapons, and get the key for these handcuffs. Now!"

Taylor recognized Alonzo's voice. She tried to lift her head, but a hand came down on the side of her face and prevented her from moving.

"Where's the key?" a gruff voice spoke into her ear.

She didn't answer, and he placed his hand on top of her head, pushing her face into the floor. "Where. Is. The. Key?" he asked again, his voice against her ear in a sinister hiss.

Taylor didn't think she'd get anywhere by resisting. She needed time to figure out what they wanted and how she could get out of this. "Jacket pocket. Outside left," she said through gritted teeth.

"That's a good girl," he whispered and then put electrical tape over her mouth.

He turned her over, dug into her jacket pocket, and retrieved the key. "Here, boss."

Her gaze followed the man as he crouched, moved forward toward the passenger seat, and released Piquot from

the cuffs. He rubbed his wrists, looked back at her, and gave a sly smile.

Taylor closed her eyes. She needed to assess the damage. Aside from being unable to move, she wasn't physically hurt. And she was mentally aware of everything that was happening.

She couldn't be certain but guessed there were two men in the back with her. Another man drove, and Alonzo was sitting in the passenger seat.

Unable to move, Taylor lay on her side and tried to keep her breathing steady. If they thought she passed out, maybe they'd talk, and she could better evaluate her situation.

The van continued for miles over what felt like potholed roads. She had no idea where they were going, but when the van traveled over railroad tracks, she tried to get a picture of where they were. The only tracks near downtown Albany cut across to the west side. They must've been taking the back roads. But where to?

Taylor tried to keep track of the time and guessed they'd been driving for more than thirty minutes when she sensed them going up what felt like a rocky incline. They traveled that way for several minutes before she heard Alonzo speak.

"Up there, about fifty feet, take a left. Then drive about a mile. It'll be on your left. You can't miss it."

What would be on their left? Where were they taking her?

# Chapter 23

Zack was in full-blown panic mode. Taylor was missing after she'd gone to check out a lead at the Twelfth Street Albany warehouse.

"It's time to call Gil and Boyd," Max said.

Zack was so freaked out he nearly forgot he was talking to his brother on the other end of the phone line. "I thought of that. But Taylor was concerned that Boyd is in on this. Maybe we only give Gil a call. After all, he's the one we report to and the one Taylor reports to."

"You're probably right. If Gil wants to bring Boyd in—that's his call."

"I'm going to call him right now."

"Okay. Call me back after you speak with him."

Zack swiped off the phone and immediately pushed in Gil's number. The phone rang several times before it went to voice mail. He looked at the time. It wasn't even seven in the morning. Maybe he wasn't up. He fired off a text to Gil and waited for a reply. Nothing.

He called Gil's phone again. Again, it rang until it went to voice mail, and he decided to leave a message. "Hey, it's me, Zack Ramirez. Listen, I'm concerned about Taylor. She got a tip that one of the stolen laptops was being used. The signal came from the Twelfth Street warehouse in Albany.

She went there and was supposed to keep in touch, but we haven't heard from her, and I'm concerned." Zack swiped off the phone and raked a hand through his hair.

Helplessness seemed to pervade his mood. He couldn't just do nothing, so he fired off another text to Gil, but when he got no response, his anxiety levels jacked up another notch.

"I'm going to keep calling him until I get an answer." He phoned Gil one more time, and it went to voice mail. This time, he didn't leave a message. "This can't wait."

He swiped to his favorites and called Max again. Before his brother even said hello, Zack barked into the phone, "Gil's not answering."

"Time for plan B," Max said.

"Which is?"

"We gotta call Boyd. We don't have a choice."

Two hours later, Zack, Max, Rafe, and Jordan entered FBI headquarters in Albany, ready to meet with SAC Boyd.

Zack walked up to the reception desk, pent-up frustration evident in every step he took. "Special Agent in Charge, Brett Boyd is expecting us." He presented his ID. His brothers and Jordan followed suit.

The dark-haired receptionist, with a long face and deep-set eyes, held out her hand and took the IDs. She made several keystrokes on her computer and stared at the screen. "He's expecting you. If you'll stand in front of the camera, one by one, I'll prepare your security badges."

Zack clenched his hands by his side. He'd already endured an almost hour-long car ride from Hollow Lake to get here. The entire time, he continued to call Taylor but got no response. He'd also tried to reach Gil, but that, too, turned out to be a dead end. Maybe Taylor had been smart enough to call Gil and they were together. Zack didn't know. All

he knew was that the woman he loved was in trouble. He could feel it in his bones.

"Sir, please look straight into the camera."

Zack did as he was told, and within a couple of minutes, he was handed a security badge with his photo. He waited while the same task was performed for Rafe, Max, and Jordan.

"Mr. Boyd's admin is coming down to get you."

Zack shook his head. More waiting. He was ready to jump out of his skin.

Max grabbed his elbow. "*Calmaté*, bro. We are going to get Taylor. Just chill for a minute. We need your full mind. Come on."

His brother was right. If Taylor were in trouble, she'd need him to be levelheaded. Frantic and scared wasn't going to get them anywhere.

From across the lobby, he heard the ding of an elevator. A tall blond man dressed in a perfectly pressed dark blue suit and shiny black shoes walked toward them. "Hello. I'm James, Mr. Boyd's assistant. Please follow me."

Zack and the others followed him to the elevator. They got off on the second floor and were escorted to a conference room featuring a rectangular walnut table with six executive leather chairs on either side. The walls were paneled with wood, a photograph of the current President was on one wall, and a large monitor was on the other.

"Can I get you anything? Coffee? Tea? Water?"

In unison, they all said, "No. Thanks."

"Is Special Agent in Charge Boyd going to be meeting with us?" Zack looked at the clock hanging on the far wall above the mounted screen. It was almost nine, nearly three hours since anyone had been able to reach Taylor.

"He'll be right in." James left the room, and Zack paced.

And paced.

And paced.

"Where the hell is Boyd?" he said through a clenched jaw.

"Hey, bro," Rafe said. "It's only been a couple of minutes."

"Right now, every minute counts." He shoved his hands inside his pockets. "This is bull. We shouldn't be kept—"

Zack didn't get a chance to finish that sentence because Brett Boyd pushed open the conference room door, followed by Gil. For a moment, Zack was taken aback. Why hadn't Gil returned his call?

Boyd stood at the head of the conference table and turned to him. "Please, Mr. Ramirez, take a seat."

"I'm comfortable standing." Zack didn't move.

"Please." Boyd motioned to the chair. "We need to discuss the situation regarding Agent Shore."

That got Zack going, and he sat in the chair next to Rafe. "Okay. I'm sitting. What can you tell us about Taylor?"

Boyd took a seat on the other side of the table next to Gil and rested his chin on steepled hands. "Gil notified me this morning that Taylor went to the warehouse. I immediately sent two agents to the location. When they got there, all they found was one of the stolen laptops, evidence of a struggle, and tire marks that stretched from the cargo bay into the warehouse. The tracks were examined, and they were bigger than a car tire. For now, we're assuming it was a van." Boyd held up his hands. "Other than that, we don't have much else to go on at the moment."

Zack wasn't sure he heard Boyd correctly. "Did you say evidence of a struggle? What kind of evidence?"

"We found Taylor's gun and badge."

The words hit him like a knife to his heart. "How is this even possible?" Zack banged a fist on the table.

"Hang on there," Gil said.

He raised his brow and tilted his head. "Really, Gil? Because I called, left messages, and sent you several texts but got no response. In fact, I'm surprised to see you here. Why didn't you get back to me?"

Gil sat forward. "I don't answer to you. But if you must know, when I listened to your messages and saw your texts, I thought it would be quicker if I went to Boyd directly."

"Okay, okay. Let's deal with what's important," Boyd said. "And that's getting Agent Shore back."

What Gil had said didn't sit right with Zack. However, now was not the time to get into it. Boyd was right. They needed to find Taylor. "Do you have any leads?"

"Ten minutes ago, Agent Clancy here—" Boyd pointed to Gil "—received a text telling him to stand by for information about Taylor Shore."

"Did you trace where the text came from?" Jordan asked.

"Our cyber team is working on that now," Boyd said.

"Is there any way I can help?" she said.

He shook his head. "Afraid not. This is FBI business. In fact, we wouldn't even have you here, except for the fact that the text Gil received also requested that you all be in the room when they contacted us."

Zack looked at his brothers and Jordan. They appeared as mystified as he felt. "Why did whoever is behind this ask for us to be here?"

Boyd shrugged. "We're about to find out. They said they'd be calling us at ten o'clock." He checked his watch. "That's about fifty minutes from now. In the meantime, I'm going to find out if the cyber team has any more information on the text. They also left behind the stolen laptop that you traced to the warehouse. We're cross-checking the fingerprints left on the keyboard with our criminal database.

We may have some answers on that." Boyd stood. "Try and remain calm. We're doing everything we can to find her."

"Agent Boyd," Jordan called out, "my offer still stands if you need my help tracing that text."

He turned to face her. "My answer is still the same. This is an internal matter, and we can't allow civilians to enter our cybercrime area. But thank you." Boyd walked out, leaving Gil behind.

Zack was in shock. The woman he loved was missing and evidently had fought for her life. He knew Taylor was strong. She'd kickboxed her way out of a fire, but how many assailants had she been up against? He closed his eyes at the thought of Taylor being taken away in a van. The whole situation made his stomach roil.

Gil sat across from Zack, texting on his phone, and that annoyed him. Shouldn't Gil be doing something to help save Taylor?

"Hey, Gil. Why didn't you return my calls?"

The agent looked up. He seemed surprised. "I told you—I went straight to the source. I called Boyd. I knew that would be the fastest way to help Taylor."

"Yeah, yeah, I get that. But why wouldn't you call me back and let me know you did that?"

Gil didn't answer.

"Actually," Max said, "it's an honest question. You had to know we'd be worried out of our minds."

"Like I said, I don't have to answer to you."

"But by not answering, it kinda makes it look like you're hiding something."

Gil scoffed. "Me hiding? You guys are nuts." He waved them away with a hand.

Zack was about to get out of his chair when he felt Max's hand on his forearm.

*"Déjalo,"* Max whispered.

Zack knew he should drop it, just like his brother said, but he couldn't. Something was off.

He stood. "Why do I think you know something you're not saying?"

"Are you accusing me of something? I'm a federal agent."

"I don't care what you are. You're hiding something."

The van finally came to a stop, but Taylor didn't open her eyes.

"Wake up." The voice was low and gravelly.

She didn't move right away and felt a kick in her back. Her eyes shot open, and Alonzo sneered at her. "We're almost there. Release her legs. We have some walking to do. But watch out—she's feisty."

One of the thugs who threw her into the van grabbed her by her arm and sat her up. One side of his head was shaved to the scalp, stark and bare, while the other side spilled a curtain of straight, coal-black hair down to his shoulders. His exposed ear bore a dozen earrings. He ripped off the electrical tape around her ankles. "Get out," he yelled.

Taylor shimmied her way to the door of the van, hung her legs over the side, and jumped down where the second knuckle dragger waited.

He was shorter and stout, with a spiked strip cut down the center of his head. He, too, wore a leather jacket that covered his arms, leaving his hands, neck, and face exposed, featuring dozens and dozens of images in black ink.

"What are you looking at?" he growled.

Taylor slowly shifted her gaze over his shoulder. She didn't want any of them to think she was the least bit intimidated. Her only thought since she'd been pushed into that van was how to get out. The first thing she needed to

do was scope out her surroundings. They were somewhere in the woods. The leaves on the trees were in full autumnal mode. The road the van drove on seemed to be a hiking trail that abruptly ended.

Something about this place seemed oddly familiar. Maybe it was just wishful thinking.

"Hey, what are you waiting for?" Piquot yelled. "Let's go."

Taylor turned and, with the two thugs on either side of her, followed Piquot and the driver up an incline into the woods.

Without a trail, they were forced to bend under low-hanging branches and step over fallen tree trunks and through years of dead leaves. With her mouth taped and her hands tied behind her back, her balance wasn't steady on the steep incline, and several times, she tripped. Each time, one of the thugs yanked her up hard by her arm.

Taylor had no idea how long they had walked before she heard the familiar sound of rushing water. There must've been a creek nearby. Without being too obvious, she continued to scan the area, knowing it was important to familiarize herself with the terrain.

The farther they walked, the more something about this place seemed familiar, but she couldn't yet place it, partly because her heart was racing, and she knew she didn't have much time to figure a way out of this.

While they continued on the steep incline, she scanned the area, trying to find any familiar markings. When they got to the top of the rise she realized they were high on a cliff, and on her left was the Hudson River.

Her mind scrambled to figure out their exact location. But before she could look around, the man with the spiked strip

cut yanked her by the arm and pulled her to the right. That was when she saw the sign: *THIS IS A RESTRICTED AREA*

Taylor nearly cried out. She knew this place. Her gaze darted all around, taking in the landscape. She wanted to be sure she wasn't imagining things. Granted, it looked different this time of year, but there was no mistaking she knew this place, and she'd been here before.

A year ago, at the beginning of the summer, when the trees were lush and at their peak and a riot of wildflowers stretched across the grounds, she and Zack had come to this exact spot. Taylor swallowed hard as the memories of that day flooded back.

*They'd decided to continue their newfound love of wine and have a picnic at this state park in Germantown, New York. The drive had been beautiful. But when they got on the trail, they realized the highest point, where you could view the Hudson River, was closed off.*

*Deciding that the rules did not apply to them, they disregarded the restricted-area sign. They chose the perfect spot toward the edge of the cliff where they could see clear to the other side of the river. They spread out their blanket and sat. From the picnic basket, Taylor pulled out a bottle of wine, an assortment of cheeses, prosciutto, and a loaf of ciabatta bread. Just as she was adding the glasses, napkins, and utensils, a park ranger approached them.*

*She was tall, had an athletic build, and looked very official in her uniform. "Hey, there, folks." She tilted her hat back. "Didn't you see the sign back there? This area is off-limits."*

*Taylor remembered Zack fumbling for the right thing to say, but he couldn't come up with a good reason to explain why they disregarded the sign. So, he told her the truth. "Well, you see, Ranger, we're celebrating."*

*"Really?" She raised a brow. "What's the occasion?"*

*"We've been together for almost a year," Zack said.* Taylor remembered that had made her smile. It had made her feel special that he celebrated anniversaries. That wasn't something she was used to. Her parents had never been around for her or her sister's birthdays. When it came to their wedding anniversary, they'd typically jet set off to some European isle to celebrate. She and Emily were never included.

*"Well, I'm happy for you both. Nevertheless, you're in a restricted area, and I'm going to have to fine you." She reached into her back pocket and pulled out her citation book.*

*"That's fair," Zack said. "Do you mind telling me why this is a restricted area?"*

*The park ranger looked up from what she was writing and pointed behind Zack. Taylor turned to find they were sitting about fifty yards from what appeared to be a log cabin.*

*"That there was one of our ranger stations," she said. "It's going to be replaced with a more modern unit. Unfortunately, this location got the order to shut down before all the paperwork for the new construction was in. So, now we wait. In the meantime, kids have been using it for parties, drugs, and all kinds of activities we don't need in the park. So we've made this a restricted area until we can get the permit to tear the station down."*

"Hey, hurry it up," the man with the spike hairdo yelled and pushed her from behind, bringing her back to the present.

As they marched forward, Taylor spied the abandoned log cabin and figured that was where they were headed. Her heart picked up speed while her gaze frantically searched for any places she might hide once she escaped.

Because now that she knew Alonzo Piquot was behind the sextortion ring, Taylor was certain that if she didn't escape, he would kill her.

# Chapter 24

After several seconds of staring at each other and Zack's refusal to back down, Gil left the room, leaving him more convinced that the agent was hiding something. He turned to his brothers. "You know there's something not right with that guy."

"Hey, bro," Max said, "this is a tense situation. I get it. But you think you might be overreacting a bit?"

"Hell to the no." Zack began to pace again.

"He's Taylor's partner. What makes you not trust him?" Rafe asked.

He pointed to the door. "Did you see the way he walked out? As if I offended him by asking a very legit question. Why didn't he return my calls? I mean, he knew Taylor was in trouble." Zack shook his head. "If he was so busy, why not shoot me a text saying he got it and was on it? But no, we ended up calling Boyd because Gil couldn't or wouldn't return the calls. And when I pressed him, he acted like *he* was the injured party. It doesn't add up."

"Zack's got a point," Jordan said.

"Yeah. When you put it like that, I'm going to have to agree," Rafe said.

Max nodded. "Yeah, I'm with you, but for some reason, the guy seems to have gone mute, and since he's the FBI

agent, it's not like we're going to pull it out of him. For the moment, Gil has the upper hand."

"I know. And that's what pisses me right off." He checked the clock on the wall. "All we can do now is wait."

"And wonder why whoever is behind this wanted all of us here," Max said.

At five minutes to ten, the conference room door opened, and Boyd marched in, followed by Gil and Boyd's assistant, James.

James hit the lights, picked up a remote, and turned on the monitor at the far end of the room.

"A video call should be coming through from the kidnappers at ten. We'll patch the audio to that speakerphone." A sleek, black, disc-like shape about eleven inches in diameter sat in the center of the table. "The video will appear on the wall monitor."

Zack sat next to Boyd. He clenched and unclenched his hands as the second hand rounded the clock on the wall. Finally, at precisely ten, the phone rang.

Boyd reached over and punched a red button on the speaker. "This is Boyd." As he announced himself, a fuzzy, dark image appeared on the screen. It took several seconds for it to focus, and when it did, Zack nearly jumped out of his seat.

Slumped and strapped to a chair, with each of her legs bound, sat Taylor.

"Oh, my God. What the—"

"Easy, there." Boyd grabbed Zack's arm and pulled him back down.

The camera moved, and Alonzo Piquot's face filled the frame. "Well, isn't this nice? You all came. What a treat. Hello, Special Agent in Charge." Alonzo took a bow. "I

know I've been on your most-wanted list for a while." He scoffed. "I'd like to give you credit for persistence, but we both know persistence and actually getting the job done are two different things. And when it comes to getting the job done, I think we both know that's been an epic failure on the part of the FBI." Alonzo laughed. "Now we find ourselves in this awkward position—" He held up a hand. "Let me rephrase that. The Bureau finds itself in this awkward position."

"And what position is that?" Boyd asked, outwardly appearing calm and collected.

"Well. I seem to have one of your agents."

"We're aware. And we want Agent Shore back. Unharmed." Boyd's tone was threatening.

"I figured."

"So, what needs to happen?"

"You'll turn over five million in unmarked bills, and I'll return your agent."

Zack swallowed hard. All his attention was on Boyd and what he would say next.

Boyd cleared his throat. "I think you know the FBI has a no-concessions policy. We do not negotiate on ransom demands."

"I thought you might say something like that. I don't think you realize I'm serious. Either you fork over the money, or she dies."

"You son of a bitch!" Zack jumped out of his seat. "You lay one hand on her, and I will hunt you down, and there will be nowhere you can go where I won't find you."

Piquot put a hand to his heart. "Oh, now I really am scared." He shook his head. "Save it. You'll never find me. But enough about me. Let's talk about Special Agent in Charge Boyd. Why is it that Agent Shore's direct supervi-

sor doesn't have the same passion you have for getting her back? It looks like he's going to follow company policy and not negotiate with me."

"Hold on a second," Boyd jumped in. "Agent Shore is very important to me and the Bureau. But I need to speak with the governor first. Then you'll need to give us some time to arrange for the money transfer. We don't have that kind of cash sitting in a drawer."

"That all sounds reasonable," Piquot said. "As a little enticement, you might want to remind the governor how Agent Shore came into my possession. She was looking for the people who extorted nude photos of his underage son. I don't think he wants that information out in the public. Not with his re-election campaign about to kick off. Do you?" He chuckled. "I'll tell you what. I'll give you until five o'clock today to convince the governor to agree to our terms and release the funds. Then I'll tell you where to deposit them."

"That's not all!" Zack yelled.

Piquot huffed. "What is it now?"

"I want to speak with Taylor," he demanded.

Piquot pursed his lips. "Awww, true love. Isn't it disgusting?" He turned around, then turned back. "All right if you must." He looked off to his right and, in a lower voice, said, "Bring the camera over there."

In a herky-jerky movement, the camera moved closer to reveal Taylor. The camera was put on a tripod positioned in front of her.

"Is she awake?" Piquot asked.

Zack watched as a hand pulled her hair to position her head upright.

Piquot slapped her face a couple of times. "Come on—time to wake up. Wakey, wakey."

He whispered to Boyd, "Did they drug her?"

"Looks like it."

Taylor blinked and looked around.

"Looks like your lover boy wants to say hello," Piquot said. "Do you understand what I'm saying to you?"

Her eyes got wide, and she nodded.

Zack's heart was about to break seeing the woman he loved in such a vulnerable position. Every second he helplessly watched, his hatred for Piquot grew like a weed inside his chest, choking off the oxygen. As far as Zack was concerned, Alonzo Piquot needed to be scourged from the earth, and he had every intention of being the one to take him out. "I want to hear her speak."

"You're becoming a pain in my ass," Piquot said.

"I don't care. You want five million. I want to know we're getting all of Taylor back."

Without ceremony, Piquot ripped the electrical tape off her mouth, and Taylor gasped.

Zack knew that must have hurt.

"Are you okay?" he asked, knowing it was a stupid question, but all he wanted to do was hear her voice.

"Yes. Yes." She coughed. "I was thinking about that wine picnic where we got fined."

Zack leaned forward. Why was she talking about a wine picnic? It must've been the drugs. From what he could tell, she seemed out of it, and he had no idea what she was talking about. Before he could ask, one of Piquot's men was taping her back up.

"Wait, I'm not done!" he yelled.

"I am." Piquot's face filled the frame once again. "So no more. Boyd, you have your marching orders. Don't mess around with me, or you'll never see Agent Shore again." The screen went black.

Boyd stood.

"What's the plan? Are you going to speak to the governor?" Zack asked.

"I'm going to call him right now. We can't lose Agent Shore. But you must know we can't pay the ransom."

"You can't pay the ransom? But you just told him you'd talk to the governor." He slapped the table.

"And I will because he needs to know what's happening. But that didn't mean we'd turn over any money. We don't pay ransoms."

"Really? Because the threat to expose the governor's son sounded real. Don't you think he'll want to know about that? Doesn't that change anything?"

Boyd pursed his lips. "Look, I know what our policy is, but this does seem to be an unusual circumstance. All I can do is give the governor the facts. I'm not sure he'll authorize the deal."

"Then what's the plan to get her back?" Zack demanded.

"We're calling in our top hostage negotiator. I've got agents working on tracing that call, and we're going to use every possible resource to get her back." Boyd stared down at him. "We will get her back."

## *Chapter 25*

Taylor sat in the middle of the abandoned park ranger station. Her hands and legs were tied to the chair with duct tape. While the station had once served as a rest stop and a place to get information for hikers on the trail, from the looks of things, it was clear it had been used by the homeless and teenagers who'd wanted to party. Even though the place was in disrepair, much of the original furnishings remained, including a waist-high reception desk with aged pamphlets of the area, where Piquot positioned himself with a laptop.

On the far right wall was a wooden table with four chairs, where Piquot's two men and driver now sat playing cards.

The wood floor was littered with candy wrappers, cigarette butts, and empty beer bottles. The grime on the windows was thick, but from what she could gather, there seemed to be plenty of daylight.

Whenever she wasn't being watched, Taylor desperately tried to wiggle her hands free, but all she'd managed to do was burn the skin around her wrists. Knowing that Alonzo Piquot would sell his own mother, it was up to her to escape. Unfortunately, she was alone in this, and her odds didn't look great.

Piquot stood behind the reception desk with his laptop and was busy typing. He looked up and sneered at Tay-

lor. "Let's see if your precious FBI thinks you're worth the trouble."

The look on his face made her skin crawl.

"You're never going to get away with this. You know that?" Taylor spoke with a confidence she didn't quite feel. "I mean, the FBI does not negotiate. So what's your plan? You gonna kill me?"

"I will have no problem getting rid of you." He looked at his nails as if he were admiring a new manicure. "In fact, maybe I just shoot you now, and I still collect the money."

"You don't have the guts to kill me and still ask for the money."

"Oh, no?"

"If nothing else, Zack Ramirez will want proof I'm still alive."

Piquot laughed. "Ah, yes. The boyfriend. He has become a pain in my ass. What you fail to realize is that I'm very good at what I do. I've created an entire empire because I'm that good."

"You think what you do is something to be proud of?"

"I am very good at moving goods. In fact, maybe we don't kill you." He looked over at his two henchmen. "Hey, how 'bout we traffic her. I mean, she's not bad looking."

His men smiled and nodded.

"We could get a pretty penny," Piquot continued. "It would serve her right. After all, fair is fair. She tried to infiltrate our sex trafficking ring, and now we make her a real part of it." He threw his head back and laughed.

Taylor knew she should be afraid, but all he had managed to do was jack up her anger. If she could free herself from this chair, she would kick his ass. "It might be too soon for you to take a victory lap. Like I said, the FBI doesn't negotiate."

"Shut up!" Piquot sprung from his chair. "Do you hear me? Shut up!" He paced the room. "You're really starting to annoy me." He walked up to her chair and bent at the waist so their faces were inches apart. "You don't seem to understand who has the upper hand here. Do you?" He pointed at himself. "I do. I'm in charge. And you are nobody. Don't you get that? A pawn for me to do with as I wish." He straightened. "Get her out of my sight."

Two of his men stood, and Piquot pointed to the door behind the reception desk. "Lock her in that room. She disgusts me."

Before Taylor could react, the two men picked up the chair and carried her past the reception desk toward a door to the right. They put the chair down, and one of the men opened the door, while the other kicked her chair into the room.

Taylor fell with the chair onto the floor sideways. The men laughed, then she heard the door close and lock.

Lying on her side, she closed her eyes and tried to catch her breath. She had to find a way out of this chair. Difficult as it was, she lifted her head and tried to take in her surroundings.

Before her stood a green metal desk and a chair on wheels. To the right of the desk, on a bulletin board, hung a map of what looked like the park. Behind the desk, high on the wall, was a transom window about eighteen inches high and four feet wide. Despite the smallness of the window, it gave Taylor hope.

With all her strength, she sucked in her core and shimmied her way across the floor until she was perpendicular to the desk. Taylor took a moment to think and to catch her breath. She hoped that if she could hook the chair's leg around the leg of the desk she might be able to snap off a

piece of the chair and free her own legs. She wasn't sure what to do after that, but it was a start.

Slowly and as quietly as she could, she contorted her body so that she was able to hook the leg of the chair where it needed to be. But that wasn't the most challenging part. Now she needed to push away from the desk and pull as hard as she could in the opposite direction with the hope that this old wooden chair would give.

Taylor took a deep breath, and then, with every last ounce of strength she possessed, she pulled her body and the chair away from the desk. Nothing happened, so she continued to pull in the opposite direction. She could feel the veins in her neck and temples bulging as she strained with all her might. After several seconds, she stopped and collapsed in the chair.

She couldn't give up but she wasn't sure how much more she had in her. Just as she was about to make another attempt at breaking the chair leg, a commotion erupted in the other room and she became dead still.

She wasn't able to make out the words, but she recognized Alonzo's voice. He was yelling something, then came the sound of footsteps running and the door slamming. Within moments, she heard the door open again. This time, Piquot and his men were all talking. She chose this moment, while they seemed to be involved in whatever was going on out there, to make her move. With all her might she pulled as hard as she could until at last, the chair leg broke free, and with it the seat of the chair came unattached. She lay there breathing hard and covered in perspiration.

This was not the time to rest. Somehow, she'd managed to destroy the chair, which gave her the ability to inch her taped hands down the spindles of the chair back.

Taylor sat up and quickly began to release her left leg by removing the tape.

Now all she needed to do was get out of this room, and the only possible escape was the transom window. She gauged the distance, and the only way up there was by getting on the desk and then, somehow, jumping to the window.

The noise level from the other room had quieted down, and she had no idea if they would come rushing in. Taylor knew it was a long shot, but it was one she needed to take and fast.

In one move, she rose to her feet and climbed on top of the desk. She would need to jump about four feet, grab onto the window, push it open, and then squeeze her way out. She knew this was crazy, but considering the circumstances, it was the only option.

Without thinking, she counted to three and jumped. Her fingers grabbed the ledge of the window as she dangled about seven feet off the ground. Taylor looked down, then closed her eyes, summoning all her strength. Slowly, she hoisted herself a little higher until her elbows rested on the window's ledge. She took another deep breath, slid open the lock bar, and pushed out as hard as she could, but the window didn't budge. "Come on, damn it," she whispered.

Taylor wasn't sure how much more she had in her. She was physically hurting and exhausted. "One more time." She urged herself on and, once again, placed her hand against the window, and, with all her might, pushed. It took a few seconds, but finally, the window opened. She smiled and sucked in the fresh air.

She knew her time was running out. With the last bit of strength she possessed, she hoisted herself over the ledge, squeezed her way through the window, and dropped to the ground.

Taylor wasted no time. The moment she caught her breath, her gaze searched the area, and staying low to the ground, she headed away from the cabin, hoping it would bring her toward the river. There she'd be able to chart a course out of the park.

When she was far enough away, she stood and began to run. She leapt over fallen logs, and bent under low hanging branches, occasionally looking behind her to make sure she wasn't being followed. Eventually, they would know she had disappeared and would come after her.

She kept the pace for several minutes before she heard something other than the sound of her own footsteps and heavy breathing. Stopping behind a large tree, she took a peek but saw nothing. But she heard the sound again—like a twig breaking under someone's foot. Not wanting to wait around to find out if there was someone following her, she took off.

After a few more yards, she definitely heard the sounds of someone running. Digging deep into whatever reserve energy she had, she picked up the pace and turned one last time to see who might be behind her. She never saw the edge of the cliff.

# Chapter 26

Zack paced the FBI conference room, not wanting to think about what was happening to Taylor at the hands of Alonzo Piquot. He only wanted to know that the FBI had decided to pay the ransom and that Taylor would be released.

In the back of his mind, he imagined a million things that could go wrong when it came to a ransom demand. Knowing Alonzo was a criminal and wouldn't think twice about killing Taylor had him nearly jumping out of his skin waiting for Boyd to return with news from the governor.

Zack continued to pace, when he felt a hand on his shoulder.

"You think I don't know what you're going through?" Rafe turned him around and grabbed his forearms, forcing him to stop and look at him. "I went through this when Mallory's crazy husband pretended to be dead and kidnapped their daughter. I know the amount of anxiety that's coursing through you is enough to fuel a rocket. But let's see what Boyd says and take it from there."

He huffed out a breath. "Thanks, bro. I appreciate you get it, but this guy is dangerous, and he's got her tied up. I can't get the image out of my head." He closed his eyes. "If I only knew where she was."

"Why don't you have a seat? Boyd should be back soon."

Reluctantly Zack sat. But his mind wouldn't shut off, replaying the image of Taylor strapped to a chair. He curled his fists tighter and tighter each time his mind went over the image. This time he also replayed her words. He hadn't understood what she was saying and attributed it to the fact that they'd probably drugged her and she wasn't yet fully aware of where she was.

*I was thinking about that wine picnic where we got fined. I was thinking about that wine picnic where we got fined.*

Zack turned to Rafe. "I can't help but wonder what Taylor meant when she said *I was thinking about that wine picnic where we got fined.*"

"It was a strange statement," his brother agreed. "Do you have any idea what she could have been talking about?"

He shook his head. "I've been going over her words again and again, and I come up blank." He leaned in closer to Rafe. "But you know Taylor. I don't care how drugged she was—there was a message in there for me. I need to quiet my mind and think." Zack stood. "I'm going to go to the restroom, splash some water on my face. I'll be back."

Rafe nodded. "Don't take too long. Boyd could be back any minute."

Zack waved a hand at him and continued out the door.

Walking down the corridor, he passed several cubicles. On one desk he noticed several brochures from local state parks. It struck him as odd, and he imagined that either the agent who belonged to this cubicle was preparing for a camping trip or working on an assignment. Zack shrugged and continued toward the restroom.

The idea of traipsing through the woods and being subjected to poison ivy, ticks, or any type of disease was not his idea of fun. As much as he hated working out, he'd take that any time over hiking. That was one of the things he

and Taylor had agreed on. And was the reason they took up wine tasting.

Zack pushed open the swinging door to the men's room, stood at the sink, and looked at himself in the mirror. He studied the dark circles under his eyes and wondered what Taylor was suffering at that very moment. And that was when it hit him. What Taylor had been trying to tell him—the one and only time they'd gone on a picnic at the state park. That must've been what she was hinting at.

He slammed his hand on the edge of the sink and knew exactly what he had to do, and that did not include waiting around for Boyd and the governor to make decisions. Not when he knew where she was.

"Oh, hey," Gil called out as he entered the washroom. "I guess we both needed a break from waiting around."

Zack took a step back and tried to act natural. Something about Gil made his stomach clench. Taylor had been suspicious of Boyd, but she'd never said anything about Gil. However, after this morning's events, Zack thought—no, he felt in his bones—Gil was hiding something. Trusting his gut, he made the snap decision not to say that he knew where Piquot was keeping Taylor. With FBI agents being suspect, this was something he was going to have to do on his own.

"Yeah. It's been nerve-racking sitting in that conference room. I thought if I came in here and splashed some water on my face it would calm my nerves." Zack shook his head. "Didn't work." He shoved his hands into his pockets. "Boyd's not back yet, is he?"

"No. I think it'll be a little while. I mean, it is five million."

"Yeah. I think maybe I'll walk around outside for a few minutes, get some fresh air."

Gil nodded.

"Okay. See you in a few." Zack brushed past him and left.

He was about to text Rafe and let him know where he was going but decided it would be best to text him once he got to the park. The FBI didn't need to know where he was going. Not just yet anyway.

Zack marched down the corridor and headed straight for the elevators before anyone could spot him or stop him. He hustled across the lobby, pushed through the revolving doors, jogged straight toward the visitor's parking lot, and got into his car. After pulling up a map app on his dashboard, he peeled out of the lot.

Within minutes, he was speeding south along the New York State Thruway. According to the app, the state park was only a few exits away, with an estimated arrival time of forty-five minutes. When his phone pinged, Zack glanced at the screen on the dashboard and shook his head. Rafe had been blowing up his phone with texts and calls from the moment he'd gotten in his car. By now his brothers knew he'd left. He just wondered if the FBI knew he was MIA. Zack decided to stand by his earlier decision. He'd let Rafe know where he was when he arrived at the location.

His concentration had been so focused on his destination that he hadn't noticed he was driving twenty miles over the speed limit. Zack quickly checked his mirrors and eased his foot off the gas pedal. When the car slowed to a reasonable speed, he checked his mirrors again. While he wanted to get to the park without delay, the last thing he needed was to be stopped by the New York State Police for speeding.

When he reached the exit, he flipped his blinker and slowed the car. He passed through the turnstile and took the first exit on the right. The app indicated he was five miles from the park entrance.

As he got closer, his mind settled. He needed to plan

his next move. He wasn't armed, and he knew he was no match against Alonzo Piquot and whatever henchmen he had with him.

Zack drove as far into the park as was allowed and parked. He pressed a button that opened the trunk and got out of the car. The area looked different this time of year yet somewhat familiar from when he and Taylor were here in the summer. He walked to the trunk, picked up the tire iron, and closed the lid.

When his phone rang, he checked the caller ID to discover it was Rafe calling again. This time he decided to take the call. "Hey."

"Bro. Where the hell are you? Boyd is furious. Not to mention Gil is missing, too."

"Wait, what? Did you say Gil is missing? Where did he go?"

"We don't know, but he never came back to the conference room, and Boyd can't reach him on his cell."

"Shoot. This isn't good."

"What's going on, Zack?"

"Listen carefully. That cryptic message from Taylor... well, I figured it out. Alonzo is keeping her at an abandoned ranger station at the Clermont Park in Germantown."

"Is that where you are?"

"I just got here, and I'm going after her."

"Wait. Don't do that. Hold up. Let me tell Boyd—"

Zack swiped off the call. The fact that Gil was missing gave him a sense of increased urgency, and he quickly began marching up the path. He had no idea how far the abandoned station was, but he recalled they'd walked awhile. They'd even laughed about it since neither of them had enjoyed the trek.

He trudged forward and had only been walking for about

five minutes when he heard what sounded like footsteps behind him. Zack turned, tire iron in hand, and could just make out a tall figure several yards away coming toward him at a rapid pace. If he wasn't mistaken, the figure bore a resemblance to Gil.

Without thinking, Zack spun on his heels and began sprinting up the hill. For several yards, he ran full out. He had no idea if Gil was gaining on him, but he knew he needed to keep going. It wasn't until he heard the sound of a gun go off that he realized he was being shot at.

Frantic, Zack looked around for cover. Spying a group of dense evergreen bushes to his left, he dove under them, then shimmied on his belly as he tried to get farther from the path. He tried not to breathe as he lay pressed against the ground beneath the bushes. Zack couldn't imagine why Gil would be shooting at him. And with that thought, his mind nearly exploded with the realization that it was Gil, not Boyd, who was in on the sextortion scheme.

He crawled his way to the edge of the cliff looming over the Hudson River. Before he could assess his next move, he heard the sound of heavy footsteps.

"Zack. I know you're around here. Make it easy on yourself, and show me where you are. I'm not going to hurt you. We need to find Taylor."

Zack didn't move. He tried to slow his heart rate and not make a sound. Gil was the enemy, and Zack knew he had no intentions of helping him or Taylor.

"Hey, Zack. Don't be stupid. Come on out. You're not going to make it out of here alive on your own. Let me help you. Come on, man. I can talk to Piquot. I know the guy. I can save Taylor."

Through the thick underbrush, he could see Gil's shoes. From the looks of it, he was only about twelve feet from

where Zack was hiding. Digging his fingers into the dirt, Zack slowly dragged himself toward the cliff.

"Come out! Now!" Gil yelled.

Zack heard a shot fired, and taking his chances, he crawled to the very edge of the cliff, looked over it, and found a small ledge about four feet down. Rolling over, he held on to some protruding pine roots as he slowly lowered himself onto the ledge.

With his arms stretched out to the sides and his body plastered against the rock wall, he stood on the four-foot-wide ledge and held on for dear life.

"Zack! Where are you! No use in fighting it. Come on out. We're bound to find you. You're only making this harder on you and Taylor."

Despite Gil's warnings, Zack continued to hug the rock as he moved inch by inch to his left. When he came around a corner, he nearly fell hundreds of feet into the river below when he found a barely conscious Taylor lying on her side on a six-foot-wide ledge.

Taylor looked up. For a split second, she couldn't believe her eyes. She'd never been so happy to see Zack in all her life and couldn't imagine how he'd gotten here. Before she could speak, Zack put a finger over his mouth, indicating she should be quiet, and then mouthed the words *It's Gil* and pointed above himself.

Taylor frowned. *Gil?* she mouthed back.

Zack nodded.

She'd heard what she thought were gunshots but never imagined it was Gil who was doing the shooting. A shiver ran down her spine. All this time, her partner, Gil Clancy, was working on the inside? Gil was the leak? It was almost unbelievable. Why would he do it?

Zack reached her, kneeled beside her, and took her into his arms. "Are you okay?"

"I'm fine," she whispered into his ear. "I just got the wind knocked out of me when I fell. Did you say Gil shot at you?"

Again, he nodded, and Taylor raised her brows.

They continued to speak in whispered tones as Zack checked to make sure she didn't have any broken bones.

"Listen. I don't hear Gil anymore," Taylor said. "He's probably gone to get Alonzo and his men. We need to get out of here, and the only way out is if we climb back up the cliff and head down the trail."

Zack looked up. "It's a stretch."

She looked out over the ledge. The drop into the river was at least two hundred feet. "Look, we don't have a choice. There's no way we'd survive that jump. We need to go up. I'll go first."

He backed up a foot so Taylor could stand and face the rock. Flexing her fingers, she tested the rough surface for any solid grip until she found a crack big enough for her fingers to grab. Gritting her teeth, Taylor dug her fingers in and hoisted herself up, using her feet to help her scale the rock wall. When the top of the cliff was within reach, she threw her right arm over and, with all her strength, hoisted herself up and over.

Keeping flat against the ground, she turned her body around and leaned over the edge. "Zack, can you make it?" she whispered-shouted.

Zack nodded and did precisely as Taylor had done. Once he was safely up, Taylor pointed to the same bushes he had hidden under. "Let's head for those and stay as low as we can for as long as we can," she said into his ear.

He turned and nodded. "On the count of three. One, two, three."

They took off at a run, staying low to the ground until they reached the bushes and slid under them.

"Fan out. I want them both found now, damn it. And no excuses. Bring them both to me."

"That's Piquot," Taylor whispered. "They're close."

"It sounds like they're going up the hill. Let's keep moving," Zack said.

They continued to make their way down the hill on their stomachs until Zack abruptly stopped. Taylor gave him a questioning look. He held up a finger. She watched as he patted the ground around him, then turned to her with a tire iron in his hand. She had no idea where he got it, but she smiled.

For several more minutes, they slowly crawled beneath the cover of the bushes until there was no more cover. Taylor looked at Zack and whispered, "Run on three." She lifted one finger, a second finger, and finally a third. Simultaneously, they jumped up and began running down the hill.

With adrenaline spurring her on, Taylor ran like she'd never run before, keeping pace with Zack. They were nearly down the mountain when, twenty yards ahead, Gil sprang out from behind a tree, pointing a gun at them.

"Stop!"

Taylor slowed to a walk, Zack at her side.

"You—" he pointed the gun at Zack "—drop the tire iron. Now!"

They were breathing heavily. Zack dropped his only hope of a weapon, and Taylor bent at the waist, putting her hands on her knees. She looked up and, between deep breaths, stared at Gil. "Seriously? It was you the whole time. You're the inside man? What does Piquot have on you?"

"Shut up. Both of you turn around." Gil inched closer,

his gun trained on Zack. "If you don't shut up, I'll shoot him first."

Taylor slowly stood straight. "Why?"

"Both of you put your hands over your heads, turn around, and start marching back up the hill."

"Gil, you owe me that much. How long have you been…" She paused. "You're the reason the sex trafficking case was lost. You're the one who warned Piquot."

"Well, aren't you the smart one?" Gil stepped closer, his gun trained on Zack. "Now I told you—turn around and start walking, or I put a bullet in your boyfriend's head."

Taylor couldn't believe that her partner, someone she'd trusted with her life, had betrayed her the entire time they'd worked together. "Tell me one thing. You owe me that. Is Boyd involved?"

Gil laughed. "You mean Mr. Boy Scout, who follows the rules no matter what?"

That was enough of an answer to reassure her that her SAC wasn't involved. She needed to take care of Gil before Piquot and his men arrived. "Look, you don't need to do this. Just let us go, and I won't say anything."

"Do you know how lame you sound?" he sneered. "I want a piece of that five million. So, sorry—you're coming with me. Now move!" He waved his gun, indicating she should start walking in front of him.

Taylor took one step to her right, then she spun. Her left leg lashed out in a lightning-fast roundhouse kick, knocking the gun from his hand. Without hesitation, her left knee dove into his ribs, and he doubled over.

Zack picked up his tire iron and raised it over Gil's head—

"Stop!" Piquot commanded. "Drop it, now."

He turned toward Alonzo, who was coming closer, gun in hand.

"I said now!" Alonzo looked over at Gil. "Get up, you."

As Gil struggled to stand, Taylor didn't move, fists clenched as she watched Zack lower the tire iron and then look at her. He seemed to be giving her a signal with his eyes while his fingers tapped the tire iron. It took a few seconds, but she figured out what he was trying to communicate. He wanted to count to three with his fingers on the tire iron. She nodded, and he began the count. One finger. Two fingers. Three fingers.

As Gil was standing up, Taylor kicked him in the jaw, and he fell back with a loud groan.

She turned to face Piquot, who was moving toward her. Zack raised the tire iron and ran toward Piquot, bringing the tire iron down across his back. Piquot fell to his knees, pointed his gun at Taylor, and shot her.

## Chapter 27

"FBI. You're surrounded!" Boyd charged up the hill, leading a team of agents with weapons drawn. "Do not move!"

Zack dropped the tire iron, ran to Taylor, and took her in his arms. "Hey, over here. We need help. Taylor's been shot." He checked her over. There was an excessive amount of blood coming from her thigh. "Hurry. Please."

Boyd reached them first. "Tie those two up," he said, pointing to Gil and Piquot, who were both lying on the ground. "And Diaz, call the medics now."

Taylor's eyes were closed, and she made a moaning sound.

"Baby, you're going to be fine. Hang in there."

"Where's Piquot?" Taylor asked in a whispered voice.

"He's being taken away."

"And Gil?"

"He's being taken away, too." Zack looked up at Boyd. "We don't have time to wait for the medics. She needs attention right now."

Boyd nodded. "We brought medics with us. They're right here." As he spoke, two burly medics came rushing toward them with a stretcher.

"Please, sir, give us some room," the taller medic said.

Zack kissed Taylor on the temple. "Hang in there, baby."

With reluctance, he stepped away and let the medics do their job.

As Zack stood, he saw several more agents come down the hill with Piquot's men cuffed and surrounded.

Boyd approached him. "You did a very dangerous thing."

He looked at the ground. "Yeah. I know. But I didn't feel I had a choice."

"Why is that?"

"Because we suspected this was an inside job."

Boyd looked around and then pursed his lips. "How'd you figure that?"

"Too many things didn't add up. Not to mention the sextortionists were always a few steps ahead of us."

"Yeah. That sounds about right." Boyd sucked in a breath. "Unfortunately, I've suspected Gil for a while."

Zack turned to face him and raised his brows. "You did? Why didn't you stop him?"

"He's got years of service. He's got commendations coming out of his ears. And damn, I was his mentor. Part of me didn't want to believe he'd turned. But that last op... The sex trafficking op should have been textbook, and it wasn't. That's when I knew something was wrong. That's when I suspected he might be on the take. But I had no proof and no way of getting any."

"And you let Taylor continue to work with him?" Zack couldn't believe what Boyd was saying.

"Excuse me, sir," the tall medic said. "We're ready to take Agent Shore to the hospital."

"I'm going with her." Zack stepped forward, and Boyd grabbed his arm.

"We'll finish this conversation later."

"No. We won't," Zack said. "This is a conversation you should be having with Taylor."

Boyd nodded. "Okay."

\* \* \*

Taylor was immediately wheeled into surgery as soon as the ambulance arrived at the hospital, leaving Zack alone with his thoughts. He'd sent a text to Max letting him know what had happened. Now all he could do was wait.

An hour later, tired of pacing the same twenty steps in the waiting room, and probably annoying the other people who were likely just as nervous as he was while they waited for news on their loved ones, Zack decided he needed some fresh air.

Outside the hospital, he continued to pace, but being outside gave him a wider berth and the feeling that he had more room to think. And think he did. He thought about the last few years and about his happiest times. Those times all came down to being with Taylor. She was the one person who had brought him the most joy.

Unfortunately, Taylor had been through so much, and now this. It wasn't fair. Life hadn't exactly dealt her the happy family card or an easy time in her career. At that moment, he realized he hadn't been fair to her. He didn't have the right to tell her what she could or couldn't do. He didn't have the right to try to change someone. If this was the career she wanted, so be it. Either he took her for what she was or he didn't. He needed her. That much was clear. He only hoped she needed him, too. He didn't want to live without her. He loved her—all of her and all of her choices.

Calmer, he walked back into the hospital and sat in the waiting room with all the other anxious people.

It wasn't long before Max, Jordan, Rafe, and Mallory walked in.

"What are you guys doing here?"

"Bro," Rafe said, "where else would we be?" He sat next

to Zack, put his arms around his shoulder, and pulled him in close.

"Any word?" Mallory asked.

"Nah," Zack said.

"How long has she been in there?" Max asked.

He checked his watch. "About three hours."

"Okay. So we wait." Jordan sat, as did the others.

"Anyone need a coffee?" Max asked.

No one responded, so Max sat next to Jordan and held her hand.

One hour later, a petite brown-eyed woman with a surgeon's cap came toward him. "Mr. Ramirez?"

Zack stood. "Yes. How is she?"

"Agent Shore will be fine."

He blew out a breath.

"We were able to remove the bullet. It was lodged in the bone, but fortunately, nothing shattered. There is, however, extensive muscle damage, and she'll need lots of physical therapy to fully recover the use of her leg."

"When can I see her?"

"She's still in recovery. The nurse will come out and get you when she's in a room."

"Thank you, Doctor." Zack turned to Rafe, who embraced him. "Thank God." He whispered into his brother's chest.

Zack looked up when Boyd entered the room. "What are you doing here?"

Boyd took a step back. "She's my agent. I wanted to make sure she's being well cared for."

He was torn between giving Boyd information and freezing him out. The fact that Boyd had suspected Gil all along and never said a word to Taylor infuriated him. Could all this have been avoided if Boyd had just questioned Gil in

the first place? He supposed those were all questions Taylor would ask. For now, he didn't need Boyd upsetting her.

"Listen, the doctor just spoke to us. Taylor's in recovery, and they'll let us know when we can see her," Zack said. "Let me suggest you talk to her when she's feeling better. I think you've got some things she'll want to hear. But for today, let's let her rest."

Boyd rubbed his jaw. "Yeah. I suppose you're right. I'll be back."

Zack watched him turn and walk away.

## Chapter 28

Taylor stared out the window. The wind was blowing, and a flurry of multicolored leaves fell from their branches and danced in swirls before descending to the ground. She loved this time of year and wished she was outside instead of being cooped up in this room for the last three days. She hated hospitals.

The pain meds made her sleepy, and she fought to keep her eyes open. She didn't want to be unconscious when Zack came to visit.

She turned away from the window and stared at the ceiling. Yesterday the physical therapist told her it would take several months of therapy before she could go back to work. She hadn't even asked about kickboxing for fear the wait time would only further depress her.

"Hello, Shore," Boyd said, knocking on the door. "How are you feeling today?"

Taylor frowned. "Like I was shot at and then sat on. How about you?"

Boyd stepped into the room. "May I?" He pointed to the chair next to her bed.

Taylor nodded, and her gaze followed him as he walked across the room and maneuvered the chair to face her. While she'd been anxious to find out what had happened, Zack had

suggested she wait to speak with Boyd to give him time to get more answers.

Over the last three days, she'd spent a lot of time in and out of pain and, for the most part, sleeping. But now she was fully awake and wanted to know exactly what Boyd knew.

"So," Boyd said as he sat, "first things first. Do you need anything?"

"Yeah. Some answers."

He clasped his hands. "Okay. You want to get right into it, then?"

"Damn straight." Taylor didn't want to wait one more minute.

Boyd rubbed his chin. "I suspected something was off during the earlier sex trafficking operation."

"How so?"

"During the first three weeks, when you initially went undercover for that op, you were making progress. Then, suddenly, everything dried up. Alonzo Piquot went into hiding. It struck me as odd, but I put it on the back burner, figured it wasn't our time for that op. But then, you get a hot call soon after. That's what really perked up my ears. I thought it was strange. And Gil was acting a little too excited about this one, insisting that you go back out there—"

"And you didn't think to tell me this?"

Boyd held up a hand. "Your security was always a priority for me. That's why I didn't tell you. I figured the less you knew, the more you'd be able to act the part without any second guessing. I was prepared to pull you out at any moment. Please believe that."

"I guess we'll never know."

"Okay—" he shrugged "—I deserved that."

"Yes, you did." Taylor looked up at the ceiling. "So what happened next?"

"I did a lot of digging. It took some time, but Gil hadn't covered his tracks as well as he thought he had." Boyd spread his hands, palms up. "Turns out all those weekend fishing trips he told us about…he'd actually been fishing at the craps tables in Atlantic City. He's not a very good gambler. Addicted, but not good. He racked up a quarter of a million in debt to a loan shark out there, and…well… it was time to pay up."

"Did you say a quarter of a million?" Taylor tried to whistle, but her mouth was too dry. "I need some water— would you mind?"

Boyd stood and poured her a glass of ice water from the pitcher on the side table and handed it to her.

Taylor drank deeply and handed him back the glass. "That's a lot of cash. How did Piquot get involved?"

"That's where it gets interesting. Seems Piquot was on the lookout for any federal official who was in financial trouble. Figured they'd be an easy bribe to make sure his operations stayed below the radar. He also has a lot of connections to loan sharks. You know, all those scum mix in the same social circles. So, he got word from one of his loan shark friends that he had a debt that hadn't been repaid and the guy was a fed. And it didn't look like it was going to be repaid anytime soon. So, Alonzo bought the loan."

"He bought the loan? What does that mean?"

"Gil now owed Alonzo a quarter of a million, with interest, which he had no way of paying back. So it was either pay back the money, which he couldn't, be killed in some horrible torturous way, or play ball by doing Piquot's bidding."

"Oh, my god. This is like out of a bad movie."

Boyd nodded. "A tragically bad movie."

"I'm not sure how much more of this I can take."

He stood. "Are you okay? Can I get you something?"

"Look at me. I'm in a bed with a serious leg injury. No, I'm not okay." She rolled her eyes. "And now you're telling me some pretty out-there stuff about a partner I thought I knew. But it was all a lie. And you knew about it." Taylor blew out a heavy breath. "Listen, boss, I'm pissed. So, just get on with the story so I can see where this goes, and then I'll decide *my* next moves. 'Cause this whole thing is turning my stomach."

Boyd sat and stared at the floor for a moment.

"Come on." She slapped a hand on the blanket. "Don't keep me waiting. Just tell me."

"We've gotten a good deal of information from Gil. He knows he needs to play ball. But Piquot has lawyered up, trying to make a deal."

"You're not seriously considering giving him a deal, are you?"

"Nah. No way. But it's all part of the negotiation. For now, I'll tell you what we know."

"Piquot had Gil give us just enough information on the sex trafficking ring to make it look like the op was moving forward. But when you got too close, that's when Gil helped pull the plug, and the operation went bust."

Rage poured through Taylor's veins. The months she'd worked on that assignment, away from everything she knew, away from Zack, only to have it yanked out from under her by her partner.

"With Gil now being such a good foot soldier for Piquot, when the governor's kid was taken to the hospital, and the sextortion case was front and center, Piquot gave him the task of making sure we got thrown off by looking overseas."

In Taylor's mind, all the pieces were falling into place. "That all makes sense, except how did he manage to do this all on his own?"

"He didn't. He had help."

"Help?"

"You know Roger Abbot, manager of the cyber tech team?"

"You mean surly Roger? The one you sent to sweep my car after the laptops were stolen?"

Boyd nodded. "*Surly*'s a good description. Poor guy's been overlooked for a promotion for years, and he made no bones about sharing his grievances. So, Gil approached him, knowing he'd need someone good at tech and who could easily get around the Bureau with no questions asked."

"Are you kidding me? Roger was in on this?"

"No, no." Boyd waved a hand. "Roger came right to me, told me he'd been offered money to work with Gil. Roger didn't know it was for Alonzo Piquot, but he knew it had to do with the governor's son's case. Anyway, I told Roger to play along with Gil. Pretend like he was all in. And when the laptops got stolen, I specifically sent Roger to the scene to make it look like you may have somehow been involved so I could get you off the case. I knew it wasn't safe to be around Gil anymore."

"But…but… I had my own plan to get off the case. We already figured out something was wrong." Taylor could feel heat rising to her cheeks. "Well, we thought it was you." She closed her eyes. "Sorry, boss."

"Yeah, we were all dancing around each other on this one." He paused. "Look, we're getting more information as we go forward. Gil's facing prison, and regardless of how many lawyers Piquot wrangles into his corner, he'll be going away for a very, very long time."

Boyd's words seem to satisfy Taylor. A quiet settled over her, knowing that in the end, Alonzo Piquot, the destroyer of so many lives, would be put away where he couldn't do

any more damage. As for Gil…she was still sorting out her feelings. For now, hatred was at the top of the list.

"Knock, knock."

Taylor turned to find Zack at the door.

"Am I interrupting?"

"No," she said. "We were just wrapping up."

He raised a brow. "Is everything okay?"

"It will be," Taylor said and smiled.

# *Epilogue*

*Two Weeks Later*

Zack parked his car across the street from Rafe's house and turned to Taylor. "You ready?"

"Sure. Why shouldn't I be?"

"There's a lot of people in there who are all going to be happy to see you. You up for that?"

"I'll be happy to see them, too. But this party isn't about me. This is Max and Jordan's engagement party, and I think they'll be too busy celebrating that to fawn all over me."

Zack smiled. "I'm just saying, you know how touchy-feely my family can be."

"Well, believe it or not, I'm in the mood for touchy-feely. But I don't want the fact of me being here to take away from what's really important today—Max and Jordan."

"All right. Let me help you out." Zack got out of the car, went around to the passenger door, and opened it.

With one hand, Taylor grabbed hold of his arm and, with the other, pushed herself up and out of the seat with her cane. She'd recently graduated from crutches, and it was sometimes slow going with the pain. But every day she was getting better.

For early November, the day was unusually warm, and

the windows at Rafe's house were wide open. Music and conversation spilled out onto the sidewalk. "I think the party's already in full swing," Taylor said.

"Good, 'cause I'm hungry." Zack smiled and helped her up the steps of the front porch. The door instantly swung open, and they were greeted by Zack's aunt, Ellie.

"Oh, you made it! I'm so happy to see you both." Ellie gave Taylor a sad look. "*Probrecita*. How do you feel? How's the leg? Can I give you a hug?"

Taylor smiled. "Of course. And I'm happy to see you, too."

She stepped forward and gently embraced Taylor. "I'm so relieved you're safe," she whispered into her ear.

Taylor felt a lump rise in her throat. This was one of the warmest, loving families she'd ever known.

"Let's get you both inside." Ellie ushered them in, where the music and conversation were louder.

Once inside the foyer, Zack glanced around at the full house. To the left, in the living room, several of his cousins were gathered around a buffet table. "Wow, looks like everyone is here. Where are the guests of honor?"

"Right here, bro," Max said, stepping into the foyer with Jordan at his side. He embraced Taylor. "How are you feeling?"

"I feel good." She smiled. "But this party is all about you." Taylor kissed Jordan on the cheek. "Congratulations."

"Thanks," Jordan said. "And it is great to see you up and around. Listen, there's plenty of food and drink. And everyone's dying to see you and say hello. Why don't you start in the dining room?"

"Hey, Zack! Taylor! Come on in." Rafe was sitting at the dining room table next to their father, Judge Emilio Ramirez.

"Oh, my, it's Taylor!" Emilio rushed over to greet them. "I'm so happy to see you." He, too, embraced her. "You gave us all a scare. But I'm so happy you're doing well now. Are you in much pain?"

"No. No. I'm fine."

"Come in and sit down." Emilio ushered Taylor into the dining room and pulled out a seat for her. Within minutes, she was surrounded by Zack's relatives. Tía Ellie's three children, Marisa, Carlos, and Javier, owners of a software-development company, greeted her with warm embraces. They were soon joined by his aunt Claudia and her sons, New York City police detectives Jack and Andres.

Zack and Taylor had spent time with all his cousins during the year they'd been together. Going out to dinner, concerts, ball games, and just hanging out. Taylor laughed and joked with everyone as if they'd only just seen each other. The mood was natural, filled with love.

Zack took it all in. This was what he wanted his life to be. This suited him. He wanted his family, and he wanted Taylor to be a part of that forever.

Mallory soon waltzed out of the kitchen carrying a big cake. "Attention, attention. Everyone, come on in. It's time to pay tribute to Max and Jordan." Several more adults, in-laws, aunts, uncles, and children straggled into the dining room. As Mallory placed a large white cake in the center of the table, Rafe walked in, carrying Lucas in one arm and holding Justine's hand in the other. "I think that's everyone."

Mallory looked over at Emilio. "The floor's all yours, Pop."

The judge stood. He resembled a handsome, older Max with a shock of white hair. "Thank you. Well, here we are. Another family gathering. We haven't really had one like

this since Rafe and Mallory. But I'm very happy to still be here for this one."

"You'll outlive us all," Tía Ellie exclaimed.

Everyone chuckled.

"Be that as it may, I'm very happy to be here tonight as we toast the engagement of my eldest son and his incredibly talented, smart, beautiful fiancée, Jordan."

Max put his arm around her and pulled her in close.

"Jordan, as you can see," Emilio continued, "we're a big noisy, nosy, in-your-face bunch. And if you can put up with that, we can promise you a family that will always be by your side and always love you. So, for that, I'm wishing you and Max a million years of happiness together." He looked around the room. "Zack, can you pop that bubbly over there so we can raise a glass?"

"Sure, Pop." Zack rushed over to the sideboard, and with help from his cousin Javier, they opened three bottles of champagne and poured everyone a glass.

"All right now," Emilio said. "Let's toast the newest couple to soon become a permanent fixture in this family."

Everyone in the room raised their glasses and, in a chorus, shouted, "To Max and Jordan!"

The cake was cut, and for an hour, the music played, more champagne was consumed, and the conversation was plentiful.

Zack looked over at Taylor and smiled. "Hey, you. It's still warm out—wanna sit on the back porch and get some air?"

She smiled. "Sounds like a good idea."

They made their way through the crowd to the kitchen back door and onto the porch. They sat on the cushioned two-seater. "Comfortable?" he asked.

Taylor nodded. "This was nice. I'm glad I came." She

turned to face him. "Your family is great. I forgot how much I liked spending time with them."

"Even though, like my pop said, we're noisy, nosy, in-your-face?"

"Yeah. That's the best part."

Zack laughed. "I guess you're right." He scratched the back of his head. "It may be too soon to talk about you and me. I mean, since you're still recovering—"

"No. It's not too soon. I've been thinking about it, too, especially since I've been living at your place for the last week." Taylor maneuvered her body to face him. "I think it's time to get into it." She paused. "You know, for years, I've been pushing on a career because I thought it would help me bring some closure to what happened to my sister, Emily. And for the most part, believe it or not, it has. But I learned some things. I learned that I've been blaming my parents and even Emily's disappearance on why I couldn't ever really be fully there for someone else." She glanced away and shifted in her seat.

"I think that's all changed," she continued. "I mean, after I got shot and learned everything about Gil's betrayal. I mean he stole the laptops and then tried to kill me by setting the fire." She looked off and pursed her lips. "Well, it got me thinking. Really thinking about what I want in life. Don't get me wrong—I still want to chase bad guys. It makes me feel all warm and fuzzy inside when they get their due. But I also want this." She pointed inside the house. "A family."

Zack smiled. "Funny—I want that, too." He nodded toward the house. "I want that with you."

"Even if I come with a job that terrifies you?"

He looked up. "Yeah. Believe it or not, even if it comes with your terrifying job, I want you."

Taylor smiled. "I'm happy to hear that. But I think you'll

probably be pleased to know that I'm not going into the field anymore."

Zack frowned. "You're not?"

"Look at this leg. Even the physical therapist said it's never going to be one hundred percent. And I don't work with anything less."

"What are you going to do?"

"Well, I've spoken to Boyd, and I want to work on the cybercrime team as an analyst. It's a desk job, but at least I'm still involved."

Zack's grin widened. "So you'd still be with the Bureau, but you'd be sitting in an office?"

"That's right. So what do you think?"

"As long as you're happy." He put his arm around her.

"But I want you to be happy, too."

"Well, I'll tell you what would make me really happy."

"What's that?"

"How about we spend the rest of our lives together—you, me, and this crazy, mixed-up family of mine?"

"Zack Ramirez, is that a proposal?"

"Taylor Shore, will you marry me?"

"I thought you'd never ask."

Zack turned to Taylor, took her face in his hands, and looked into her eyes. "Taylor Shore, I love you now, and I will love you forever." Slowly, he pressed his lips to hers for a long, slow kiss.

\* \* \* \* \*

# Get up to 4 Free Books!

**We'll send you 2 free books from each series you try PLUS a free Mystery Gift.**

Both the **Harlequin Intrigue®** and **Harlequin® Romantic Suspense** series feature compelling novels filled with heart-racing action-packed romance that will keep you on the edge of your seat.

---

**YES!** Please send me 2 FREE novels from the Harlequin Intrigue or Harlequin Romantic Suspense series and my FREE gift (gift is worth about $10 retail). After receiving them, if I don't wish to receive any more books, I can return the shipping statement marked "cancel." If I don't cancel, I will receive 6 brand-new Harlequin Intrigue Larger-Print books every month and be billed just $7.19 each in the U.S. or $7.99 each in Canada, or 4 brand-new Harlequin Romantic Suspense books every month and be billed just $6.39 each in the U.S. or $7.19 each in Canada, a savings of 20% off the cover price. It's quite a bargain! Shipping and handling is just 50¢ per book in the U.S. and $1.25 per book in Canada.* I understand that accepting the 2 free books and gift places me under no obligation to buy anything. I can always return a shipment and cancel at any time by calling the number below. The free books and gift are mine to keep no matter what I decide.

Choose one:
- ☐ **Harlequin Intrigue Larger-Print** (199/399 BPA G36Y)
- ☐ **Harlequin Romantic Suspense** (240/340 BPA G36Y)
- ☐ **Or Try Both!** (199/399 & 240/340 BPA G36Z)

Name (please print)

Address                                                                                     Apt. #

City                            State/Province                              Zip/Postal Code

**Email:** Please check this box ☐ if you would like to receive newsletters and promotional emails from Harlequin Enterprises ULC and its affiliates. You can unsubscribe anytime.

**Mail to the Harlequin Reader Service:**
**IN U.S.A.:** P.O. Box 1341, Buffalo, NY 14240-8531
**IN CANADA:** P.O. Box 603, Fort Erie, Ontario L2A 5X3

Want to explore our other series or interested in ebooks? Visit www.ReaderService.com or call 1-800-873-8635.

---

*Terms and prices subject to change without notice. Prices do not include sales taxes, which will be charged (if applicable) based on your state or country of residence. Canadian residents will be charged applicable taxes. Offer not valid in Quebec. This offer is limited to one order per household. Books received may not be as shown. Not valid for current subscribers to the Harlequin Intrigue or Harlequin Romantic Suspense series. All orders subject to approval. Credit or debit balances in a customer's account(s) may be offset by any other outstanding balance owed by or to the customer. Please allow 4 to 6 weeks for delivery. Offer available while quantities last.

**Your Privacy**—Your information is being collected by Harlequin Enterprises ULC, operating as Harlequin Reader Service. For a complete summary of the information we collect, how we use this information and to whom it is disclosed, please visit our privacy notice located at https://corporate.harlequin.com/privacy-notice. Notice to California Residents – Under California law, you have specific rights to control and access your data. For more information on these rights and how to exercise them, visit https://corporate.harlequin.com/california-privacy. For additional information for residents of other U.S. states that provide their residents with certain rights with respect to personal data, visit https://corporate.harlequin.com/other-state-residents-privacy-rights/.

# Exploding the Israel Deception

## Steve Wohlberg

A Jewish believer exposes false prophecies about Israel, the temple, and Armageddon

Copyright © 2000 by
Steve Wohlberg

All Rights Reserved
Printed in the USA

Published by:
**Amazing Discoveries**
7051 McCart Avenue
Fort Worth, Texas 76133

Edited by Debra J. Hicks/Russ Holt
Proofread by Arlene Clark
Cover design by Allen Hrenyk/Craig Branham
Cover photo by Don Satterlee

ISBN 1-58019-139-8

# FOREWORD
## BY
## DOUG BATCHELOR
### DIRECTOR OF AMAZING FACTS
### RADIO AND TELEVISION MINISTRIES

The Bible is a book for all people, but it revolves around a specific people, the Jews. It is impossible to have a clear picture of final events without first having a correct understanding of the true place of the Jewish nation in prophecy.

As a Jewish Christian, I am deeply concerned about the widely accepted distortions regarding modern Israel and prophecy. When Jesus came the first time, the Jewish people were not prepared to receive Him because they had misunderstood the prophecies regarding His kingdom. When He died on the cross, even His own disciples were bewildered. They were looking for a literal kingdom, in which the Messiah would overthrow their enemies so they could regain the earthly glory of Solomon's time. But when Jesus came the first time, He came to establish a spiritual kingdom (Luke 17:21).

Now, just before His second coming, the Christian world is repeating the Jewish nation's mistake. People

are reversing the spiritual things to literal and then spiritualizing the plain letter! The tragedy is that in the process, they are setting themselves up for a devastating disappointment.

Steve Wohlberg courageously exposes these popular yet dangerous misconceptions in a clear and progressive style that is irrefutable for honest Bible students. Pray, read, and then hold onto your seat!

—Doug Batchelor

# TABLE OF CONTENTS

| Chapter | Page |
|---|---|

Author's Introduction ............................ 7

1 ~ Wrestling with an Angel ................... 13

2 ~ A New Look at Jesus Christ ............... 19

3 ~ The Shocking Principle of Two Israels! 25

4 ~ "Choice" and the Chosen Nation ......... 35

5 ~ The "70ᵀᴴ Week of Daniel" Delusion .... 41

6 ~ The Divine Divorce .......................... 49

7 ~ When the Wall Came Tumbling Down ... 55

8 ~ 1948—An "Unsinkable" Doctrine? ....... 63

9 ~ Titanic Truths About the Temple ........ 77

10 ~ When the River Euphrates Runs Dry ... 93

11 ~ Frogs, Fables, and Armageddon .......... 105

12 ~ Thunder From Heaven's Temple .......... 111

13 ~ 144,000 Israelites Indeed ................... 119

# Author's Introduction

*[handwritten: World View]*

When January 1, 2000 finally arrived, it became obvious that doomsday prophecies about <u>Y2K</u> had failed. Earnest predictions about massive computer chaos, power disruptions, bank failures, stock markets crashing, nuclear missiles launching, and the resulting global terror, all proved to be <u>false prophecies.</u>

*Is it possible that certain <u>popular</u> <u>end-time</u> <u>prophecies</u> about <u>Israel will also fail?</u>*

On New Year's Eve, 1999, Israeli police assembled in record numbers inside Jerusalem. They were determined to keep the peace in the midst of growing concerns about terrorism and the possible explosive actions of religious fanatics. Hundreds of thousands of pilgrims and worshippers were crowding toward the Wailing Wall and the Temple Mount. News reporters from around the world swarmed throughout the City of David. With the approach of the long expected new millennium, apocalyptic interest was at its height. A

lot of people were thinking, "If the arrival of the year 2000 has anything to do with the end of the world, then surely Jerusalem is the place to be!"

*Yet nothing happened.*

Why are the eyes of so many people fixed upon Jerusalem? There are many reasons, yet one big one is clear. The truth is that literally millions of Christians who are interested in Bible prophecy believe that earth's final events will one day center around the Middle East, Jerusalem, and the Jews. According to what is commonly understood, what happens to the nation of Israel is *very definitely* connected with the final battle of Armageddon, the return of Jesus Christ, and the end of the world.

The November 1, 1999 issue of *Newsweek*, in its comments about Y2K and Christian concerns, reported, "...the predominant issue in Christian prophecy is the return of the Jews to the Holy Land and the rebuilding of the Jerusalem temple."[1]

Today, well-respected Christian scholars such as Hal Lindsey, Jack Van Impe, Dave Hunt, Peter Lalonde, Irvin Baxter Jr., and Tim LaHaye, all teach the significance of Israel in prophecy. The milestone Christian film, *Left Behind: The Movie,* which begins with a Russian surprise attack against Israel, continues this trend of associating the book of Revelation's end-time prophecies with a rebuilt Jewish Temple on the Temple Mount.

## Author's Invitation     9

While there are differences of opinion among Christian scholars who teach about Bible prophecy, the majority firmly believe the following five events have been definitely predicted by God to occur before the second coming of Jesus Christ: (1) The rebirth of the state of Israel in 1948, (2) A soon coming "Seven Year Period of Great Tribulation," (3) The rebuilding of a third Jewish temple on the Temple Mount inside Jerusalem, (4) The rise of a mysterious man, the Antichrist, who will enter this rebuilt Jewish temple, proclaiming himself as God, (5) A final war against the nation of Israel, resulting in a Middle East battle of Armageddon.

It may sound like blasphemy to some, but the purpose of this book is to re-examine the accuracy of these popular teachings, in the light of Scripture.

Before we go any further, let me tell you a little about myself. I am Jewish, and I love Jewish people. I also believe Jesus Christ is my Messiah. Out of love for the human race, "Christ died for our sins." 1 Corinthians 15:3. He rose from the dead, and has ascended to heaven. He will one day return to this earth, as He promised, *and everything truly predicted in Bible prophecy will be fulfilled.* The battle of Armageddon will be fought. And yes, there will be an "end of the world." Matthew 24:14.

Yet I have come to a rather frightening conclusion. I am convinced that in the midst of today's popular

prophetic teachings about the end-times, there are actually *gigantic errors* which are really not in harmony with the words of Jesus Christ or with the true meaning of the book of Revelation. The Master has warned us, "Take heed that no man deceive you." Matthew 24:4. I have taken this warning seriously.

Y2K prophecies have failed.

No terrorist explosions took place in Jerusalem on the eve of the new millennium.

You are about to discover solid New Testament proof that many Christian predictions about Israel will also fail.

The goal of this book is to *explode* these false prophecies, before it is too late.

Please read it prayerfully.

Its message could save your life.

---

[1] Kenneth L. Woodward, "The Way the World Ends," *Newsweek*, Nov. 1, 1999, p. 73.

> "And he gathered them together into a place called in the Hebrew tongue Armageddon.
>
> And the seventh angel poured out his vial into the air; and there came a great voice out of the temple of heaven, from the throne, saying, It is done.
>
> And there were voices, and thunders, and lightnings; and there was a great earthquake, such as was not since men were upon the earth, so mighty an earthquake, and so great.
>
> And the great city was divided into three parts, and the cities of the nations fell: and great Babylon came in remembrance before God, to give unto her the cup of the wine of the fierceness of his wrath.
>
> And every island fled away, and the mountains were not found."
>
> Revelation 16:16-20

# Chapter 1

# Wrestling with an Angel

Have you ever heard of a wrestling match between a human being and an angel? As far as we know, it has happened only once in history. The details of this ancient story, which is recorded in Genesis chapter 32, will soon take on explosive significance in our study of Israel and Bible prophecy.

Abraham lived about 4,000 years ago. He eventually had a son named Isaac, then Isaac had a son named Jacob. It was Jacob who wrestled with the angel. As a result of that wrestling match, the angel changed Jacob's name to "Israel." In order to understand why this strange encounter took place and its deep meaning for us today, we must first study some history about Isaac, Rebekah, Esau, and Jacob as recorded in Genesis chapter 27.

"When Isaac was old, and his eyes were dim, so that he could not see," he decided to bless Esau, his

firstborn son, before he died (Genesis 27:1-4). But first he sent Esau out to the field to hunt for a tasty meal. Isaac's wife, Rebekah, had other plans. Realizing the importance of her husband's "final blessing upon the firstborn," she coveted that blessing for her younger son, Jacob, who was more spiritual than Esau. While Esau was out hunting in the field, Rebekah quickly prepared a meal and convinced Jacob to take the food to Isaac while pretending to be Esau (Genesis 27:5-17).

When Jacob took the meal to his father, he lied, saying, "I am Esau thy firstborn; I have done according as thou badest me: arise, I pray thee, sit and eat of my venison, that thy soul may bless me." Verse 19. When Isaac inquired how it was that he had killed an animal so quickly, Jacob lied again, saying, "Because the Lord thy God brought it to me." Verse 20. Suspiciously, Isaac asked, "Art thou my very son Esau?" Jacob then lied a third time, saying, "I am." Verse 24. Isaac finally believed this deception and gave the firstborn's blessing to Jacob (verses 25-29).

Soon afterward Esau returned from his hunting trip, and then Isaac realized that he had been tricked. He said to Esau, "Thy brother came with subtilty, and hath taken away thy blessing." Verse 35. Then "Esau hated Jacob" and said in his heart, "I will slay my brother Jacob." Verse 41. However, Rebekah discovered Esau's plot and sent Jacob away to her relatives in a far country, where he remained for 20 years (Genesis 27:43; 31:41). Jacob never saw his mother again.

## WRESTLING WITH AN ANGEL 15

Genesis chapter 32 describes what happened to Jacob 20 years later on his journey back home. Surrounded by a large caravan of family and servants, Jacob sent messengers ahead of the group to tell Esau that he was coming. When these men returned with the news that Esau was on his way to meet them and that 400 soldiers were accompanying him, terror struck Jacob's heart. He felt a deep sense of guilt over his past sin of deception and was terrified for the safety of his family. So Jacob "rose up that night" and "was left alone" to plead with God for forgiveness and deliverance (Genesis 32:22, 24).

Then "there wrestled a man with him until the breaking of the day." Verse 24. Hosea 12:4 says this "man" was really an angel. Supposing that this might be his angry brother Esau, Jacob struggled for his life all night. Then, at the crack of dawn, this powerful stranger revealed himself, not as a foe, but as one sent from heaven. He touched Jacob's thigh, "and the hollow of Jacob's thigh was out of joint, as he wrestled with him." Verse 25.

Jacob suddenly realized that this powerful man was now possibly his only hope. Broken and helpless, he clung to him, saying, "I will not let thee go, except thou bless me."

"The angel then asked, "What is thy name?

"And he said, Jacob.

"And he said, Thy name shall be called no more Jacob, *but Israel*: for as a prince hast thou power with God and with men, and hast prevailed." Verses 26-28, emphasis added.

This is the first time the name "Israel" is used in the Bible. The context reveals its deep spiritual significance. In the beginning, "Israel" was a special name given to only one man, Jacob, by the angel of God. In the Bible, people's names mean more than they do today. Back then, names were often descriptions of people's characters. Jacob literally meant "Deceiver" or "Crook." When Esau discovered Jacob's sin of deception, he said to Isaac, "Is he not rightly named Jacob?" Genesis 27:36. Thus the name "Jacob" was a description of his character and of his sin. When the Angel said, "What is your name?" He already knew the answer. But He wanted Jacob to say his own name, which represented a humble confession and turning away from his sin. Jacob passed the test, repented, and placed his entire dependence upon God's mercy.

The response, "Thy name shall no more be called Jacob, but Israel," revealed that God had given him a new character! The word "Israel" literally means, "prince of God." Thus the name "Israel" was *a spiritual name*, symbolizing Jacob's spiritual victory over his past sin of deception. In other words, the man "Jacob" was now a spiritual "Israel." As we shall soon see, this

truth about a spiritual Israel will take on explosive significance in our study of Israel and Bible prophecy.

Israel had 12 sons "which came into Egypt." Exodus 1:1-5. One son, named Joseph, had many dreams (Genesis chapter 37), and I will come back to this point later. The children of Israel multiplied in Egypt and were forced into slavery until the time of Moses. Then God told Moses, "Say unto Pharaoh, Thus saith the Lord, Israel is my son, even my firstborn. ... Let my son go." Exodus 4:22, 23. Here is an important development in biblical thought. The name "Israel" is now being expanded. It no longer refers only to Jacob, but also to his descendants. *The nation is now called "Israel."* Thus, the name "Israel" first applied to a victorious man, then to a people. It was God's desire that this new nation of Israel should also be victorious, as was Jacob, through faith in Him. God called this new nation of Israel, "my son ... my firstborn." Remember this. It will become significant later on in our study.

The next paragraph below contains little phrases about the nation of Israel which may seem dry to you at first. But amazing things can happen when you water a dry seed. Those little phrases will soon sprout and grow into trees of towering significance when we turn to the New Testament. Take special note of them.

Israel was called "a vine" that God brought "out of Egypt." Psalm 80:8. God said, "But thou, Israel, art my

servant, ... the seed of Abraham." Isaiah 41:8. God also spoke of "Israel mine elect" in Isaiah 45:4. Again, God said through Isaiah, "Behold my servant, whom I uphold; mine elect, in whom my soul delighteth; I have put my spirit upon him: he shall bring forth judgment to the Gentiles. He shall not cry, nor lift up, nor cause his voice to be heard in the street. A bruised reed shall he not break, and the smoking flax shall he not quench: he shall bring forth judgment unto truth." Isaiah 42:1-3. All of these words originally applied to the nation of Israel. Don't forget that.

In about 800 B.C., the Lord said through the prophet Hosea, "When Israel was a child, then I loved him, and called my son out of Egypt." Hosea 11:1. Yet by this time the nation of Israel, which God loved, had failed to live up to the spiritual meaning of its own name. She had not lived victoriously, as a "prince of God." God sadly declared, "They sacrificed unto Baalim, and burned incense to graven images." Hosea 11:2. Yet God had a special plan. The sentence "When Israel was a child, then I loved him, and called my son out of Egypt" is actually like a time bomb. In Chapter 2 of this book, that verse will explode with tremendous importance as we turn to the New Testament.

## Chapter 2

# A New Look at Jesus Christ

In this chapter, we will begin to push the button that will explode the "Israel Deception."

Approximately 800 years had passed since the time of Hosea the prophet. Finally, heaven's prophetic clock struck twelve. Then "Jesus was born in Bethlehem of Judæa in the days of Herod the king." Matthew 2:1. Because King Herod felt threatened by this newly born potential rival to his throne, he sent soldiers who "slew all the children that were in Bethlehem." Matthew 2:16. Yet God warned Joseph in advance of the slaughter. "Behold, the angel of the Lord appeareth to Joseph in a dream, saying, Arise, and take the young child and his mother, and flee into Egypt, and be thou there until I bring thee word." Verse 13. So the family arose and "departed into Egypt." Verse 14.

The next sentence after Matthew 2:14 is like an atomic bomb in its prophetic implications. Under the inspiration of the Holy Spirit, Matthew wrote that

Joseph, Mary, and Jesus remained in Egypt "until the death of Herod: that it might be fulfilled which was spoken of the Lord by the prophet, saying, Out of Egypt have I called my son." Verse 15.

*Do you realize what you just read?* Matthew is quoting Hosea 11:1, which, in its historical context, referred to the nation of Israel being called out of Egypt in the time of Moses. Yet here the Gospel writer picks up this text and then declares it "fulfilled" in Jesus Christ! Here Matthew is beginning to reveal a principle that he develops throughout his book. The apostle Paul also taught the same principle, as we shall soon see.

Remember, the first time the name "Israel" is used in the Bible, it is a spiritual name given to one man, whose name was Jacob (Genesis 32:28). That name had to do with Jacob's spiritual victory. It means, "prince of God." Even so in the beginning of the New Testament that same name is beginning to be applied to one Man, to the Victorious One, to Jesus Christ, *the Prince of God*.

There are amazing parallels between the history of Israel and the history of Jesus Christ. In Hebrew history, a young man named Joseph, who had dreams, went to Egypt. In the New Testament we find another man named Joseph who had dreams and then went to Egypt. When God called Israel out of Egypt, He called that nation "my son." Exodus 4:22. When Jesus came out

of Egypt, God said, "Out of Egypt I have called my son." When the nation of Israel left Egypt, the people went through the Red Sea. They were "baptized ... in the sea." 1 Corinthians 10:2. In the third chapter of Matthew, we read that Jesus was baptized in the Jordan river "to fulfill all righteousness." Verse 15. Then God called Jesus, "my beloved Son." Verse 17.

After the Israelites passed through the Red Sea, they spent 40 years in the wilderness. Immediately after Jesus was baptized in the Jordan river, He was "led up of the Spirit into the wilderness" for 40 days (Matthew 4:1, 2). At the end of the 40 days, Jesus resisted the devil's temptations by quoting three Scriptures. All were from Deuteronomy, the very book that God gave to Israel at the end of their 40 years in the wilderness! What does this mean? It means that in Matthew's book, Jesus is repeating the history of Israel, point by point, and is overcoming where they failed. He is becoming the new Israel, the Prince of God, the one victorious Man who overcomes all sin.

After healing a large number of people, Jesus "charged them that they should not make him known: That it might be fulfilled which was spoken by Esaias the prophet, saying, Behold my servant, whom I have chosen; my beloved, in whom my soul is well pleased: I will put my spirit upon him, and he shall shew judgment to the Gentiles. He shall not strive, nor cry;

neither shall any man hear his voice in the streets. A bruised reed shall he not break, and smoking flax shall he not quench, till he send forth judgment unto victory." Matthew 12:16-20.

Here Matthew is doing the same thing he did with Hosea 11:1. He is quoting Isaiah 42:1-3, which, in its original context, referred to God's "servant," which was "Israel ... my servant." Isaiah 41:8. Once again, under inspiration from the Holy Spirit, the writer of the first New Testament book declared that Isaiah 42:1-3 had been "fulfilled" by God's "servant," Jesus Christ!

What about those other seemingly dry little phrases about the nation of Israel? It is time to water them, too. They must now grow into trees that reach heaven. In Psalm 80:8, Israel was called a "vine." Yet Jesus Christ declared, "I am the true vine." John 15:1. God referred to the nation of Israel as "my son, even my firstborn." Exodus 4:22. Yet the apostle Paul later called Jesus Christ "the firstborn of every creature." Colossians 1:15. The prophet Isaiah called Israel "the seed of Abraham." Isaiah 41:8. Yet Paul wrote, "Now to Abraham and his seed were the promises made. He saith not, And to seeds, as of many; but as of one, And to thy seed, which is Christ." Galatians 3:16.

That last text is the clearest and most explosive of them all! In the Old Testament, God definitely called "Israel ... the seed of Abraham." Isaiah 41:8. Yet here Paul wrote that Abraham's seed does not refer to

"many," but to "one, ... which is Christ." Thus we discover that, in the New Testament, what originally applied to the nation of Israel is now applied to Jesus Christ. The Messiah is now the "seed." Therefore, Jesus Christ is Israel!

Yet there is more. In Genesis and Exodus, the name "Israel" not only refers to one victorious man, to Jacob, but also to his descendants, who became Israel. The same principle is revealed in the New Testament. Right after the statement about Jesus being "the seed," Paul then told his Gentile converts, "And if ye be Christ's, then are ye Abraham's seed." Galatians 3:29. Thus in the New Testament, the name Israel not only applies to the one Victorious Man, the True Seed, Jesus Christ, but also to those who are in Christ. Believers in Jesus become part of "the seed." In other words, true Christians are now *God's spiritual Israel*.

God made a covenant with the twelve tribes of Israel at the foot of Mount Sinai. Animal sacrifices were offered. Then "Moses took the blood, and sprinkled it on the people, and said, Behold the blood of the covenant, which the Lord hath made with you." Exodus 24:8. At the end of His ministry, Jesus Christ made a new covenant with the twelve apostles in an upper room on Mount Zion. Before offering Himself as the great Sacrifice, our Lord declared, "This is my blood of the new testament [covenant], which is shed for many for

the remission of sins." Matthew 26:28. What does this mean? It means that Jesus Christ, the True Seed, was there making a new covenant with a new Israel!

These fundamental New Testament facts will soon take on explosive significance when we examine what the book of Revelation *really teaches* about Israel, the temple, Babylon the Great, and Armageddon.

*May I suggest you put your seatbelts on?*

# Chapter 3

# The Shocking Principle of Two Israels!

Have you ever been hit so hard on the head that you started seeing double? Well, from what I have studied, the Christian world needs to get hit hard on the head with the truth of the New Testament! Then more Christians will start seeing double about the subject of Israel. According to the New Testament, there are now two Israels! The proof? Paul wrote, "They are not *all Israel,* which are *of Israel.*" Romans 9:6, emphasis added. In this chapter, we will discover that there is an Israel "according to the flesh" (Romans 9:3) and an "Israel of God" (Galatians 6:16) composed of both Jews and Gentiles who have personal faith in Jesus Christ.

Paul wrote, "Even as Abraham believed God, and it was accounted to him for righteousness. Know ye therefore that they which are of faith, the same are the children of Abraham." Galatians 3:6, 7. Paul's argument is that Abraham had faith, therefore those who have

faith are his children. We might call this the concept of "faith lineage." This truth is like a key that can open a lock in our heads. Once the lock is open, then we can understand the shocking principle of two Israels.

John the Baptist understood and boldly preached the truth of "faith lineage." "In those days came John the Baptist, preaching in the wilderness." "But when he saw many of the Pharisees and Sadducees come to his baptism, he said unto them ..." "Think not to say within yourselves, We have Abraham to our father: for I say unto you, that God is able of these stones to raise up children unto Abraham. And now also the axe is laid unto the root of the trees: therefore every tree which bringeth not forth good fruit is hewn down, and cast into the fire." Matthew 3:1, 7, 9, 10.

Those Pharisees and Sadducees were part of Israel according to the flesh. They did not have faith like Abraham did, yet they thought they were his children. John the Baptist exposed this delusion. He thundered, "Don't think that!" John then laid the "axe" to the root of the trees by saying that if those men did not bear "good fruit" through faith like Abraham did, then they would be "hewn down, and cast into the fire." Verse 10. Thus natural lineage by itself is not enough. Without faith and a spiritual connection with God, those men were doomed.

Jesus Christ taught the same truth. A certain group of Jews once said to Him, "Abraham is our father."

## The Shocking Principle of Two Israels!

Jesus responded, "If ye were Abraham's children, ye would do the works of Abraham." John 8:39. They claimed to be Abraham's children, but they had no faith. By saying, "If ye were Abraham's children," Jesus denied their claim. Christ continued, "But now ye seek to kill me, a man that hath told you the truth. This did not Abraham. Ye do the deeds of your father." John 8:40, 41.

They responded, "We have one Father, even God." Then "Jesus said unto them, If God were your Father, ye would love me: for I proceeded forth and came from God." "Ye are of your father the devil, and the lusts of your father ye will do. He was a murderer from the beginning, and abode not in the truth, because there is no truth in him. When he speaketh a lie, he speaketh of his own: for he is a liar, and the father of it." "He that is of God heareth God's words: ye therefore hear them not, because ye are not of God." John 8:41, 42, 44, 47.

What an atomic text! Here Jesus Christ Himself spoke words that blast into shivers a large portion of the prophetic theories currently held in the evangelical world. Jesus was talking to people who claimed to be Israelites, the children of Abraham. Yet they were only the Israel of the flesh! Jesus said they were not really Abraham's children at all. Because they had no faith and were following lies, their lineage actually went back to Satan, the father of lies! Soon we will separate

God's truth from Satan's lies when we look at what Revelation really teaches about Israel, the 144,000, Babylon, and Armageddon.

Jesus Christ also taught this same concept of "faith lineage" in John chapter 1. A spiritually minded Jew named Nathanael was wondering whether Jesus of Nazareth was really the Messiah. Retiring to a favorite spot under a fig tree, he prayed about the matter. Soon a friend introduced him to the Saviour. When Jesus saw Nathanael coming to Him, He said, "Behold an Israelite indeed, in whom is no guile!" John 1:47.

Nathanael had a natural lineage that went back to Abraham. Yet he had more. In his spiritual life, he had gained victories over guile, which means deception. When Jesus discerned Nathanael's spiritual lineage to Abraham and Jacob, He called him "an Israelite indeed." Therefore, just as the man Jacob became a spiritual Israel, even so had this man Nathanael become an Israelite indeed. He was part of God's true spiritual Israel.

Just as there are now two Israels, even so are there now two kinds of Jews. There are Jews in the flesh and Jews in the Spirit. In words of warning to certain Jews who were breaking the Ten Commandments, Paul wrote, "Behold, thou art called a Jew, and restest in the law, and makest thy boast of God." "For circumcision verily profiteth, if thou keep the law: but if thou be a breaker of the law, thy circumcision is made

# THE SHOCKING PRINCIPLE OF TWO ISRAELS! 29

uncircumcision. Therefore if the uncircumcision [Gentiles] keep the righteousness of the law, shall not his uncircumcision be counted for circumcision?" "For he is not a Jew, which is one outwardly; neither is that circumcision, which is outward in the flesh: But he is a Jew, which is one inwardly; and circumcision is that of the heart, in the spirit, and not in the letter; whose praise is not of men, but of God." Romans 2:17, 25, 26, 28, 29.

*Did you catch that?* Someone who is "called a Jew" because he is a physical descendant of Abraham, and yet who lives as a lawbreaker, "is not a Jew." His "circumcision is made uncircumcision." To God, he is a Gentile. And the believing Gentile, who through faith keeps "the righteousness of the law," his uncircumcision is "counted for circumcision." Thus to God, he is a Jew. The teachings of John the Baptist, Jesus Christ, and Paul all agree that natural lineage is not enough. Whether or not someone is "an Israelite indeed" depends upon that person's faith and spiritual character. Paul summarized, "For we are the circumcision, which worship God in the spirit, and rejoice in Christ Jesus, and have no confidence in the flesh." Philippians 3:3. Anyone today can become one of these "Jews," even if their father was Adolf Hitler!

These concepts of "faith lineage," Jews being counted as Gentiles and Gentiles being counted as Jews, lead us into one of the biggest issues now facing the

evangelical world. This issue is at the core of prophetic interpretation. In it we are faced with two options. One is the truth, the other a lie. One leads to heaven, the other, possibly, to hell.

The big question is "What about the promises God made to Israel in the Old Testament?" If we conclude that those promises must be fulfilled to the Israel of the flesh, then we must conclude that Jerusalem and the modern Jewish nation will eventually become the center of the final battle of Armageddon. But if we conclude that those promises can legitimately be fulfilled to God's Israel in the Spirit, then we must restudy the book of Revelation to discover how its end-time prophecies apply to Christians.

Paul deals with this highly explosive issue in Romans 9:2-8. His words require careful thought. With "continual sorrow" in his heart, Paul wrote about his Jewish "kinsman according to the flesh: Who are Israelites; to whom pertaineth the adoption, and the glory, and the covenants, and the giving of the law, and the service of God, *and the promises*." Verses 2-4, emphasis added. God did make promises to Israel in the Old Testament. Yet, what if some Jews do not believe in Him? Can God fulfill His promises to an unbelieving Israel in the flesh? If not, has His Word failed?

Paul's answer to these important questions is clear. "Not as though the word of God hath taken none effect.

## THE SHOCKING PRINCIPLE OF TWO ISRAELS! 31

For they are not all Israel, which are of Israel." Verse 6. Notice that the concept of "two Israels" is Paul's assurance that God's Word will not fail! Look carefully: "They are not all Israel [the Israel of God], which are of Israel [the Jewish nation]." Thus a Jew can be of the Jewish nation, and yet not be part of the Israel of God. Now, here is the highly explosive question. To *which* Israel will God fulfill His promises?

Paul continues, "Neither, because they are the seed of Abraham, are they all children: but, In Isaac shall thy seed be called." Verse 7. Since not all physical descendants of Abraham are automatically God's children, therefore His promises are for those "in Isaac." Abraham had two sons. The first was Ishmael, who was born after the flesh. The second was Isaac, who was born when Abraham had faith in God's promise (Genesis 16:1-3, 15; 21:1-3; Romans 4:18-21). In Galatians 4:22-31, Paul reveals that Ishmael *represents* unbelieving Jews, while Isaac *represents* both Jews and Gentiles who have faith! "Now we, brethren, as Isaac was, are the children of promise." Galatians 4:28. The children of promise are those who "receive the promise of the Spirit through faith." Galatians 3:14. Therefore, the Israel that is "in Isaac" is the Israel of God in the Spirit!

Paul concludes, "That is, They which are the children of the flesh, these are not the children of God: but the children of the promise are *counted* for the

seed." Romans 9:8, emphasis added. Here is a summary of Paul's reasoning: (1) In the Old Testament, God made promises to "the seed of Abraham," (2) This "seed" would continue "in Isaac," (3) Isaac was born through faith, (4) Isaac represents those who have faith, (5) All who have faith—Jews and Gentiles—"are counted for the seed," (6) This seed is the "Israel" of God, (7) God will fulfill His promises *to this Israel,* and (8) Therefore, "the word of God" to Israel has not been made of "none effect," even though some natural Jews do not believe!

Thus we have the answer to the issue that means so much in prophetic interpretation. The Bible is clear. God will fulfill His Old Testament promises to those "in Isaac," that is, to His Israel in the Spirit. Those who are only "the children of flesh, *these are not the children of God:* but the children of the promise are counted for the seed." Romans 9:8, emphasis added. We should not expect God to fulfill His promises to an unbelieving Israel in the flesh, unless, of course, those natural Israelites choose to believe in Jesus Christ.

We will examine one more atomic section before we close this chapter. What about Paul's question, "Hath God cast away his people?" Romans 11:1. This verse is being quoted around the world to prove that God has not cast away the Israel of the flesh. Yet notice Paul's answer: "God forbid. For I also am an Israelite, of the seed of Abraham." Notice that Paul uses himself

## The Shocking Principle of Two Israels! 33

as an example to prove that God has not "cast away his people." Who are "his people"?

In the next three verses, Paul refers to ancient Israel's apostasy in the days of Elijah. God said to Elijah, "I have reserved to myself seven thousand men, who have not bowed the knee to the image of Baal." Verse 4. In Elijah's time there were also two Israels. One followed Baal, while the other followed God. Then Paul made this application. "Even so then at this present time also there is a remnant according to the election of grace." Verse 5. Just as in Elijah's time there was a faithful remnant of Israel, even so in Paul's time there was also a faithful remnant of believing Jews, who, like himself, had been saved by grace. These are God's people. It is *this faithful remnant of spiritual Israel* whom God has certainly not "cast away."

Soon we will see this exact issue addressed in the book of Revelation. As in the days of Elijah, we are now in the midst of a terrible apostasy. Yet today God has His "seven thousand" who have not "bowed the knee to Baal." They are His faithful remnant, *His Israel in the Spirit.* Like Elijah, they will be on the side of Jesus Christ and the truth at Armageddon!

# Chapter 4

# "Choice" and the Chosen Nation

From the top of Mount Sinai, the Almighty said to Moses: "Thus shalt thou say to the house of Jacob, and tell the children of Israel; Ye have seen what I did unto the Egyptians, and how I bare you on eagles' wings, and brought you unto myself. Now therefore, if ye will obey my voice indeed, and keep my covenant, then ye shall be a peculiar treasure unto me above all people: for all the earth is mine: And ye shall be unto me a kingdom of priests, and an holy nation." Exodus 19:3-6.

Notice the words "if" and "then." God said that "if" Israel obeyed, "then" they would be His peculiar treasure. That tiny word "if" involves a big issue. That word has to do with *conditions*. God loved Israel. He chose them apart from any obedience on their part. He brought them out of Egypt, bore them on eagles' wings, and brought them to Himself. Yet, contrary to popular opinion, God's use of the word "if" made it clear that

the continuation of His favor to the Israelites was conditional upon their response to His goodness, upon their choices to obey. In other words, the members of the chosen nation must themselves choose correctly, or the consequences would be disastrous!

Forty years later, Israel entered the Promised Land and remained there for about 800 years. During this period, many responded to God's love by obeying His voice. But the majority strayed from the path of righteousness. Again and again, God manifested His mercy by raising up prophets and pleading with Israel to return to the covenant. Yet apostasy continued and deepened. Finally, after hundreds of years of warning, disaster struck. In 722 B.C., the northern tribes were carried away by the cruel Assyrians. In 586 B.C., Judah was taken to Babylon. Such was the result of wrong choices.

In 586 B.C., the armies of Babylon demolished Jerusalem and burned the temple with fire. The Jews were removed from their land and carried into captivity. Yet, in the mercy of God, this exile was not to be permanent. The prophet Jeremiah predicted that God "would accomplish seventy years in the desolations of Jerusalem." Daniel 9:2. After 70 years the Jews would leave Babylon, return to their land, and rebuild their temple and their city. God had decided to give His chosen nation another chance to respond to His love.

In simple terms, the Lord was saying: "You blew it. Let's try again!"

This "second chance" granted to the nation of Israel is revealed in the prophecy of the "seventy weeks." Near the end of the Babylonian captivity, the angel Gabriel told Daniel, "Seventy weeks are determined upon thy people and upon thy holy city, to finish the transgression, to make an end of sins, and to make reconciliation for iniquity, and to bring in everlasting righteousness, and to seal up the vision and the prophecy, and to anoint the most Holy." Daniel 9:24. This 70-week period was "determined" for Daniel's people, the nation of Israel. During that period, the chosen nation would have another opportunity to come into harmony with God. Near the end of this period, something big would happen. The Messiah would come "to bring in everlasting righteousness." As we shall see in Chapter 6, Israel's destiny as a nation would at that time be determined by her choice to receive or reject that Messiah!

Math was never my favorite subject in school. Yet we must apply ourselves to some mathematics in order to understand this particular prophecy.

70 weeks = 490 days

God said to Ezekiel, who was a contemporary of Daniel, "I have appointed thee each day for a year." Ezekiel 4:6. The 70-week prophecy must be "a day for

a year" because it would reach down hundreds of years to the coming of the Messiah. Thus 490 days equals 490 years. When did it start? Gabriel tells us in the next verse, "Know therefore and understand, that from the going forth of the commandment to restore and to build Jerusalem unto the Messiah the Prince shall be seven weeks, and threescore and two weeks." Daniel 9:25.

Persia conquered Babylon in 538 B.C. Then King Cyrus issued a decree for the Jews to return to their land and to rebuild their temple (Ezra 1:1-3). Later, King Darius issued another decree that led to the completion of the temple (Ezra 6:1, 8). Still later, King Artaxerxes gave Nehemiah permission to rebuild the wall around the city (Nehemiah 1:3; 2:1-9). Yet the predicted "commandment to restore and to build Jerusalem" did not occur until Persian King Artaxerxes issued a lengthy decree giving Ezra official authority to "set magistrates and judges" over Jerusalem and to "execute judgment" upon all who refused to follow the laws of God and the king (Ezra 7:21, 25, 26). This was the only decree which fully restored civil authority to Jerusalem and to the Jewish state.

That commandment occurred "in the seventh year of Artaxerxes." Ezra 7:7. The date was 457 B.C., as many Bibles state in the margin of Ezra chapter 7. Gabriel said, "From the going forth of the commandment to restore and to build Jerusalem unto the Messiah the Prince shall be seven weeks [49 years],

and threescore and two weeks [434 years]." Daniel 9:25.

49 years + 434 years = 483 years

Going forward 483 years from 457 B.C. comes to A.D. 27, the time of "the Messiah the Prince." The word "Messiah" means "Anointed One." In A.D. 27, which was the very year specified in prophecy, Jesus Christ was "anointed" by the Holy Spirit at His baptism (Matthew 3:16, 17; Acts 10:38)! Then Jesus said, *"The time is fulfilled, ...* repent ye, and believe the gospel." Mark 1:15, emphasis added. Jesus knew that He was fulfilling the prophecy of Daniel chapter 9!

The total period mentioned by Gabriel in Daniel 9:24 was "seventy weeks," or 490 years. Gabriel then subdivided this total period into three smaller periods—7 weeks (verse 25), 62 weeks (verse 25), and 1 week (verse 27).

7 weeks + 62 weeks + 1 week = 70 weeks

We have seen that 7 weeks plus 62 weeks brings us down to A.D. 27, the time of Christ's anointing as the Messiah. That leaves one final week of the prophecy. Gabriel said, "He shall confirm the covenant with many for one week." Daniel 9:27. One week equals 7 days, which means 7 years. This famous 7-year period is often called "the 70th week of Daniel." In the next chapter, we will focus our attention on this controversial 70th week.

# Chapter 5

# The "70th Week of Daniel" Delusion

In 1945, after months of agonizing deliberation, President Harry Truman finally decided to drop an atomic bomb upon Japan. Right or wrong, the ultimate goal of his decision was to end World War II and to prevent the death of millions. So, on August 6, a bomb called the "Little Boy" fell on Hiroshima. Three days later, another bomb called the "Fat Man" dropped on Nagasaki. Approximately 130,000 people were instantly vaporized. Many have argued whether or not it was the right thing to drop those bombs. But in the minds of those who made that decision, it was for the ultimate good of America.

Dear friend, it is for the ultimate good of the entire evangelical world for God's bomb of truth to now drop upon a gigantic prophetic delusion that is presently believed by millions. It is time to drop the "Little Boy." We will save the "Fat Man" for a later chapter.

The Bible says, "He shall confirm the covenant with many for one week: and in the midst of the week he shall cause the sacrifice and the oblation to cease." Daniel 9:27.

Have you ever heard of the "seven-year period of great tribulation"? The whole idea is rooted in two words of the above sentence! The two words are "one week." Supposedly, that period of "one week" applies to a final seven-year period of great tribulation at the end of time. Right now, all over planet Earth, in books, in magazines, in videos, on the radio, in seminaries, on the Internet, and at Bible prophecy conferences, Christians are talking about events they firmly believe will occur during that final seven years of tribulation.

According to the popular interpretation of Daniel 9:27, the "he" refers to a future Antichrist who will eventually make a covenant, or peace treaty, with the Jews during the final seven years of tribulation. In the "midst" of this tribulation, this Antichrist will cause "the sacrifice ... to cease." In order for the sacrifices to cease, they must have been restarted. Therefore, according to countless modern interpreters, there must be a rebuilt third Jewish temple on the Temple Mount in Jerusalem.

A popular Christian magazine called *Endtime* reflects this current view: "Three and one-half years

after the confirming of the covenant [by the Antichrist] the Jews' Third Temple must be completed and sacrifice and oblation be in progress. We know this because Daniel 9:27 states that in the middle of the seven years the Antichrist will cause the sacrifice and the oblation to stop."[1]

Much of the Christian world is now locked in a fierce debate about whether Jesus will return for His church before the 7 years (the pre-tribulation view), in the midst of the 7 years (the mid-tribulation view), or at the end of the 7 years (the post-tribulation view). Yet by far the most explosive question, which few seem to be asking, should be "Is an end-time 'seven-year period of great tribulation' really the correct interpretation of Daniel 9:27 in the first place?"

Historically, Protestant scholars have not applied Daniel 9:27 to a future period of tribulation at all! Neither have they applied the "he" to the Antichrist. Rather, they applied it to Jesus Christ! Notice what the world-famous Bible commentary written by Matthew Henry says about Daniel 9:27: "By offering himself a sacrifice once and for all he [Jesus] shall put an end to all the Levitical sacrifices."[2] Another famous Bible commentary, written by Adam Clarke, says that during the "term of seven years," Jesus would "confirm or ratify the new covenant with mankind."[3] Finally, another well-respected old commentary declares: "He

shall confirm the covenant—Christ. The confirmation of the covenant is assigned to Him."[4]

The following 10 points provide logical and convincing evidence that the "one week" spoken of in Daniel 9:27 does not apply to any future seven-year period of tribulation at all. Rather, this great prophetic period has already been definitely fulfilled in the past!

1. The entire prophecy of Daniel 9:24-27 covers a period of "seventy weeks." This period applies to one complete, sequential block of time. This prophecy would start during the Persian period and would end during the time of the Messiah.

2. Logic requires that the 70th week follow immediately after the 69th week. If it does not, then it cannot properly be called the 70th week!

3. It is illogical to insert a 2,000-year gap between the 69th and the 70th week. No hint of this gap is found in the prophecy itself. There is no gap between the first 7 weeks and the following 62 weeks. Why insert one between the 69th and the 70th week?

4. Daniel 9:27 says nothing about a seven-year period of tribulation, or about any Antichrist.

5. The focus of this prophecy is the Messiah, not the Antichrist. Modern interpreters have applied "the people of the prince" who would come to "destroy the city and the sanctuary" (verse 26) to the Antichrist. Yet the text does not say this. In the past, that sentence has

been applied to the Romans, who under Prince Titus did "destroy the city and the sanctuary" in A.D. 70.[5]

6. "He shall confirm the covenant." Jesus Christ came "to confirm the promises made unto the fathers." Romans 15:8. Nowhere in the Bible is Antichrist ever said to make or confirm a covenant with anyone! The word "covenant" *always applies* to the Messiah, never to the Antichrist!

7. "He shall confirm the covenant with many." Jesus said, "This is my blood of the new testament, which is shed for many." Matthew 26:28. Jesus used the same words, because He knew that He was fulfilling Daniel 9:27!

8. "In the midst of the week he shall cause the sacrifice and the oblation to cease." The 70th week was from A.D. 27 to 34. After three and a half years of ministry, Christ died in A.D. 31, "in the midst [middle] of the week." At the moment of His death, "the veil of the temple was rent [torn] in twain from the top to the bottom." Matthew 27:51. This act of God signified that all animal sacrifices had at that moment ceased to be of value. The Great Sacrifice had been offered!

9. "For the overspreading of abominations he shall make it desolate." Jesus plainly applied this "abomination of desolation, spoken of by Daniel the prophet" (Matthew 24:15) to the time when His followers were to flee from Jerusalem before the

destruction of the second temple in A.D. 70. Jesus told His 12 disciples, *"When ye shall see* Jerusalem compassed with armies [the Roman armies led by Prince Titus], then know that its *desolation* is near." Luke 21:20, emphasis added. Those disciples did "see" those very events. Christ's very last words to the Pharisees from inside the second temple were, "Behold, your house is left unto you desolate." Matthew 23:38. Thus Daniel's prophecy about Jerusalem becoming "desolate" was exactly fulfilled in A.D. 70! Jesus understood this perfectly.

10. Gabriel said that the 70-week prophecy specifically applied to the Jewish people (Daniel 9:24). From A.D. 27 to A.D. 34, the disciples went only "to the lost sheep of the house of Israel." Matthew 10:6. At the end of the 70 weeks, in the year A.D. 34, Stephen was stoned by the Jewish Sanhedrin (Acts chapter 7). Then the gospel began to go to the Gentiles. In Acts chapter 9, Saul became Paul, "the apostle of the Gentiles." Romans 11:13. Then in Acts chapter 10, God gave Peter a vision revealing that it was now time to preach the gospel to the Gentiles (Acts 10:1-28). Read also Acts 13:46.

The explosive evidence is overwhelming! Point by point, the events of the 70th week have *already been fulfilled in the past!* The following eight words found in Daniel 9:27: "confirm ... covenant ... many ... midst ... sacrifice ... cease ... abominations ... desolate" all find

a perfect fulfillment in Jesus Christ and in early Christian history.

One reason why the Jewish nation as a whole failed to receive its Messiah was because its leaders and scholars failed to correctly interpret the 70-week prophecy. They failed to see Jesus Christ as the Messiah who *died* in the midst of the 70th week. The same thing is happening today! Amazingly, sincere Christian scholars are now misinterpreting the very same prophecy.

The entire "seven-year period of great tribulation" theory is a grand illusion. It may go down in history as the *biggest evangelical misinterpretation* of the 20th century! It can be compared to a big, fat hot air balloon. Inside, there is no substance, only air. As soon as Daniel 9:27 is understood correctly and the pin of truth is inserted, the balloon will pop. The fact is that no text in the Bible teaches any "seven-year period of great tribulation." If you look for it, you will end up like Ponce de Leon, who tirelessly searched for the famous fountain of youth but never found it.

The current debate and tremendous confusion over pre-tribulation, mid-tribulation, or post-tribulation is really a smoke screen of the enemy which is hiding the real issue. What is the real issue? We will find out when we study what the book of Revelation actually teaches about Israel, the temple, Babylon the Great, and Armageddon.

¹Irvin Baxter, Jr., "Have the Final 7 Years Begun?" *Endtime* Magazine, May/June 1997, p. 17.

²*Matthew Henry's Commentary on the Whole Bible,* Vol. IV—Isaiah to Malachi, Complete Edition (New York: Fleming H. Revell Co.) 1712, notes on Daniel 9:27, p. 1095.

³*The Holy Bible* with a commentary and critical notes by Adam Clarke, Vol. IV—Isaiah to Malachi (New York: Abingdon-Cokesbury Press), notes on Daniel 9:27, p. 602.

⁴Rev. Robert Jamieson, Rev. A.R. Fausset, and Rev. David Brown, *A Commentary Critical and Explanatory on the Whole Bible,* Complete Edition (Hartford, Conn.: S.S. Scranton Co.), notes on Daniel 9:27, p. 641.

⁵See notes on Daniel 9:26 in commentaries by Matthew Henry (p. 1095), Adam Clarke (p. 603), and Jamieson, Fausset and Brown (p. 641).

# Chapter 6

# The Divine Divorce

Then came Peter to him, and said, Lord, how oft shall my brother sin against me, and I forgive him? till seven times? Jesus saith unto him, I say not unto thee, Until seven times: but, Until seventy times seven." Matthew 18:21, 22. Jesus always chose His words carefully. His response to Peter contains an important lesson. "Seventy times seven" equals 490, which is a perfect reference to the 70-week prophecy of Daniel chapter 9!

The 70-week period in Daniel 9:24-27 represented a second opportunity for the chosen nation to demonstrate faithfulness to God. Israel's first temple had been destroyed and her children carried to Babylon because she had rejected the warnings God had given by His prophets. Yet through divine love and mercy, another opportunity would be granted to come into harmony with God. Israel returned to her land and built a second temple.

Though she had sinned at least "seven times," God's forgiveness toward the nation was extended to "seventy times seven." Near the close of this period, Someone greater than the prophets would come. Then Israel's destiny as a nation would be determined by her response to God's Son.

Near the end of Jesus Christ's earthly life, He beheld Jerusalem "and wept over it, Saying, If thou hadst known, even thou, at least in this thy day, the things which belong unto thy peace! but now they are hid from thine eyes. For the days shall come upon thee, that thine enemies shall cast a trench about thee, and compass thee round, and keep thee in on every side, And shall lay thee even with the ground, and thy children within thee; and they shall not leave in thee one stone upon another; because thou knewest not the time of thy visitation." Luke 19:41-44.

When Jesus spoke to Peter about forgiveness being extended "until seventy times seven," He knew that the 70-week prophecy was soon to end. He knew the significance of this prophecy to Israel as a nation, to Jerusalem, and to the second temple. Chapters 21-23 of Matthew reveal the sad, final, and explosive encounters between Jesus Christ and the leaders of His chosen people. It is now time to see the true meaning of those encounters.

During the week prior to His crucifixion, Jesus "went into the temple of God, and cast out all them that sold and bought in the temple, and overthrew the tables

of the moneychangers, and the seats of them that sold doves, And said unto them, It is written, My house shall be called the house of prayer; but ye have made it a den of thieves." Matthew 21:12, 13. At this point, Jesus still called the second temple "My house." But a change would come.

"In the morning as he returned into the city, he was hungered. And when he saw a fig tree in the way, he came to it, and found nothing thereon, but leaves only, and said to it, Let no fruit grow on thee henceforward for ever. And presently the fig tree withered away." Verses 18, 19. Here the fig tree was a symbol of the Jewish nation. The "seventy times seven" countdown was nearing its close.

"When he was come into the temple, the chief priests and the elders of the people came unto him as he was teaching." Verse 23. Their plan was to expose Jesus as a false Messiah and then put Him to death. Jesus told those leaders a parable that outlined the entire history of Israel in one sweep. "There was a certain householder [God], which planted a vineyard [Israel], and hedged it round about [God's love], and digged a winepress in it, and built a tower [the temple], and let it out to husbandmen [the Jewish leaders], and went into a far country. And when the time of the fruit drew near, he sent his servants [the prophets] to the husbandmen, that they might receive the fruits of it. And the husbandmen took his servants, and beat one, and killed another, and stoned another. Again, he sent other

servants more than the first [continued mercy]: and they did unto them likewise. But *last of all* he sent unto them his son [at the close of "seventy times seven"], saying, They will reverence my son. But when the husbandmen saw the son, they said among themselves, This is the heir; come, let us kill him, and let us seize on his inheritance. And they caught him, and cast him out of the vineyard, and slew him [their final sin]." Verses 33-39, emphasis added.

Then Jesus asked those leaders, "When the lord therefore of the vineyard cometh, what will he do unto those husbandmen? They said unto him, He will miserably destroy those wicked men, and will let out his vineyard unto other husbandmen, which shall render him the fruits in their seasons." Verses 40, 41. Did they realize what they were saying? Hardly! They had just pronounced their own doom!

Looking His murderers straight in the eye, Jesus sadly declared in words of burning truth, "Therefore I say unto you, The kingdom of God shall be taken from you, and given to a nation bringing forth the fruits thereof." Verse 43. The Master Himself said it. The kingdom of God would soon be "taken" away from an unbelieving Israel in the flesh and given to another "nation." Why? *Because of their final sin of crucifying "the Son"* (verses 38, 39).

In His next parable, Jesus outlined the same historical sequence but added details of the destruction of Jerusalem and the call of the Gentiles. "The kingdom

of heaven is like unto a certain king, which made a marriage for his son, And sent forth his servants to call them that were bidden to the wedding: and they would not come. Again, he sent forth other servants, saying, Tell them which are bidden, Behold, I have prepared my dinner: my oxen and my fatlings are killed, and all things are ready: come unto the marriage. But they made light of it, and went their ways, one to his farm, another to his merchandise: And the remnant took his servants, and entreated them spitefully, and slew them. But when the king heard thereof, he was wroth: and he sent forth his armies, and destroyed those murderers, and burned up their city." Matthew 22:2-7. This literally took place when Jerusalem and the second temple were destroyed by the Romans in A.D. 70. Daniel's prophecy was fulfilled that said: "The people of the prince that shall come shall destroy the city and the sanctuary." Daniel 9:26. Continuing the parable, Jesus said, "Then saith he to his servants, The wedding is ready, but they which were bidden were not worthy. Go ye therefore into the highways, and as many as ye shall find, bid to the marriage." Matthew 22:8, 9. Thus Christ represented the call of the Gentiles at the end of the 70 weeks.

Matthew chapter 23 contains the Saviour's final words in tears and agony over His chosen people. Eight times during His last public exchange with Israel's leaders, Jesus cried out, "Woe to you, scribes and Pharisees, hypocrites!" Finally, with a broken heart, the Son of the Infinite God declared: "O Jerusalem,

Jerusalem, thou that killest the prophets, and stonest them which are sent to thee, how often would I have gathered thy children together, even as a hen gathereth her chickens under her wings, and ye would not! Behold, your house is left unto you desolate." Matthew 23:37, 38. This time God was not saying: "You blew it. Let's try again." Israel's decision to crucify Christ would have permanent consequences. The result was a searing separation—a painful, divine divorce.

Then "Jesus went out, and departed from the temple [He never returned]: and his disciples came to him for to show him the buildings of the temple. And Jesus said unto them, See ye not all these things? Verily I say unto you, There shall not be left here one stone upon another, that shall not be thrown down." Matthew 24:1, 2. In A.D. 70, the second temple was destroyed by the Romans, and more than one million Jews perished. Such was the terrible results of that divine divorce. Today, the Muslim Dome of the Rock stands on the Temple Mount. Will there be a third temple?

According to Daniel 9:24-27 and the teachings of Jesus Christ, the prophecy of "seventy times seven" represented the limits of national forgiveness for the Jewish nation—as a nation. What would happen next? A new day had come. It was time for the wall to come tumbling down.

# Chapter 7

# When the Wall Came Tumbling Down

In 1989, the Berlin Wall came down. Today there is nothing left of it. No longer is there a physical separation between East and West Germany. The two have become one. According to the Bible, this is exactly what Jesus Christ accomplished for Jews and Gentiles. As it is written, "For he is our peace, who has made both one, and has broken down the middle wall of partition between us." Ephesians 2:14.

The truth of the New Testament is often quite different from what is taught in seminaries and discussed in theological circles. One of the biggest areas of confusion concerns the issue of Jews and Gentiles. Many have been taught that God has two separate plans—one for the Jews, the other for the Gentiles. God's plan for the Gentiles is often seen as being fulfilled in "the church age." This idea of "two plans" is now being taught all over the world. Yet the big

question is, "Does the New Testament really teach this popular two-plan theory?"

First, we must back up a little. The ending of the "seventy times seven," those woes on the Pharisees, the transfer of the kingdom, the divine divorce, and the destruction of the second temple did not mean that all Israel had rejected its Messiah! Nor is it fair to simply say, "The Jews killed Christ." No! This idea has terribly, unjustly, and cruelly fueled anti-Semitism for almost 2,000 years. It was not "the Jews" who killed Christ. It was human nature. It was your nature and mine. Jesus Christ died "for the sins of the whole world." 1 John 2:2.

Many Jews welcomed their Messiah. The 12 disciples were all Jewish. The Holy Spirit on the day of Pentecost fell only on Jews. It was 3,000 Jews who were then baptized (Acts 2:5, 22, 36, 41, 46). The early Church in Jerusalem was Jewish. Soon "a great company of the priests were obedient to the faith." Acts 6:7. With the exception of Luke, the entire New Testament was written by Jews. The question must be asked, "Should we call this group of early Jewish believers in Jerusalem 'Israel' or 'the Church'?" It is obvious that they were both!

As the early Jewish Church expanded in the book of Acts, these questions were eventually raised: "Is our Messiah only for us? What about the Gentiles?" After the Holy Spirit fell unexpectedly on the Gentiles (Acts

## When The Wall Came Tumbling Down 57

10:44, 45), narrowness and prejudice slowly began to break down. A Jewish council of believers convened in Jerusalem to discuss "the Jew and Gentile" question (Acts chapter 15). Finally, the Holy Spirit broke through the fog and revealed to the apostles what had actually been accomplished by Jesus Christ. A new day had dawned. The wall had come down. It had been demolished by the cross!

A number of years later, Paul wrote to believing Gentiles: "Wherefore remember, that ye being in time past Gentiles in the flesh, who are called Uncircumcision by that which is called the Circumcision in the flesh made by hands; That at that time ye were without Christ, being aliens from the commonwealth of Israel, and strangers from the covenants of promise, having no hope, and without God in the world: But now in Christ Jesus ye who sometimes were far off are made nigh by the blood of Christ. For he is our peace, who hath made both one, and hath broken down the middle wall of partition between us ... to make in himself of twain one new man, so making peace; And that he might reconcile both unto God in one body by the cross." Ephesians 2:11-16. Here Paul is quite clear. Believing "non-Jews" were "in time past Gentiles ... aliens from the commonwealth of Israel." But "now in Christ Jesus," Jews and Gentiles have become "one." It is the *truth*. So let's come out of the fog! The wall came tumbling down at the cross!

Paul was enraptured by this theme. He wrote a lot about it. "Whereby, when ye read, ye may understand my knowledge in the mystery of Christ Which in other ages was not made known unto the sons of men, as it is now revealed unto his holy apostles and prophets by the Spirit; That the Gentiles should be fellow heirs, and of the same body." Ephesians 3:4-6. Here Paul called this uniting of Jews and Gentiles into "the same body" the "mystery of Christ," which is "now" being revealed "by the Spirit." This mystery is more important than any mystery movie you might watch on TV. Again, Paul wrote, "There is neither Jew nor Greek, there is neither bond nor free, there is neither male nor female: for ye are all one in Christ Jesus." Galatians 3:28. As pastors often say during marriage ceremonies, "What God has joined together, let no man separate!" This now applies to Jews and Gentiles in Jesus Christ!

According to the New Testament, believing Jews and believing Gentiles are now one. The two combined are "Abraham's seed." Galatians 3:29. This is now "the Israel of God." Galatians 6:15, 16. This "mystery" has been accomplished through the cross. Jesus Christ did it. When He died, He broke down the wall. Now think about it. Should Christians rebuild a wall that Jesus Christ died to abolish?

Yet what about Paul's statement in Romans 11:26 that "all Israel shall be saved"? Some have applied this to a mass conversion of the Jewish nation at

Armageddon. Yet the context reveals otherwise. When Paul wrote that "all Israel shall be saved," he did not mean that at some point "every Jew would be saved." In the same chapter he wrote, "If by any means I may provoke to emulation them which are my flesh, and might save *some* of them." Verse 14, emphasis added. Again, in the same chapter, Paul declared "And they also, if they abide not still in unbelief, shall be grafted in." Verse 23.

It is true that "all Israel shall be saved." But, as we studied in Chapter 3 of this book, the big question is "Which Israel?" Remember, "they are not all Israel, which are of Israel." Romans 9:6. There is a natural Israel according to the flesh, and there is an Israel in the Spirit made up of Jews and Gentiles who believe in Jesus Christ. To apply the "all Israel" which "shall be saved" to a group of Jews who are separate from the Church is to rebuild the wall which Jesus Christ died to abolish!

Who then is the "all Israel" in Romans 11:26? The answer is in the context. Paul wrote, "I speak to you Gentiles, inasmuch as I am the apostle of the Gentiles, I magnify mine office: If by any means I may provoke to emulation them which are my flesh, and might save some of them." Verse 13, 14. Paul hoped that as the Gentiles responded to his preaching about the Messiah, that this would "provoke ... some" of his Jewish countrymen to re-examine the claims of Christ.

Hopefully, this would lead "some of them to believe in Jesus. Then this combined group of believing Jews and believing Gentiles would form the "all Israel" which shall be saved.

Now for the entire context. "For I would not, brethren, that you should be ignorant of this mystery, lest you should be wise in your own conceits; that blindness in part is happened to Israel, until the fullness of the Gentiles be come in. And so all Israel shall be saved: as it is written, There shall come out of Sion the Deliverer, and shall turn away ungodliness from Jacob: For this is my covenant unto them, when I shall take away their sins." Verses 25-27. The context clearly reveals that the "all Israel" in verse 26 is a united group of believing Jews and believing Gentiles who have responded to the gospel. To believe otherwise is to deny the context, reject "the mystery," and to rebuild the wall that Jesus Christ died to abolish.

God Almighty told Moses on Mount Sinai that "if" the Israelites obeyed His voice, "then" they would be "a peculiar treasure... a kingdom of priests, and an holy nation." Exodus 19:5, 6. In his first letter to believers, Peter used these same words that God had spoken to Israel, and he applied them to the Church. "But *ye* are a chosen generation, a royal priesthood, and holy nation, a peculiar people... Which in time past were not a people, but are now the people of God." 1 Peter 2:9, 10, emphasis added.

In the Old Testament, God spoke about "Israel mine elect." Isaiah 45:4. In the New Testament, Paul wrote "to the saints and faithful brethren in Christ" in Colosse (Colossians 1:2). After reminding them that there is now "neither Greek nor Jew," Paul then specifically told the believers that they were "the elect of God." Colossians 3:11,12.

Thus Peter and Paul agreed. They both took the exact words that God spoke in the Old Testament about Israel and applied them to Jews and Gentiles who believe in Jesus Christ! They both taught that believing Jews and Gentiles, combined, "are now the people of God" (1 Peter 2:9,10; Colossians 3:11, 12; Galatians 6:16). The "two" are now "one" and are of "of the same body." Ephesians 2:14-16; 3:6. Through His cross, Jesus Christ Himself has performed this mysterious wedding ceremony. Therefore, what God has joined together, let no man seperate!

Heavy fog on a highway can be dangerous. It often results in fatal car wrecks. As we shall soon see, if we do not come out of the fog of falsehood about Jews and Gentiles, we just might crash at Armageddon!

## Chapter 8

# 1948 — An "Unsinkable" Doctrine?

When the horrors of World War II were finally over and Adolf Hitler's Third Reich had come to an end, the world awoke to the full result of the German dictator's "Final Solution." Approximately six million innocent Jews had been brutally murdered. Public opinion then favored the return of the Jews to their ancient homeland.

The British controlled Palestine until May of 1948. On May 14, by resolution of the General Assembly of the United Nations, the Jewish Zionist Movement proclaimed the rebirth of the State of Israel. For almost 2,000 years the Jewish people had been "wanderers among the nations." Now they were home. Yet their struggles had just begun.

An Arab League composed of Egyptians, Iraqis, Syrians, and Jordanians quickly invaded Palestine in an attempt to crush out the new nation. The fighting was

heavy. Yet by 1949 the Arabs were defeated, and Israel was still in the land. In May of 1967, Egypt, Jordan, and Syria prepared for another attack. The Israelis struck first, and the war was over in six days. In 1973, at the beginning of the Jewish season of Yom Kippur, the Egyptians and Syrians attacked again. The battles were fierce and bloody. Yet by 1974, Israel was again on top and still in the land.

For more than 50 years these astonishing events have gripped the attention of much of the Christian world. A conclusion has been reached by millions. This must be the fulfillment of Bible prophecy. Today this conviction is being expressed all over planet Earth. The rebirth of the State of Israel in 1948 is now considered by countless Christians to be the most significant prophetic event of the 20th century!

An example of this conviction may be found in the popular book *The Next 7 Great Events of the Future.* Author Randal Ross declares: "I call the establishment of the State of Israel 'the ultimate prophecy time bomb,' because when Israel became a legitimate state in the eyes of the world in May 1948, that single, seemingly isolated incident started the prophetic timeclock ticking down toward the 'zero hour' and the end of time."[1] Hal Lindsey echoed, "Since the restoration of Israel as a nation in 1948, we have lived in the most significant period of prophetic history."[2] It is not an under-

# 1948—An "Unsinkable" Doctrine?

statement to say that the vast majority of current Christian beliefs about the end-times rest firmly upon this 1948 platform.

On April 10, 1912, the Titanic set sail from England for America. The largest ship in the world at that time, she was considered to be unsinkable. Then, after four days of smooth sailing, she hit the ice. Three hours later she was under water, on her way down to the bottom of the Atlantic Ocean. In many ways, the 1948 theory is like the Titanic. In the minds of countless Christians, it is considered to be unsinkable. However, in a few moments, this popular theory is going to hit the ice of God's Word. If it begins to sink, then we should abandon ship as soon as possible!

There are three main arguments now being used to support the theory that Bible prophecy was fulfilled in 1948. It is time to carefully examine these arguments.

## 1. The "Fig Tree" Argument

Hal Lindsey wrote: "Jesus predicts an extremely important time clue. He says, 'Now learn a parable of the fig tree' [Matthew 24:32, 33 quoted]. ... The most important sign in Matthew has to be the restoration of the Jews to the land in the rebirth of Israel. ... When the Jewish people ... became a nation again on 14 May 1948 the 'fig tree' put forth its first leaves. Jesus said that this would indicate that He was 'at the door,' ready to return."[3]

Is this really what Jesus said? In a parallel passage, Luke records: "And he spake to them a parable; Behold the fig tree, and all the trees; When they now shoot forth, ye see and know of your own selves that summer is now nigh at hand. So likewise ye, when ye see these things come to pass, know ye that the kingdom of God is nigh at hand." Luke 21:29-31.

Because Luke wrote, "and all the trees; when they now shoot forth," we can clearly see that Jesus did not have in mind just one tree representing Israel in 1948. In Matthew, Jesus explained His parable of the fig tree. He said, "So likewise ye, when ye shall see all these things, know that it is near, even at the doors." Matthew 24:34. When fig trees, and all trees, start blooming at the end of winter, we know that summer is near. "So likewise," said Jesus, when we see "all these" various signs given in Matthew chapter 24 occurring at the same time, then we may know that His return is near. The fig tree is not the sign. It simply represents "all" the signs in Matthew chapter 24, none of which is the specified rebirth of Israel in 1948. The ice of God's Word has just ripped the first hole in the bottom of the 1948 ship!

## 2. The "Israeli Victories" Argument

The idea is often expressed that the Israeli victories over the Arabs in 1949, 1967, and 1973 is strong

evidence that God had regathered Israel and was now fighting in behalf of His chosen nation, even though the leadership of that nation still does not believe in Jesus Christ. Again, let's examine the argument.

First of all, the Bible says that Jesus Christ is the same yesterday, today, and forever (Hebrews 13:8). God says, "I am the Lord, I change not." Malachi 3:6. Let's examine the Scriptures with this principle in mind. Was God able to fight for Israel in the Old Testament when they were in unbelief?

After the Exodus, God promised to bring Israel into the Promised Land (Exodus 33:1-3). Twelve men were sent in to spy out the territory. Yet after all the people heard the "evil report" about "the giants" in the land, they "murmured against Moses," saying, "let us return into Egypt" (Numbers 13:32, 33; 14:2, 4). Then God Himself pronounced this judgment: "But as for you, your carcasses, they shall fall in the wilderness. And your children shall wander in the wilderness forty years. ... And ye shall know my breach of promise." Numbers 14:32, 34. Thus, because of Israel's unbelief, God was unable to fulfill His promise to that generation.

Sadly, the ancient Israelites were unwilling to accept that 40-year sentence. The people then proposed to go up anyway "unto the place which the Lord hath promised." Numbers 14:40. But Moses said, "It shall not prosper. Go not up, for the Lord is not among you.

... Therefore the Lord will not be with you. ... But they presumed to go up. ... Then the Amalekites came down ... and smote them." Numbers 14:42-45. This passage is full of instruction. Because of Israel's unbelief, God could not fight for them. Years later, when Israel again "forsook the Lord ... they could not any longer stand before their enemies." Judges 2:13, 14. This basic Bible truth is repeated many times in Joshua, Judges, Samuel, Kings, Chronicles, Jeremiah, etc.

God does not change. All throughout sacred history, He could not fight for Israel while they were in unbelief. Thus He could not have been fighting for the Jewish nation in 1949, 1967, and 1973! Just because a nation wins battles, this is not evidence in itself that God is fighting for that nation. Was God fighting for Hitler when he won so many battles? Was the Lord on the side of the Nazis when they cruelly murdered six million Jews? Obviously not! Dear friend, the "Israeli Victory" argument is not based on a thorough study of the Word of God. Ice has just ripped hole number two in the hull of this "unsinkable" theory!

## 3. The End-Time Regathering Argument

This is "the big one." The idea is now being expressed all over the world that ancient prophecies found in the Old Testament, which predict a regathering of Israel back into their land, were fulfilled in 1948. The

## 1948—An "Unsinkable" Doctrine?

main prophecy used to support this conclusion is found in Ezekiel chapters 36-38.

In *The Late Great Planet Earth,* Hal Lindsey gives the following three reasons why Ezekiel's prophecy must point to a 1948 fulfillment: (1) God said concerning Israel: "I will take you from among the heathen, and gather you out of all countries, and bring you into your own land." Ezekiel 36:24. (2) The phrase "out of all countries," applies to a "world wide dispersion," and therefore cannot apply to the time of the Babylonian captivity. (3) Ezekiel's prophecy will be fulfilled "in the latter days" (38:16), which, according to Hal Lindsey, is a "definite" term applying to "the time just preceding" the second coming of Jesus Christ.[4] These three reasons have been accepted by countless Christians as "unsinkable" evidence in favor of a 1948 fulfillment.

The following five arguments not only cast doubt upon the three points just listed, but also prove that Bible prophecy could not have been fulfilled in 1948!

1. God specifically told ancient Israel that He would gather them "from all the nations" *immediately* "after seventy years be accomplished at Babylon." Jeremiah 29:10, 14, 18.

2. The time period right after the Babylonian captivity is also called "the latter days" (Jeremiah 29:10-14; 30:24; 27:2-7; 48:47; 49:39; 50:1). Thus, the

phrase "the latter days" is not always a "definite term" that applies to "the time just preceding" the second coming of Jesus. Moses told ancient Israel, "I know that after my death ... evil will befall you in the latter days." Deuteronomy 31:29.

**3.** Three times in Ezekiel chapter 38, the regathered Israelites are described as a people who "dwell safely all of them" (verse 8), "are at rest, that dwell safely, all of them dwelling without walls" (verse 11), and "my people of Israel dwelleth safely" (verse 14)." These words definitely do not apply to modern Israelis, who now "dwell" in the midst of terrorism, Arab hostility, bomb threats, and the plots of the PLO.

**4.** The reason why the Israelites were scattered in the Old Testament was because they forsook God, broke His law, and disobeyed His word (Jeremiah 16:10-13; 29:18, 19). If you search carefully, you will discover that, according to the Bible, Israel must first repent of her sins *before* such a regathering can be accomplished by God.

Here is the proof. God said to Israel: "It shall come to pass, when all these things are come upon thee, the blessing and the curse ... and thou shalt call them to mind among all the nations, whither the Lord thy God hath driven thee, And shalt *return* unto the Lord thy God, and shalt *obey* his voice ... *then* the Lord thy God will turn thy captivity ... and will return and gather thee

## 1948—AN "UNSINKABLE" DOCTRINE? 71

from all the nations." Deuteronomy 30:1-3, emphasis added.

According to these inspired words, when God scatters Israel among "all the nations," if they *return* and *obey* His voice, *then* He will regather them. If they do not return and obey, then this prophecy cannot be fulfilled by God! Because the Messiah has come, this "return to the Lord" must be a return to Jesus Christ. It is clear that Jewish Zionism did not meet this spiritual condition in 1948.

Again, God told ancient Israel, "If ye transgress, I will scatter you abroad among the nations: But if ye turn to me ... yet will I gather them." Nehemiah 1:8, 9. "And ye shall seek me, and find me, *when* ye shall search for me with all your heart. And I will be found of you, saith the Lord: and I will turn away your captivity, and I will gather you from all the nations." Jeremiah 29:13, 14, emphasis added. These Scriptures are very plain. Israel must first repent, *then* God will gather her. Once again, this condition was not met by the Zionist movement in 1948. The "unsinkable" theory is starting to go down. "Lower the lifeboats" is the cry from heaven!

The most important "regathering prophecy" found in Ezekiel chapter 36 also contains the conditional elements taught in Scripture. Notice carefully, "Thus saith the Lord God. *In the day* that I shall have cleansed

you from *all* your iniquities *I will also cause* you to dwell in the cities, and the wastes shall be builded." Ezekiel 36:33, emphasis added. Thus, "in the day" that God cleanses Israel from "all" her sins, in that day He would "also cause" her to dwell in her cities. This did not happen in 1948! Israel as a nation was not cleansed from "all" her iniquities at that time. It had not confessed and forsaken its past sin of rejecting the Son (Matthew 21:37-39).

Jonah predicted, "Yet forty days, and Nineveh shall be overthrown." Jonah 3:4. Yet 40 days later, Nineveh was not overthrown. Why? Because the prophecy was conditional. Nineveh repented, so God's judgment was deferred. As we have seen, the same conditional elements are also found in the regathering prophecies. Because Israel did not first repent and return to the Lord Jesus Christ, the promises of regathering could not have been fulfilled by God in 1948.

5. The prophet Ezekiel declared: "And the word of the Lord came unto me, saying, Son of man, set thy face against Gog, the land of Magog." "In the latter years thou shalt come into the land that is brought back from the sword, and is gathered out of many people." "Thou shalt ascend and come" "upon the people that are gathered out of the nations." "And it shall come to pass at the same time when Gog shall come against the land of Israel, saith the Lord God, that my fury shall

come up in my face." "I will rain upon him, and upon his bands, and upon the many people that are with him, an overflowing rain, and great hailstones, fire, and brimstone. ... And they shall know that I am the Lord." Ezekiel 38:1, 2, 8, 9, 12, 18, 22, 23.

Chapter 5 of *The Late Great Planet Earth* is called "Russia Is a Gog." There Hal Lindsey applied the words of Ezekiel chapter 38 to the restoration of Israel in 1948 and then to a final Middle East battle between Russia and the Jewish nation. Yet the explosive truth is that the book of Revelation actually applies Ezekiel's prophecy to a global event that will occur at the end of the millennium.

In Chapter 2 of this book we discovered how Matthew took Hosea 11:1, which originally applied to the nation of Israel, and then declared it "fulfilled" in Jesus Christ (Matthew 2:15). We also saw how Paul made a similar "Old Testament to New Testament application" when he applied "the seed of Abraham," which was definitely "Israel," to "one ... which is Christ" (Isaiah 41:8; Galatians 3:16). Fasten your seatbelts! The book of Revelation does the same thing with Ezekiel chapter 38!

Revelation 20:7-9 says: "And when the thousand years are expired, Satan shall be loosed out of his prison, And shall go out to deceive the nations which are in the four quarters of the earth, Gog and Magog,

to gather them together to battle: the number of whom is as the sand of the sea. And they went up on the breadth of the earth, and compassed the camp of the saints about, and the beloved city: and fire came down from God out of heaven, and devoured them."

The major elements are the same. Both Ezekiel chapter 38 and Revelation chapter 20 speak about Gog, Magog, a great army, a final gathering for battle against Jerusalem, and fire from heaven. Yet Revelation chapter 20 applies these things to the end of the millennium, to a global Gog and Magog, and to a final global battle against the camp of the saints and the beloved city, which is the new Jerusalem (Revelation 3:12; 21:10; Hebrews 12:22). Thus Revelation chapter 20 takes what originally applied to the literal Jewish nation and then applies it to a final global battle against the saints of Jesus Christ, who are inside the new Jerusalem at the end of the millennium.

Why does Revelation do this? For the same reason we discussed in Chapter 3 of this book. So that the "word of God" will not be made of "none effect" through the unbelief of many natural Jews. (See Romans 9:6.) God did promise in Ezekiel chapter 38 (and in Zechariah chapter 14) that He would defend Israel and Jerusalem during a final battle. And He will. He will defend His Israel in the Spirit, which will dwell inside the new Jerusalem at the end of the millennium!

## 1948—AN "UNSINKABLE" DOCTRINE? 75

According to Revelation 20:7-9, this is how Ezekiel chapter 38 will be fulfilled. Therefore, the big question is "Are we willing to accept the New Testament's application of Old Testament prophecies?" If not, then we are not being faithful to the entire Word of God!

On April 15, 1912, at 2:20 a.m., the unsinkable Titanic was fully underwater. About a third of her passengers were in lifeboats, while the majority were on their way to the bottom of the Atlantic Ocean. How about us? Will we abandon the "1948 Ship" before it is too late? Our Captain is now pleading, "Get into the lifeboats!" If we refuse, we may go down to the bottom of the sea!

---

[1] Randal Ross, *The Next 7 Great Events of the Future*, (Lake Mary, Fla.: Creation House), © 1979, p. 23.
[2] Hal Lindsey with C.C. Carlson, *The Late Great Planet Earth* (Grand Rapids, Mich.: Zondervan), 1970, p. 51.
[3] *Ibid.*, p. 43.
[4] *Ibid.*, pp. 49, 50.

# Chapter 9

# Titanic Truths About the Temple

On April 15, 1912, the Titanic sank to the bottom of the Atlantic Ocean. There it remained, undiscovered for decades. In 1980, a rich Texas oilman decided to fund a search for the lost ship. Two expeditions went out to sea, yet they found nothing. In 1985, another group of researchers set sail from France. They pinpointed a 12-mile area in which they thought the ship had rested. After two months of deep-sea surveying, their sophisticated ocean-scanning devices located a large object on the sea floor. As the outlines of a ship became clearer, the shout finally rang out: "This is it! We have found the Titanic!" The discovery was reported in newspapers around the world.

In this chapter, we will continue to survey the hidden depths of the Word of God. We do not need any sophisticated equipment, though—only open hearts. As we set sail into the following paragraphs, we will

discover things more shocking than what those researchers uncovered in 1985. Are you ready? It is now time to discover Titanic truths about the temple!

It is a fact that several Jewish organizations in Jerusalem are now preparing for the rebuilding of a third Jewish temple on the Temple Mount. A popular Christian book called *The Edge of Time,* by Peter and Patti Lalonde, gives the following report: "A model of the Third Temple has been constructed and sits on exhibit in old Jerusalem. Even a computerized list of candidates who fulfill the requirements of a Temple priest has been drawn up, and rabbinical students have been training for ancient Jewish temple rites and sacrifice."[1] Many religious Jews want another Temple. Millions of Christians now believe the Bible definitely predicts one will be built. *But does it really?* Is it possible that the "third temple" theory is yet another grand delusion of the last days?

First of all, let's focus on what happened before the second temple was destroyed. When Jesus Christ died, "the veil of the temple was rent in twain from the top to the bottom; and the earth did quake." Matthew 27:51. By ripping the veil, God Almighty showed all mankind that the value of animal sacrifices was over. The earthly temple service was coming to an end. Why? Because the great Sacrifice had just been offered! A few years later, Paul wrote in reference to the earthly temple, "Now that which decayeth and waxeth old is ready to

## TITANIC TRUTHS ABOUT THE TEMPLE    79

vanish away." Hebrews 8:13. In A.D. 70, the second temple was demolished by the Romans.

Now think for a moment. Would the providence of God ever lead the Jewish people to rebuild a third temple? Would the Father ever initiate the restarting of sacrifices that ended with the death of His Son? When Jesus cried out, "It is finished" (John 19:30), He abolished all sacrifices. He was the final Sacrifice! Therefore, would not the restarting of sacrifices be an open denial that Jesus Christ is the Messiah? If Israel ever did rebuild a third temple and begin to offer sacrifices, would not this be another official, national rejection of the Saviour? What happened 2,000 years ago when the leaders of Israel officially rejected their Messiah? The result was disaster! More than a million Jews perished.

Three main sections of Scripture are being used today by Christians to support the "third temple" theory. They are Daniel 9:27, assorted "temple texts" in the book of Revelation, and 2 Thessalonians 2:4. Yet in all three of these sections, nothing is said about any temple being "rebuilt." In the Old Testament, major portions of Scripture are devoted to the building of the wilderness tabernacle, the first temple, and the second temple (Exodus chapters 35-40; 1 Kings chapter 6; Ezra chapters 3-6). Yet concerning the *literal rebuilding* of a third Jewish temple, we find nothing.

## Argument 1—The use of Daniel 9:27

Popular prophecy scholars today argue that when Daniel 9:27 describes the coming of one who will "cause the sacrifice ... to cease," this must refer to an end-time Antichrist who will stop the sacrifices of a rebuilt Jewish temple. Yet we proved in Chapter 5 of this book that it was Jesus Christ who already caused "the sacrifice ... to cease" 2,000 years ago through His death on the cross. Matthew Henry faithfully declared that it was Jesus who would "cause the sacrifice and oblation to cease. By offering himself a sacrifice once and for all he shall put an end to all the Levitical sacrifices."[2] Therefore, when people use Daniel 9:27 as a foundation text to support the idea of a "rebuilt third temple," they are actually trying to build a house on sand. Worse yet. They are building on top of a major earthquake fault line!

## Argument 2—"Temple texts" in the book of Revelation

These texts all concern the heavenly temple, not a rebuilt third temple on earth. Revelation 11:19 says, "The temple of God was opened in heaven." Revelation 14:17 says that "another angel came out of the temple which is in heaven." Revelation 15:5 declares that "the temple ... in heaven was opened," and Revelation 16:17 says, "There came a great voice out of the temple of heaven." Thus there is a temple in heaven. And it is in

this temple that Jesus Christ, our Great High Priest, now ministers His blood in our behalf (Hebrews 8:1, 2; 9:12, 14). It is also to this temple that Paul counsels Christians to look (Hebrews 10:19-22). We will study this subject more thoroughly in Chapter 12 of this book.

### Argument 3—The use of 2 Thessalonians 2:4

This is probably the most important passage used to support the "third temple" theory. Here Paul wrote that the Antichrist would sit "in the temple of God, shewing himself that he is God." 2 Thessalonians 2:4. Hal Lindsey comments: "It is certain that the Temple will be rebuilt. Prophecy demands it. ... "[The Antichrist] takes his seat in the temple of God, displaying himself as being God" (2 Thessalonians 2:4). ... We must conclude that a third Temple will be rebuilt upon its ancient site in old Jerusalem."[3]

2 Thessalonians 2:1-8 is one of the most controversial passages in the Bible. It is time to examine this section carefully. In this analysis, I will draw on the past insights of historic Protestants, which was commonly accepted doctrine in Europe, England, and America for over 300 years—since the time of the Reformation.

## AN ANALYSIS OF 2 THESSALONIANS 2:1-8

**Verse 1**—"Now we beseech you, brethren, by the coming of our Lord Jesus Christ, and by our gathering

together unto him." Jesus is "coming" to gather His children. The Greek word used here for "coming" is *parousia,* which clearly refers to the second coming of Jesus Christ (Matthew 24:27).

**Verse 2**—"That ye be not soon shaken in mind, or be troubled, neither by spirit, nor by word, nor by letter as from us, as that the day of Christ is at hand." Here Paul warned the Thessalonians not to be troubled by anyone who would suggest that "the day of Christ" on which He would "gather" His children was "at hand" in the first century. No. Something big must happen first.

**Verse 3**—"Let no man deceive you by any means: for that day [when Jesus comes to gather His children] shall not come, except there come a falling away first, and that man of sin [Antichrist] be revealed, the son of perdition." Here Paul is very clear. "That day" when Jesus comes to "gather" us shall not come until there is first "a falling away" and the Antichrist is revealed! Thus, contrary to popular opinion, Antichrist comes *before* Jesus comes to gather His people! Paul warned, "Let no man deceive you by any means" into believing anything else.

The phrase, "a falling away," is from the Greek word "apostasia," which means "a falling away" from the truth. Thus, there would be in the history of Christianity, as in the history of Israel, a major "falling away" from God's Word that would result in the rise

of Antichrist. Paul called this Antichrist "that man of sin." These words actually point to an earlier prophecy found in Daniel chapter 7.

Daniel chapter 7 predicted the rise of a "little horn" with "eyes like the eyes of a man." Daniel 7:8. Daniel did not say the little horn would be a man, but that it would have "eyes like the eyes of a man." This horn would arise out of "the fourth beast," or "fourth kingdom" (verse 23), which was the Roman Empire. It would arise "among" the 10 horns in Europe (verse 8), would speak proud words against God (verses 8, 25) and would make "war with the saints" (verse 21) in Christian history.

Paul also called the Antichrist "the son of perdition," which is what Jesus Christ called Judas (John 17:12). Judas was an insider, an apostle, one of the twelve. Judas kissed Jesus, calling him "Master" (Mark 14:45). Yet it was a kiss of betrayal. By calling Antichrist "the son of perdition," Paul gives us a clue in that this deceiver would not be a pagan dictator like Adolf Hitler, but rather a professed apostle of Jesus Christ. Yet in reality, he would be a false apostle. (See 2 Corinthians 11:13.)

**Verse 4**—"Who opposeth and exalteth himself above all that is called God, or is worshipped; so that he as God sitteth in the temple of God, shewing himself that he is God." Paul did not say, as so many believe, that Antichrist will walk into a temple and say, "I am

God." Rather, he would sit "as God ... showing himself that he is God." The difference is subtle, yet very important. The Antichrist will not "say it," for this would be too obvious. Yet he will "show it" by his actions.

The Antichrist will "sit." This does not mean he will "sit down" on some chair. In the language of the Bible, to "sit" means to sit in a position of authority. Jesus Christ now "sits" at the right hand of God (Mark 16:19). He is our supreme authority, the only Mediator between God and men (1 Timothy 2:5). According to Paul, the Antichrist will also deceptively "sit" in a position of authority. Yet this "sitting" will actually be in opposition to the supreme authority of Jesus Christ!

Antichrist will even "sit in the temple of God." Here is the key text! Millions of sincere Christians, like Hal Lindsey, apply this to a rebuilt third Jewish temple in Jerusalem. But is that right? Think about it. Let's say that a group of Jewish people, who do not believe in the great sacrifice of Jesus Christ, were to rebuild a third temple on the Temple Mount. Could that temple ever really be called "the temple of God"? No! For that temple would be in itself a denial of Jesus Christ! Notice what the famous Christian commentator Adam Clarke had to say about Paul's words: "By the temple of God the apostle could not well mean the temple of Jerusalem; because that, he knew, would be destroyed within a few years. After the death of Christ the temple

of Jerusalem is never called by the apostles *the temple of God."*[4]

The Greek word Paul used here for "temple" is "naos." One Titanic truth about the temple is that every time Paul used the word "naos" in his letters, he always applied it *not* to a building in Jerusalem, but to the Church! Paul wrote to "the church of God which is at Corinth," saying, "Know ye not that ye are the temple ["naos"] of God?" 1 Corinthians 1:2; 3:16. (See also 2 Corinthians 6:16; Ephesians 2:19-22.) Thus, to Paul, "the temple of God" is the Christian Church! Again, Adam Clarke commented: "Under the gospel dispensation, the *temple of God* is the Church of Christ."[5] And this is where Antichrist will sit! He will deceptively enter the Church, like Judas, who was one of the twelve! Then he will "sit" in a position of supreme, apparently infallible authority, which will ever so subtly counterfeit the supreme authority of Jesus Christ!

If you were the devil, wouldn't you try to do the same thing? You wouldn't spend most of your time hanging out in a bar. Your goal would be to try and deceive Christians! If you were Satan, wouldn't you want to sneak into the Church, get behind the pulpit, and then preach a sermon? (See Acts 20:28-31; 1 Timothy 4:1; 2 Timothy 4:3, 4.) This is exactly what Paul says the Antichrist will do! He will cleverly enter the temple of God, which is the Christian Church, and

then he will "sit" in a position of apparently supreme authority as he makes pronouncements on matters of Christian doctrine.

The world-famous Matthew Henry, whose roots were firmly planted in historic Protestantism, commented: "[Paul] speaks of some very great apostasy. ... No sooner was Christianity planted and rooted in the world than there began to be a defection in the Christian church. ... He is called the man of sin, ... the son of perdition. ... These names may properly be applied, for these reasons, to the papal state. ... The bishops of Rome not only oppose God's authority, ... but have exalted themselves above God. ... The antichrist here mentioned is some usurper of God's authority in the Christian church, ... and to whom can this better apply that to the bishops of Rome?"[6]

The above view was shared by John Wycliffe, William Tyndale, Martin Luther, John Calvin, the translators of the King James Bible, John Wesley, Sir Isaac Newton, Charles Spurgeon, Bishop J.C. Ryle, Dr. Martyn Lloyd-Jones, and countless other Protestant reformers. Have we not just discovered a Titanic truth?

**Verses 5, 6**—"Remember ye not, that, when I was yet with you, I told you these things? And now ye know what witholdeth [restrains] that he might be revealed in his time." This is a very controversial sentence. Multitudes of prophecy scholars today believe that the Holy Spirit inside the Christian church is the restrainer.

They teach that when the Church is removed at the rapture, then the Antichrist will appear. They also teach that after this Antichrist shows up, he will then enter the rebuilt Jewish temple in Jerusalem and proclaim that he is God. This will supposedly happen during "the seven years of tribulation." Yet from what we have studied so far, can you not see that there is something wrong with this picture?

Paul did not specify in this letter "what" was restraining Antichrist. Yet the Thessalonians knew, for Paul said in verse 6 that he had previously "told" them. A study of the writings of the early Church fathers, who were Christian leaders living after the apostles, reveals exactly what the early church believed. "The early Church—from whom *alone* we can learn what Paul told them by word of mouth, but refrained from committing to writing—has left it on record that the Apostle had told them that this hindering power was the dominion of the Roman Caesars; that while they continued to reign at Rome, the development of the predicted power of evil was impossible. ... While the Caesars reigned he [the Antichrist] could not appear, but when they passed away he would succeed them."[7]

Based on historical research, Matthew Henry agreed. "This is supposed [believed] to be the power of the Roman empire, which the apostle did not think fit to mention more plainly at that time; and it is notorious that, while this power continued, it prevented

the advances of the bishops of Rome to that height of tyranny to which soon afterwards they arrived."[8] Thus, the force that "witholdeth," or restrains, was the imperial power of the Roman Empire ruled by the Caesars. It was only after Rome fell, in A.D. 476, that the popes were free to rule. This used to be a common interpretation among Lutheran, Baptist, Presbyterian, and Methodist scholars for 300 years after the Reformation. But times have changed. New scholars are here with new ideas.

**Verse 7**—"For the mystery of iniquity doth already work: only he who now letteth [restrains] will let, until he be taken out of the way." In Paul's day, because of the restraining power of the Roman empire, the Antichrist's rise to power was being hindered. Yet Daniel's previous prophecy predicted the eventual fall of the fourth beast (the Roman Empire), which would then allow the "little horn" (Antichrist) to fully spring into action (Daniel 7:7, 8). In his epistle to the Thessalonians, Paul did not specify in writing that the Roman Empire would eventually be "taken out of the way." The reason was because his letter might be discovered by Roman authorities, which might have resulted in more "persecutions and tribulations" against his converts for their perceived disloyalty to Caesar. (See 2 Thessalonians 1:4.) This view fits with prophecy and history. Not only that, it makes perfect sense!

In Paul's day, the "mystery of iniquity" was already working. Yet it was largely hidden. It was not until the Roman Empire finally fell in A.D. 476 that this "mystery" was fully revealed for what it was to the eyes of the world. Then came the Dark Ages, when Europe was held in a grip of terror for almost 1,000 years. Historians estimate that the "Holy Office of the Inquisition" was responsible for the brutal torture and deaths of 50-100 million Christians. And this was done in the name of Jesus Christ! Surely Antichrist has entered the temple of God.

**Verse 8**—"And then shall that Wicked be revealed, whom the Lord shall consume with the spirit of his mouth, and shall destroy with the brightness of his coming." Thus "the mystery of iniquity" would start in the days of Paul and would continue to the end. Then it will be destroyed by the "brightness of his coming." The Greek word for "coming" used in verse 8 is the same word for "coming" used in verse 1. That word is *parousia,* which clearly refers to the second coming of Jesus Christ. Thus, according to verses 1 and 8, it is at the second coming, *after* Antichrist is revealed, that Jesus Christ will come to "gather" His children.

## A Simple Summary of 2 Thessalonians 2:1-8

**Verse 1**—Jesus Christ is "coming" [the *parousia*] to "gather" His children.

**Verse 2**—Paul told the early Thessalonian believers not be "shaken" by false ideas that this "day of Christ" was "at hand" in the first century.

**Verse 3**—Before "the day of Christ" comes, "a falling away" must come *first*, then the prophesied "man of sin" would be revealed.

**Verse 4**—This "man of sin" will exalt himself and will even sit in "the temple of God," *which is the Church*, "shewing himself that he is God."

**Verse 5**—Paul had previously warned the Thessalonians about this.

**Verse 6**—The Thessalonians knew "what" was then restraining the Antichrist.

**Verse 7**—The Antichrist was already working secretly in the first century. Soon the restraining power would be "taken out of the way."

**Verse 8**—Then the Antichrist would be fully "revealed." *After* his revelation, he would continue until the second coming of Jesus. Then he will be "destroyed" by the "brightness" of Christ's "coming" [the *parousia*]. And it is at this second coming, at the *parousia*, *after* the Antichrist is revealed, that Jesus Christ will "gather" His children who have remained faithful to the truth!

So what have we discovered in the deep waters of the Bible? Something much bigger than what those researchers uncovered in 1985. We have discovered Titanic truths about the temple! We have learned that

there is nothing in Scripture about the rebuilding of a third Jewish temple on the Temple Mount! When Revelation speaks of a temple, it is always referring to "the temple of heaven." Revelation 16:17. And when Paul wrote about the Antichrist entering the temple of God, he was talking about his entrance into the Church! If certain people who reject the final sacrifice of Jesus Christ ever do rebuild a third temple on the Temple Mount inside Jerusalem, it definitely will not be "the temple of God"!

So don't be fooled. Millions today are expecting some tricky Antichrist to show up after all the Christians are raptured away from this world. Books that teach this are best sellers. Videos that promote this are eagerly watched all over America. Few seriously question these ideas. Even less are looking for deception to occur *inside* the Church! Yet Paul was writing to us when he warned, "Let no man deceive *you* by any means." 2 Thessalonians 2:3, emphasis added. That word "you" means *you and me*! May God help us to stay close to Jesus Christ and to avoid the deceptions of those who have "fallen away" from the truth.

---

[1]Peter and Patti Lalonde, *The Edge of Time*, p. 41.

[2]*Matthew Henry's Commentary on the Whole Bible*, Vol. IV—Isaiah to Malachi, Complete Edition (New York: Fleming H. Revell Co.) 1712, notes on Daniel 9:27, p. 1095.

[3]Hal Lindsey with C.C. Carlson, *The Late Great Planet Earth*, (Grand Rapids, Mich.: Zondervan), 1970, pp. 45, 46.

[4]*The New Testament of Our Lord and Saviour Jesus Christ*, with a commentary and critical notes by Adam Clarke, Vol. 11—Romans to the Revelations (New York: Abingdon-Cokesbury Press), notes on 2 Thessalonians 2:3, 4, p. 602.

[5]*Ibid.*

[6]*Matthew Henry's Commentary on the Whole Bible*, Vol. VI—Acts to Revelation, Complete Edition (New York: Fleming H. Revell Co.), notes on 2 Thessalonians 2:3, 4, p. 798.

[7]H. Grattan Guiness, *Romanism and the Reformation* (Rapidan, Va.: Hartland Publications), © 1995 (originally published in 1887), p. 51.

[8]*Matthew Henry's Commentary on the Whole Bible*, Vol. VI—Acts to Revelation, Complete Edition (New York: Fleming H. Revell Co.), notes on 2 Thessalonians 2:5-7, p. 798.

# Chapter 10

# When the River Euphrates Runs Dry

We have reached the heart of this book. It is finally time to study the book of Revelation. As we open its sacred pages, we discover statements about mount Sion (14:1), the twelve tribes of Israel (7:4-8), Jerusalem (21:10), the temple (11:19), Sodom and Egypt (11:8), Babylon (17:5), Gog and Magog (20:8), the Euphrates river (16:12), and Armageddon (16:16). Thus, it is obvious that Revelation uses the terminology and geography of the Middle East in its prophecies. Yet what is happening right now all over planet Earth is that sincere evangelical scholars are applying most of these terms literally—to those literal places, and to the Jewish nation in the Middle East. Once again, here is the "highly explosive" question: Does God want these prophecies to be applied to the Israel in the flesh, or to His Israel in the Spirit?

One example of such Middle East literalism is the following interpretation of Revelation 16:12. The Bible says, "The sixth angel poured out his vial upon the great river Euphrates; and the water thereof was dried up, that the way of the kings of the east might be prepared." Revelation 16:12. A popular Christian magazine called *Endtime* comments: "EUPHRATES RIVER TO BE DRIED UP: In Revelation 16:12, the Bible predicts that the Euphrates River will be dried up to prepare the way for the kings of the east to invade Israel. This will happen at the time of the battle of Armageddon. ... On January 13th, 1990, the *Indianapolis Star* carried the headline 'Turkey will cut off flow of Euphrates for 1 month.' The article stated that a huge reservoir had been built by Turkey. While filling up the reservoir, the flow of the Euphrates would be stopped for one month and a concrete plug for a diversion channel built. These things have now been done. With this newly built dam, Turkey has the ability to stop the Euphrates River at will. The conditions for fulfilling this 1900-year-old prophecy are now in place!"[1]

When many Christians read about the Euphrates drying up, the apply this literally. The kings of the east are often assumed to be China. When modern Turkey built a dam on the Euphrates river, many concluded that soon a massive Chinese army would be able to cross a dry river bed in order to attack Israel at Armageddon. This is supposedly how Revelation 16:12 will be

## WHEN THE RIVER EUPHRATES RUNS DRY  95

fulfilled. Yet we cannot help but wonder, why would the Chinese ever launch such an army? And if they ever did attack Israel, why would they worry about crossing this river? Why not just send planes and drop bombs? Hasn't the Persian Gulf War taught us that ground armies don't accomplish much in this high-tech age of ours?

We are about to learn from the Bible that such Middle East literalism actually fails to understand the true meaning and genius of the book of Revelation. It fails to discern that Revelation is simply using Old Testament terms, history, and geography as symbols that are then meant to be applied spiritually and globally at the end of time! On August 9, 1945, the United States government finally decided to drop an atomic bomb called the "Fat Man" upon Nagasaki. It is now time to drop our version of the "Fat Man" upon the popular Middle East method of interpreting Bible prophecy.

"The sixth angel poured out his vial upon the great river Euphrates; and the water was dried up, that the way of the kings of the east might be prepared." Revelation 16:12. In order to correctly understand this prophecy, we must first study some ancient Bible history about Israel and Babylon. In 605 B.C., "Nebuchadnezzar king of Babylon" came "unto Jerusalem, and besieged it." Daniel 1:1. Jerusalem was conquered and Israel was taken captive for 70 years (Daniel 9:2). After those 70 years, an amazing set of

circumstances occurred. The Euphrates was dried up, Babylon was conquered from the east, and Israel was delivered. As we shall soon see, this history forms the background for a *true* understanding of Revelation 16:12.

Ancient Babylon sat on the river Euphrates (Jeremiah 51:63, 64). A wall surrounded the city. The river Euphrates ran through Babylon, entering and exiting through two spiked gates whose bars reached down to the riverbed. When these double doors were shut and all other entrances were closed, Babylon was impregnable. Ancient Babylon was "most proud," "a golden cup ... that made all the earth drunken ... of her wine." Jeremiah 50:32; 51:7. Yet she was to fall suddenly and be destroyed (Jeremiah 51:8). Then God would call Israel, saying, "My people, go ye out of the midst of her." Jeremiah 51:45. As we shall soon see, these exact words are repeated in the book of Revelation to spiritual Israel about the importance of coming out of modern Babylon (Revelation 17:4,5; 18:2-8).

In 538 B.C., on the night of ancient Babylon's fall, her king and subjects were drunk with wine (Daniel chapter 5). So were the guards, and they forgot to fully close the double doors. Over 100 years earlier, God had predicted concerning Babylon and the Euphrates, "I will dry up thy rivers." Isaiah 44:27. The Lord also spoke about "Cyrus," who conquered Babylon, saying, "I will

... open before him the two leaved gates; and the gates shall not be shut." Isaiah 45:1. Moreover God called Cyrus "my shepherd" and "his anointed" (Isaiah 44:28; 45:1). Thus Cyrus was a type of Jesus Christ. And he came "from the east" Isaiah 46:11!

Inside the British Museum in London lies the famous Cyrus Cylinder. It describes how Cyrus, a general of Darius, conquered Babylon. Cyrus and his army dug trenches upstream alongside of the river Euphrates. By diverting the water, the river gradually went down as it ran through the city of Babylon. No one noticed. At night, at the height of Belshazzar's drunken feast, the water became low enough for Cyrus and his men to quietly slip under the double doors, which had been left open. Quickly they overran the doomed city, killed the king (Daniel 5:30), and conquered Babylon. Then Cyrus issued a decree to let Israel go (Ezra chapter 1).

The book of Revelation uses the events, geography, and terminology of the Old Testament, and then applies them universally to Jesus Christ, the Israel of God, and modern Babylon at the end of time. A failure to discern this principle has resulted in a massive misunderstanding of Revelation, a false Middle-East focus, *and deception!*

In Revelation chapter 17, a holy angel said to the apostle John: "Come hither; I will shew unto thee the judgment of the great whore that sitteth upon many

waters." "So he carried me away in the spirit into the wilderness: and I saw a woman sit upon a scarlet coloured beast, full of names of blasphemy, ... having a golden cup in her hand." "And upon her forehead was a name written, MYSTERY, BABYLON THE GREAT, THE MOTHER OF HARLOTS AND ABOMINATIONS OF THE EARTH." Revelation 17:1, 3, 4, 5. John saw this woman when he was "in the spirit." Even so must we be "in the Spirit" in order to understand this prophecy!

Notice carefully. John saw a Mystery Babylon who "sitteth upon many waters." She also has "a golden cup," just like we read in Jeremiah! Yet this "Mystery Babylon" is not the same as the ancient city of Babylon in the Middle East. And the "many waters" that she sits upon certainly do not refer to the literal river Euphrates that today trickles through modern Iraq. No! Revelation's angel interpreter said, "The waters which thou sawest, where the whore sitteth, *are peoples, and multitudes, and nations, and tongues*." Revelation 17:15, emphasis added.

The genius of Revelation is that it uses the history of the Old Testament and then applies it spiritually to a Mystery Babylon, which now sits upon the "many waters" of a spiritual river Euphrates! According to the angel interpreter, this river of "many waters" actually represents "peoples, and multitudes, and nations" around the world that support Mystery Babylon and her

global deceptions (Revelation 17:15; 18:23). Echoing the ancient words of the prophet Jeremiah, yet applying them spiritually and globally, Revelation says, "Babylon is fallen, is fallen, that great city, because she made all nations drink of the wine of the wrath of her fornication." Revelation 14:8.

The error of those who adopt the "literal Middle East" method of interpreting Revelation's prophecies stems from: (1) the belief that those prophecies must apply to the Israel of the flesh, (2) a failure to study the Old Testament's "root history" behind Revelation's prophecies, and (3) a failure to apply that history spiritually and universally to the Israel in the Spirit and to the Lord's global enemies. Modern interpreters usually apply the words "Babylon," "Euphrates," and "kings of the east" to a literal city, a literal river, and literal armies in the Middle East. Yet Revelation speaks of that "which spiritually is called Sodom and Egypt," about a "Mystery, Babylon," and about "waters" that *represent* "peoples, and multitudes, and nations, and tongues." Revelation 11:8; 17:1, 5, 15.

This issue can be compared to the wearing of two different pairs of glasses. If we put on the "literal Middle East glasses" and then read Revelation, we will "see" these prophecies as applying to the Israel in the flesh. But if we put on the "Middle East *symbolism* glasses" and then read Revelation, we will "see" these prophecies as applying to the Israel in the Spirit. Paul

wrote to Christians, "But ye are not in the flesh, but in the Spirit." Romans 8:9. If we put on the wrong glasses and interpret prophecy according to the flesh, we will end up more blind than a bat. But if we put on the right glasses and interpret prophecy according to the Spirit, then we will say, "I was blind, now I see." John 9:25.

A woman in prophecy represents a church. The Church of Jesus Christ is called "his wife" who makes "herself ready" for the marriage supper of the Lamb (Revelation 19:7, 8). That woman called "MYSTERY, BABYLON" represents a false form of Christianity which has fallen away from God and is now leading "peoples, and multitudes, and nations, and tongues" away from the truth of Jesus Christ! Just like ancient Israel during her darkest days, this modern Babylon is now "playing the harlot." Ezekiel 16:1, 2, 15, 35. She is even now making "all nations" drunk with "her wine," which represents her false doctrines. This Mystery Babylon is now denying "the mystery of Christ" that we studied about in Chapter 7. She has rebuilt a wall between Jews and Gentiles—a wall that Jesus Christ abolished at the cross (Ephesians 2:14-17).

In the Old Testament, when Cyrus dried up the *literal* river Euphrates, God told *literal* Jews to come out of *literal* Babylon. "My people," the Lord pleaded, "go ye out of the midst of her, and deliver ye every man his soul from the fierce anger of the Lord." Jeremiah 51:45. This very same call is now being given in

Revelation to those in the midst of *spiritual* Babylon. God says, "Come out of her, my people, that ye be not partakers of her sins, and that ye receive not of her plagues." Revelation 18:4.

Inside spiritual Babylon today are large numbers of true Christians who are serving the Lord to the best of their ability. This applies to many who are even now teaching false prophecy. Yet God still calls them "my people." The Lord mercifully sees them as part of His spiritual Israel. But they are confused! The word "Babylon" means "confusion." Because of today's global religious confusion, especially about Bible prophecy, millions of the Lord's people now believe false theories about the end of time! Yet according to Revelation 18:4, Jesus Christ is now calling us all to "come out" of spiritual confusion and *into the truth of His Word.* We must all leave Babylon before it is too late! Soon the river will run dry!

"The sixth angel poured out his vial upon the great river Euphrates; and the water thereof was *dried up.*" Revelation 16:12, emphasis added. "Babylon the Great" now sits on "the great river Euphrates." This river represents "peoples, and multitudes" around the world who, refusing to come out, continue to support the false doctrines of Mystery Babylon. Soon "the sixth angel" will pour out "his vial upon the great river Euphrates." This vial is one of the seven "vials of the wrath of God." Revelation 16:1. Thus, it is the wrath of God, not

modern Turkey, that will dry up the Euphrates! What does it mean? Brace yourself. It means that God's wrath will be soon poured out upon *people* who continue to support the deceptions of Babylon!

When the "peoples, and multitudes, and nations" that have supported modern Babylon up to the end finally experience God's wrath, then they will realize that they have been deceived. Then they will "hate the whore, and shall make her desolate and naked, and shall eat her flesh, and burn her with fire." Revelation 17:16. Their support for Babylon will vanish. *This is how Babylon's water will dry up,* preparing the way for the "kings of the east." Revelation 16:12.

Cyrus came from "the east" to conquer ancient Babylon (Isaiah 44:26-28; 46:11). The word "east" means "sun rising." The name "Cyrus" means "sun." Cyrus was a type of Jesus Christ, "the Sun of righteousness." Malachi 4:2. In Revelation, God's angels come from the east (Revelation 7:2). Jesus said, "As the lightening cometh out of *the east,* and shineth even unto the west; so shall also the coming of the Son of man be." Matthew 24:27, emphasis added. Jesus is coming from the east with the armies of heaven as "KING OF KINGS, AND LORD OF LORDS." Revelation 19:14, 16. Thus, the "kings of the east" are not the Chinese, but King Jesus and His armies, which will soon descend from the eastern skies to conquer modern Babylon and to deliver Israel at Armageddon!

Which Israel will Jesus deliver? It will surely be an Israel in the Spirit, which, having chosen to walk in the Spirit and to interpret prophecy according to the Spirit, has also chosen to "come out" of Mystery Babylon and to forsake its fleshy ideas (Galatians 5:16, 25; Revelation 18:4). Let's be part of that Israel!

---

[1]*Endtime* Magazine, January/February 1998, p. 2.

# Chapter 11

# Frogs, Fables, and Armageddon

Most people don't like frogs, but I used to catch a lot of them when I was a boy. Did you know that the book of Revelation talks about frogs? Amazingly, it connects them with the battle of Armageddon.

John wrote, "I saw three unclean spirits like frogs come out of the mouth of the dragon, and out of the mouth of the beast, and out of the mouth of the false prophet. For they are the spirits of devils, working miracles, which go forth unto the kings of the earth and of the whole world, to gather them to the battle of that great day of God Almighty." "And he gathered them together into a place called in the Hebrew tongue Armageddon." Revelation 16:13, 14, 16. The dragon, the beast, and the false prophet represent the three parts of Mystery Babylon (verse 19). A careful reading of this passage reveals that Armageddon has to do with a final

global battle between these three froglike spirits, the kings of the whole world, and God Almighty!

The third of those "three unclean spirits like frogs" is described as coming "out of the mouth of the false prophet" and going to "the whole world" prior to Armageddon (verses 13, 14, 16). What could this highly symbolic language about a froglike spirit speaking globally through a false prophet represent? Could it represent a worldwide system of false prophecy that is now deceiving millions into thinking that Armageddon is only a Middle East conflict that does not involve them?

A plague of frogs was one of the 10 plagues of Egypt. The Bible says, "Aaron stretched out his hand over the waters of Egypt; and the frogs came up, and covered the land of Egypt." Exodus 8:6. This incident forms the background for Revelation 16:13. In the Old Testament, the frogs came up from "the waters of Egypt." In Revelation 16:12, 13, the three frogs come up from "the great river Euphrates," whose waters represent the "peoples, and multitudes, and nations" that support Mystery Babylon. The *third frog* speaking through the false prophet represents a gigantic system of false prophecy that even now covers the land.

The *third frog of false prophecy* is now teaching a literal Middle East Armageddon involving the literal river Euphrates, China, Russia, the Jewish nation, and a rebuilt third temple in old Jerusalem. Dear friend, this

## FROGS, FABLES AND ARMAGEDDON    107

is all false prophecy. It is part of "the wine" of Babylon, which deceives all nations (Revelation 14:8; 18:23). The apostle Paul plainly predicted that the time would come when the majority would "turn away their ears from the truth, and shall be turned unto fables." 2 Timothy 4:3, 4. Yes, we are now living in a time of frogs and fables!

Have you read the fable of a handsome prince who was turned into a frog? What a disaster! Yet this frog-prince still had the power of speech. One day the unfortunate frog-prince happened to meet a beautiful princess. He opened his mouth, spoke, and convinced the maiden to give him a kiss. Then, presto! The frog became a prince again! What is the moral of this story for us today? The moral is that if we have come under the subtle influence of frogs and fables, it is high time to be turned back into a prince! We need the kiss of royalty. The Bible says, "Kiss the Son." Psalm 2:12. Through the words of truth that fall from the lips of King Jesus, we can be delivered from the third frog of false prophecy!

"And he gathered them together into a place called in the Hebrew tongue Armageddon." Revelation 16:16. This is the only time the word "Armageddon" is used in the Bible. The truth is that there is no literal place called "Armageddon" anywhere in the world. This mysterious word is a combination of two words: (1) "Ar," which means "mountain," and (2) "Mageddon," which reminds us of the ancient valley of Megiddo

(2 Chronicles 35:22). In the Old Testament, the valley of Megiddo was a place of bloody battles and great slaughters. Thus, the mysterious word "Armageddon" suggests a mountain of slaughter.

In Bible prophecy, the word "mountain" is used symbolically to refer to the global kingdom of God that will one day "fill the whole earth" (Daniel 2:35, 44, 45). In Revelation 16:14, we read about a global gathering of "the kings of the earth and of the whole world" to a final battle. These worldwide forces of Satan compose his global kingdom. They will all be gathered to "Armageddon," to the Mountain of Slaughter. Thus, we conclude that "Armageddon" refers to a worldwide battle in which Satan's global kingdom will finally be slaughtered by the approaching kingdom of God Almighty!

The actual slaughter of Satan's global kingdom is described immediately after the word "Armageddon" is used. Revelation 16:16-20 says: "And he gathered them together into a place called in the Hebrew tongue Armageddon. And the seventh angel poured out his vial into the air; and there came a great voice out of the temple of heaven, from the throne, saying, It is done. And there were voices, and thunders, and lightnings; and there was a great earthquake, such as was not since men were upon the earth, so mighty an earthquake, and so great. And the great city was divided into three parts, and the cities of the nations fell: and great Babylon

## FROGS, FABLES AND ARMAGEDDON 109

came in remembrance before God, to give unto her the cup of the wine of the fierceness of his wrath. And every island fled away, and the mountains were not found." Contrary to the popular teaching of the third frog, these words clearly describe divine wrath upon Babylon and a global slaughter that reaches far beyond the geography of the Middle East!

Prior to Armageddon, the three froglike spirits "go forth unto the kings of the earth and of the whole world, to gather them to the battle of that great day of God Almighty." Revelation 16:14. This same gathering is described in Revelation chapter 19. John wrote, "I saw the beast, and the kings of the earth, and their armies, gathered together to make war against him that sat on the horse, and against his army." Revelation 19:19. Thus, the gathering for Armageddon is a gathering of the world forces of Mystery Babylon against Jesus Christ and against His army. Who will make up His army? It will be an army of angels who return with Jesus at His second coming (Matthew 16:27; 24:31).

The following passage clearly describes the actual battle of Armageddon, the victory of Jesus Christ, and the final slaughter. "And I saw heaven opened, and behold a white horse; and he that sat upon him was called Faithful and True, and in righteousness he doth judge and make war. His eyes were as a flame of fire, and on his head were many crowns. ... And he was clothed with a vesture dipped in blood: and his name

name is called The Word of God. And the armies which were in heaven followed him upon white horses. ... And out of his mouth goeth a sharp sword, that with it he should smite the nations: and he shall rule them with a rod of iron: and he treadeth the winepress of the fierceness and wrath of Almighty God. And he hath on his vesture and on his thigh a name written, KING OF KINGS, AND LORD OF LORDS." Revelation 19:11-16.

This is the truth of the Word of God. The world forces of Satan's global kingdom will soon come crashing down at Armageddon, the Mountain of Slaughter. In the midst of the ruins will lie the third frog of false prophecy. That frog will never become a prince. But you and I can! So let's turn away from all frogs and fables in order to follow the King!

# Chapter 12

# Thunder From Heaven's Temple

He gathered them together into a place called in the Hebrew tongue Armageddon.

And the seventh angel poured out his vial into the air; and there came a great voice out of the temple of heaven, from the throne, saying, It is done. And there were voices, and thunders, and lightnings; and there was a great earthquake." Revelation 16:16-18. Immediately after the word "Armageddon" is used, the next verse focuses on "the temple of heaven." Then there are voices, thunders, lightnings, and a great earthquake. God is definitely trying to get our attention! From the context, the voice of the Almighty is now saying to us, "Look up" toward the temple in heaven!

The *third* frog is now telling us to look down toward a *third* temple on earth. This is a strategy called diversion. In 1991, during Operation Desert Storm, the allies built up their forces to the east of Iraq in the

Persian Gulf. Thus, Sadaam Hussein thought an attack was coming from the east. However, the allies attacked from the west! This attack was successful because Sadaam was not looking in that direction. Today, the third frog is doing the same thing! He wants us to look in the wrong direction toward a rebuilt third temple on earth. If we follow his croaking counsel, then we will fail to learn life-saving truth that comes from another direction!

Again John wrote, "The temple of God was opened in heaven, and there was seen in his temple the ark of his testament: and there were lightnings, and voices, and thunderings, and an earthquake." Revelation 11:19. Here are the same manifestations of God's power that we just read about in Revelation chapter 16. Yet now these fireworks are connected with the seeing of "the ark" in heaven's temple. Millions have seen the movie *Raiders of the Lost Ark*. In it, Indiana Jones finds the lost ark of the covenant. That movie was fantasy, yet Revelation is reality! As a result of the third frog's strategy of diversion, the knowledge of the heavenly ark has been lost. Isn't it time to regain that knowledge?

The same manifestations of God's power described twice in Revelation also occurred when the Almighty came down on Mount Sinai to give the Ten Commandments (Exodus 19:16-18; 20:1-17). The Ten Commandments were called "tables of testimony, tables of stone, written with the finger of God." Exodus 31:18.

(See also Exodus 34:28, 29.) After Moses received the tables, he then "came down from the mount, and put the tables in the ark." Deuteronomy 10:5. Because those two tables were placed in the ark, that special box was called "the ark of the testimony." Exodus 40:20, 21.

Revelation 11:19 says, "The temple of God was opened in heaven, and there was seen in his temple the ark of his testament." Inside that ark are the Ten Commandments. This is a truth that God wants us to see! Yet the devil is determined to blind us. This is the reason for his strategy of diversion. Through the *third frog of false prophecy*, the great deceiver is now trying to divert our minds toward a rebuilt *third* temple on earth. Why? Because that temple has no ark! If we follow his croaking counsel, we will look in the wrong direction, bypass heaven's temple, and thus fail to "see" the present importance of the Ten Commandments!

Mystery Babylon has not only rebuilt a wall between Jews and Gentiles, but she also teaches that the Ten Commandments were given only for Israel and not for the Church! Yet Jesus Christ, the Author of the Church, declared: "Think not that I am come to destroy the law, or the prophets: I am not come to destroy, but to fulfill. For verily I say unto you, Till heaven and earth pass, one jot or one tittle shall in no wise pass from the law, till all be fulfilled. Whosoever therefore shall break one of these least commandments, and shall teach men so, he shall be called the least in the kingdom of heaven:

but whosoever shall do and teach them, the same shall be called great in the kingdom of heaven." Matthew 5:17-19. In these words, Jesus plainly said we should "do" and "teach" the "commandments." We should not even "break one" of them!

A few verses later, in Matthew 5:27, Jesus quoted the seventh commandment: "Thou shalt not commit adultery." Christ commented, "Whosoever looketh on a woman to lust after her hath committed adultery with her already in his heart." Matthew 5:28. Here Jesus revealed the spiritual depth of the seventh commandment, and He also applied that commandment to everyone.

A few chapters later, Jesus rebuked the Pharisees for their deceptive practice of getting around the fifth commandment. He told them, "Thus have ye made the commandment of God of none effect by your tradition." Matthew 15:6. Here Jesus stood up for the Ten Commandments and condemned others for breaking them. Yet, today many professed Christians place Jesus in opposition to the law of God. Are they really referring to the Jesus of the New Testament? Well might we ask the question, "Will the real Jesus please stand up?"

James wrote to Christians, "Whosoever shall keep the whole law, and yet offend in one point, he is guilty of all. For he that said, Do not commit adultery, said

also, Do not kill. Now if you commit no adultery, yet if thou kill, thou art become a transgressor of the law." James 2:10, 11. Think about it. How can a Christian "become a transgressor" of a law that does not exist? Can a speeding driver receive a speeding ticket for transgressing a speed law that does not exist? Of course not. Speed laws definitely do exist. And if we will but slow down and read carefully the words of Jesus and of James, we will discover that the Ten Commandments still exist and *apply to Christians!*

Paul is very clear in his writings that Christians are not saved by the law, but by the grace of Jesus Christ. "For by grace are ye saved through faith." Ephesians 2:8. Again, we are "justified by faith without the deeds of the law." Romans 3:28. Yet, Paul is equally clear in those very same writings that the Ten Commandments continue to exist and have a purpose. What is this purpose? Paul declared: "By the law is the knowledge of sin." Romans 3:20. Again he said, "I had not known sin, but by the law." Romans 7:7.

The law is like a mirror. Most of the time when people get up in the morning and look in the mirror, they don't like what they see! Yet the mirror is important. We need to look at it! It is the same with God's law. If we have the courage to look into it, we may not like what we see, but this uncomfortable revelation will help us to feel our need for Jesus Christ.

As it is written, "The law was our schoolmaster to bring us unto Christ, that we might be justified by faith." Galatians 3:24.

The Bible says, "Christ died for our sins." 1 Corinthians 15:3. Yet what exactly are "our sins"? God's answer is, "Sin is the transgression of the law." 1 John 3:4. Again, Paul wrote, "By the law is the knowledge of sin." Romans 3:20. Thus, when we look at the law, we see "our sins," and once we understand "our sins," then we can understand why Jesus died on the cross! Two thousand years ago, outside Jerusalem on the crest of a hill called Calvary, Jesus Christ experienced all of our sins of breaking the Ten Commandments! "Our sins" entered His mind and broke His heart! Through infinite love for us, Jesus paid the full price for our breaking of the Big Ten. It is the *truth*. Jesus Christ died on Mount Calvary because we have broken the Ten Commandments given on Mount Sinai!

God gave "another law" on Mount Sinai that had to do with the earthly temple and the sacrificing of animals. This law involved "sacrifice and offering and burnt offerings ... which are offered by the law." Hebrews 10:1, 8. According to Paul, it was this very "law of commandments contained in ordinances" that formed "the middle wall of partition" between Jews and Gentiles (Ephesians 2:14-16). When Jesus died, He "caused the sacrifice ... to cease." Daniel 9:27. But that

law of sacrifices that ceased was not the Ten Commandments. The Big Ten are eternal, were written on stone, and are now inside the ark in heaven's temple (Revelation 11:19). Modern Babylon, which means "confusion," has not only rebuilt a wall between Jews and Gentiles, but it has also mistakenly nailed the Ten Commandments to the cross!

"God is not the author of confusion." 1 Corinthians 14:33. In order to overcome the wiles of modern Babylon, we must accept the words of Jesus (Matthew 5:17-19), of Paul (Romans 3:19, 20; 7:7, 12, 13), of James (James 2:10-12) and of John (1 John 3:4) regarding the continuation of the Ten Commandments. We must look square into the Big Ten and *realize that we are sinners*. Then, losing all self-confidence, we must repent of our sins and trust fully in the blood, merits, and worthiness of Jesus Christ! Only then can we have the promise of full forgiveness for all of our sins. As it is written, "If we confess our sins, he is faithful and just to forgive us our sins, and to cleanse us from all unrighteousness." 1 John 1:9. Jesus loves us. If we trust Him fully, He will pardon us completely!

Through faith in Jesus, believers "receive the gift of the Holy Ghost." Acts 2:38. He is called "the Spirit of truth" in John 16:13. The Spirit of truth is like a miniature atomic bomb that can explode sin and deception out of our hearts! Through the Spirit's power, believers are supernaturally enabled to keep the Ten

Commandments. Paul wrote, "That the righteousness of the law might be fulfilled in us, who walk not after the flesh, but after the Spirit." Romans 8:4. The Holy Spirit also brings the tender love of Jesus Christ into our hearts (Romans 5:5). And Jesus said, "If ye *love* me, *keep* my commandments." John 14:15, emphasis added.

This brings us to the very heart of the issue that will ultimately divide God's Israel in the Spirit from Mystery Babylon. The issue is *love for Jesus Christ* that is practically demonstrated by *keeping the Ten Commandments!* In Revelation chapter 14, this very issue is symbolically represented as being shouted to the whole world by a *third angel*. "And the third angel followed them, saying with a loud voice," "Here is the patience of the saints: here are they that keep the commandments of God, and the faith of Jesus." Revelation 14:9, 12. This same issue is repeated in Revelation 12:17 and Revelation 22:13-15 (King James Version). This issue will be understood by all who overcome the third frog's strategy of diversion, who look to the right temple, and who see the heavenly ark of the covenant (Revelation 11:19).

Dear friend, the true "Israel of God" (Galatians 6:16) will focus on the true "temple of God" (Revelation 11:19) and will keep "the commandments of God" (Revelation 14:12) through Jesus Christ. Let's not allow the *third frog* to lead us away from the *third angel's* message to a false *third temple* that has *no ark!*

# Chapter 13

# 144,000 Israelites Indeed

"The dragon was wroth with the woman, and went to make war with the remnant of her seed, which keep the commandments of God, and have the testimony of Jesus Christ." Revelation 12:17. "Here is the patience of the saints: here are they that keep the commandments of God, and the faith of Jesus." Revelation 14:12. Just as a "remnant" of ancient Israel came out of ancient Babylon and rebuilt a second temple (Haggai 1:12), even so will a final "remnant" of spiritual Israel come out of modern Babylon in order to keep the Ten Commandments which are in the ark in heaven's temple (Revelation 11:19).

This final remnant is referred to in prophecy as the 144,000 (Revelation 14:1-5). They are described as coming from "all the tribes of the children of Israel." Revelation 7:4. Does this mean they are all literal Jews? Millions think so. Some popular teachers liken this

group to "144,000 Jewish Billy Grahams" who will evangelize the world during the tribulation. But is this right? We have previously seen that Paul wrote that Jews and Gentiles are now "one" and are part of "the same body" through Jesus Christ (Ephesians 2:14; 3:4-6). Does the last book in the Bible contradict the words of Paul? Does Revelation rebuild a wall between Jews and Gentiles that Jesus Christ abolished at the cross? Of course not.

Let's put on our "New Testament glasses" and take a closer look. The 144,000 are described as standing on "mount Sion" with Jesus Christ (Revelation 14:1). Mount Zion is where Jerusalem sits. Yet in Revelation, "mount Sion" does not refer to any mountain in the Middle East. John wrote, "And he carried me away in the Spirit to a great and high mountain, and showed me that great city, the holy Jerusalem, descending out of heaven from God." Revelation 21:10. As John was "in the Spirit," even so must we be "in the Spirit" in order to see the truth about Mount Sion and the 144,000. Paul wrote to believers, "But ye are come unto mount Sion, and unto the city of the living God, the heavenly Jerusalem ... To the general assembly and church of the firstborn, which are written in heaven." Hebrews 12:22, 23. Here mount Sion is the place where the new Jerusalem sits. It is the home of the Church. And this is where John saw the 144,000!

## 144,000 ISRAELITES INDEED   121

In the New Testament, James wrote his letter "to the twelve tribes which are scattered abroad." James 1:1. Who were these twelve tribes? In the next sentence James called them, "My brethren." Then he wrote to them about "the trying of your faith." James 1:3. Thus, these "twelve tribes," which James wrote to as a unit, were believers in Jesus Christ! In the same letter, he counseled those from among these "twelve tribes" who were sick to "call for the elders of the church" for special prayer (James 5:14). Thus, it is clear that, to James, the "twelve tribes" were part of the Church!

The 144,000 "follow the Lamb whithersoever he goeth." Revelation 14:1, 4. Thus, they are Christians who love Jesus. They are "not defiled with women; for they are virgins." Revelation 14:4. This does not mean that the 144,000 are made up of only literal, Jewish, unmarried or celibate men! No! For this would be teaching mass celibacy, which Paul called "doctrines of devils" in 1 Timothy 4:1, 3. In 2 Corinthians 11:2, Paul also used the word "virgin," and he applied it to the Church! What about the 144,000 not being "defiled with women"? This is talking about the symbolic women of Revelation chapter 17.

The atomic truth is that the 144,000 represent a final remnant *of God's Israel in the Spirit,* composed of believing Jews and Gentiles, who are not "defiled" by the deceptions and false prophecies of the mother and

daughters of Mystery Babylon (Revelation 17:5). The reason Revelation refers to them as coming from "all the tribes of the children of Israel" is because, in the process of leaving modern Babylon and all deception, they have gone through a similar "wrestling experience" with the Lord as did Jacob when the Lord changed his name to Israel in Genesis chapter 32!

At the beginning of this book we noticed that the name "Jacob" literally meant "crook" or "deceiver." This name was an accurate description of his character. Jacob stole his father's final blessing from his brother Esau. He purposefully lied to Isaac three times (Genesis 27:19-24). As a result of his wicked deception, Jacob went into exile for 20 years. On his way back home, Jacob discovered that Esau was coming with 400 men to meet him (Genesis 32:6). Filled with guilt, shame, and terror, Jacob thought he was about to die for his sin.

Then came that lonely night of wrestling with the Angel of God. Finally, just before dawn, Jacob gave up on himself, repented of his sin, and clung to the heavenly messenger, saying, "I will not let thee go, except thou bless me." Genesis 32:26. Then came this response came from the Angel: "Thy name shall be called no more Jacob, but Israel: for as a prince hast thou power with God and with men, and hast prevailed." Verse 28. Through repentance, humility, and faith, Jacob overcame his naturally deceptive nature. God gave him

## 144,000 ISRAELITES INDEED   123

a new heart, a new name, a new character. He had gained the victory!

That very experience that transformed Jacob into a "spiritual Israel" is a type of the transforming experience that will produce the 144,000! This is a deep thought, yet it is true. This insight is more significant than the discovery of the Titanic in 1985. And it applies to us. By nature we are all like Jacob—sinful, crooked, and deceptive. Maybe, while reading this book, you have discovered the shocking truth that you have deceived others about Bible prophecy. The thought is terrifying! The Bible says, "A false witness shall not be unpunished, and he that speaks lies shall not escape." Proverbs 19:5. Just as Esau was coming to meet Jacob, even so will God Almighty come to meet Mystery Babylon and to punish her for her lies (Revelation 18:8). Those who "love and make a lie" will be outside the new Jerusalem (Revelation 22:15). "All liars" will end up in the lake of fire (Revelation 21:8). Thus, the truth about these Israel issues is a matter of life and death!

Yet Jesus Christ loves us! On a cruel cross He agonized, suffered, bled, and died for all of our sins, including our sins of deception! Then He rose from the dead and ascended to heaven. And now, as our great High Priest in heaven's temple, Jesus Christ has given us the book of Revelation to teach us the truth! At this very moment, the Good Shepherd is pleading with us

to leave the lies of Mystery Babylon before it is too late. "Come out of her, my people," is His final call from heaven (Revelation 18:4, 8). Soon modern Babylon will be "utterly burned with fire: for strong is the Lord God who judgeth her." Revelation 18:8.

This is now our night for spiritual wrestling! Yet soon the night will end. It was at the breaking of the day when the heavenly Messenger finally touched Jacob's thigh (Genesis 32:24, 25). It was then that Jacob's self-confidence was finally broken. It was then that he clung for dear life to the Angel of God. So it may be with us. According to Bible prophecy, we are even now at "the breaking of the day." Jesus Christ is coming soon! Oh, may the Master touch us now and break us! May the Holy Spirit explode all our pride! Let's cling to Jesus for our lives and say, "I will not let You go, unless You bless me!"

As with Jacob, if we humble ourselves, repent of our sins, and depend entirely upon God's mercy, the King of Israel will not forsake us. If in simple faith we cling to Jesus, He will definitely forgive us, change us, and give us a new name. By faith we can hear the Master say, "Thy name shall be called no more Jacob, but Israel: for as a prince hast thou power with God and with men, and hast prevailed." Genesis 32:28. Jesus Christ is the true Seed of Abraham. He is the Victorious One! Through faith in Him, God will cause "us to triumph in Christ." 2 Corinthians 2:14. Through Jesus,

we can escape the snares of Mystery Babylon. Through God's grace, we can each become, like Jacob, a "spiritual Israel."

The Bible specifically says about the 144,000: "In their mouth was found no guile [deception]: for they are without fault before the throne of God." Revelation 14:5. Like Nathanael, they are "Israelite[s] indeed, in whom is no guile." John 1:47. They overcame Mystery Babylon, her deceptions, and her false prophecies. The 144,000 are like Jacob. They prevail over their own deceptive natures through the grace of Jesus Christ!

The above passage in Revelation 14:5 about the 144,000 finds its root in the Old Testament. "The *remnant of Israel* shall not do iniquity, nor speak lies; neither shall a deceitful tongue be found in their mouth." Zephaniah 3:13, emphasis added. Thus the final remnant of Israel will be made up of people who speak the truth. They must be one with Jesus Christ, who is "the truth." John 14:6. They must also be guided by "the Spirit of truth." John 16:13. Composed of both Jews and Gentiles who believe in the Messiah, they will be God's final Israel in the Spirit. It is my personal opinion that the number "144,000" is symbolic. Yet whether literal or symbolic, I hope we will all "be in that number, when the saints go marching in."

This book is called *Exploding the Israel Deception*. Its purpose is not to promote anti-Semitism against Jewish people, or to offend sincere Bible believing

Christians. Rather, its goal is to enlighten minds and save souls. At this very moment, the Christian church is filled with gigantic misinterpretations of prophecy which are actually out of harmony with Jesus Christ and the New Testament. For the good of all, *this explosion must succeed!*

If you have been led to believe that the prophecies in the book of Revelation apply to an Israel in the flesh, these lies must be unmasked. If you have been taught that Revelation's statements about Jerusalem, mount Sion, the temple, Gog, Magog, Babylon, and the Euphrates River apply to those literal places in the Middle East, these errors must be shattered. If you have accepted the idea that the Antichrist will one day walk into a rebuilt Jewish temple during a final seven-year period of tribulation, this false theory needs to be blown up. If sincere people have convinced you that Armageddon centers around Russia, China, and the modern State of Israel, then someone must push the button which reads, "Destroy Global Delusions." It is now time to flee from all frogs and fables!

Every one of these supposedly "unsinkable" theories will soon hit the ice at Armageddon. All such lies will go down just like the Titanic! "Abandon ship" is the cry from our Captain! "Come out of her, my people!" is the plea of our soon-coming Deliverer (Revelation 18:4). Instead of looking toward an earthly Temple Mount in the Middle East, let's focus on the

true temple in heaven where our loving High Priest now ministers His blood in our behalf. Jesus is the true Israel, the Seed of Abraham (Isaiah 41:8; Galatians 3:16). "And if ye be Christ's, then are ye Abraham's seed, and heirs according to the promise." Galatians 3:29. Never forget these words!

May God help us all to be among Revelation's final remnant of Israel in the Spirit, of whom it is written, "Here is the patience of the saints: here are they that keep the commandments of God, and the faith of Jesus." Revelation 14:12. May Paul's words apply to us: "But ye are not in the flesh, but in the Spirit." Romans 8:9. Let's live in the Spirit and *interpret prophecy according to the Spirit*. Through the love and mercy of Jesus Christ, may each one of us become "an Israelite indeed, in whom is no guile." John 1:47.

Please share this truth with others. Jesus just might use you to push the red button.

# Additional Resources
# (With Steve Wohlberg)

- ❖ **Israel in Prophecy**— A audio or video series based on this book.

- ❖ *New Book!* **The Left Behind Deception**— Discover shocking facts about the Rapture and the Antichrist (also in audio or video).

- ❖ **Jewish Discoveries in Scripture**— An eight-part video series where Messianic Jews share their faith.

- ❖ **Amazing Discoveries Bible Prophecy Seminar**— A power-packed 24-part series about Earth's final days (audio or video).

To order:

Call 1-800-795-7171

Or write:

Texas Media Center

P.O.Box 330489

Fort Worth, TX 76163

www.israelinprophecy.com

ment essentiel de *La modification*. Plus nettement inspiré du roman de Kierkegaard, à mon avis, est l'exercice que réussit Cécile dans le train qui la ramène de Paris à Rome avec Léon Delmont : il semble qu'elle arrive à croire qu'elle ne connaît pas l'homme qui est en face d'elle, qui va lui parler, qui deviendra son amant; elle recommence ainsi, en repartant de zéro, tout son amour pour Léon Delmont (p. 225). Léon Delmont, lui aussi, se livre à ce même petit jeu (p. 256-257). Or, c'est bien une répétition de ce genre que le héros de Kierkegaard se flattait d'obtenir, sans y arriver. Le roman danois, à travers un commentaire de l'histoire biblique de Job, va beaucoup plus loin que le nôtre, mais les ressemblances me paraissent indéniables. Et qu'est, après tout, *La modification*, sinon une suite de voyages aller et retour Paris-Rome qui se répètent, sans se répéter, et dont on souhaite qu'ils se répètent, mais autrement qu'ils ne le font en réalité ? J'en viens à me demander si c'est par hasard que les deux titres se font écho, et si la modification n'est pas une solution proposée consciemment par Butor à l'insoluble quête d'une répétition.

Terminons ces suggestions par une réflexion d'un autre ordre. Quand on songe que Butor avait montré subtilement dans son essai de 1950 que, la fiancée de Sören Kierkegaard s'étant mariée - avec un autre - pendant que le philosophe élucubrait *La répétition*, ce roman s'en était ressenti, on est en droit de se demander comment s'insère *La modification*, parabole de la fidélité conjugale contre vents et marées, dans la vie de Michel Butor à un moment où il projetait sans doute de se marier. Les amateurs de fine psychologie pourront tirer de là un malin plaisir.

## LE TÉMOIN PRIVILÉGIÉ, LÉON DELMONT

Même dans le cadre d'une lecture traditionnelle, on peut éliminer certaines naïvetés d'interprétation. En particulier il y a longtemps que les romanciers nous ont habitués à comprendre que les personnages ne sont pas vraiment tels qu'ils apparaissent dans le récit. Nous ne les voyons le plus

souvent que par les yeux d'un des héros ou par ceux d'un narrateur qui est lui-même un personnage romanesque. Henriette Delmont n'est peut-être pas aussi rancie et affreuse que Léon Delmont nous le dit, et en revanche Cécile pas aussi merveilleuse qu'il se le figure. Nous retrouvons l'éternel problème de la distance entre le point de vue de l'auteur, qui sait tout, ou qui peut, s'il le veut, tout savoir de ses personnages, et le point de vue des personnages eux-mêmes qui se voient les uns les autres déformés par leurs passions. D'une certaine manière *La recherche du temps perdu* de Proust est une perpétuelle contestation des portraits qu'elle contient : l'image que nous nous faisions de Swann, ou de Françoise, ou de M$^{me}$ Verdurin doit être sans cesse remplacée par une autre, dont nous soupçonnons qu'elle n'est pas plus vraie que la précédente. Par un procédé qui est loin d'être propre à Butor, ce sont les adjectifs qualificatifs qui alertent le lecteur et suscitent ses doutes. Il ne s'agit pas tant des qualifications péjoratives appliquées à Henriette, que des qualifications élogieuses que fait naître Cécile. Henriette n'est d'ailleurs qualifiée directement que de pauvre (p. 38, 178), de malheureuse (p. 43); c'est par la bande qu'Henriette est jugée, ce sont ses traits qui sont « tirés, soucieux, soupçonneux » (p. 18), c'est sa politique qui est « timorée, mesquine » (p. 82). Il arrive aussi que Cécile soit exaltée indirectement : Léon Delmont nous parle de son « superbe amour » (p. 55) ou « d'une merveilleuse vie d'aventure » *(ibid.)*, mais toute précaution sera abolie page 163 où nous lisons : « Ne suis-je donc pas dans ce train, en route vers Cécile merveilleuse ? » La banalité de l'adjectif, et sa valeur hyperbolique le rendent suspect. Si l'on remarque en outre que la jeune femme du compartiment, que Léon Delmont appelle Agnès, est dite « gracieuse » (p. 30), « belle » (p. 260), que l'Italienne inconnue a un « admirable dos » (p. 256) et un « admirable visage » *(ibid.)*, nous savons que ce n'est pas l'auteur qui parle, mais Léon Delmont. Et cependant, en dessous, par l'ironie perceptible, nous entendons la voix de Butor qui se moque de son personnage. Le cas de « Cécile merveilleuse » est, remarquons-le en passant, encore plus complexe, car, à ce moment, Léon Delmont, malgré ses efforts, ne croit plus que Cécile soit merveilleuse : il s'est avoué (p. 111) que le dernier sourire de Cécile était « aigre » et qu'il se tranformera en sar-

casme lors de ses prochains voyages à Rome. La mauvaise foi du personnage se superpose ici à l'ironie de l'auteur. Quoi qu'il en soit, ces contrepoints à l'audition desquels le lecteur entend deux timbres en lisant le même mot sont classiques : on en trouverait jusque dans les romans de Voltaire.

## LE THÈME DE L'EAU

Pour des raisons que je vous exposerai plus loin, je crois qu'il est légitime de faire rentrer dans les aspects traditionnels de *La modification* l'obsession de l'eau qui hante l'imagination de Léon Delmont. Butor a été l'élève de Gaston Bachelard. Or celui-ci a montré dans des ouvrages devenus classiques, *La psychanalyse du feu* et *L'eau et les rêves*, par exemple, que tout poète ressent dans la profondeur de l'objet la présence d'un des quatre éléments des sciences primitives, l'eau, le feu, la terre et l'air. Quand on lit *L'emploi du temps*, roman écrit par Butor juste avant le nôtre, on est frappé du fait que Bleston, la ville qui, peut-être plus que Jacques Revel, est l'héroïne du roman, est la ville du feu; c'est suggéré avec insistance, par tous les moyens, à chaque page. Si l'on passe à *La modification*, on s'aperçoit, mais il faut y mettre un peu plus d'attention, que la rêverie de Léon Delmont s'organise autour du thème de l'eau. Voici la preuve de ce changement : chacune des briques dont sont bâties les maisons de Bleston est imaginée comme du feu enfermé dans un parallélépipède de terre; dans *La modification* les briques évoquent un liquide, le sang. Nous trouvons par exemple page 45 : « la ville paraissant dans toute sa rougeur profonde, le sang ancien suant de toutes ses briques, teignant toute sa poussière ». Il faut bien comprendre que, dans ces conceptions alchimistes, l'eau est la substance fluide qu'on retrouve dans tous les liquides : le sang, le vin, l'huile, le lait, le pétrole sont des eaux de couleurs, de saveurs et de viscosités diverses; la neige est de l'eau solide; une vitre, un miroir sont aussi de l'eau durcie puisque nous leur donnons le nom de glace. L'important, c'est que le même objet, une brique, qui était du feu éteint, devienne un liquide figé.

Il est certain que le feu n'est pas absent de *La modification;* nous verrons tout à l'heure sous quelle forme. Examinons donc la place qu'occupe l'eau. Commençons par des remarques en apparence futiles, mais dont l'accumulation est curieuse. Il n'est pas anormal qu'il pleuve beaucoup pendant le voyage de Léon Delmont : nous sommes en novembre; mais enfin il pleut beaucoup. On note que les parapluies et les imperméables sont nombreux, ce qui ne signifie peut-être rien en soi. Nous pouvons nous étonner cependant que sur les six camions que Léon Delmont aperçoit sur les routes le long de la voie, cinq soient des camions de pétrole ou de lait (p. 14, 44, 98, 100, 258); et l'aube, c'est l'heure où dans les villages italiens roulent « pesamment les voitures des laitiers » (p. 249). Avez-vous remarqué qu'on se lave souvent dans *La modification?* On s'y lave les mains pages 39, 81, 84, on s'y baigne pages 44 et 63, ou bien l'on y fait une simple toilette pages 85, 143, 271, tandis que les dames s'y « rafraîchissent » pages 113, 165, 264; quant à s'essuyer les mains ou la bouche, nous y reviendrons. Passons à d'autres eaux : il est certain que l'on ne peut aller de Paris à Rome par chemin de fer sans longer un lac, la mer, sans longer ou traverser des fleuves; mais on peut noter que le récit signale à peine les autres éléments du paysage, mise à part la forêt sur laquelle nous aurons à nous expliquer; je ne vais prendre qu'un exemple : ouvrons *La modification* à la page 47; par la fenêtre nous verrons déboucher un motocycliste « entre une grange et un bosquet *près d'une mare* »; d'un village nous retiendrons le clocher, évidemment, et aussi le château d'eau; de Joigny nous ne connaîtrons que le reflet du bourg dans l'Yonne. Je vous laisse chercher d'autres passages semblables. Je compte plus de dix évocations directes des fontaines de Rome, ce qui est naturel car les fontaines de Rome sont justement célèbres; mais on peut se demander si Butor n'a pas voulu lier subtilement l'amour de son personnage pour Rome et le thème de l'eau dans le roman. Il est probable aussi que parmi les motifs qui provoquent l'intérêt de Léon Delmont pour Julien l'Apostat on peut mettre le fait que la construction des thermes de Lutèce est attribuée à cet empereur; le voyage part du voisinage des thermes de Julien pour aboutir au voisinage des thermes de Dioclétien.

En tout cas, comme on se lave fréquemment, on boit beaucoup au fil des pages, si l'on y mange assez peu ; à mon compte, on boit 7 fois du café, 6 fois du café au lait, 8 fois du thé, 7 fois du vin, 3 fois de l'alcool et 3 fois des boissons « rafraîchissantes » diverses ; si Léon Delmont rêvasse sur les réclames contenues dans l'indicateur des chemins de fer, c'est la Verveine du Velay qui attire son attention au point qu'il se promet d'en faire l'essai (p. 29). Ce qui frappe surtout, c'est que jamais Butor n'indique les effets de la nourriture sur le corps, alors qu'à plusieurs reprises est décrit le bien-être causé par la boisson (par exemple, p. 189 ou 195) ; autrement dit, se nourrir est un acte indifférent mais boire fait pénétrer en nous une substance agissante. Tout naturellement donc l'angoisse qui étreint Léon Delmont dans ses songes se traduira par la vieille métaphore de la soif (p. 236-237). Car l'eau et tout le vocabulaire qui se rattache à cette notion vont fournir d'innombrables métaphores dans *La modification*. Je ne saurais en dresser ici la liste complète. Voici quelques exemples. Notons tout d'abord, sans qu'on puisse parler de métaphore proprement dite, que les rêves de Léon Delmont sont pleins de l'image d'un fleuve (p. 206, 211, 219). Au fil des pages, nous rencontrons « une lente houle de coteaux » (p. 63), un fleuve de voitures place du Théâtre-Français (p. 65), ou l'idée qu'en 1955 s'achève « une des grandes vagues de l'histoire » (p. 277). Il n'est pas jusqu'aux losanges de la grille chauffante qui ne deviennent des « vagues » (p. 96), et les draps du lit qui ne deviennent « une infranchissable rivière de lin » (p. 43). La fraîcheur, si elle n'est pas excessive, est une vertu, d'ailleurs imprécise, pour une chambre (p. 123), pour une lumière (p. 131). La voix de Virgile « baigne » de fastueuses demeures (p. 72), tandis que la présence de Cécile « baignait » les souffrances physiques de Léon Delmont et les apaisait (p. 257). Et ce même Léon Delmont ne se lave pas seulement le corps, mais l'âme, encrassée par toute sorte de cauchemars (p. 250). Enfin, comme nous pouvions nous y attendre, bain et fontaine se rencontrent dans le mythe de la fontaine de Jouvence, esquissé page 109, explicite page 98, par exemple, d'autant plus que les amants ont rendez-vous non loin du palais Farnèse, près d'une fontaine « en forme de baignoire » *(ibid.)*.

## • *L'eau, la forêt et le feu*

Il nous faut préciser maintenant les rapports entre l'eau, la forêt et le feu dans *La modification*. La forêt occupe dans les paysages qui défilent devant la vitre du compartiment presque autant de place que la mer et les rivières. Si étonnant que cela puisse paraître au premier abord, la forêt est un élément aquatique : il faut partir du fait qu'il s'agit de la forêt de Fontainebleau, et que dans Fontainebleau, il y a fontaine : la forêt sera donc un lieu humide (p. 116, 211), pourrissant (p. 204), et même une sorte de mer qui se referme derrière le promeneur égaré (p. 198, 202). C'est ainsi que le fantôme du Grand Veneur pourra devenir dans les rêves de Léon Delmont un passeur d'eau, un nautonier démoniaque (p. 219). La forêt de Fontainebleau n'est jamais vue que sous la pluie (p. 116, 137), même au printemps, lors du premier voyage avec Henriette; bien qu'il ne soit pas dit qu'alors il ait plu pendant que le couple traversait la forêt, la notation « la forêt de Fontainebleau toute en pousses vives » est immédiatement suivie de « les averses vous précédant » (p. 228); mais le lien est si fort entre l'eau et les bois que Léon Delmont ne peut plus imaginer les uns sans l'autre, jusque dans le futur : « Vous regarderez, au travers des vitres noires peut-être couvertes de milliers de gouttes de pluie, surgir de l'ombre absolue, au passage des fenêtres du corridor éclairé, les talus couverts de feuilles pourrissantes, les fragments des troncs par centaines dans la forêt de Fontainebleau » (p. 204).

Nous pouvons découvrir dans *La modification* une assimilation du même ordre entre l'eau et le feu, bien que ce soit encore plus inattendu que l'assimilation entre l'eau et la forêt. Mettons à part le point rouge de la cigarette; les moments où le paquet de Léon Delmont est vide et où il n'a plus d'allumettes coïncident avec ses pires dépressions : lors du malheureux retour à Rome en compagnie de Cécile (p. 211-212), et, pendant le voyage actuel, il ne lui reste plus que huit cigarettes à Modane (p. 159), deux entre Novi Ligure et Gênes (p. 213), après quoi il erre lamentablement dans le train pour se réapprovisionner au wagon-restaurant, qui a d'ailleurs été détaché du train (p. 237); en revanche, pendant le voyage heureux du 6 novembre, Léon Delmont, la « poche bien garnie de gauloises », fume « cigarette sur cigarette »

dans le couloir (p. 247). Partout ailleurs, nous assistons à une sorte de fusion entre l'eau et le feu. En principe ces deux éléments sont ennemis, mais lisons attentivement la page 211 : nous voyons que les feuilles mortes qu'on brûle dans les jardins, au bas de la page, sont semblables à celles de la forêt, dont il est dit dans le haut de la même page qu'elles sont mouillées ; ainsi se justifie la fumée dont il est question au troisième paragraphe ; la fumée devient vapeur, nuages, brume aux pages 214-215, produit d'un feu dans une salle « suintante » ; nous retrouverons ce thème, implicite, dans les pages 219 et 222. L'eau et le feu peuvent aussi s'unir plus heureusement en une substance unique : partout, dans *La modification*, le feu est un feu liquide, qu'il se présente sous la forme d'un feu ondoyant et fluide, c'est-à-dire sous forme de flamme, ou caché dans une eau de feu, c'est-à-dire dans le vin ou l'alcool, peut-être aussi dans le pétrole. Nous ne reviendrons pas sur le vin et l'alcool, mais à mon compte la flamme paraît treize fois dans *La modification*, soit par référence à une flamme réelle (la flamme d'une raffinerie de pétrole, p. 273, par exemple), soit dans un rêve de Léon Delmont (p. 219, 231, 232), soit par métaphore (« flamme de soupçon », p. 41 ; « une chevelure de ternes flammes », p. 116 ; « votre flamme interne », p. 137, etc.) ; les autres formes du feu ne paraissent probablement pas aussi souvent.

Roman de l'eau donc. Mais Bachelard avait fait observer que lorsque nous rêvons ces substances nous attachons une valeur morale à la puissance que nous leur prêtons. Autrement dit, l'eau est-elle bénéfique ou maléfique dans *La modification* ? La réponse n'est pas évidente parce que, si nous considérons l'antagoniste de l'eau, le feu, il est le plus souvent générateur d'une chaleur bienfaisante (par exemple, p. 195), mais aussi il peut être cause d'horribles brûlures (p. 237) ; l'aridité, la sécheresse sont en général affreuses (par exemple, p. 141, la main de « M^{me} Polliat » est « sèche, agrippeuse »). Mais tout compte fait, je crois bien que l'eau est un élément pernicieux dans notre roman. On s'en aperçoit d'abord en examinant les rapports de l'eau avec l'air comme nous venons de le faire des rapports de l'eau avec la forêt et avec le feu. En fait, ce que redoute surtout Léon Delmont - ou Butor - c'est l'asphyxie ; comme chez Racine, « respirer » signifie se sentir vivre avec plaisir (p. 166, 218) ; à la seule pensée du

bonheur de vivre avec Cécile, Léon Delmont respire un « coup de cet air futur » (p. 38); Cécile est « cette gorgée d'air » qui le sauvera des « fonds asphyxiés de cet océan d'ennui, de démission, de routines » (p. 42). L'eau est le symbole de la noyade, et même la pluie peut être associée à une respiration pénible (p. 202). Dans une eau où normalement on pourrait respirer il ferait bon nager : cette eau épurée, débarrassée de son pouvoir oppressant, cette eau subtile, c'est l'air où l'on rêve de flotter (par exemple, p. 217) et même de plonger, car Butor en vient à écrire : « Vous vous enfoncerez tout à loisir dans cet air splendide romain » (p. 45). Inversement, si l'air est « épais » (p. 201, 271), il devient aussi horrible que l'eau. Il y a mieux : l'élément le plus éthéré, s'il s'épaissit, devient un milieu accablant, étouffant; c'est le cas de la lueur de la veilleuse dans le compartiment. Cette lumière est bleue, ce qui évoque l'eau, évocation renforcée par l'aspect de la petite ampoule que Léon Delmont compare à une « perle bleue » (p. 169), c'est-à-dire à un objet tiré de la mer; dès lors il ne sera plus question que de l'« épaisse lumière bleue » (par exemple, p. 252), terrifiante (p. 238-239); enfin la lumière bleue devient - en songe, il est vrai - une eau visqueuse, figée, « un caillot » (p. 262). Bref, l'eau est un milieu hostile, et tout milieu est hostile dans la mesure où il ressemble à l'eau. En outre, nous reconnaissons à un autre signe que l'eau est défavorable, c'est le sens des métaphores groupées autour de la notion d'eau. Nous venons de faire allusion au caillot; le mot revient plusieurs fois (p. 245, 258, 259 et 262); cette masse de liquide coagulé est toujours dans *La modification* un obstacle pesant. Voici deux autres métaphores dont la valeur est la même, c'est-à-dire péjorative : le « marécage de poix et d'ennui » (p. 82) où s'enlise la triste Henriette n'a rien de plaisant, tandis que le désarroi de Léon Delmont au cours de son voyage est ressenti par lui comme une « hideuse déliquescence » (p. 209). Remarquons d'ailleurs qu'il y a pis que la sécheresse dont nous parlions tout à l'heure, c'est, sous la sécheresse, une humidité en profondeur, image de la pourriture cachée : les rapports entre Léon et Henriette sont un « désert », un « granit » froid et rugueux d'où jaillirait une purulence si l'on incisait la surface (p. 110); nous retrouvons cette image sous la forme du « pus stupidement doré » qui, selon Cécile, caractérise le Vatican (p. 168).

Quittons les métaphores pour le sens propre des mots : il est un état de l'eau qui est répugnant, c'est l'humidité ; la sueur « presque sèche » (p. 236), le chocolat qui fond entre les mains d'un enfant (p. 106) ; sans commentaire, mais ce n'en est sans doute que plus probant, Léon Delmont note que, coup sur coup, en arrivant chez lui, il voit « Henriette arriver en s'essuyant les mains à son tablier gris », puis Thomas qui essuie « subrepticement ses mains sur sa culotte de velours à côtes avec le geste de sa mère » (p. 79) ; on soupçonne alors que, lorsqu'il voit Cécile, à Rome, se retourner « en s'essuyant les mains avec un torchon à raies de trois couleurs » (p. 174), le pauvre homme perçoit un écho désagréable de la scène parisienne, quelque gai que soit un torchon de trois couleurs par comparaison avec une blouse grise. Et si Léon Delmont songe que son départ matinal l'a obligé à emporter dans sa valise son « blaireau encore humide » (p. 28), c'est bien la preuve d'un certain écœurement, de mauvais augure pour ce voyage. C'est un cauchemar de rêver du « suintement » sur les parois de la maison de Néron, des « taches vertes visqueuses » (p. 255). Quant à l'adjectif « gluant », il en vient à signifier seulement *couvert de manière à faire horreur* (p. 203).

• *Transparence et opacité*

Cependant, c'est dans la transparence de l'eau à la lumière et dans son opacité que gisent les bienfaits et les méfaits de l'eau. La transparence fait la principale vertu de la nouvelle gare Termini à Rome (p. 113) ; au contraire, l'encre symbolise les souffrances du mauvais rêve (p. 201). Même si l'eau brille par reflet, elle est source de joie : la neige, quand Léon Delmont imagine son bonheur futur, sera « illuminée », « et le compartiment sera envahi par la réverbération, par la résonance claire et fraîche de la lumière, baignant de solennelle gaieté tous les voyageurs » (p. 130-131) ; et lors du voyage de noces, « les averses vous précédant, faisant briller toits et trottoirs, les prairies éblouissantes sur les montagnes » (p. 228) restent dans la mémoire de Léon Delmont comme un souvenir de jeunesse et de bonheur.

Mais il n'est quasi pas de page du roman où la pluie n'obscurcisse le ciel et les vitres du wagon, où la brume ne noie les villes et les campagnes, parallèlement à la tristesse

et au désespoir du héros. Nous nous apercevons que l'eau est perfide, trompeuse. L'eau nous empêche de percevoir clairement la réalité : « Au-delà de la fenêtre noyée tournent, au milieu du paysage semblable à des reflets dans un étang, les triangles obscurs de toits et d'un clocher » (p. 100-101); les images que l'on voit à travers l'eau ou réfléchies par l'eau sont également brouillées. Si l'on admet que le mot *glace* évoque l'eau, dans son compartiment où tant de spectacles ne viendront à lui qu'à travers les glaces des fenêtres ou reflétées par les miroirs et les verres protecteurs des photographies, la situation de Léon Delmont sera la situation d'un homme qui se noie. Dès la page 12, les glaces nous livrent une vision ambiguë, à demi image réelle, à demi reflet virtuel, et caricatural : « A travers la vitre, à travers une autre vitre, vous apercevez assez distinctement à l'intérieur d'un autre wagon de modèle plus ancien aux bancs de bois jaune, aux filets de ficelle, dans la pénombre au-delà des reflets composés, un homme de la même taille que vous, dont vous ne sauriez ni préciser l'âge, ni décrire avec exactitude les vêtements, qui reproduit avec plus de lenteur encore les gestes fatigués que vous venez d'accomplir. » Cette phrase, placée au début du roman, est une phrase d'appel d'un thème qui occupera une place notable dans la seconde moitié; page 163, la vitre translucide deviendra au passage d'un tunnel un miroir incertain : « Au-delà de la fenêtre on ne voit plus que le reflet brouillé de ces objets et de ces visages. » Je vous laisse le soin de trouver d'autres exemples de ces jeux d'images. Dans la nuit on voit sur la vitre à la fois les reflets de l'intérieur et les lumières de l'extérieur du compartiment (p. 179). Par ces illusions d'optique, les cheveux d'une voyageuse deviennent des flots où voguent les bateaux de la photographie de Concarneau placée au-dessus de sa tête (p. 208 sqq.). Le comble de ces confusions se trouve à la page 256 : « De nouveau au-dessus des cheveux d'Agnès, dans la vitre de la photographie invisible qui représente des bateaux à quai dans un petit port, le reflet déformé de la lune est semblable à l'empreinte de quelque bête nocturne, non pas simplement à l'empreinte, aux griffes mêmes qui se détendent et se retendent comme impatientes d'agripper; il se déplace vers le bord, vers la fenêtre, disparaît, mais à travers la vitre c'est la lune pleine elle-même qui se découvre à vous, se fixant frémissante au

centre, et dont la lumière droite envahit tout d'un coup le compartiment à tel point qu'entre vos deux souliers elle fait briller, ranime les écailles losanges du tapis chauffant métallique. » - Mais c'est surtout dans « l'épaisse lumière bleue » que le malheureux va se noyer, si vous avez admis que cette lumière marine était un véritable liquide. Tout d'abord Léon Delmont souhaite ne pas trop attendre le moment où « la perle bleue dans son centre diffuse ses sombres rayons apaisants » (p. 169); pourtant, lorsque le plafonnier sera éteint, ce sera pis : « La lumière était dure et brûlante, mais les objets qu'elle éclairait présentaient du moins une surface dure à laquelle vous aviez l'impression de pouvoir vous appuyer, vous accrocher, avec quoi vous tentiez de vous constituer un rempart contre cette infiltration, cette lézarde, cette question qui s'élargit, vous humiliant, cette interrogation contagieuse qui se met à faire trembler de plus en plus de pièces de cette machine extérieure, de cette cuirasse métallique dont vous-même jusqu'à présent ne soupçonniez pas la minceur, la fragilité,

tandis que ce bleu qui reste comme suspendu dans l'air, qui donne l'impression qu'il le faut traverser pour voir, ce bleu aidé de ce perpétuel tremblement, de ce bruit, de ces respirations devinées, restitue les objets à leur incertitude originelle, non point vus crûment mais reconstitués à partir d'indices, de telle sorte qu'ils vous regardent autant que vous les regardez,

vous restituant vous-même à cette tranquille terreur, à cette émotion primitive où s'affirme avec tant de puissance et de hauteur, au-dessus des ruines de tant de mensonges, la passion de l'existence et de la vérité.

Vous considérez cette ampoule bleue insistante, comme une grosse perle, non point claire à proprement parler, mais source dans son épaisse couleur murmurante de doux échos sur toutes les mains et sur tous les fronts des dormeurs » (p. 238-239). En rapprochant les deux derniers textes, celui-ci et celui de la page 169, nous constatons que la lumière bleue n'est point présentée comme vraiment bienfaisante, mais comme « apaisante » ou « douce », et qu'au-delà de cette apparence bénigne se cache un pouvoir destructeur. A vrai dire, nous devinons bien que cette destruction n'est qu'une étape nécessaire sur le chemin du salut final que Léon Delmont

envisagera en arrivant à Rome. Il reste que l'eau bleue de la lumière a troublé les images du monde et l'âme du héros.

L'eau nous apporte un soulagement momentané et l'illusion du bonheur. En songe, lorsque Léon Delmont étanche enfin sa soif, il avale un poison brûlant (p. 237). « L'ombre délicieuse » de la place Navone que rafraîchit la fontaine du Bernin (p. 120) est trompeuse ; trompeuse également la fontaine de Jouvence dont Cécile fait boire l'eau à Léon Delmont. Et si les amants, à Paris, tentent de se réfugier dans les îles de la Seine, cette barrière d'eau est une faible protection contre leur tristesse et leur déception (p. 176 sqq.). *La modification* est le roman d'un homme qui s'aperçoit qu'il fait fausse route. Le thème de l'eau et de ses charmes mensongers est profondément lié à l'un des projets fondamentaux que poursuit Butor dans cet ouvrage.

## CONCLUSION

La question que nous nous posons maintenant est celle de savoir si ces rêves du feu et de l'eau ont une authenticité dans les écrits de Butor. Si l'écrivain est hanté par le rêve d'une substance, il ne peut changer d'obsession chaque fois qu'il entreprend un ouvrage nouveau. Pour Bachelard cette hantise fait l'unité souterraine de l'œuvre d'un artiste. En vérité il faudrait une analyse plus fine que celle que nous venons d'esquisser pour décider si les thèmes de l'eau et du feu sont enracinés au plus profond du projet poétique de Michel Butor, ou s'il s'agit d'artifices de fabrication destinés à donner une coloration à chacun de ses romans.

Quoi qu'il en soit, faisant suite à un roman rouge et or, *L'emploi du temps*, *La modification* est un roman vert et bleu, couleur de l'eau : qu'il nous suffise de rappeler qu'en 1955, la plupart des compartiments de 3ᵉ classe étaient verts, que la valise de Léon Delmont est verte (p. 9), que son costume est bleu (p. 12), sans parler de l'« épaisse lumière bleue ». Et qui sait si les robes rouges ou orange de Cécile (p. 68), son manteau de pluie « jaune clair » (p. 175) ne mettent pas une fausse note dans les teintes froides où baigne l'ensemble.

Il est sûr qu'il y a, de *L'emploi du temps* à *La modification*, une baisse de tension, ou plutôt de densité poétique. Le feu

était caché dans les pierres mêmes de la ville de Bleston, vrai protagoniste de *L'emploi du temps;* si nous avions étudié cet ouvrage, nous aurions été obligés de mettre le thème du feu parmi les aspects « nouveau roman » parce que cette substance y existe sur un mode objectif. Dans *La modification* l'obsession de l'eau n'est plus, je crois, qu'un trait du caractère ou du tempérament de Léon Delmont : nous rentrons dans le domaine du psychisme des personnages, qui fait partie de la poétique la plus traditionnelle du roman.

On a parfois trouvé une analogie entre la longue phrase de Butor, avec ses rebondissements, et la lente volute des phrases proustiennes. Si cela était, les romans de Butor seraient encore plus tournés vers le passé que nous ne venons de le dire. Mais, excepté la longueur, je ne vois pas grand-chose de commun aux deux tournures de phrase, et nous parlerons plus loin de la manière dont Butor construit les siennes.

Même du point de vue qui vient d'être provisoirement le nôtre, on ne peut pas dire que *La modification* soit un roman sans valeur. Nous nous intéressons à ce Français moyen, au sujet duquel certains critiques se sont demandé comment il avait réussi à séduire deux femmes et à diriger un réseau de vente important. L'air circule autour de Léon Delmont, comme le disait Balzac des personnages de *La chartreuse de Parme.* Surtout le réseau des images est si habilement tissé que tout baigne dans une atmosphère parfaitement spécifique et plausible.

| 3 | Un nouveau roman

Mais *La modification* a aussi la réputation d'être un « nouveau » roman. En 1957 les critiques hostiles au nouveau roman ne s'y sont pas trompés et ont décrié le choix du jury Renaudot.

Il me faut donc maintenant essayer de vous expliquer ce qu'on peut entendre sous l'appellation de nouveau roman. Naturellement on s'est querellé pour savoir si l'on a le droit de parler ou non d'une *école* du nouveau roman. Comme, lorsqu'on y regarde de trop près, l'école classique, l'école romantique, l'école naturaliste, etc., s'en vont en fumée, ne nous interdisons pas d'employer la dénomination commode d'école du nouveau roman, en nous rappelant toujours ce qu'en vaut l'aune. Disons que vers 1950 quelques romanciers ont refusé certaines des données essentielles du roman issu des conceptions de Balzac, et qu'ils l'ont fait pour des raisons fort semblables. Nathalie Sarraute, dans *L'ère du soupçon*, et Robbe-Grillet dans les plus anciens des articles réunis plus tard sous le titre de *Pour un nouveau roman* s'accordent sur un certain nombre d'idées; Butor, à travers son recueil intitulé *Répertoire*, ne les contredit pas, sauf sur un point : Butor conteste que Balzac ait donné du roman une formule absolument contraire aux recherches modernes. Mais revenons à Nathalie Sarraute et à Robbe-Grillet.

## MORT DU HÉROS DE ROMAN

Il saute aux yeux d'abord que tous deux proclament la mort du héros de roman. Voici ce qu'en dit Nathalie Sarraute : « Il était très richement pourvu, comblé de biens de toute sorte, entouré de soins minutieux; rien ne lui manquait, depuis les boucles d'argent de sa culotte jusqu'à la loupe veinée au bout de son nez. Il a, peu à peu, tout perdu : ses

ancêtres, sa maison soigneusement bâtie, bourrée de la cave au grenier d'objets de toute espèce, jusqu'aux plus menus colifichets, ses propriétés et ses titres de rente, ses vêtements, son corps, son visage, et, surtout, ce bien précieux entre tous, son caractère qui n'appartenait qu'à lui, et souvent jusqu'à son nom [1]. » Nous trouvons presque les mêmes termes sous la plume de Robbe-Grillet [2]. Il subsiste cependant dans les romans des noms propres, parfois réduits à une simple initiale, comme dans les œuvres de Kafka, parfois réduits à un prénom interchangeable, comme dans *Le bruit et la fureur* de Faulkner ; mais ces noms ne désigneront plus « que de simples supports, des porteurs d'états encore inexplorés que nous retrouvons en nous-mêmes [3] ». Si l'on peut encore parler de personnage, il est seulement le siège d'une pulsion obsédante, d'un désir, d'un projet anxieux, c'est un être indéfini sinon par une direction psychique. Ni Nathalie Sarraute, ni Robbe-Grillet ne prétendent avoir inventé de faire disparaître le héros ; ils constatent que c'est le terme d'une évolution commencée depuis longtemps ; Robbe-Grillet se contente d'ajouter quelques noms à la liste des romanciers en qui Nathalie Sarraute reconnaît des précurseurs.

## SUPPRESSION DE L'INTRIGUE

L'accord se fait également sur l'abolition de l'intrigue classique dans le roman : « Quelle histoire inventée pourrait rivaliser avec celle de la séquestrée de Poitiers [4] ou avec les récits des camps de concentration ou de la bataille de Stalingrad ? » se demande Nathalie Sarraute [5], tandis que Robbe-Grillet consacre quatre pages [6] à montrer qu'il n'est plus possible aujourd'hui de raconter ce qu'on appelle généralement une histoire, c'est-à-dire une suite d'événements ordonnés selon des conventions littéraires : « Il ne lui suffit

---

1. *L'ère du soupçon* (cf. bibliographie, p. 78), p. 57.
2. *Pour un nouveau roman* (cf. bibliographie, p. 78), p. 27.
3. Nathalie Sarraute, *op. cit.*, p. 40.
4. C'est André Gide qui a raconté l'histoire de *La séquestrée de Poitiers* (Gallimard, 1930). En 1901, à Poitiers, dans la maison d'une famille de bonne bourgeoisie, on découvrit une femme de cinquante-deux ans, Mélanie Bastian, enfermée depuis vingt-quatre ans, sans air, au milieu d'ordures. On ne sut jamais si la famille avait voulu dissimuler que la malheureuse était folle ou si elle était devenue folle parce qu'elle avait été séquestrée par sa mère, dont le moins qu'on puisse dire est qu'elle était autoritaire et bizarre.
5. *Ibid.*, p. 66.
6. Robbe-Grillet, *Pour un nouveau roman*, p. 29 à 32.

pas [à l'anecdote] dans les romans du XIXᵉ siècle d'être plaisante, ou extraordinaire, ou captivante ; pour avoir son poids de vérité humaine, il lui faut encore réussir à persuader le lecteur que les aventures dont on lui parle sont arrivées vraiment à des personnages réels, et que le romancier se borne à rapporter, à transmettre, des événements dont il a été témoin. Une convention tacite s'établit entre le lecteur et l'auteur : celui-ci fera semblant de croire à ce qu'il raconte, celui-là oubliera que tout est inventé et feindra d'avoir affaire à un document, à une biographie, à une quelconque histoire vécue. Bien raconter, c'est donc faire ressembler ce que l'on écrit aux schémas préfabriqués dont les gens ont l'habitude, c'est-à-dire à l'idée toute faite qu'ils ont de la réalité [1]. » Robbe-Grillet ajoute que l'auteur doit éviter la moindre contradiction, car le lecteur veut trouver « l'image d'un univers stable, cohérent, continu, univoque, entièrement déchiffrable [2] ». Le nouveau romancier ne s'interdira certes pas de présenter des événements, mais il ne les groupera pas de telle sorte que leur suite soit un enchaînement certain, tranquillisant.

## DÉSENGAGEMENT

Il est un troisième point dont Nathalie Sarraute ne parle guère dans *L'ère du soupçon*, quoique la lecture de ses romans ne laisse pas de doute sur son adhésion. Le nouveau roman est désengagé. On sait que la théorie de l'engagement littéraire se trouve dans *Situations, II*, de Sartre, sous la rubrique *Qu'est-ce qu'écrire ?*, première des études de *Qu'est-ce que la littérature* [3] ? ; je vous renvoie à ce texte. Toutefois, voici le passage que je crois le plus important pour nous en ce moment : « L'écrivain « engagé » sait que la parole est action : il sait que dévoiler c'est changer et qu'on ne peut dévoiler qu'en projetant de changer. Il a abandonné le rêve impossible de faire une peinture impartiale de la Société et de la condition humaine. L'homme est l'être vis-à-vis de qui aucun être ne peut garder l'impartialité, même Dieu [4]. » En vérité Sartre

---
1. *Ibid.*, p. 29-30.
2. *Ibid.*, p. 31.
3. Sartre, *Situations, II*, Gallimard, 1949, p. 57-88.
4. *Ibid.*, p. 73.

ne prétend point qu'un roman doive prouver une thèse philosophique ou politique; il prétend seulement qu'en décrivant la réalité sans chercher à rien dissimuler de ce qu'il croit vrai, le romancier force son lecteur à prendre conscience des vices de la société. Il n'en reste pas moins que le but de l'œuvre romanesque est de contester le monde, ce qui n'est pas le but de la peinture, de la musique et de la poésie. Robbe-Grillet va prendre le contre-pied de ces théories : « L'art ne peut être réduit à l'état de moyen au service d'une cause qui le dépasserait [1] »; et Robbe-Grillet considère qu'un roman est une œuvre d'art, ce que Sartre au fond niait. Le roman n'explique rien, ne démontre aucune vérité préexistante, ne trouve aucune justification par le sens qu'on voudrait lui donner avant qu'il soit écrit : « L'œuvre d'art, comme le monde, est une forme vivante : elle *est*, elle n'a pas besoin de justification. Le zèbre est réel, le nier ne serait pas raisonnable, bien que ses rayures soient sans doute dépourvues de sens. Il en va de même pour [...] un roman [2]. » Robbe-Grillet n'en a pas moins horreur de la gratuité de l'œuvre d'art, de l'art pour l'art. En réalité, il voudrait donner de l'engagement une définition nouvelle : « L'engagement c'est, pour l'écrivain, la pleine conscience des problèmes actuels de son propre langage, la conviction de leur extrême importance, la volonté de les résoudre de l'intérieur. C'est là, pour lui, la seule chance de demeurer un artiste et, sans doute aussi, par voie de conséquence obscure et lointaine, de servir un jour peut-être à quelque chose - peut-être même à la révolution [3]. »

## L'ALIÉNATION EN LITTÉRATURE

Si donc, à lointaine échéance, le romancier et ses romans peuvent servir à quelque chose, ce ne sera qu'en libérant les lecteurs. Robbe-Grillet et Butor veulent tous deux lutter, avec leurs moyens d'écrivains, contre l'aliénation des hommes et des femmes de notre temps. Mais il s'agit dans la pensée de Robbe-Grillet - car les vues de Butor ne sont pas tout à fait les mêmes - d'une aliénation littéraire, d'une aliénation

---

1. Alain Robbe-Grillet, *op. cit.*, p. 35.
2. *Ibid.*, p. 41.
3. *Ibid.*, p. 39.

des hommes et des femmes en tant que lecteurs et lectrices. L'engagement sartrien datait d'une époque où Sartre espérait être lu par les ouvriers et où il pensait à créer l'équivalent français du réalisme socialiste qui régnait alors sans conteste en Russie. Robbe-Grillet avoue qu'il lui faut bien écrire pour des lecteurs « bourgeois », appartenant à cette fraction d'intellectuels bourgeois et de bourgeois tout court qui se posent des questions sur la légitimité et la pérennité de la société. Tout ce que peut faire le romancier, c'est de montrer que le roman peut échapper aux règles, aux conventions romanesques comme on les pratiquait au siècle dernier ; bref, en contestant les fondements du roman « bourgeois », on peut rendre les lecteurs actuels disponibles pour d'autres romans, nés dans d'autres sociétés.

C'est ainsi que se justifie la place qu'occupent les objets dans les œuvres des écrivains de cette école et l'étrange façon dont ils en parlent. Bien que l'essai de Robbe-Grillet que nous allons maintenant utiliser soit postérieur à *La modification*, nous allons nous y référer parce que nous y trouverons l'explication d'un aspect important de notre roman. Il s'agit de *Nature, humanisme, tragédie* (paru en 1958), dans *Pour un nouveau roman*[1]. Nous avons le sentiment, dit Robbe-Grillet, de vivre dans un univers tragique, et c'est en cela que nous ne sommes pas libres, que nous sommes aliénés. Or rien ne nous prouve que l'univers soit objectivement en proie au tragique, et assurément il n'est pas nécessaire que nous le ressentions tel. Voici comment, dans un très beau texte, Robbe-Grillet expose la naissance en chacun de nous de cette conviction que nous sommes victimes de la fatalité :

« Retraçons, à titre d'exemple, le fonctionnement de la « solitude ». J'appelle. Personne ne me répond. Au lieu de conclure qu'il n'y a personne - ce qui pourrait être un constat pur et simple, daté, localisé, dans l'espace et le temps -, je décide d'agir comme s'il y avait quelqu'un, mais qui, pour une raison ou pour une autre, ne répondrait pas. Le silence qui suit mon appel n'est plus, dès lors, un *vrai* silence ; il se trouve chargé d'un contenu, d'une profondeur, d'une âme - qui me renvoie aussitôt à la mienne. La distance entre mon cri, à mes propres oreilles, et l'interlocuteur muet (peut-être

---

1. *Ibid.*, p. 45-67.

sourd) auquel il s'adresse, devient une angoisse, mon espoir et mon désespoir, un sens à ma vie. Plus rien ne comptera désormais pour moi, que ce faux vide et les problèmes qu'il me pose. Dois-je appeler plus longtemps ? Dois-je crier plus fort ? Dois-je prononcer d'autres paroles ? J'essaie de nouveau... Très vite je comprends que personne ne répondra ; mais la présence invisible que je continue à créer par mon appel m'oblige, pour toujours, à lancer dans le silence mon cri malheureux. Bientôt le son qu'il rend commence à m'étourdir. Comme envoûté, j'appelle de nouveau..., de nouveau encore. Ma solitude, exacerbée, se transmue à la fin, pour ma conscience aliénée, en une nécessité supérieure, promesse de mon rachat. Et je suis obligé, pour que celui-ci s'accomplisse, de m'obstiner jusqu'à ma mort à crier pour rien.

« Selon le processus habituel, ma solitude n'est plus alors une donnée accidentelle, momentanée, de mon existence. Elle fait partie de moi, du monde entier, de tous les hommes : c'est notre nature, une fois de plus. C'est une solitude pour toujours [1]. »

Que peut faire le romancier pour arracher ceux qui liront ses œuvres à un piège si spécieux ? En 1956, Robbe-Grillet avait déjà montré que dans le roman d'autrefois les objets n'étaient pas les objets, mais que l'auteur pensait d'abord à ce qu'il voulait signifier, et qu'il imaginait ensuite la chose, le geste, la scène, qui donnerait une apparence sensible à cette signification. Il pensait, par exemple, à une insulte : il faisait faire un pied de nez par son personnage. Mais supposons que l'expression « pied de nez » ne figure pas dans le texte que je lis, que j'y lise la description minutieuse de la position d'une main, placée dans un plan vertical, le pouce posé sur un nez, les doigts écartés, etc., je serai forcé de convenir que si je vois dans cette image le signe d'une insulte, c'est moi, lecteur, qui l'y aurai mis ; je prendrai conscience de tout l'arbitraire, de tout le conventionnel de mon interprétation : l'insulte ne sera plus objectivement dans le geste évoqué. Voici maintenant ce que dit Robbe-Grillet et les exemples qu'il donne lui-même : dans le roman d'autrefois « les objets et les gestes qui servaient de support à l'intrigue disparaissaient complètement

---

1. *Ibid.*, p. 54-55.

pour laisser la place à leur seule signification : la chaise inoccupée n'était plus qu'une absence ou une attente, la main qui se pose sur l'épaule n'était plus que marque de sympathie, les barreaux de la fenêtre n'étaient que l'impossibilité de sortir... Et voici que maintenant on *voit* la chaise, le mouvement de la main, la forme des barreaux. Leur signification demeure flagrante, mais, au lieu d'accaparer notre attention, elle est comme donnée en plus; en trop même, car ce qui nous atteint, ce qui persiste dans notre mémoire, ce qui apparaît comme essentiel et irréductible à de vagues notions mentales, ce sont les gestes eux-mêmes, les objets, les déplacements et les contours, auxquels l'image a restitué d'un seul coup (sans le vouloir) leur *réalité* [1] ». Est-il quelque chose de plus tragique qu'une chaise vide ? Efforçons-nous donc de parler de sa couleur, de sa structure, pieds, barreaux, siège, dossier : ce ne sera plus qu'une chaise. Et nous nous promènerons dans un monde neutre, à qui nous ne demanderons plus de nous être favorable, un monde, en tout cas, et c'est le principal, qui ne pourra plus nous être hostile.

## UN ENCHAINEMENT DE CONSÉQUENCES

Ainsi le reproche que l'on a fait souvent à la nouvelle « école » d'accorder trop d'importance aux problèmes de forme n'est pas justifié. Vous voyez maintenant que cette transformation de la forme, c'est-à-dire de la manière de présenter les choses, est capitale pour elle : comme le romancier « classique », ils évoqueront une chaise vide, mais par un artifice d'écriture, ils obtiendront l'effet qu'ils recherchent, cette chaise ne sera pas le symbole de toute la misère humaine.

Je pense qu'il est inutile désormais de vous expliquer pourquoi les romanciers dont nous parlons ont eu besoin de modifier les autres éléments de la technique romanesque telle qu'elle était pratiquée au XIX$^e$ siècle. Tout se tient. A cause de la place prise par l'objet indépendamment de ce que l'homme voit en lui, le personnage de roman, faisceau d'interprétations humaines et de significations subjectives,

---

1. Alain Robbe-Grillet, *Pour un nouveau roman*, Édit. de Minuit, 1963, p. 19.

s'est effacé. - Laissons de côté la question de savoir si ces artistes ne subissent pas tout simplement l'envahissement de notre univers par les choses, la réification, en langage marxiste ; on trouve une analyse très bien faite de ce point dans *Pour une sociologie du roman*, de Lucien Goldmann [1]. Ce qui nous importe en ce moment, c'est de bien voir que le projet essentiel du romancier entraîne nécessairement des conséquences comme l'évanouissement du héros. Il en est de même pour l'intrigue : si le roman doit nous déshabituer du tragique, l'histoire suivie, structurée selon des règles dramatiques, avec un début (un jour, se produit un événement insolite), et une fin (le héros meurt, ou se marie, ou est abandonné par sa femme), cette histoire est remplacée par une séquence de faits qui en soi ne constitue pas une tragédie.

En outre on ne nous demande plus de croire que l'histoire que nous lisons est une histoire « vraie », et que le héros a existé. Depuis longtemps déjà nous sommes reconnaissants aux poètes de ne plus prétendre qu'une nymphe est cachée dans le puits de notre jardin ; depuis longtemps nous rions du maître de Jacques le Fataliste qui serre les dents et s'agite quand Jacques lui raconte comment il a été victime d'une injustice du sort. Devant notre besoin croissant de distinguer la fiction de la réalité, Nathalie Sarraute et Robbe-Grillet se contentent de prendre les devants et n'exigent plus que nous ajoutions foi à ce qu'ils nous racontent au point de croire que c'est arrivé.

---

1. Lucien Goldmann, *Pour une sociologie du roman*, N.R.F., 1964, p. 189 sqq.

# 4 | Application de la théorie à « La modification »

Essayons maintenant de chercher dans *La modification* l'application de ces points théoriques.

## L'INTRIGUE

Commençons par l'intrigue. A proprement parler il n'y a pas d'intrigue dans notre roman, bien que cela ne saute pas aux yeux d'abord. C'est une illusion habilement ménagée par l'auteur qui fait croire au lecteur que *La modification* a un début, un milieu et une fin. Cet artifice consiste à délimiter nettement le récit par deux petits faits : un homme entre dans un compartiment à Paris, il quitte ce même compartiment à Rome. Nul ne peut prétendre que le premier de ces faits est un de ces tournants lourds de signification par quoi commence une époque nouvelle; ni que le second boucle un cycle d'événements remarquables. Comparez ces deux bornes du récit d'une part avec la décision prise par M. de Rênal d'engager le jeune Sorel comme précepteur et d'autre part avec la mort de Julien sur l'échafaud : *Le rouge et le noir* est un drame, *La modification* n'en est pas un. Butor n'a pas découpé une « tranche de vie » dans le déroulement du temps : entre deux faits qui ne veulent rien dire, un homme a bavardé intérieurement. Ce monologue intérieur était déjà commencé quand il a mis le pied sur la rainure de cuivre du panneau coulissant; le monologue peut se poursuivre quand il sera sorti de la gare Termini. Qui nous dit qu'il ne va se précipiter chez sa maîtresse Cécile dès que nous l'aurons perdu de vue à la dernière ligne du roman ? Il ne s'est rien passé. Un nommé Léon Delmont a fait le voyage de Paris à Rome en chemin de fer; tout le monde peut en faire autant; ce n'est pas une histoire.

Mais n'oublions pas que l'intrigue du roman « classique » suppose que le lecteur fasse semblant de croire que l'histoire

est arrivée. Nul n'a séparé plus nettement que Butor, en théorie, le monde réel et le monde romanesque. Je vous renvoie aux pages 7 et 8 de *Répertoire*[1]. Les faits vrais sont l'objet du récit historique; ces faits sont vérifiables par des recoupements avec des réalités non écrites, et le château de Versailles porte témoignage de l'existence de Louis XIV. *Les Mémoires* de Saint-Simon ne sont pas un roman. Mais dans le roman, les choses sont seulement possibles, vraisemblables; le roman et le romancier sollicitent du lecteur une étrange adhésion, car au cours de notre lecture nous acceptons tel événement et nous refusons tel autre selon que nous sommes préparés ou non à recevoir l'un et non l'autre; cette préparation est obtenue lorsque l'auteur a savamment disposé un réseau de recoupements internes à son récit. Je n'ajoute pas créance aux extraordinaires propos du père Grandet mourant devant ses écus parce que ces propos sont vrais, mais parce que j'y ai été préparé par un tissu serré d'anecdotes montrant, donnant l'illusion de prouver, *prouvant* l'avarice du bonhomme : supposons que nous lisions le récit de sa mort à quelqu'un qui n'aurait pas connaissance du début du roman, nous ne provoquerons chez notre auditeur qu'ahurissement et scepticisme ou indifférence. Mais, dans *La modification*, nous acceptons de lire sans difficulté, page 220 : « Les bateaux voguent sur la tête d'Agnès endormie. » Nous devinons que l'obsession de l'eau qui hante la cervelle de notre Léon Delmont est le facteur déterminant de notre adhésion. A force de parler de l'eau dans son roman, Butor a fait passer une image insolite. De même nous croyons volontiers que Cécile ne se détachera pas facilement de Léon Delmont, comme il est dit, entre autres, page 241, parce que nous avons lu page 263 comment les amants se sont réconciliés après le triste séjour de Cécile à Paris : « Enfin elle vous a vu, s'est arrêtée, a poussé un cri, a laissé tomber son sac, et sans même se baisser pour le ramasser s'est précipitée dans vos bras. » Tout cela fait partie des procédés traditionnels de la littérature, romans ou pièces de théâtre.

Mais voici en quoi la tendance du nouveau roman va se retrouver dans *La modification*. Butor construit son

---

[1]. Voir bibliographie, p. 78.

récit de telle sorte que notre adhésion soit toujours l'adhésion à une fiction et non à une vérité. Nous savons par des confidences de Balzac comment il imaginait une intrigue pour l'œuvre qu'il allait écrire : il inventait des aventures d'après l'attitude, le visage, le vêtement d'un passant rencontré dans la rue. Jamais ce secret de fabrication n'est avoué dans *La comédie humaine*. Au contraire, les meilleures pages de *La modification* nous montrent Léon Delmont en train de fabuler sur l'aspect de ses voisins de compartiment, c'est-à-dire que nous trouvons, dans le roman même, le mécanisme par lequel naît l'imaginaire. Et de place en place une petite phrase nous rappelle que tout est mensonger : à propos d'un des Italiens, « Et qui vous dit qu'il soit Romain ? » (p. 128), à propos de la femme âgée accompagnée d'un petit garçon, « elle n'est peut-être pas veuve, elle ne s'appelle pas Madame Polliat ». (P. 141.) Par là le récit est contesté et renvoyé aux incertitudes de la fiction. D'ailleurs les inquiétudes de l'ecclésiastique (p. 118) pourraient aussi bien être attribuées au professeur, tandis que les amours de « Madame Polliat » (p. 129) sont si peu distinctes de celles de « Pierre » et d' « Agnès » (pp. 138-139) qu'on les confond vite.

L'allure même des phrases rejette la narration loin de la vérité historique. Des phrases courtes, des verbes nombreux, au passé simple, voilà le style de l'histoire : « Toutes les places qui bordent le Rhin et l'Issel se rendirent. Quelques gouverneurs envoyèrent leurs clefs dès qu'ils virent seulement passer de loin un ou deux escadrons français » écrivait Voltaire pour raconter le passage du Rhin. La phrase longue est une transposition du monologue intérieur qui dans sa continuité ignore la ponctuation; les redites, les retours en arrière, les remises en question, les sinuosités traduisent le balbutiement intime. Quant aux temps des verbes, *La modification* est normalement au présent et au passé composé; à la rigueur on pourrait prétendre que ces deux temps sont des substituts du passé simple : présent de narration et passé composé comblant le vide laissé par la quasi-disparition du passé simple. En fait, ce n'est pas tout à fait vrai. Le présent est un vrai présent, celui du monologue intérieur, « vrai » présent, si l'on peut dire, car ce « vrai » est conventionnel : les actions et les pensées sont parlées au moment même où elles surviennent : « Vous vous introduisez

par l'étroite ouverture » (p. 9). Le passé composé marque l'antériorité par rapport à ce présent; mais il est impossible d'employer à sa place le passé simple : p. 17, Butor ne pouvait écrire « Votre premier mouvement [...] *fut* d'étendre le bras », et encore moins « vous *vîtes* les cheveux autrefois noirs d'Henriette » : c'est Léon Delmont qui parle et non Butor qui écrit. L'imparfait, en plus de ses emplois normaux, va tendre à remplacer et le présent et le passé composé, teintant la narration d'une nuance de style indirect : « Il ne fallait pas que quelqu'un sût chez Scabelli que c'était vers Rome que vous vous échappiez pour ces quelques jours » (p. 10), voilà pour le présent et, pour le passé composé, « Si vous aviez peur de le manquer, ce train au mouvement et au bruit duquel vous êtes maintenant déjà réhabitué, ce n'est pas que, etc. » (p. 17), « aviez » est bien l'équivalent du passé composé, car il est repris page 20 par « Si vous avez eu peur de le manquer, ce train [...] c'est parce que, etc. ». Dans tous ces cas, l'écran du discours s'interpose de manière sensible entre l'événement et le lecteur, alors que le passé simple prétend abolir toute autre distance qu'un intervalle de temps : « Louis XIV passa sur un pont de bateaux », c'est comme si nous avions assisté à la scène. - L'abondance des participes présents, qui est dans les habitudes du nouveau roman, produit un effet un peu différent, mais convergeant avec les glissements de temps dont nous venons de parler. Lorsque nous lisons « celui que vous appelez Pierre s'éveillant, décollant ses épaules du dossier, appuyant ses coudes sur ses genoux, regardant défiler le sombre paysage » (p. 260), nous ne songeons ni à ces actions, ni au temps où elles se sont passées, mais à l'image d'un homme en train de les accomplir, image fixée comme sur une photographie : l'événement n'est plus daté dans le passé, il est éternellement présent quand nous l'imaginons. - C'est peut-être l'emploi des temps dans *La modification* qui maintient sourdement, mais constamment, le ton de la fiction. Ce style n'est pas le style d'une intrigue classique.

Le dernier trait enfin qui caractériserait une intrigue classique, c'est qu'elle devrait être un lien fort assemblant les personnages en un tout indissoluble. Nous allons voir qu'ici il n'en est rien. Revenons aux voyageurs réunis dans le compartiment. Léon Delmont va peu à peu les faire entrer

dans son roman, le roman qu'il vit et le roman qu'il fabrique. Le professeur sera un homme qui a choisi librement un métier qu'il aime, ce qu'il n'a pas fait, lui, Léon Delmont (p. 52-55). L'ecclésiastique médite peut-être de quitter l'Église comme Léon Delmont médite de rompre avec Henriette (p. 90). Les deux représentants de commerce, le Français et l'Italien, ont la mine d'hommes qui trompent leur femme (p. 108 et 171). M$^{me}$ Polliat, c'est Henriette dans quelques années (p. 106), ou plutôt c'est Cécile dans vingt ans (p. 129). Agnès et Pierre, ce sont Henriette et Léon il y a vingt ans (p. 138 à 140). Les deux garçons, ce sont les enfants de Pierre et d'Agnès dans vingt ans (p. 141), c'est-à-dire les enfants de Léon et d'Henriette aujourd'hui. Ce que devient le temps dans cette fabulation, nous le verrons tout à l'heure. Mais il nous faut revenir à l'essentiel : Butor, en tout cela, n'a d'autre but que de désamorcer la machine à produire du tragique. Giraudoux faisait remarquer que la tragédie, c'est une cage centrale où viennent se déchirer les grands fauves, les monstres sacrés que sont les héros tragiques. Butor va rassembler tout son monde dans un immeuble *(Passage de Milan)*, dans un espace urbain sans issue *(L'emploi du temps)*, dans un lycée *(Degrés)*, et, évidemment, ici, dans l'étroite boîte d'un compartiment de chemin de fer. Toutefois de cette rencontre des personnages, aucun tragique ne peut naître. C'est très clair dans *Passage de Milan* où rien ne permet de savoir si la mort de la jeune fille, à l'aube, est un meurtre ou un accident. Cela tient à ce que les personnages tragiques ne se rencontrent pas dans un même lieu par hasard. La fatalité qui les poursuit les lie à jamais entre eux par les liens du sang, par l'amour, par la haine, par le besoin de se venger. Je ne puis m'étendre : songez seulement que pour se débarrasser d'Agrippine, Néron n'a d'autre moyen que de la tuer. Butor met en présence des gens qui ne se connaissent pas entre eux et qui ne s'intéressent pas les uns aux autres, les locataires d'un immeuble parisien, les habitants d'une ville industrielle, les voyageurs d'un compartiment, les élèves d'un lycée; c'est l'intérêt qu'elles prennent au lieu qui les rassemble qui justifie ces communautés de hasard, besoin de s'y loger, d'y travailler, d'y être véhiculées, de s'y instruire. Le plus bel exemple de ces agglomérations d'êtres qui persistent à se sentir étrangers les uns aux autres

est celui des foules qui viennent visiter un haut lieu du tourisme, disons les chutes du Niagara; c'est le thème d'une autre œuvre de Butor : *6 810 000 litres d'eau par seconde*. Il me semble que par cette intention constante et profonde Butor demeure fidèle à l'un des projets fondamentaux du nouveau roman. Dans *La modification*, nous sommes avertis par l'annonce de coïncidences, au sens propre du terme, insignifiantes : « De l'autre côté du corridor, une onze chevaux noire s'arrête devant la mairie » (p. 17); « De l'autre côté du corridor, une onze chevaux noire démarre devant une église, suit une route qui longe la voie, rivalise avec vous de vitesse, se rapproche, s'éloigne, disparaît derrière un bois, reparaît, traverse un petit fleuve avec ses saules et une barque abandonnée, se laisse distancer, rattrape le chemin perdu, puis s'arrête à un carrefour, tourne et s'enfuit vers un village dont le clocher bientôt s'efface derrière un repli de terrain » (p. 21). Comme les hommes et les femmes dans la vie, l'auto et le train se sont côtoyés, ont fait un bout de chemin ensemble et se perdent de vue : où est le tragique ?

Je dois avouer que j'éprouve ici une certaine gêne. Butor mêle deux sortes de hasards et je trouve que l'un nuit à l'autre. Il est vrai que le 15 novembre 1955 un train est parti de la gare de Lyon à 8 h 10; le 15 place du Panthéon existe, ainsi que l'hôtel Quirinale, via Nazionale, à Rome. Il serait exagéré de prétendre que nous sommes revenus aux sottises du roman historique, qui nous obligeait à admettre que le comte Alfred de Vigny, se documentant pour *Cinq-Mars*, était à quatre pattes cent cinquante ans avant sa naissance sous la table du cabinet où Louis XIII et Richelieu discutaient des affaires du royaume. Nous n'avons pas à lire *La modification* comme *Les trois mousquetaires*. Les faits précis réels utilisés dans *La modification* sont assez banals pour que nous les confondions avec le décor, non moins réel, que Léon Delmont voit ou imagine : Paris, Rome, le port de Gênes aperçu de la voie ferrée. Toutefois, en regard de ces réalités prises au hasard, le hasard qui rassemble deux jeunes mariés, un prêtre, un professeur, etc. dans le compartiment du roman sent un peu l'artifice. Il est dangereux de confronter ces personnages qui ont bien l'air d'être imaginaires avec un événement « historique », fût-ce le trajet quotidien d'un train. J'aimerais savoir que, ce jour-là, c'est

Butor et non Léon Delmont qui est bien monté dans un wagon en partance à la gare de Lyon et qu'il y a bien trouvé les compagnons de route qui nous sont présentés. L'histoire de Léon Delmont serait alors née de la rêverie du romancier sur la petite société où il est plongé. Quoi qu'il en soit, on sollicite ma confiance et mon adhésion par deux moyens : la référence au monde réel et un système de cohérences internes au monde romanesque. Faut-il aller jusqu'à dire que le jeu littéraire est légèrement faussé ?

## LE HÉROS

Passons au « héros ». Malgré les apparences encore, Léon Delmont n'existe pas au sens où le père Goriot existait. Je vous ai dit que nous savions sur lui toutes sortes de menus faits. Mais Butor ne nous livre aucun portrait physique de son personnage. Nous ignorons son origine sociale, son enfance et sa jeunesse ; tout au plus peut-on se figurer, par recoupements, qu'il est quelque chose comme ancien élève des H.E.C. L'auteur ne nous présente rien que le flot d'idées et d'images qui coulent dans une conscience pendant que le train va de Paris à Rome. Léon Delmont n'est que le support de ces états de conscience, le lieu où ils défilent ; il n'existe pas plus que le lit d'un fleuve. La modification de ses projets ne se fait pas par un mécanisme psychologique, mais par l'effet, le poids des objets qui tombent sous ses yeux : « S'il n'y avait pas eu ces gens, s'il n'y avait pas eu ces objets et ces images auxquels se sont accrochées mes pensées de telle sorte qu'une machine mentale s'est constituée, faisant glisser l'une sur l'autre les régions de mon existence au cours de ce voyage différent des autres, détaché de la séquence habituelle de mes journées et de mes actes, me déchiquetant, s'il n'y avait pas eu cet ensemble de circonstances, cette donne du jeu, peut-être cette fissure béante en ma personne ne se serait-elle pas produite cette nuit » (p. 274).

C'est ici que Butor et Robbe-Grillet se séparent, mais beaucoup moins qu'on ne le croirait : les quelques lignes que je viens de citer sont à la fois très loin d'une page de Robbe-Grillet, et très proches. Il suffit d'ouvrir *Le voyeur* ou *La*

*jalousie* de Robbe-Grillet pour constater que le personnage témoin ne fait rien que noter l'aspect, la place des objets ou des fragments d'objets qui tombent sous son regard; son angoisse naît directement de cette simple et pure conscience des objets perçus. Butor intercale un chaînon, c'est l'imagination de son « héros ». Léon Delmont ne peut s'empêcher de faire ce que nous faisons tous : il ajoute un sens aux sons qu'il entend, aux couleurs qu'il voit, aux odeurs qu'il sent, et c'est cette fable surajoutée qui le bouleversera. Le mécanisme est donc le suivant : en voyant la silhouette épaisse d'un homme dont on devine bien qu'il est vulgaire et pauvre, Léon Delmont qui gagne sa vie dans les services de vente d'une firme industrielle, et qui va rejoindre sa maîtresse, imagine que ce gros homme est représentant de commerce et qu'il est allé à Paris pour « voir une femme lui aussi, quel genre de femme, dans quelle rue sordide, quel hôtel meublé ? » (p. 107); là-dessus, Léon Delmont remarque : « Il a une alliance » *(ibid.)*, et se laisse aller à lui fabriquer une épouse « qu'il croit tromper si habilement mais qui n'ignore rien en réalité de ce qui l'attire à Paris, qui le laisse mentir le plus souvent sans le contredire, pour avoir la paix, mais qui de temps en temps explose » (p. 108). Butor n'insiste pas. Léon Delmont s'est renvoyé à lui-même sa propre image déformée, caricaturale, et nous comprenons que cette image est purement illusoire, mais l'adultère a pris une hideuse apparence pour l'amant de Cécile : la modification est en marche. L'essentiel est que le processus a été déclenché par la présence - moins encore, par l'aspect extérieur - d'un voyageur. Ce penchant à fabuler apparaît dans *La modification* comme un vertige; le pauvre Léon Delmont, comme s'il avait lu les romans de Robbe-Grillet, voudrait bien avoir la simplicité du Voyeur, par exemple : « Il faut fixer votre attention sur les objets que voient vos yeux, cette poignée, cette étagère, et le filet avec ces bagages, cette photographie de montagnes, ce miroir, cette photographie de petits bateaux dans un port, ce cendrier avec son couvercle et ses vis, ce rideau roulé, cet interrupteur, cette sonnette d'alarme, [...] afin de mettre un terme à ce remuement intérieur, à ce dangereux brassage et remâchage de souvenirs » (p. 157). Tout le malheur de l'homme vient de ce qu'il ajoute des symboles au spectacle des choses. C'est ce que

dit Robbe-Grillet, c'est ce que dit Butor; le premier escamote les symboles, le second montre comment ils naissent et nous torturent.

Cependant Léon Delmont, dans ce jeu de miroirs déformants, tend à s'évanouir. S'il se voit en chacun des voyageurs masculins du compartiment, il finit par se fondre en un être collectif. Cécile et Henriette, elles aussi, s'éparpillent dans toutes les femmes que Léon Delmont a sous les yeux. Des figures qui les représentent tous trois se trouvent réunies simultanément en un même lieu. Le temps n'existe plus, Léon, Cécile et Henriette perdent du coup cet élément de sa personnalité, fondamental pour un héros de roman, son histoire. S'ils peuvent s'incarner momentanément aujourd'hui à différents âges de leur vie en d'autres êtres semblables à eux, eux-mêmes ne sont plus que des incarnations fugitives dans la chaîne des générations humaines. Le roman du XIX$^e$ siècle campait des individus; les individus ont disparu du roman moderne.

A la rigueur, cette fusion de l'individu pourrait être obtenue par les moyens du roman traditionnel. Mais c'est un procédé d'écriture qui va permettre à Butor de dissoudre radicalement Léon Delmont. La première chose qui surprend le lecteur de *La modification*, c'est que le « héros » y est presque partout désigné par la 2$^e$ personne du pluriel. Normalement une page de roman suppose un trio, l'auteur, le personnage dont on parle, et le lecteur. C'est implicite au XIX$^e$ siècle, mais tout à fait explicite dans *Pantagruel*, ancêtre de nos romans. Quand il lui arrive de parler de lui, l'auteur emploie la 1$^{re}$ personne; s'il s'adresse à son lecteur, il emploie la 2$^e$; la 3$^e$ est essentiellement attribuée au personnage. Nous en savons déjà assez pour comprendre que le « nouveau roman » va bouleverser les rapports dans cette sorte de triangle : on ne peut pas grand-chose sur l'auteur et sur le lecteur, qui résistent comme tous les êtres vivants; le seul moyen de changer leurs situations relatives, c'est donc, une fois de plus, de détruire le personnage autant que faire se peut. Le héros de roman était un intermédiaire entre l'auteur et le lecteur, car le premier avait mis beaucoup de lui-même dans sa créature (faut-il rappeler le mot de Flaubert : « Madame Bovary, c'est moi »?), et le « bon » lecteur, celui qui jouait le jeu, se mettait dans la peau du héros, ou de l'héroïne, selon le cas.

Voilà bien une des aliénations dont Nathalie Sarraute, Robbe-Grillet, Butor et les autres voudraient soulager le lecteur. Laissons donc de côté le ton d'accusation que la 2[e] personne du pluriel donne au texte : rappeler à quelqu'un ce qu'il a fait, et dont il ne veut plus se souvenir, ou qu'il ne veut pas avouer, c'est opérer comme un juge qui instruit un procès. En ce sens, *vous*, qui force à reconnaître la vérité, est le moteur même de la modification. Laissons aussi de côté la question de savoir qui parle dans *La modification* : il est sûr que nous entendons d'abord la voix de Léon Delmont se tancer lui-même, découvrir sa vérité qui lui était restée cachée jusqu'à ce malheureux voyage en 3[e] classe. Ces problèmes ont été éclaircis, entre autres, par Butor lui-même dans *Répertoire II*[1]. Je n'insisterai pas non plus sur l'effet pathétique du passage de « vous » à « je » pages 190-191 et page 196 : « Que ferais-je, à quel saint, quelle sainte me vouerais-je ? », « (je ne suis pas vieux, j'ai décidé de commencer à vivre, j'ai repris des forces, tout cela est passé) ». L'accusé se défend et nie, la victime crie de douleur sous la persécution du bourreau. Mais relisons de suite plusieurs pages de *La modification*; peu à peu se produit un glissement; la répétition entêtante de ce « vous » finit par viser le lecteur. Cet accusé piteux n'est plus un fantoche, Léon Delmont, mais chacun de nous, lecteurs, dans nos médiocrités, nos rêves de velléitaires, nos désirs de ne pas être ce que nous sommes, nos dégoûts, nos amertumes, nos petitesses. Léon Delmont a complètement disparu. Dans les moments de sa lecture où le lecteur parvient à ce sentiment, il ne se met pas dans la peau du personnage, il se trouve seul, en face de lui-même : Léon Delmont n'existe pas.

## L'ALIÉNATION. L'ENGAGEMENT

Je suppose que vous voyez comment Butor prétend libérer le lecteur de son asservissement aux habitudes de la littérature française. Les conventions ne sont respectées qu'en apparence dans *La modification*, mais on voit qu'elles y sont contestées dès qu'on remarque des anomalies qui donnent à réfléchir.

1. P. 61 à 72 (voir bibliographie, p. 78).

Cependant Butor ne s'en tient pas là; il ne se contente pas de lutter contre l'aliénation du lecteur par les procédés d'écriture, il va lui présenter un personnage aliéné lui-même, non seulement parce qu'il a tendance à fabuler, mais encore aliéné dans la vie sociale que l'auteur lui attribue. L'essentiel de cela est dit pages 54-55 : « Comment peut-on être directeur de la branche française de la maison Scabelli ? [...] avant d'entrer chez Scabelli, il est bien clair que vous vous moquiez éperdument des machines à écrire et de leur vente; [...] il est entendu que ce sont de bonnes machines, tout aussi bonnes que les autres, de très beaux objets qui fonctionnent bien, mais cela est tout à fait en dehors de votre département, de vos attributions et de vos soucis, car vous ne vous occupez nullement de la production, il s'agit simplement pour vous d'obtenir que les gens achètent une Scabelli au lieu d'une Olivetti ou d'une Hermès, et cela sans raison véritable naturellement, jeu assez amusant parfois, jeu harassant, jeu qui ne vous laisse pas de répit, jeu qui rapporte, jeu qui pourrait vous anéantir entièrement, tel un vice »; certes Léon Delmont gagne bien sa vie, mais « vous n'avez pas tout à fait assez d'argent, vous n'avez pas assez de liberté en face de l'argent, sinon vous seriez en première ». Tout y est, depuis le manque d'intérêt du travail payé jusqu'à la perpétuelle insatisfaction du salarié devant l'insuffisance de ce qu'il gagne, en passant par l'humiliation de celui qui ne produit pas devant celui qui produit. Cependant, pour en revenir à nos problèmes, il faut bien voir que cette analyse de l'aliénation est un retour aux procédés traditionnels du roman. L'aliénation n'est pas combattue par la nouveauté de la technique narrative, mais par la description d'un personnage exemplaire, d'un homme pris dans un engrenage de servitudes qui nous donnera conscience par réflexion de celui où nous sommes pris nous-mêmes. - C'est la réapparition de l'engagement exactement tel que l'envisageait Sartre, même si les moyens auxquels songe Léon Delmont pour se libérer sont bien loin de ceux que Sartre propose. A vrai dire, ce retour à des procédés anciens pour mettre en œuvre un des projets essentiels de l'auteur me paraît grave. *L'emploi du temps* était sûrement d'un style beaucoup plus pur.

# Le salut par l'écriture | 5

## MODIFICATION. PRISE DE CONSCIENCE. REPENTIR

Maintenons-nous provisoirement à ce point de vue d'où *La modification* nous paraît comme un roman engagé. C'est l'histoire de la correction d'une erreur : l'amour de Léon Delmont pour Cécile ne peut lui donner ce qu'il en attendait, une mise en ordre de l'univers.

Il nous faut élargir, pour comprendre cette exigence, notre enquête sur la pensée de Butor. En consultant la liste de ses ouvrages, vous trouverez un livre, publié en 1958, qui s'appelle *Le génie du lieu*. Cette notion de génie des lieux est une des clefs de l'œuvre entière. La Terre n'est plus telle qu'elle était au premier jour : les hommes y ont vécu et y ont laissé leur trace, surtout dans les endroits où ils se sont concentrés pendant des siècles, voire des millénaires. Butor a passé huit mois en Égypte. En contraste avec le désert, figure du néant, la vallée du Nil est un « lieu » : un fleuve, une végétation, des cultures, des animaux, des édifices faits de main d'homme, des hommes. Notez que les limites de ce lieu sont très précisément marquées : c'est la crête des falaises de part et d'autre de la vallée. Le génie du lieu est d'abord comme un fonds religieux qui s'accumule et persiste d'âge en âge [1]; c'est pourquoi il y a pour Léon Delmont une sorte de continuité entre la Rome païenne et la Rome chrétienne; le Panthéon est le signe visible de cette synthèse religieuse. Le génie

---

1. Michel Butor, *Le génie du lieu*, Grasset, 1958, p. 150 sqq.

du lieu peut être seulement une sorte d'influx spirituel né de la présence des hommes : dans notre roman, il n'est pas de site traversé par le chemin de fer où ne surgissent des souvenirs, celui de Lamartine devant le lac du Bourget (p. 70), celui d'un autre voyage en passant, par exemple, à la gare de Sennecey (p. 111). Dès *L'emploi du temps*, la notion de génie du lieu avait pris toute sa force. Il est évident qu'à part la vallée du Nil c'est dans les villes que se ressent surtout l'influence de ceux qui ont habité là autrefois. Signalons au passage que *L'emploi du temps* et, plus encore, *La modification* font apparaître une antithèse entre deux lieux de génie opposés. Les grandes villes industrielles de l'Europe du Nord, les villes où l'on travaille dans l'aliénation vont être hantées par un génie sombre, feu noir pour Bleston, la cité imaginaire de *L'emploi du temps*, pluie et brume pour Paris dans *La modification*. Il est bien naturel dès lors que l'on y rêve de contrées lumineuses, ensoleillées, pays de loisirs et de liberté, pays vers lesquels on se tourne pour avoir une raison de vivre : la Crète et toute la Méditerranée dans le premier roman, Rome dans le nôtre. Butor avoue d'ailleurs que dans son imagination il se fait une sorte de transfert de l'Égypte à Rome [1]. *La modification* est un essai pour superposer deux villes, celle où l'on travaille, Paris, et celle dont on rêve, Rome.

En tout cas, le génie du lieu ne sera ressenti qu'à l'arrivée d'un étranger. Il n'est pas perçu normalement par les autochtones pour qui il est une seconde nature ; il ne sera perceptible que si un nouveau venu décèle en lui une vertu qui le distingue de tous les autres lieux de la terre, si le nouveau venu perçoit une étrangeté et un mystère dont il voudra percer le secret. Le mythe de Thésée et du Labyrinthe est sûrement fondamental dans l'esprit de Butor ; vous le trouverez explicitement évoqué dans *L'emploi du temps*. Mais ce mythe est complété par celui d'Ariane, la jeune fille qui guidera le héros dans les galeries ténébreuses du palais inconnu. Et cela aussi est très clairement dit dans *L'emploi du temps*. Vous comprenez alors ce qu'est l'amour de Léon pour Cécile : « Elle est pour vous le visage de Rome, sa voix et son invitation, [...] elle y est toujours votre introductrice, la porte de

---

[1] *Ibid.*, p. 199-200.

Rome, comme on dit de Marie dans les litanies catholiques qu'elle est la porte du ciel » (p. 237-238). Vous comprenez également pourquoi cet amour est voué à l'échec : les pages 276-277 sont particulièrement révélatrices : hors de Rome, Cécile « perd ses pouvoirs d'intermédiaire », d'une part, et, d'autre part, Thésée et Ariane ne peuvent s'aimer « dans cette espèce de substitut de mariage que vous avez l'intention d'instaurer » après avoir quitté Henriette, car les amants doivent rester au fond étrangers l'un à l'autre : leur amour ne dure que le temps de l'initiation de l'homme au génie du lieu qu'habite la femme.

Pis encore : dans le cas de Cécile et de Rome, peut-être le lieu a-t-il perdu son génie ; Rome n'est plus le centre d'un monde. « Si puissant pendant tant de siècles sur tous les rêves européens, le souvenir de l'Empire est maintenant une figure insuffisante pour désigner l'avenir de ce monde, devenu pour chacun de nous beaucoup plus vaste et tout autrement distribué.

« C'est pourquoi, lorsque vous avez tenté personnellement de le faire s'approcher de vous, son image s'est délabrée ; c'est pourquoi, lorsque Cécile arrive à Paris, elle redevient semblable aux autres femmes » (p. 277). Léon Delmont est un homme d'ordre. On se tromperait si l'on considérait comme hors-d'œuvre les considérations sur la destinée des empires qu'on lit dans cette même page 277 : « Une des grandes vagues de l'histoire s'achève ainsi dans vos consciences, celle où le monde avait un centre, qui n'était pas seulement la terre au milieu des sphères de Ptolémée, mais Rome au centre de la terre, un centre qui s'est déplacé, qui a cherché à se fixer après l'écroulement de Rome à Byzance, puis beaucoup plus tard dans le Paris impérial, etc. » Ces grandes vues cosmiques, qui seraient un peu boursouflées s'il fallait les attribuer à Butor, attribuons-les à Delmont. N'y voyons pas non plus des idées sur la condition humaine, mais l'inquiétude actuelle d'un Européen en 1955, peu conscient sans doute de vivre dans un empire, l'empire américain. En tout cas nous touchons à l'un des besoins profonds de Léon Delmont, trouver un centre au monde dans lequel il vit.

Cécile a peut-être été une bonne prêtresse du génie de Rome, à ceci près qu'elle veut ignorer la Rome chrétienne - elle aurait pu l'être si Rome n'avait perdu son génie. Il faut conti-

nuer à osciller entre Paris et Rome (p. 280). L'astre qui est le symbole de Cécile est la lune : Cécile n'a point de lumière propre, elle réfléchit la lumière romaine (p. 276); lorsque Léon Delmont arrive à Rome à l'aube, il ne voit plus la lune pleine *(ibid.)* qu'il avait vue par la fenêtre du wagon pendant presque tout ce voyage nocturne; et quand il sortira tout à l'heure de la gare, la lune aura disparu (p. 273). Quand il s'aperçoit que l'émerveillement qui émane encore du nom de Rome n'est qu'un vain prestige, impossible à transporter dans une autre capitale, « par exemple Paris » (p. 277), Léon Delmont se détache de Cécile. Ne nous demandons pas trop si cette conception de l'amour qui fait de la femme l'intermédiaire entre l'homme et le monde respecte l'égalité des sexes. L'important est que son amour n'a été pour Léon Delmont ni une libération ni un fil conducteur dans le Labyrinthe. C'est au cours de ce voyage du 15 novembre qu'il le découvre. Et il en tire la conclusion que si l'amour est sans pouvoir, rien dans la vie ne lui donnera le moyen de vaincre l'aliénation et le désordre. Sans foi religieuse ni révolutionnaire, comment chercher le salut ? « Je ne puis espérer me sauver seul », se dit Léon Delmont (p. 274). Logiquement il ne reste qu'une solution, écrire.

## ÉCRIRE

Pour Butor l'homme est un animal qui écrit. Si l'on met bout à bout, sans trop se soucier de la chronologie, les *Entretiens* III et VI de Georges Charbonnier [1], et le dernier essai de *Répertoire III* [2], on obtient *grosso modo* la théorie suivante : les animaux émettent des sons significatifs qui leur permettent de communiquer entre eux, mais on n'a pas encore constaté qu'aucun d'eux ait jamais exécuté un dessin porteur d'un message; seul l'homme le fait. C'est toujours le vieux rêve humaniste qui veut trouver une différence radicale entre l'homme et les autres êtres animés. Cependant, dessiner, c'est introduire dans le monde que nous voyons des structures voulues par l'homme : un jardinier qui dessine un jardin, un

---

[1]. Georges Charbonnier, *Entretiens avec Michel Butor*, Gallimard, 1967, III et VI, p. 37, 69, 71.
[2]. Michel Butor, *Répertoire III*, Éditions de Minuit, 1968; « La littérature, l'oreille et l'œil », p. 399.

architecte qui fait le plan d'un édifice imposent à la matière un ordre humain. L'écriture n'est évidemment qu'un cas particulier du dessin. Je résume : par le langage écrit l'homme met dans le chaos du monde un ordre qui lui permet d'y voir clair. Mais comme la réalité est perpétuellement mouvante, le langage cesse très vite d'être efficace : le langage d'hier ne rend plus compte de la réalité d'aujourd'hui. La plupart des hommes ou bien ne se rendent pas compte que les moyens d'expression figés dont ils se servent sont périmés, ou bien ne s'en soucient pas. Celui qui est pris d'un malaise en s'apercevant que quelque chose fonctionne mal et qui essaiera de maîtriser et d'ordonner efficacement la réalité de son temps, celui-là sera un écrivain. Tout écrit vraiment neuf aide l'auteur et les lecteurs à devenir des hommes authentiquement hommes.

*La modification* sera donc l'histoire d'une inspiration littéraire : prenant conscience d'une « lézarde » (p. 18, 239), d'une « fissure » (p. 27, 191), ou « craquelure » (p. 27), « déchirure » (p. 191), Léon Delmont va peu à peu être subjugué par la présence physique de ce livre qu'il a acheté à la gare de Lyon, simple volume dont on ne sait ni le titre ni l'auteur, qui va redevenir en rêve un cahier de feuilles blanches quand « la pluie en lave les pages » (p. 202). Il va lui falloir remplir la « forme » de ce livre (p. 283) par un livre dont il ne savait même pas « qu'il était en [sa] possession » (p. 229). Mais si l'envie d'écrire prend l'écrivain quand il ressent une certaine inadaptation du langage passé, il n'est pas de livre nouveau qui ne soit la remise en question d'un livre passé. Le livre d'hier apparaît alors comme une esquisse incomplète du livre futur ; il y a en fin de compte entre eux le même rapport qu'entre un livre de prophéties et un livre qui raconte comment les destins ont été accomplis. Les allusions au VI$^e$ chant de *l'Énéide* (p. 83, 215) sont une des clefs de *La modification* : on sait qu'à la fin de ce VI$^e$ chant, Anchise dévoile à Énée le sort futur de Rome. Léon Delmont consulte les deux livres qui sont les livres de prophéties d'un voyageur du xx$^e$ siècle : l'indicateur des chemins de fer (p. 41), et le *Guide bleu (passim)*. Les autres ouvrages dont il est question dans *La modification*, de la méthode *Assimil* aux lettres de Julien l'Apostat, ne me semblent jouer de rôles qu'épisodiques, au moins du point de vue qui est le nôtre en ce moment.

Volume dont Léon Delmont ne lira pas le texte, *Indicateur Chaix*, *Guide bleu*, ces évocations nous ramènent toujours au même fait : un livre est d'abord un objet composé de plusieurs cahiers de papier reliés, papier couvert de signes noirs dont les agencements divers présentent des sens divers. Cet objet est tout à fait semblable à une peinture qui ne nous procure pas de plaisir parce qu'elle représente telle ou telle vue du monde réel, mais parce qu'elle offre aux regards un arrangement harmonieux de taches colorées : le peintre n'a pas peint un paysage, il a peint un tableau. Devant la façade de la cathédrale de Chartres ou le chevet d'une église romane il ne nous vient pas l'idée absurde de chercher quel objet réel l'artiste a voulu imiter, nous portons simplement notre attention sur la convenance réciproque des parties, leur équilibre, leurs symétries et dissymétries. Si nous prenons quelque plaisir à lire *La modification*, comment pouvons-nous croire que nous le tirons de l'histoire assez plate d'un employé de commerce usé par une femme abrutie et quatre enfants médiocres, et qui se console dans les bras d'une dactylo-secrétaire anticléricale ?

Nous trouvons donc la source de notre plaisir dans l'architecture du livre, dans l'agencement et la répétition des motifs, dans les contrastes et les analogies des phrases. Ce thème de l'eau, dont nous parlions tout à l'heure, nous pouvons le trouver intéressant en lui-même, le suivre dans ses métamorphoses, plus ou moins surprenantes, d'un caillot de sang à une lumière bleue. Vous sentez bien que le rythme de ses apparitions, les contrastes qu'il forme avec d'autres thèmes, ou les ressemblances, tout cela nous procure une jouissance esthétique. Butor a voulu créer un objet dont l'effet soit autant que possible comparable à celui que produit, par exemple, la diction d'un vers. Il y a dans

« Le vierge, le vivace et le bel aujourd'hui »

la superposition d'un réseau de sons (v et i), d'une cadence marquée par la répétition de l'article, d'un jeu de contrastes entre les sens des adjectifs, etc. Et en outre il a fallu à Mallarmé conserver les douze syllabes de l'alexandrin classique. J'abrège. Butor veut composer ses romans en faisant jouer les éléments de la narration entre eux comme le poète fait jouer les divers éléments du vers.

# Architecture | 6

C'est cette architecture qu'il nous faut maintenant examiner.

## REMARQUES PRÉLIMINAIRES

Nous devons faire cependant deux remarques préliminaires. D'abord *La modification* n'est pas le livre dont la genèse nous est racontée justement au cours des pages de *La modification*. Nous n'y trouvons rien de semblable à ce qui se passe dans *L'emploi du temps*. Le vrai temps présent de l'homme qui noircit des feuilles de papier n'apparaît pas ici : il est convenu que le présent, c'est le moment où Léon Delmont pense à ceci ou à cela. Et pourtant, c'est bien *La modification* qu'écrira Léon Delmont dès l'après-midi, dans sa chambre d'hôtel, puisqu'il tentera « de faire revivre sur le mode de la lecture cet épisode crucial de [son] aventure, le mouvement qui s'est produit dans [son] esprit accompagnant le déplacement de [son] corps d'une gare à l'autre à travers tous les paysages intermédiaires » (p. 283). Léon Delmont se refuse à « poétiser » la réalité qu'il a vécue, comme il y avait un instant songé (p. 280). A la dernière page du roman, le livre futur nous est présenté comme le pur compte rendu d'une aventure arrivée. Nous retrouvons sur ce plan encore l'ambiguïté de *La modification*, roman traditionnel si c'est le compte rendu d'une aventure arrivée, nouveau roman si un homme, Butor ou Delmont, rassemble en une fiction des éléments disparates : un indicateur Chaix, un livre qu'il ne lit pas, les silhouettes des voyageurs enfermés dans un compartiment.

Nous pouvons remarquer en outre que le déplacement du héros dans l'espace selon un horaire strict suscite quelque difficulté, s'il a des avantages que nous verrons plus loin. La difficulté est la suivante : puisque l'on prétend nous donner le flux même d'une conscience, notre lecture devrait durer le temps d'un parcours de Paris à Rome, et en plus devrait se faire au même rythme que ce flux d'états de conscience, parfaitement chronométré. Or il n'en est rien : nous mettons six heures à lire de suite *La modification;* nous sommes loin des vingt et une heures trente-cinq du trajet. L'écart est estompé par deux moyens, l'indétermination du temps que Léon Delmont passe hors du compartiment, et l'indétermination du temps pendant lequel il dort. Vous avez sans doute vu que le texte nous donne la vie de Léon Delmont seulement dans le compartiment; les blancs qui séparent les parties et les chapitres sont occupés par les moments où il quitte sa place. Vraisemblablement, ces blancs représentent quatre heures et demie au plus. Notre homme aurait donc dormi plus de dix heures; il aurait fait, en plusieurs fois, une bonne nuit ! ce qui n'est pas. En cherchant encore davantage à couper les cheveux en quatre, on s'aperçoit que le débit du roman devient de plus en plus rapide au fil des pages : par exemple nous repartons de Dijon à 11 h 18, page 97 : il nous a fallu lire 1/3 du volume pour faire 1/7 du voyage. Il est 15 h 30 à la page 156 : nous avons dépassé la moitié du volume et nous ne sommes qu'au tiers du voyage, la vitesse du roman a encore diminué. Heureusement car cela réduit le décalage entre la durée de la méditation de Léon Delmont dans son compartiment et le temps de notre lecture. Cette lenteur est due à ces descriptions minutieuses des choses et des gens qui donnent tant de ressemblance - superficielle - entre les œuvres de Robbe-Grillet et le début de *La modification*. On a reproché à ces descriptions d'être plus longues que l'examen que le personnage fait de l'objet; cela ne me paraît pas bien juste puisque la lenteur de débit du texte traduit la lenteur d'une contemplation fascinée. Cependant le roman se précipite à partir du milieu, d'une part grâce à la disparition des descriptions de menus objets, d'autre part grâce aux moments d'inconscience de Léon Delmont dont les sommeils commencent, semble-t-il, page 202, au début du chapitre VII, ce qui permet au train

de faire davantage de kilomètres par page de roman : il est en gare de Gênes, vers 22 h 30, à la page 233, soit aux 2/3 du trajet quand le roman en est aux 4/5 de ses pages. Après quoi Léon Delmont dormant de plus en plus, nous fonçons vers Rome au cours du chapitre VIII : six heures et demie de voyage en 34 pages ! Ces savants calculs vous semblent peut-être mesquins. Cependant nous sommes en droit de les faire à partir du moment où le roman prétend ne dérouler que le contenu d'une conscience.

Mais le déplacement dans l'espace va avoir deux avantages, dont l'un est capital. En premier lieu, le déroulement romanesque ne demandera aucun artifice de datation. Butor évite les *ensuite* et les *le lendemain*. Une fois pour toutes, on nous a fourni, avec l'horaire des chemins de fer, la correspondance entre l'espace, qui n'a aucune réalité pour nous, lecteurs assis dans nos fauteuils, et le temps qui seul nous importe. Il suffira donc à Butor de dire que Léon Delmont est à Dijon ou à Modane pour que nous suivions l'écoulement du temps. Pour des chronologies plus fines, Butor superposera un mouvement à un autre, par exemple pendant que le train roule, la lente translation du contrôleur de compartiment en compartiment (p. 56-57). Mais surtout ce déplacement du héros permet de conserver la solide base continue d'un temps que l'on parcourt comme un chemin, tout en bouleversant l'ordre chronologique du passé vers le futur. C'est un merveilleux procédé pour composer le roman sans violenter les habitudes du lecteur.

Et nous voici parvenus à l'architecture de *La modification*.

## COMPOSITION

*La modification* est divisée en 9 chapitres distribués 3 par 3 entre 3 parties. Dans la 1re partie, les chapitres sont de longueur croissante : 15, 24 et 40 pages dans le tirage en 10/18. Puis viennent 3 chapitres d'égale longueur (31, 32 et 33 p.). Enfin les 3 chapitres de la 3e partie, de longueur décroissante, 38, 34 et 12 pages. La 3e partie est à peu près égale à la 1re (84 p. contre 79), mais l'avant-dernier chapitre (34 p.) est nettement plus long que le 2e (24 p.). Ces mesures

ont leur importance parce qu'elles indiquent les contraintes que l'écrivain s'est imposées, comme le poète s'impose la contrainte de l'alexandrin. Butor considère que c'est indispensable à l'imagination créatrice : sachant qu'il faut boucler tel épisode en tant de pages, l'auteur doit modeler ses songes en conséquence, échappant aux suggestions de ses souvenirs et au laisser-aller de la rêverie. *La modification* offre donc une belle façade classique, symétrique, assez semblable à celle du château de Versailles vers les jardins : un corps de logis, distribué en trois éléments par la décoration de la façade, est placé entre deux ailes à peu près semblables, elles aussi subdivisées chacune en trois parties par le même relief de colonnes et de statues.

Comme nous l'avons dit, Léon Delmont sort du compartiment à toutes les fins de chapitre et y rentre au début du suivant, la page blanche représentant une durée très variable, un repas au wagon-restaurant ou le temps de quelques pas sur le quai pendant un arrêt en gare. Ainsi la masse du texte est comme aérée et le lecteur prend du repos pendant les silences.

A l'intérieur de chaque chapitre, trois moments sont en concurrence : le présent romanesque, le souvenir et l'anticipation [1]. De l'anticipation, ou des anticipations de Léon Delmont, je ne crois pas qu'il y ait grand-chose à dire : il s'agit d'un futur soit immédiat (son séjour à Rome, son retour à Paris), soit un peu plus lointain (la vie en commun avec Cécile); mais je ne crois pas qu'on puisse distinguer plusieurs plans dans l'imprécision de l'imaginaire. Le présent, c'est ce que le personnage voit, entend, ressent dans le compartiment; il faut y joindre les cauchemars, ou plutôt les fins de cauchemars dont Léon Delmont a conscience au réveil; cela complique un peu ce présent en y mêlant un élément intemporel, le monde du rêve, et peut-être une analyse plus fine que la nôtre devrait-elle faire une place spéciale à ces rêves. Il faut noter que toujours, lorsque le roman passe du futur au passé, ou d'un des plans du passé à un autre, il y a passage par le présent. Toute confusion entre des épi-

---

[1]. L'étude qui va suivre, jusqu'au tableau de la p. 59, était écrite quand j'ai pu me procurer, - avec peine, - l'essai de Roudaut, *Répétition et modification dans deux romans de Michel Butor* (voir bibliographie, p. 78). J'ai constaté avec plaisir que j'avais retrouvé le découpage proposé par un des spécialistes les plus avertis du nouveau roman.

sodes distincts est évitée. Butor emprunte à la peinture un de ses procédés : lorsque deux couleurs risquent sur une toile d'interférer fâcheusement à cause du voisinage, le peintre les sépare par un trait noir. Cette délimitation des diverses pièces du récit facilite beaucoup la lecture de *La modification*. Restent les évocations du passé. Ce passé est discontinu. Je vous propose de distinguer six laps de temps passés dont nous pouvons reconstituer sans trop d'efforts le déroulement. Nous les désignerons par la lettre P suivie d'un exposant :

1º Voyage de noces de Léon et d'Henriette à Rome ; printemps 1936 - $P^1$.

2º Deuxième voyage à Rome de Léon et d'Henriette ; hiver 1951-1952 - $P^2$.

3º Début de la liaison entre Léon et Cécile en 1953 ; fin août ($1^{re}$ rencontre dans le train), fin septembre - début octobre ($2^e$ rencontre par hasard à Rome), hiver (Léon devient l'amant de Cécile) - $P^3$.

4º Voyage de Cécile à Paris ; octobre - novembre 1954 - $P^4$.

5º Avant-dernier voyage de Léon à Rome ; du 6 au 11 novembre 1955 - $P^5$.

6º Dernier séjour de Léon Delmont à Paris ; du 11 au 15 novembre 1955 - $P^6$.

Seul $P^3$ n'est pas un laps de temps d'un seul tenant, mais il forme un massif romanesque, l'entrée de Cécile dans la vie de Léon Delmont.

Nous allons maintenant essayer de voir comment ces éléments sont agencés à l'intérieur de chaque chapitre. Nous appellerons C les passages qui décrivent la vie dans le compartiment et qui sont le présent romanesque. Nous appellerons A tous les passages d'anticipation, projets, rêves d'avenir, prévisions de notre personnage.

• Le $1^{er}$ **chapitre** est très simple :

C (p. 9 à 17) - $P^6$ (p. 17 à 21) - C (p. 21 à 23)

• Les choses se compliquent dès le $2^e$ **chapitre**. Alignons-en d'abord les diverses phases :

C (p. 25 à 33) - A (p. 33 à 35) - C (p. 35) - $P^6$ (p. 35 à

38) - A (p. 38) - P⁶ (p. 38 à 41) - A (p. 41 à 43) - P⁶ (p. 43) - C (p. 43-44) - A (p. 44 à 47) - C (p. 47 à 49)

Les A des pages 38 et 41 à 43 sont de nature un peu spéciale : il est inutile de les cerner par des passages C, car c'est une méditation sur l'indicateur des chemins de fer, que Léon Delmont tient dans ses mains, et qu'il avait déjà dans sa serviette lors de P⁶. Ces deux passages A renferment un jeu très subtil sur les temps des verbes, jeu qui suggère une sorte de style indirect libre, avec un glissement final au futur. Il est évident que ce chapitre est construit comme le livre entier, symétriquement par rapport à un centre : C-A-C-P⁶-A-P⁶-A-P⁶-C-A-C. Le 1ᵉʳ chapitre s'est en quelque manière gonflé comme une éponge par des injections de A dans les trois massifs C, P⁶ et C; on pourrait dire également que le 1ᵉʳ chapitre s'est déployé comme un éventail pour donner le 2ᵉ. Remarquons en outre que seul un passé est évoqué, le plus proche.

• Le **3ᵉ chapitre** est presque plus simple :

C (p. 51 à 58) - A (p. 58 à 62) - C (p. 62-63) - P⁶ (p. 63 à 67) - C (p. 68) - P³ (p. 68 à 71) - C (p. 71) - P⁶ (p. 71 à 84) - C (p. 84-85) - A (p. 85 à 87) - C (p. 87 à 91)

Il faut toutefois signaler que le long P⁶ de la page 71 à la page 84 est coupé par deux fois comme pour offrir un repos au lecteur : pages 74-75, un paragraphe commence au futur, continue au passé et finit au conditionnel; pages 81-82, trois paragraphes où l'on glisse du présent au futur par le détour d'une phrase au passé. Il s'agit de méditations assez voisines des passages des pages 38 et 41 à 43 que j'ai désignées par A dans le 2ᵉ chapitre parce qu'elles m'ont semblé plus nettement détachées du contexte que celles du 3ᵉ chapitre. En tout cas, le schéma reste le même, mais au centre du chapitre apparaît une narration P³; l'éventail s'est encore un peu ouvert. Au point où nous en sommes, du moins, c'est la rencontre avec Cécile (P³) qui contraste le plus avec l'affreuse dernière semaine (P⁶) auprès d'Henriette : P³ s'installe à la place d'honneur, repoussant de part et d'autre P⁶.

• La 2ᵉ partie semble bâtie autrement. Le **chapitre 4** aurait la structure suivante :

C (p. 95 à 98) - A (p. 98 à 100) - C (p. 100-101) - P$^5$ (p. 101 à 103) - C (p. 103) - A (p. 103 à 106) - C (p. 106 à 108) - P$^5$ (p. 109 à 111) - C (p. 111-112) - P$^3$ (p. 112 à 114) - C (p. 114) - P$^5$ (p. 114 à 117) - C (p. 117 à 119) - P$^3$ (p. 119 à 121) - C (p. 121) - P$^2$ (p. 121-122) - C (p. 122) - P$^3$ (p. 122 à 124) - C (p. 124 à 126)

Peu de remarques : le passage P$^5$ des pages 101 à 103 contient deux brèves allusions au présent, mais, dans nos préoccupations actuelles, cela paraît sans conséquence. La symétrie dans ce chapitre est plus difficile à voir et il faut opérer quelques substitutions. Pourtant, au centre, nous trouvons maintenant le passage P$^3$ des pages 112 à 114, encadré par deux passages P$^5$, ce qui nous donne un noyau composé ainsi : C-P$^5$-C-P$^3$-C-P$^5$-C (de la p. 106 à la p. 119). Ce noyau est précédé d'un groupe C-A-C-P$^5$-C-A; et il est suivi par P$^3$-C-P$^2$-C-P$^3$-C. Il saute aux yeux que ces deux groupements sont construits de la même manière, avec des éléments différents : P$^5$ est au milieu du 1$^{er}$, encadré par A, P$^2$ est au milieu du 2$^e$, encadré par P$^3$. Ainsi ce 4$^e$ chapitre commence par C-A-C, comme le 2$^e$ et le 3$^e$; il gravite autour de P$^3$, comme le 3$^e$ chapitre. Butor ne passe donc pas d'un chapitre à l'autre par un contraste, mais par variation du rythme. Ce chapitre 4 est le chapitre de l'amour de Léon pour Cécile, pris dans ses débuts et au point où il en était arrivé lors du dernier voyage de Léon à Rome. Ajoutons que cependant P$^2$ apparaît à l'un des centres secondaires du chapitre; mais ce malheureux séjour d'Henriette à Rome en hiver est tout à la gloire de Cécile.

• Voici le plan du **chapitre 5** :

C (p. 127 à 130) - A (p. 130-131) - C (p. 131) - P$^5$ (p. 131-132) - C (p. 132) - P$^4$ (p. 132 à 134) - C (p. 134) - P$^5$ (p. 134-135) - C (p. 135) - A (p. 135 à 137) - C (p. 137 à 141) - P$^5$ (p. 142-143) - C (p. 143) - P$^4$ (p. 143 à 145) - C (p. 145) - P$^2$ (p. 145 à 150) - C (p. 150) - P$^4$ (p. 150 à 152) - C (p. 152-153) - P$^5$ (p. 153 à 156) - C (p. 156 à 158)

Il faut noter que le passage P$^5$ des pp. 142-143 contient deux allusions au futur, mais imaginées dans le cadre du séjour de Léon à Rome du 6 au 11 novembre 1955. Nous devons bien admettre que nous trouvons des rappels, des

échos d'un plan du récit à un autre, quelque nettes que soient les coupures dans *La modification*. Le début du chapitre est celui du chapitre 4 : C-A-C-P$^5$-C; le centre est un passage C, celui des pages 137 à 141. La structure d'ensemble est celle du chapitre 4 : de part et d'autre de C, deux suites dont la première a pour centre P$^4$ (p. 132 à 134) et la seconde gravite autour de P$^2$ (p. 145 à 150). Voici la première :

C-A-C-P$^5$-C-P$^4$-C-P$^5$-C-A

et la seconde :

P$^5$-C-P$^4$-C-P$^2$-C-P$^4$-C-P$^5$-C

C'est donc une description de la vie dans le compartiment qui est au centre de ce chapitre, et par là même au centre du roman : Léon Delmont y raconte ses amours avec Henriette sous couleur d'imaginer celles de « Pierre » et d' « Agnès »; faut-il voir là le signe d'un retour vers Henriette ou celui d'un irrémédiable détachement ? Nous sommes au moment où tout peut basculer d'un côté ou de l'autre. P$^2$ est toujours au centre de la seconde moitié du chapitre. Mais P$^4$, le voyage de Cécile à Paris, fait son apparition, d'abord au centre de la 1$^{re}$ moitié du chapitre, puis pour encadrer, épisode désastreux lui-même, le désastreux voyage d'Henriette à Rome en 1951-1952. L'amour de Léon pour Cécile est sur la pente descendante.

• Passons au **6$^e$ chapitre**; en voici le schéma :

C (p. 159 à 161) - A (p. 161 à 163) - C (p. 163) - P$^5$ (p. 163-164) - C (p. 164-165) - P$^4$ (p. 165-166) - C (p. 166-167) - P$^5$ (p. 167 à 169) - C (p. 169 à 171) - P$^5$ (p. 171 à 174) - C (p. 174-175) - P$^4$ (p. 175 à 179) - C (p. 179) - P$^2$ (p. 179 à 183) - C (p. 183) - P$^4$ (p. 183 à 188) - C (p. 188 à 192)

Nous retrouvons le début de chapitre caractéristique de la 2$^e$ partie : C-A-C-P$^5$-C. Le centre du chapitre est encore C, le C des pages 169 à 171. Cette fois il s'agit des rapports « du signor Lorenzo » avec sa femme, sa dactylo, son patron, et c'est la caricature de la vie de Léon. Ce passage C est au milieu d'une suite tout à fait symétrique : C-P$^4$-C-P$^5$ d'un côté et P$^5$-C-P$^4$-C de l'autre. Dans la 2$^e$ moitié du chapitre, P$^2$ reste encadré par deux P$^4$, comme au chapitre 5. Toutefois il n'y a pas symétrie exacte entre la

1$^{re}$ moitié du chapitre et la 2$^e$, car dans la 1$^{re}$ nous avons bien P$^4$ encadré par deux P$^5$, mais ce centre secondaire est en 6$^e$ position à partir du début alors que le centre secondaire P$^2$ est en 4$^e$ position à partir de la fin. En fait tout le glissement par rapport au chapitre précédent est dans le passage de « Pierre et Agnès » au « signor Lorenzo »; le reste reprend les mêmes éléments dans une disposition presque semblable, après suppression de deux groupes C - P$^5$.

• Nous abordons la 3$^e$ partie. Deux éléments nouveaux apparaissent : les sommeils de Léon Delmont et ses projets d'écrire. Nous allons conserver notre système de découpage, mais il est probable qu'on pourrait utiliser ces deux éléments pour trouver une autre composition à cette dernière partie. Quoi qu'il en soit, voici le plan du **chapitre 7** :

C (p. 195 à 200) - A (p. 200 à 204) - C (p. 204-205) - P$^5$ (p. 205 à 208) - C (p. 208-209) - P$^4$ (p. 209 à 213) - C (p. 213 à 218) - P$^5$ (p. 218 à 220) - C (p. 220) - P$^4$ (p. 220 à 226) - C (p. 226-227) - P$^1$ (p. 227 à 230) - C (p. 230 à 233)

Rien n'est changé dans la structure du début, et c'est toujours un passage C qui est au centre (p. 213 à 218). Dans la seconde moitié, nous retrouvons P$^5$ et P$^4$, dans un ordre qui est le même que dans la 1$^{re}$ moitié, au lieu d'être inversé pour la symétrie. Mais la grande innovation de ce chapitre, c'est pour la première fois l'évocation de P$^1$ qui fait pendant à A, d'un bout du chapitre à l'autre. Le voyage de noces avec Henriette (P$^1$), par cette symétrie, est comme ramené du passé vers l'avenir : Henriette va reprendre sa place. Il est probable d'ailleurs qu'il faudrait ordonner les temps dans *La modification* comme ils sont ordonnés dans l'Évangile selon saint Luc, c'est-à-dire les ranger d'après le cycle annuel des saisons : nous sommes en novembre, l'été et l'automne viennent de finir, tristement, dans la pluie; l'hiver et le printemps sont encore à venir, gonflés d'espoir. Or tous les souvenirs de Léon Delmont concernant Cécile sont datés de l'été ou de l'automne, mais c'est en hiver et au printemps qu'Henriette est venue à Rome. En tout cas la construction du chapitre 7 semble montrer que l'avenir s'ouvre de nouveau devant Henriette.

• Le **chapitre 8** est la répétition à peu près exacte du 7e, avec les mêmes éléments. Toutefois les deux passages $P^5$ viennent dans la 1re moitié, et les deux $P^4$ dans la 2e :

C (p. 235 à 239) - A (p. 239 à 246) - C (p. 246-247) - $P^5$ (p. 247 à 249) - C (p. 249 à 253) - $P^5$ (p. 253 à 256) - C (p. 256) - $P^4$ (p. 256 à 259) - C (p. 259 à 261) - $P^4$ (p. 261 à 263) - C (p. 264) - $P^1$ (p. 264 à 267) - C (p. 267 à 269)

Le centre, un très bref passage C à la page 256, évoque la substitution de la lune elle-même à son image réfléchie dans la vitre protectrice d'une photographie : une réalité remplace une vaine image et sa lumière « fait briller, ranime les écailles losanges du tapis chauffant métallique ». Henriette chasse Cécile.

• Le découpage du **chapitre 9** que je vous propose demandera quelques justifications. Le voici :

C (p. 271-272, jusqu'à « c'est déjà la banlieue romaine ») - A (p. 272-273) - C (p. 273-274) - $P^5$ (p. 275) - C (p. 276 à 278) - $P^4$ (p. 278-279) - C (p. 279 à 281) - $P^1$ (p. 281-282) - C (p. 282-283)

J'ai fait rentrer dans le premier passage C deux paragraphes au futur. Vous pouvez constater qu'il ne s'agit pas du même futur que celui que nous lisons à partir de « Vous allez arriver », que je place sous la rubrique A : d'abord ces anticipations A portent sur un futur assez prochain, ce qui n'est pas le cas des 3e et 4e paragraphes de la page 272, et surtout les anticipations A représentent toujours des images dont Léon Delmont essaie la vraisemblance en tâchant de se les figurer, alors que les futurs de la page 272 sont les conséquences d'un raisonnement : « Je continuerai par conséquent. » Cela dit ce chapitre est très simple : il commence par la suite habituelle, il a pour centre le C des pages 276 à 278 où se trouvent les grandes considérations politiques de Léon Delmont. De part et d'autre, à $P^5$ répond $P^4$ et à A répond $P^1$, comme dans toute la fin du livre.

Une dernière remarque : le nombre des éléments d'un chapitre n'est pas tout à fait libre : il est évident qu'il doit être impair; mais en outre, l'élément C ne peut venir au centre que s'il y a 5, 9, 13, 17 ou 21 éléments.

Pour y voir clair, je vous propose de dresser le tableau suivant où les symétries et les parallélismes sautent aux yeux :

| N° DU CHAPITRE | COMPOSITION | | | NOMBRE D'ÉLÉMENTS |
|---|---|---|---|---|
| 1 | C | $= P^6 =$ | C | 3 |
| 2 | C A C | $P^6 A = P^6 = A P^6$ | C A C | 11 |
| 3 | C A C | $P^6 C = P^3 = C P^6$ | C A C | 11 |
| 4 | C A C - $P^5$ - C A | $C P^5 C = P^3 = C P^5 C$    $P^3$ C - $P^2$ - C $P^3$ C | | 19 |
| 5 | C A C $P^5$ C - $P^4$ - C $P^5$ C A = C | $= P^5 C P^4 C - P^2 - C P^4$    C $P^5$ C | | 21 |
| 6 | C A C $P^5$ C    $P^4$ | C $P^5 = C = P^5$ C    $P^4$ | C $P^2$    C $P^4$ C | 17 |
| 7 | C A C $P^5$ C | $P^4 = C = P^5$ | C $P^4$    C $P^1$ C | 13 |
| 8 | C A C $P^5$ C | $P^5 = C = P^4$ | C $P^4$    C $P^1$ C | 13 |
| 9 | C A C $P^5$ | $= C =$ | $P^4$    C $P^1$ C | 9 |

## MOTIVATIONS : STRUCTURE ET SIGNIFICATION ROMANESQUE; STRUCTURE ET SENS DES MOTS

Voilà un fastidieux étalage de lettres et de chiffres. Pour simplifier j'ai cru pouvoir omettre les premiers et les derniers mots de chaque élément; il m'a semblé que nulle part il n'y avait à se tromper sur l'endroit de la coupure. Mais quand je vous disais que *La modification* est un ouvrage d'architecture, vous n'étiez pas forcés de me croire sur parole et il me fallait donner des preuves. D'ailleurs il est bien entendu que l'on peut faire des analyses plus fines : je vous renvoie à l'étude de M<sup>me</sup> Van Rossum-Guyon[1], et aussi à un essai de Jean Roudaut[2]. Il y a sûrement beau-

---

1. Françoise Van Rossum-Guyon, *op. cit.*
2. Jean Roudaut, *op. cit.*

coup d'autres ordonnances systématiques à découvrir dans notre roman : quand ce ne serait que le tissu des répétitions de mots, des retours d'expressions, des symétries dans l'évocation des situations ; un seul exemple, pour vous mettre sur la piste : page 173, à Rome, Cécile dit à Léon : « Embrasse-moi », et le malheureux répond : « Pas ici ; dans la *pizzeria* », et page 175, à Paris, à une invite analogue, il se fait écho à lui-même : « Pas ici, pas dans ce quartier, ma chérie. » Mais avais-je besoin de vous signaler ce cas ? Butor nous alerte directement par la longue méditation de son héros devant deux toiles symétriques de Pannini, d'autant plus clairement que ces toiles sont médiocres (p. 66-67 et 71-72). Bref, cherchez et vous trouverez.

Il doit être bien entendu qu'au point où nous sommes parvenus nous sommes au seuil de l'essentiel. Ces jeux de puzzle que je vous propose vous paraissent peut-être assez vains. Un roman est fait pour être lu et non pour être disséqué. Mais dès la première lecture, nous avons le sentiment net que *La modification* est agencée selon une organisation stricte. Il était bon de vérifier, au moins en gros, ce sentiment, c'est-à-dire de vérifier qu'on ne nous raconte pas une pseudo-histoire vraie, qu'on ne prétend pas imiter la nature, faire concurrence à quelque réalité sociale. Le livre en question est un tout harmonieux et organisé, c'est une œuvre d'art.

S'il s'agissait seulement de provoquer je ne sais quel plaisir esthétique, nous en reviendrions à votre objection : à quoi bon s'être donné tant de peine ? Bâtir une façade parfaitement belle à une maison dans laquelle on ne peut se loger est tout à fait dérisoire. Il nous reste à comprendre que si l'écrivain veut transmettre - osons dire le mot - un message, il le fait justement par la mise en place des éléments de récit : c'est la juxtaposition et le voisinage qui sont significatifs. Prenons un exemple. Voici la première rencontre de Léon et de Cécile, au 3[e] chapitre (p. 68 à 71). Si nous lisons ce passage à sa place dans le contexte, nous éprouvons une sorte d'allégresse, d'espoir vers la liberté et le bonheur. Nous sentons bien que cette joie vient en partie du fait que nous venons de lire les pages 63 à 67 où Léon Delmont erre misérablement dans Paris pour ne pas rentrer chez lui, auprès d'Henriette, des enfants et de la bonne. Après l'évo-

cation des quelques heures éblouissantes en face d'une inconnue qui sera Cécile, nous retombons dans une visite au musée du Louvre, dans un restaurant où les spaghetti ne valent rien, etc. Quand nous aborderons la 2ᵉ partie, il restera dans notre mémoire la lumière de ces pages 68 à 71, placées au milieu du chapitre que nous venons de lire. Isolons maintenant ces pages 68 sqq., oublions ce qui précède et ce qui suit : il ne reste qu'un déjeuner au wagon-restaurant pendant lequel des propos insipides ont été échangés entre un monsieur de bonne apparence et une jeune femme solitaire très intéressante ; c'est bête à pleurer. Nous avons été pris au piège ; nous partageons l'illusion de Léon Delmont pour qui Cécile apparaît comme la « porte » du bonheur. Butor a évité les deux écueils inévitables dans un roman classique : ou bien l'auteur embellissait la scène pour nous faire éprouver la joie des amours naissantes, après quoi tout serait allé à vau-l'eau quand nous nous serions aperçus que Cécile n'était que Cécile ; ou bien il nous tirait par la manche pour nous avertir que tout était grotesque et il récrivait la première conversation entre Léon et Mᵐᵉ Bovary. Butor a décrit une scène très plate, - et nous ne nous en doutons pas. Seul l'agencement des éléments du récit lui a permis de dire ce qu'il avait à dire. Je ne puis multiplier les exemples. *La modification* ne pourrait se dérouler dans un autre ordre que celui qui nous est donné.

Il faut aller plus loin. Si obscur que soit notre sentiment d'être devant une œuvre d'art composée, cela suffit : nous savons que nous sommes dans l'imaginaire. Un tableau comme celui que je viens de vous proposer nous en donne l'assurance. Il s'agit d'un art figuratif, certes, pour retourner au langage de la peinture : c'est-à-dire que les personnages et les objets sont reconnaissables aux yeux du public le plus traditionaliste ; la nouveauté de l'œuvre n'est pas là. Mais nous avons été libérés des habitudes du roman « bourgeois » du siècle dernier. Si nous avons été des lecteurs loyaux de *La modification*, ce n'est pas à Léon Delmont qu'il est arrivé quelque chose, c'est à nous, non que nous revivions les aventures romaines de Léon Delmont en amour et en politique européenne, mais il nous est arrivé ce qui nous arrive quand nous lisons un poème ou quand nous

regardons une peinture. Les romanciers ont fait la même révolution que les poètes et les peintres : depuis Baudelaire un poème est un poème, depuis les impressionnistes une peinture est une peinture. Ces romanciers des environs de 1950 tentent d'écrire des romans qui soient exclusivement des romans. Après cela, si Rimbaud en écrivant les *Illuminations* ou Picasso en peignant Guernica ont espéré faire surgir un homme nouveau, pourquoi cet espoir serait-il refusé aux romanciers ?

Reste à savoir dans quelle mesure *La modification* renouvelle notre langage. Mme Van Rossum-Guyon a tenté de montrer [1] que le mot « porte », pour quiconque a lu notre roman, n'a plus tout à fait le même sens qu'auparavant ; il est certain que le mot revient presque à chaque page du roman, soit dans un de ses innombrables sens métaphoriques : porte du compartiment, porte de Rome, arcs de triomphe, porte de communication entre la chambre de Cécile et la chambre voisine dans son appartement romain, portes fermées des églises romaines, tunnels du chemin de fer, seuils, pas à franchir, frontières et gares qui sont les modernes portes des villes ; jusqu'à Cécile elle-même qui est appelée « porte de Rome »; sans parler de toutes les portes que l'on trouve dans les cauchemars de Léon Delmont. *La modification* elle-même est une porte, celle qui ouvre sur la nécessité d'écrire. Il est certain que lorsque nous lisons « Un autre homme passe la tête par la porte et regarde des deux côtés » (p. 282), l'effet produit est exactement celui que cherche Butor : un geste insignifiant pour celui qui n'a pas lu *La modification* s'est peu à peu chargé de sens au fil des pages ; il y a eu création d'un symbole interne au roman ; cet homme, debout sur un seuil, le corps dehors et la tête dedans, explore le passé et l'avenir. J'avoue ne pas être bien convaincu : cette mise en question quasi exhaustive des emplois et sens du mot *porte* et des mots qui s'y rattachent par leur sens me paraît moins enrichissante que la lecture de deux ou trois vers d'*Alcools*, d'Apollinaire. Il faudrait faire la même enquête sur le mot *réseau* ou *grille*. Tout est réseau dans *La modification*. La critique a beaucoup blâmé la promotion d'un tapis chauffant de wagon au rang de *leit-motiv*.

---

[1]. *Op. cit.*, p. 263 sqq.

Ce tapis chauffant qui offre l'aspect d'une grille est pourtant le cœur du roman. Il se présente d'abord comme l'objet le moins signifiant ; on en parlera parce que nos yeux errent également sur un tapis chauffant, sur un prêtre et sa soutane, sur un professeur et son livre. Les diverses figures que danseront les ordures à la surface de ce tapis n'auront aucun sens ; on n'en pourra rien dire sinon « c'était ainsi tout à l'heure, c'est ainsi maintenant » ; le temps se déroule, le monde change, les objets sont ici et là. Tout cela est essentiel, car tandis que le philosophe se demande si nous sommes et pourquoi nous sommes, le romancier nous dit que nous sommes là, c'est un fait, et qu'il n'y a pas d'explication à donner. Le gibier du romancier, c'est le concret, le tapis chauffant dans un compartiment de 3$^e$ classe le 15 novembre 1955. Toutefois, ce tapis deviendra l'image même du monde, constellé d'étoiles (p. 143) : les rues dans les villes, les routes et les lignes de chemin de fer sur les continents sont des réseaux, ainsi que les rapports des hommes entre eux et la structure d'un roman ; et tantôt le réseau ou la grille sera un moyen de communiquer, tantôt ce sera l'obstacle qui s'interpose entre nous et l'objet de nos désirs (p. 160). Si nous avions le temps, je pense que nous arriverions à montrer une importante variation de valeur des mots *réseau* et *grille* pour le lecteur de *La modification*. Si c'est vrai, ce roman est à la ressemblance du monde aux yeux d'un humaniste : les objets, un tapis chauffant, ne signifient rien, ce sont les hommes qui, pour leur malheur ou pour leur grandeur, leur donnent un sens.

# Conclusion

Ces quelques pages sur *La modification* ne sont nullement une étude qui rende compte vraiment du texte. Je n'ai visé qu'à vous alerter sur la possibilité de lire un roman autrement que nous ne le faisons lorsque nous lisons les romans d'autrefois.

Je persiste à préférer *L'emploi du temps* : la résolution que prend Léon Delmont de nous raconter son périple me paraît moins belle que les balbutiements de Jacques Revel, héros de *L'emploi du temps*. Pour se retrouver dans une cité confuse, sans issue, embrasée d'un feu sombre, Jacques Revel se mettait à écrire désespérément et se perdait dans ses papiers noircis. Au contraire, tout se passe comme si écrire faisait le salut de Léon Delmont, à la recherche de la liberté et d'un ordre dans le monde, au terme d'une expérience manquée ; c'est en somme assez rassurant. *La modification* est, je crois, moins riche que *L'emploi du temps*.

Toutefois *La modification* est de tous les romans celui qui peut le mieux réduire nos habitudes de lecteurs façonnés par Balzac et par Flaubert. Il est en outre certain que c'est mieux qu'un ouvrage simplement important. La superposition de deux techniques était une gageure et Michel Butor a gagné son pari. Le roman nouveau insinué sous le roman conventionnel détruit sourdement ce dernier. Au bout du compte c'est l'esprit du lecteur qui est modifié : comme saint Christophe, mais un saint Christophe sournois et contraignant, Léon Delmont nous transporte d'une rive à l'autre, d'un univers romanesque à un pays inconnu. Il me reste à souhaiter qu'en lisant *La modification* vous trouviez plaisir à être mystifié par l'humour de l'écrivain : il ne semble nous proposer une histoire sentimentale que pour nous faire vivre une aventure intellectuelle, car nous sommes, vous et moi, les vrais héros du roman.

# Annexes

## VIE DE BUTOR
## RAPPROCHÉE DES GRANDS ÉVÉNEMENTS
## CONTEMPORAINS JUSQU'EN 1955

| | VIE ET ŒUVRE DE BUTOR | ÉVÉNEMENTS CONTEMPORAINS |
|---|---|---|
| 1926 | Naissance de Michel Butor, dans une petite ville du Nord. Il est le quatrième d'une famille de sept enfants. Milieu catholique pratiquant. Son père fait partie des cadres supérieurs du Chemin de fer du Nord. | Pour mémoire : Après la chute du franc, la droite revient au pouvoir en France. Ministère Poincaré. — L'Allemagne entre à la SDN. |
| 1929 | La famille vient s'établir à Paris, se loge rue du Cherche-Midi, dans un quartier qui est le centre intellectuel du monde catholique parisien. Michel B. fait ses études primaires à l'École paroissiale. *Passage de Milan* et *Degrés* permettent sans doute de restituer l'atmosphère de ce milieu. On fait de la musique (piano, violon) ; le père de M. B. dessine et grave. | Crise économique aux États-Unis. — La France est en pleine prospérité, au moins apparente. Débuts du cinéma parlant. — La crise mondiale ne sera sensible en France qu'à partir de 1932. La famille Butor n'a pas dû être assez touchée pour que la récession fût perceptible à l'enfant. |
| 1933 | | Hitler prend le pouvoir. Michel Butor a six ans ; il a pu comprendre qu'un malheur était arrivé. |
| 1934 | | A Paris, la droite tente de prendre le pouvoir par l'émeute du 6 février place de la Concorde. Michel Butor a probablement ressenti l'émotion générale. |
| 1936 | Sans changer de quartier, les Butor viennent habiter rue de Sèvres, en face de la fontaine du Fellah. M. B. commence ses études secondaires à l'École Saint-François-Xavier. | Le triomphe du Front populaire en France et le début de la guerre civile en Espagne n'ont certainement pas échappé à l'enfant. |
| 1938 | | Accords de Munich. |
| 1939 | Les Butor s'installent à Évreux. M. B. est élève du collège des Jésuites. | Élection de Pie XII. — Début de la guerre mondiale. *(Nous rappelons les principales phases de la guerre, bien que tout se passe, à travers l'œuvre de Butor, comme si ces années avaient été pour lui la traversée d'un désert. En revanche il nous faut noter désormais les principaux événements littéraires.)* |

| VIE ET ŒUVRE DE BUTOR | ÉVÉNEMENTS CONTEMPORAINS |
|---|---|
| **1940** Les Butor sont dans le Sud-Ouest au moment de la débâcle ; ils reviennent à Paris tout de suite après. M. B. entre en seconde au lycée Louis-le-Grand. Lectures extra-scolaires. Premiers vers. Dessins. Découverte du surréalisme en poésie et en peinture. | Invasion et défaite de la France. Départ du général de Gaulle pour Londres. Le maréchal Pétain devient chef de l'État. Armistice. |
| **1941** | Invasion de l'URSS par l'Allemagne. Entrée en guerre des États-Unis. |
| **1942** Élève de Philosophie. Par son grand-oncle, Édouard Le Roy, professeur de philosophie au Collège de France, M. B. est introduit dans les colloques philosophiques du château de la Fortelle (cf. *Portrait de l'artiste en jeune singe*). | Bataille de Stalingrad. Débarquement des Alliés en Afrique du Nord. — Camus, *L'étranger*; Fr. Ponge, *Le parti pris des choses*; Montherlant, *La reine morte*. |
| **1943** Entre en hypokhâgne à Louis-le-Grand. Lectures extra-scolaires. | Fin de la bataille de Stalingrad. Débarquement allié en Italie. — Sartre, *L'être et le néant*; Vercors, *Le silence de la mer*. — Anouilh, *Antigone*; J.-L. Barrault met en scène *Le soulier de satin* de Claudel. |
| **1944** Étudiant libre à la Sorbonne, pour y préparer la licence de Lettres classiques. | Débarquement en Normandie ; libération de la France. Gouvernement provisoire à Paris, dirigé par de Gaulle. — Sartre, *Huis clos*. — Les Français découvrent les poèmes écrits sous l'occupation, la littérature et le cinéma des alliés. |
| **1945** Échec aux examens. Premières publications. | Conférence de Yalta ; mort de Roosevelt ; capitulation de l'Allemagne ; Bombe sur Hiroshima ; capitulation du Japon. — Camus, *Caligula*; Mauriac, *Les mal-aimés*. |
| **1946** Licencié en philosophie. | Départ du général de Gaulle. Début de la guerre d'Indochine. — Jacques Prévert, *Paroles*. |
| **1947** Diplôme de philosophie, préparé sous la direction de Bachelard *(Les mathématiques et l'idée de nécessité)*. Engagé par Jean Wahl au Collège philosophique. Vacances en Allemagne. | Plan Marshall. Indépendance de l'Inde. En France, les institutions de la IVe République commencent à fonctionner : Vincent Auriol président de la République. Départ des ministres communistes ; grandes grèves. — Nathalie Sarraute, *Portrait d'un inconnu*; Boris Vian, *L'écume des jours*; Camus, *La peste*; Genet, *Les bonnes*; Audiberti, *Le mal court*. — Jean Vilar au festival d'Avignon. |

| | VIE ET ŒUVRE DE BUTOR | ÉVÉNEMENTS CONTEMPORAINS |
|---|---|---|
| 1948 | Présenté à André Breton. | A Prague, élimination des ministres non communistes. Blocus de Berlin. Assassinat de Gandhi. — René Char, *Fureur et mystère*. Montherlant, *Le maître de Santiago*. |
| 1949 | Échec à l'agrégation de philosophie. | Adhésion de la France au Pacte Atlantique. Victoire communiste en Chine. — Bernanos, *Dialogues des Carmélites*; Ionesco, *La cantatrice chauve*. |
| 1950 | Professeur au lycée de Sens. Second échec à l'agrégation. Dépose un sujet de thèse : *Les aspects de l'ambiguïté en littérature et l'idée de signification*. Vacances en Allemagne. Envoyé comme professeur de français à Minieh, en Égypte. Commence *Passage de Milan*. | Guerre de Corée. |
| 1951 | Lecteur à l'Université de Manchester. | Julien Gracq, *Le rivage des Syrtes*. |
| 1952 | Premier voyage en Italie. | Révolution en Égypte. — Beckett, *En attendant Godot*. Mauriac reçoit le prix Nobel. |
| 1953 | Retour à Paris. | Mort de Staline; Eisenhower devient Président des États-Unis; déposition du sultan du Maroc. — Robbe-Grillet, *Les gommes*. |
| 1954 | Publication de *Passage de Milan*. Professeur au lycée français de Salonique. Commence *L'emploi du temps*. | Chute du camp retranché de Dien-Bien Phu; accords de Genève. Début de la guerre d'Algérie. — Françoise Sagan, *Bonjour tristesse*. |
| 1955 | Professeur à l'École supérieure de préparation des professeurs de français à l'étranger. | Indépendance du Maroc; retour de Bourguiba à Tunis. — Teilhard de Chardin, *Le phénomène humain*. |
| 1956 | Publie *L'emploi du temps*. Professeur à l'École internationale de Genève. Y fait la connaissance de sa future femme. Commence *La modification*. Prix Fénéon. | Déstalinisation. Révolte et répression à Budapest. Expédition de Suez. Camus, *La chute*. |
| 1957 | Publie *La modification*. Le prix Goncourt est attribué à Roger Vailland (*La loi*), mais M. B. obtient le prix Théophraste-Renaudot. | Signature des traités du Marché commun et de l'Euratom. Premier Spoutnik. Robbe-Grillet, *La jalousie*. |
| 1958 | Publication du *Génie du lieu*. Voyage en Grèce. Mariage. Enthousiasme pour Mondrian. Installation à Paris. | Élection de Jean XXIII. Insurrection d'Alger. Retour du général de Gaulle au pouvoir. |

| | VIE ET ŒUVRE DE BUTOR | ÉVÉNEMENTS CONTEMPORAINS |
|---|---|---|
| 1959 | Contrat avec Gallimard. Naissance de la première fille de M. Butor. Voyage aux États-Unis. | Fidel Castro prend le pouvoir à Cuba. André Malraux ministre des Affaires culturelles. |
| 1960 | Publication de *Répertoire* et de *Degrés*. Mort du père de M. Butor. | Élection de Kennedy. Guerre civile au Congo. Claude Simon, *La route des Flandres*. |
| 1961 | Publication d'*Histoire extraordinaire*. Début de la collaboration avec Henri Pousseur. | Crise à Berlin. Le premier homme dans l'espace. Putsch des généraux à Alger. |
| 1962 | Publication de *Mobile* et de *Réseau aérien*. *Votre Faust* est donné à la Scala de Milan. | Indépendance de l'Algérie. Début du concile du Vatican. |
| 1963 | Publication de *Description de San Marco*. | Élection de Paul VI. Assassinat de Kennedy. Rupture entre l'URSS et la Chine. Ionesco, *Le roi se meurt*. |
| 1964 | Publication de *Répertoire II* et d'*Illustrations*. Séjour à Berlin. | Destitution de Khrouchtchev. Première bombe atomique chinoise. Sartre refuse le prix Nobel. Sartre, *Les mots*. |
| 1965 | Publication de *6 810 000 litres d'eau par seconde*. Installation dans la banlieue parisienne. | Bombardements sur le Vietnam du Nord. Affaire Ben Barka. Philippe Sollers, *Drame*. |
| 1966 | Voyages. | Début de la révolution culturelle en Chine. Malraux, *Antimémoires*. |
| 1967 | Publication de *Portrait de l'artiste en jeune singe*. Séjour au Brésil. | L'armée prend le pouvoir en Grèce. Guerre des Six jours entre Israël et les pays arabes. Mort de « Che » Guevara. André Pieyre de Mandiargues, *La marge*. |
| 1968 | Publication de *Répertoire III*. | Printemps de Prague et intervention des troupes du pacte de Varsovie en Tchécoslovaquie. Assassinats de Martin Luther King et de Robert Kennedy. Troubles universitaires en France et grève générale. |
| 1969 | Publication de *Les mots dans la peinture*. Départ pour New Mexico. | Départ du général de Gaulle. Deux hommes sur la Lune. |
| 1970 | Publication de *La rose des vents*. Retour en France : université de Nice. | Fin de la guerre du Biafra. Extension de la guerre dans l'ancienne Indochine. Mort du président Nasser. Mort du général de Gaulle. Troubles en Pologne. |
| 1971 | | Paroxysme des violences en Ulster. Soulèvement du Pakistan oriental et répression. Crise monétaire mondiale. Guerre indo-pakistanaise. |

# LES ANNÉES 1956 ET 1957

Butor compose *La modification* sans doute pendant la seconde moitié de 1956 et en 1957 ; le roman paraîtra en octobre, aura plusieurs voix au Goncourt et obtiendra finalement le prix Théophraste-Renaudot. (C'est *La loi* qui vaudra le prix Goncourt à Roger Vailland.) - *L'emploi du temps* avait paru en septembre 1956.

Au cours de ces deux années, le vieux tout-Paris s'en va. Meurent Mistinguett, Marie Laurencin, Curnonsky, Yves Nat, Édouard Herriot, Sacha Guitry et l'Agha Khan. Meurent aussi Toscanini et Éric von Stroheim, et parmi les écrivains, qui nous intéressent de plus près, Léautaud, E. R. Curtius, Julien Benda, Gabriela Mistral, Valéry Larbaud. Presque seul du premier demi-siècle, Picasso, toujours surprenant, reste sur la brèche.

En ouvrant le journal le matin le bon peuple s'ébahit à lire des nouvelles qui ne touchent guère que sa badauderie : la myxomatose décime les lapins, on parle encore de Minou Drouet, l'archéologie sous-marine fleurit, le prince Rainier de Monaco épouse une actrice de cinéma qui est aussi fille de milliardaire, le paquebot italien *Andrea Doria* fait naufrage, et le comte de Paris marie ses enfants, et les gardiens de prison font grève, et il y a des inondations dans les Alpes. On essaie d'expliquer au grand public ce qu'est un transistor, le mur du son, l'automation qui fait son apparition aux États-Unis, la datation par le carbone 14. Rien de tout cela ne concerne vraiment les gens.

Cependant les Français roulent en DS, en Aronde, en Frégate, en 403. S'ouvrent les premiers snack-bars. Les matières plastiques envahissent le décor de la vie. Des enquêtes révèlent une étrange égalité devant le poste de radio : la proportion d'auditeurs est la même, quelle que soit la classe sociale, et l'échelle des préférences, allant des chansons à la poésie, est la même. S'il y a peu de chose à dire du costume masculin, on peut noter que les femmes, quand elles ne sont pas en tailleur, portent des jupes amples ou bouffantes, un peu au-dessus de la cheville le jour, longues le soir ; au moment où Vadim et Brigitte Bardot vont désacraliser le corps féminin en le montrant nu ou recouvert d'une salopette quasi masculine, le flou romantique des étoffes qui embrument sa

personne fait de la femme une Dame de roman courtois ; il y paraît dans les rêves de Léon Delmont, le héros de *La modification*.

En outre la prospérité matérielle de Léon Delmont traduit la réussite économique de la IV[e] République. Depuis 1950 la production industrielle a doublé dans certaines branches. La construction de logements commence à s'accroître sensiblement. Tous les ménages parisiens possèdent un appareil de radio et un tiers un appareil de télévision. Les produits industriels et les objets qui ne sont pas de première nécessité prennent de plus en plus de place dans les achats des Français. Alors surgissent des problèmes nouveaux : il faut analyser et organiser la consommation, la productivité, les marchés agricoles ; quels modèles d'urbanisme faut-il adopter pour les nouvelles villes de banlieue ? Faut-il construire des autoroutes ?

C'est pourquoi on ne se rend guère compte que le régime politique agonise. Certes, le Maroc et la Tunisie trouvent un équilibre : Mohammed V fait reconnaître l'indépendance de son pays et est proclamé roi ; Bourguiba, président du conseil, fait destituer le bey et fonde la république tunisienne. Mais l'insoluble guerre d'Algérie empoisonne la vie de la France ; à cela s'ajoute l'échec de l'expédition de Suez bien que le rationnement de l'essence n'ait pas duré, le canal n'ayant été fermé que six mois. Sur l'Euratom, sur le Marché commun, l'opinion est divisée, incertaine. Après le gouvernement impuissant de Guy Mollet, que Mendès-France abandonne en mai 1956, viennent des ministères éphémères. De l'étranger proviennent des nouvelles inquiétantes : troubles à Chypre, troubles en Jordanie, question des Kurdes. Le monde communiste semble remuer aussi : au XX[e] congrès, Khrouchtchev dénonce le stalinisme et il entreprend une sorte de tour du monde avec Boulganine, mais d'autre part on apprend qu'il y a des émeutes en Pologne et la révolte de Budapest est énergiquement réprimée. Bref 31 % des Français déclarent ne pas avoir le temps de s'occuper de politique et 26 % trouvent que la politique ne sert à rien ; ce sont les publications féminines qui ont les plus gros tirages de toute la presse (*L'écho des Françaises*, *Marie-Claire*, *L'écho de la mode*). On comprend que Léon Delmont, malgré le confort dont il jouit, ne soit pas à l'aise dans sa peau ; il est sans doute de

ceux qui se désintéressent de la vie politique au jour le jour, mais il médite tristement sur sa condition aliénée et sur le destin des grands empires en Europe et dans le monde. Un personnage romanesque a rarement été de son temps avec une telle précision.

Il l'est également par sa passion pour Rome. Les Français de l'après-guerre ouvrent les yeux sur le monde hors de France. Ce n'est pas par une vaine curiosité qu'ils s'émeuvent d'une catastrophe minière à Marcinelle, en Belgique, ou qu'ils suivent les péripéties de l'entrée d'une étudiante noire à l'université d'Alabama. Ils ont été troublés, quel que fût leur choix politique, par l'affaire de Budapest. Ils se mettent à voyager, en Italie d'abord, en Espagne ou au Portugal ensuite.

Il nous reste à donner quelques indications sur l'état de la République des Lettres pendant que Butor écrit *La modification*. Le grand public demande encore des explications sur la littérature engagée, alors que le succès de Françoise Sagan, qui publie *Un certain sourire* en 1956, est le signe d'un désengagement. *La petite hutte* et *Bobosse* d'André Roussin triomphent sur le boulevard ainsi que *Patate* de Marcel Achard. Cependant les valeurs sûres pendant ces années 1956-1957 sont *Amers* de Saint-John Perse, *D'un château l'autre* de Céline, *Trop c'est trop* de Blaise Cendrars, et *La chute* de Camus. C'est la grande époque du TNP où l'on peut voir *Le faiseur* de Balzac et *Ce fou de Platonov* de Tchekhov; Sacha Pitoeff joue *Les bas-fonds* à l'Œuvre; en même temps, on édite Brecht en français. C'est d'ailleurs sur la scène que se produisent les plus grandes nouveautés; car le seul livre bouleversant est alors *Tristes tropiques* de Lévi-Strauss; mais Jean-Louis Barrault joue *Le personnage combattant* de Vauthier au Petit-Marigny, Blin monte *Fin de partie* de Beckett; à la Michodière on peut voir *Le square* de Marguerite Duras, et au Théâtre Antoine est représentée *La chatte sur un toit brûlant* de Tennessee Williams. - Butor nous dit qu'il ne va guère au cinéma, pourtant passent alors sur les écrans *Un condamné à mort s'est échappé* de Bresson, *Le monde du silence* de Cousteau et Malle, *Le ballon rouge* de Lamorisse, *Et Dieu créa la femme* de Vadim, avec les plus célèbres films d'Ingmar Bergman, *Sourires d'une nuit d'été*, *Le septième sceau*, *Les fraises sauvages*. En revanche, puisque

Butor est très attentif à la peinture, bien qu'il ait alors séjourné à Genève, signalons quelques expositions parisiennes : Toulouse-Lautrec, Soutine, Vlaminck, les Primitifs italiens, André Marchand, Bernard Buffet, et surtout une grande rétrospective de l'œuvre de Matisse.

## L'ACCUEIL DE LA CRITIQUE

• Le texte de Michel Leiris, *Le réalisme mythologique de Michel Butor*, que vous pouvez lire en appendice à *La modification* en 10/18, a paru dans *Critique*, février 1958.

• [...] six heures de morne ennui [...]
J'admire qu'on puisse admirer une telle esthétique, dont le principe semble être tout simplement celui de la photographie, étant bien entendu que l'opérateur met sa patience à *tout* photographier, sans choisir ni objet, ni angle de vue. Or c'est au choix que l'art commence, nous ne démordrons pas de cette conviction.
Albert Loranquin, La modification *par Michel Butor*,
*Le bulletin des Lettres*, 15 décembre 1957, p. 432-433.

• Rien, dans *La modification*, ne témoigne d'une novation quelconque dans le domaine du roman. Il s'agit une fois de plus d'une utilisation, acceptable encore qu'un peu artificielle, du temps proustien, et le monologue intérieur n'est absolument plus une nouveauté [...].

Le meilleur du récit tient dans les épisodes du voyage ; les petits faits sont bien observés, souvent significatifs ; les retours en arrière, qui changent à chaque chapitre, ne sont pas maladroits ; l'ensemble est parfaitement plausible, et de l'allure colimaçonienne du récit se dégage une sorte de force obsédante qu'on avait déjà remarquée dans *L'emploi du temps* [...].

Michel Butor n'a pas encore choisi sa voie : ce pourrait être celle du récit classique. Ce serait une heureuse « modification ».
Pierre de Boisdeffre, *Une révolution qui fait long feu*,
*La revue de Paris*, décembre 1957, p. 171.

• Comme Claude Simon, Michel Butor [...] s'efforce de rêver son roman. Hallucination du demi-sommeil, dans un train, la nuit, sous la mauve [*sic*] et changeante lumière de la veilleuse ; immenses phrases perdues, retrouvées à la page suivante ; recherche obstinée de la précision - à laquelle le lecteur se trouve un peu trop associé. Le lyrisme de Butor semble plus laborieux. Trop de détails le brisent.
Jean-René Huguenin, *Les prix littéraires 1957<br>
risquent de créer les fausses Écoles<br>
romanesques de demain*, Arts, 27 novembre 1957.

• [Malgré l'esprit de système qui provoque la lourdeur des descriptions, Butor, qui est un psychologue hors de pair, est « du côté des maîtres ». Il a réussi le roman que veut écrire l'École du Regard.]
Livre important, dans la mesure précisément où, dépassant la peinture obsédante des choses, il ramène à l'essentiel de toute littérature, qui est la peinture de l'homme, de son esprit, de ses sentiments, de ses mœurs, de ses rêves, de ses aventures. Il y a cela dans *La modification*, et c'est cet essentiel qui l'emporte finalement sur l'accessoire et le décor et les manies de M. Butor écrivain.
Émile Henriot, *La vie littéraire*,<br>
*Le monde*, 13 novembre 1957.

• On sait que l'auteur de *La modification* (Éditions de Minuit) appartient, avec Alain Robbe-Grillet et Claude Simon, à un groupe qu'Émile Henriot propose de nommer « l'École du Regard ». Se souvenant du titre d'un roman d'Alain Robbe-Grillet, *Le voyeur*, on peut écrire, sans l'offenser, que Michel Butor est un voyeur d'une rare acuité. Il le prouve ici, chaque fois qu'il décrit un paysage ou un décor bien connu, en nous y révélant des détails que nous avions négligés. Mais n'exerce-t-il pas ce don avec une application excessive ? Il reprend à maintes reprises l'inventaire du compartiment qui forme le cadre de son roman et ramène sous divers éclairages les mêmes scènes que son protagoniste se remémore, sans que son refus de choisir nous apporte toujours un enrichissement. Ce personnage même, il affecte de prendre ses distances avec lui, de le traiter avec le détachement d'un spectateur qui, non content d'observer ses gestes, verrait ses pensées muettes défiler dans son cerveau. Ainsi

le livre commence-t-il par cette phrase : « Vous avez mis le pied gauche sur la rainure de cuivre, et de votre épaule droite vous essayez en vain de pousser un peu plus le panneau coulissant. » N'y a-t-il point quelque puérilité à nous faire attendre jusqu'aux pages 53 et 98 pour nous apprendre que le nom du monsieur ainsi interpellé est Delmont et qu'il a reçu le prénom de Léon ?

Ces réserves formulées, qui ne portent que sur certains partis pris du narrateur, je puis dire que *La modification* est un des ouvrages les plus originaux et substantiels qui aient paru cette année. René LALOU, *Après la bataille*,
*Les annales - Conferencia*, janvier 1958, p. 22.

• [André Rousseaux revient sur un premier jugement publié dans *Le Figaro littéraire* du 2 novembre 1957 : l'étude de Michel Leiris lui a ouvert les yeux. Les hommes sont prisonniers du temps et de l'espace, ce que traduisent les allées et venues du récit dans le passé et le futur, ainsi que la claustration dans le compartiment.]

Un roman de Butor, jusqu'aux trois quarts ou aux trois quarts et demi, est le prodigieux échafaudage que l'on connaît, l'étonnante construction spatio-temporelle où des minutes, des jours, des années, des millénaires, s'imbriquent avec des lieux, des hommes, des aspects visuels ou tactiles, des œuvres d'art, - un roman de Butor, dis-je, est d'abord ce monument édifié avec une puissance sensorielle et mnémonique peu commune (sans parler de la richesse d'expression, bien entendu), pour que trente ou cinquante pages avant la fin ce monument romanesque s'effondre, mieux s'évanouisse, c'est-à-dire rentre dans la vanité qui était sa seule vérité propre. Car un roman est toujours une fiction, donc un mensonge. Mais un roman de Butor est un mensonge que le héros se fait à soi-même, copieusement, avec tout l'arsenal de ressources que son auteur lui prête généreusement. Et l'instant dont je parle, l'instant d'avant le dernier quart d'heure est la minute de la vérité : l'instant où l'échafaudage n'a plus qu'à s'abattre en laissant voir qu'il était fait de toiles peintes, car c'est l'instant aussi où le héros, entre ses illusions vaincues et ce qui lui reste d'espoir, est seul avec sa vérité pour lui faire face.
André ROUSSEAUX, *Michel Butor, romancier de la prison humaine*,
*Le Figaro littéraire*, 19 avril 1958.

• [Cette Note commence par une excellente analyse des effets de la 2ᵉ personne du pluriel, puis vient cette remarque que la médiocrité des personnages n'empêche pas le lecteur d'être pris par la curiosité.]

Le principal personnage de *La modification* n'est pas un homme, et n'est pas même une ville, mais l'*idée* d'une ville entre toutes, première dans notre temps, première dans nos légendes et nos mythes : Rome [...]. Que peut donc une ville, que peuvent le sol, l'air, la lumière, les pierres d'une ville, que peuvent les souvenirs d'une ville sur l'âme d'un homme ? Rien ne le dit, et tout le montre : ce qui parle à la raison est aussi parfaitement inexpliqué, cependant aussi puissant que ce qui parle au cœur; cet émerveillement, purement intellectuel, est contagieux. On ne sait pourquoi, sinon pour la simple raison que seules les passions vraies sont communicatives, et que la vraie passion du héros de Michel Butor était bien une ville, et non pas une femme. Mais l'énigme demeure : pourquoi cette passion-là, pourquoi les sentiments que lui inspire Rome sont-ils plus puissants sur le cœur du héros que son amour pour Cécile, et plus déterminants dans l'orientation de sa vie que le passage de l'amour pour sa femme à l'amour pour sa maîtresse ? Nous ne le saurons pas. La conclusion est d'ailleurs singulière : on voit le héros, au terme de ce livre qu'on est en train de lire, décider d'écrire un livre. (On se dit que le voilà, justement, on est en train de le lire.) L'énigme n'est pas éclaircie pour autant, au contraire. S'agissait-il, par ce processus bizarre, qui met en balance les lieux et les êtres, d'amener au jour un écrivain ? Alors, au bout du compte, le titre est trompeur : il n'y a pas eu modification, mais révélation, le voyage faisant le même office que le bain où l'on plonge les clichés photographiques, révélant ce qui avait toujours existé. Mais le talent ne trompe pas, ni la maîtrise dont ce livre témoigne : dans sa construction, où s'équilibrent avec une rigoureuse aisance le présent, le passé et le songe; dans son langage neuf et sobre, varié, subtil et fort, qui sait trouver un rythme, le briser, le reprendre, marquer le silence, restituer le rêve.

Dominique AURY, *Notes*, *Le roman*,<br>
*La nouvelle Nouvelle Revue française*,<br>
décembre 1957, p. 1148-1149.

• [Après avoir parlé de vérisme, Louis Barjon constate qu'il s'agit en réalité d'une évolution psychologique.]

Le véritable intérêt du livre réside dans la façon dont Butor s'efforce jusqu'à la limite de rendre compte d'un tel processus, sans prétendre jamais réussir à le découronner de son mystère. Il y a là un essai très intéressant qui s'apparente aux rigueurs des analyses stendhaliennes et aux minutieuses introspections de la littérature proustienne. Une observation clinique centrée autour des troublants problèmes de l'être, de la conscience, de la personne, des moyens d'échapper à cet émiettement de nous-même qui s'opère au travers des fragmentations du temps et des fluctuations de la mémoire.

Ce n'est pas la première fois que ce romancier s'est engagé dans pareille étude. *L'emploi du temps*, remarqué l'an dernier par la critique, s'appliquait déjà à nous décrire une évolution intérieure assez analogue.

Ne parlons pas trop tôt d'un « grand livre ». Mais osons croire qu'avec Butor nous tenons enfin un écrivain grâce auquel notre littérature romanesque saura retrouver, dans des voies nouvelles, l'originalité et la vigueur qui depuis trop longtemps lui manquaient.

Louis BARJON,
*Les prix littéraires*, Études, janvier 1958, p. 95.

• [*La modification* n'est pas un drame psychologique. Le monde de ce compartiment de 3ᵉ classe, le 15 novembre 1955, va contester d'autres réalités. Il ne s'agit pas de découvrir Léon Delmont, ce roman] est découverte, révélation de deux modes de vie inconciliables l'un avec l'autre. [...]

La tentative de Michel Butor est-elle donc tout à fait réussie ? Je ne le pense pas. Pour que sa réussite fût complète, il aurait en effet fallu que l'anecdote dont Butor est parti soit absolument transparente et que ses héros, sans poids ni épaisseur, après avoir servi de moyens d'approche de la Réalité, s'y résorbent et y disparaissent tout à fait. Certes Henriette et Cécile ne sont guère que cela, des repères ; elles ne vivent pas, elles sont seulement les signes, presque les chiffres de cette Réalité. Mais Léon Delmont, lui, n'est pas aussi neutre : il a une fonction (il est directeur de l'agence parisienne des machines à écrire Scabelli), une psychologie. Butor a beau le « gommer » au maximum, ne nous livrant de lui, à travers

ses souvenirs, la description de ses rêves, que des images quasi impersonnelles ; il a beau tout faire pour mettre entre parenthèses la personnalité de son héros, celle-ci résiste obstinément. De là, un malaise ; le lecteur ne sait plus très bien à qui il a affaire : à Léon Delmont, à Michel Butor, ou à soi-même... Quelques précisions de trop, qui sont d'un romancier classique (les airs d'*Orfeo* que ce directeur d'agence chantonne en rentrant chez lui le soir...), une incertitude quant au choix des paysages romains évoqués (tantôt, il ne s'agit que de monuments, de lieux banals bien faits pour susciter l'admiration d'un directeur commercial qui a lu son Guide Bleu ; tantôt, ce sont des lieux, des bâtiments plus rares, mieux assortis au goût de Michel Butor que de son Léon Delmont)... et le malentendu qui a fait célébrer *La modification* comme un roman psychologique, est inévitable.

[Bernard DORT préfère *L'emploi du temps.*]

Bernard DORT, *Épreuves du roman, La forme et le fond*, *Cahiers du Sud*, janvier 1958, p. 121-125.

## BIBLIOGRAPHIE SOMMAIRE

Voici d'abord deux ouvrages d'initiation :

R.-M. ALBÉRÈS, *Michel Butor*, Classiques du XXe siècle, Éditions universitaires, 1964.

GEORGES RAILLARD, *Butor*, Bibliothèque idéale, Gallimard, 1968.

Mais il faut prendre garde que cet ouvrage, qui est à ce jour la plus riche mine de renseignements sur Butor et son œuvre, contient des commentaires littéraires qui ne sont pas faciles à lire.

Il est à peu près indispensable, pour connaître Butor, d'avoir lu :

GEORGES CHARBONNIER, *Entretiens avec Michel Butor*, Gallimard, 1967. (Il s'agit d'entretiens radiophoniques enregistrés en janvier et février 1967.) Michel Butor s'explique sur bien des points, et il ne semble pas qu'il ait radicalement changé depuis lors.

On trouvera une mise en question des problèmes que soulève l'œuvre de Butor dans :

JEAN ROUDAUT, *Michel Butor ou le livre futur*, Gallimard, 1966.

JEAN ROUDAUT, *Répétition et modification dans deux romans de Michel Butor*, in *Saggi e ricerche di letteratura francese*, vol. 8, 1967, p. 309 sqq.

Rappelons qu'on ne saurait concevoir ce que veulent les adeptes du « nouveau » roman sans avoir lu :

NATHALIE SARRAUTE, *L'ère du soupçon*, Gallimard, 1956.

ALAIN ROBBE-GRILLET, *Pour un nouveau roman*, Éditions de Minuit, 1963.

Enfin il est évident que l'on trouvera de nombreux éclaircissement sur les intentions de Butor romancier en feuilletant l'œuvre de Butor critique littéraire :

- *Répertoire*, Éditions de Minuit, 1960 (Recueil d'articles parus à partir de 1948. Mais ces articles ne sont pas reproduits dans l'ordre chronologique).
- *Répertoire II*, Éditions de Minuit, 1964.
- *Répertoire III*, Éditions de Minuit, 1968.

Sur *La modification* précisément, il vient de paraître une longue étude où le roman est considéré à peu près de tous les points de vue possibles. D'ailleurs la lecture de cet ouvrage ne présente pas de difficulté :

FRANÇOISE VAN ROSSUM-GUYON, *Critique du roman*, *Essai sur « La modification » de Michel Butor*, Gallimard, 1970.

Ajoutons, pour compléter la bibliographie qui figure dans l'ouvrage de Raillard, que, depuis 1968, Butor a publié :

*La banlieue de l'aube à l'aurore. Mouvement brownien*, Montpellier, Fata Morgana, 1968.

*Illustrations II*, Gallimard, 1969.

*Les mots dans la peinture*, Genève, Skira, 1969.

*La rose des vents. 36 rhumbs pour Charles Fourier*, Gallimard, 1970.

*Dialogue avec trente-trois variations de Ludwig van Beethoven sur une valse de Diabelli*, Gallimard, 1971.

*Le génie du lieu*, Tome II, Gallimard, 1971.

# THÈMES DE RÉFLEXIONS
# ET D'ÉTUDES

- La famille bourgeoise à Paris, sur la rive gauche, dans les romans de Butor *(Passage de Milan, La modification, Degrés)*. Contre-épreuve : la solitude *(L'emploi du temps, Portrait de l'artiste en jeune singe)*.
- Quinze ans après la publication de *La modification*, l'idée que les hommes se font des femmes est-elle toujours celle qui transparaît dans les rêves de Léon Delmont ? Les rapports entre parents et enfants sont-ils ceux qu'on entrevoit au 15 de la place du Panthéon ?
- Structures comparées de l'Europe et des États-Unis dans *La modification* et dans *Mobile*. Cercle et carré; cheminements sinueux ou rectilignes.
- La ville dans l'œuvre de Butor, en prenant pour points de départ *L'emploi du temps* et *La modification*.
- Les rapports de *La modification* et des grandes œuvres romanesques sur lesquelles Butor a médité : *Comédie humaine* de Balzac, romans de Hugo, romans de Jules Verne, romans de Joyce, *A la recherche du temps perdu* de Proust. Il faut partir de ce que Butor a dit de ces auteurs dans les trois volumes de *Répertoire*.
- L'emploi du participe présent dans les autres romans de Butor, avant et après *La modification*.
- Esquisse d'une problématique : qui parle dans les romans de Butor ? Évolution du problème jusqu'à *Degrés*. Y a-t-il changement de voix quand la réponse à la question varie ?
- Le mythe d'Ariane dans *L'emploi du temps* et dans *La modification*. Épanouissement ou dégradation d'un roman à l'autre.
- La table du dîner familial dans *Passage de Milan* et le compartiment de chemin de fer dans *La modification*. Localisation relative dans l'espace et rapports humains.
- Dans ses *Entretiens* avec Georges Charbonnier, Butor affirme qu'il est « de plus en plus fasciné par le pluriel » (p. 189). Comment interpréter cette déclaration, quand on songe qu'entre *Passage de Milan* et *Degrés* prennent place deux romans qui s'organisent autour de deux individus, Jacques Revel et Léon Delmont ?
- Le feu dans *L'emploi du temps* et l'eau dans *La modification*. Ces deux substances élémentaires occupent-elles la même place dans l'un et l'autre roman ? (Cette étude suppose connus deux ouvrages de Bachelard, *La psychanalyse du feu* et *L'eau et les rêves*.)

- Conscience d'être et conscience de l'objet dans le roman contemporain : de Beckett à Robbe-Grillet ou à Butor.
- Compléter les enquêtes esquissées p. 14 à 23. Recenser les passages du roman où paraissent : la flamme, les autres formes de feu, l'air respirable ou irrespirable, l'eau dans les pays que traverse le train (étangs, fleuves, mer, marécages, lac), la lumière bleue, l'opacité et la transparence, etc. Établir la palette de Butor écrivant *La modification*, en distinguant soigneusement les teintes chaudes (rouge, orangé) et les teintes froides (vert, bleu). Reprendre dans le détail les jeux de reflets et les illusions d'optique dans le compartiment au cours du voyage des 15 et 16 novembre 1955.

(Dans la perspective qui est la nôtre, ces enquêtes devraient s'appuyer sur une statistique, celle de l'emploi des mots, mais aussi tenir compte de l'environnement pour chaque emploi de tel mot.)

- Reconstituer les diverses phases du projet que forme Léon Delmont d'écrire un livre.
- Le symbole lunaire dans *La modification*.
- Le thème de la grille ou du réseau dans *La modification*.
- Délimiter les récits de cauchemars de Léon Delmont. Y retrouver les thèmes de l'eau, de la porte, etc. La valeur dramatique de ces rêves : en quoi font-ils progresser la modification ?
- Étude des passages du récit à la 1$^{re}$ personne du singulier. Distinguer les discours qui commencent par « Vous vous dites » ou par une formule analogue, et les moments où la 1$^{re}$ personne surgit sans être annoncée. Vous trouverez probablement que les seconds ont plus de force et de valeur que les premiers.
- En partant du tableau de la page 59, étudier l'effet produit par l'ordre dans lequel se suivent les éléments de récit : montrer qu'un ordre différent donnerait un tout autre sens.

---

*Imprimé en France*, par l'Imprimerie Hérissey à Évreux (Eure)
N° d'édition : 11627 — N° d'impression : 50437 — Dépôt légal : Février 1990